2/08

DATE DUE

PRINTED IN U.S.A.

TAMARA Tilley

Abandoned Identity

E*v*ergreen
PRESS

Mobile, AL

Abandoned Identity
by Tamara Tilley
Copyright ©2007 Tamara Tilley

ISBN 978-0-7394-9040-2
For Worldwide Distribution
Printed in the U.S.A.

Evergreen Press
P.O. Box 191540 • Mobile, AL 36619

Dedication

To Walter, my wonderfully supportive husband. Thank you
for giving encouragement when I need it most. Your love and understanding
motivates me. My love for you grows everyday.

Also by Tamara Tilley:

Full Disclosure

Acknowledgments

To my wonderful kids, John, Christopher and Jennifer – You make me laugh at myself and put such fun into my life. Thank you for your love.

To my mom, Nancy and sister, April – Thank you for your love and support. Who would've thought I would grow up to not only enjoy books but to write them, too.

To my in-laws, Stan and Betty – Thank you for your prayers over the years and for giving me such a wonderful husband.

To Dr. Bob Phillips – Thank you for your constant encouragement and assurance.

To my wonderful friends – You've been such an incredible support team for me. I love hearing your reactions to my stories and how you bond with my characters. Your enthusiasm presses me forward.

To my readers – To those of you who've read *Full Disclosure*, thank you for taking a chance on me, a new author. You'll never know how much I've appreciated getting your e-mails and feedback. I hope you enjoy *Abandoned Identity* as well.

To my Lord and Savior, Jesus Christ – thank You for giving me an amazing family, supportive friends, and for loving me without condition. I pray others will see the power of Your grace and forgiveness through the stories I tell—stories that I pray will point others to You.

CHAPTER ONE

The young, blond woman stepped off the elevator, rushed past the receptionist, and quickly headed down the hallway.

"Jennifer, Mr. Lynch is looking for you," Doris called after her.

Jennifer didn't stop to acknowledge the message. She didn't have time. She could hear the warning in Doris' tone. Mr. Lynch was looking for her, knowing she was late returning from lunch. This could very well be her last day at Weissler and Schuler.

She glanced at her watch as she threaded her way through the multitude of workstations. She moved as quickly as she could, even though she knew her efforts were probably for nothing—after all, late was late. He would assume she had done it on purpose and would make good on his threat from the previous week. Lynch had given her two weeks to change her attitude or she would be fired.

She hurried past his office door, hoping against hope that she would be able to slip by without being noticed. A sideways glance told her otherwise. She continued towards her own office, knowing he would be quick on her heels. She had struggled all morning, trying to do her work, trying to keep it together, but with the way she was feeling, her resolve was beginning to crumble. She'd only had enough time to slip off her jacket before she heard his booming voice in the hallway.

"Ms. Patterson, you of all people should not be abusing time restrictions. A one-hour lunch is a one-hour lunch, not an hour and 25 minutes," he scolded her loud enough so everyone could hear him as he made his way down the hall toward her office.

Jennifer hung up her coat and purse on the rack behind her door and slumped in the overstuffed sofa that filled her office. She braced herself for the inevitable.

"You knew we needed to get started on the Yomahama account first thing after lunch," he said as he entered her office and firmly shut the door. "Obviously you don't care about this account as much as you say you do." He was poised for her counterattack but was surprised instead to hear her soft apology.

"I'm sorry. I thought I could make it home and back again. But with the snow, and the traffic, and the way I'm . . ."

What's the use explaining, she thought to herself. *He doesn't care*. She had just

1

given him the excuse he was looking for. She figured she would be packing up her personal items in less than an hour. She took a deep breath, her eyes focused downward. "I'm sorry. It wasn't intentional."

Harrison was taken aback. In the short time he'd known Jennifer, she had never apologized for her actions. Everything she did was intentionally antagonistic toward him. But somehow he sensed a difference in her mood.

"What's wrong?" he bristled, not really wanting to hear her excuse.

She glanced up at his imposing figure but lowered her eyes to the floor as she spoke. "I tried to kick something all weekend. I guess I'm just not feeling up to par."

He said nothing, waiting for her to make eye contact with him. She stiffened her back, sighed and said, "It won't happen again."

Had she brushed a tear from her cheek? *Not possible*, he thought to himself. Jennifer Patterson was tough as nails. She would never lower herself to tears in the workplace . . . that was unless she really was ill.

He waited again for her to look up at him, and when she did, he was met with vacant eyes, pallid skin, and beads of sweat that were starting to form on her brow. Just then, the intercom system went off. "Mr. Lynch, Mr. Yomahama is on the line. Shall I put him through to Miss Patterson's office or your own?"

Obviously Doris knew where to find him because of the scene he had just made. He walked around to the front of Jennifer's desk and cleared his voice before pushing the intercom button. "I'll take it in my office, Doris. Give me a minute to get there."

Lynch gave Jennifer one last stern look and then marched from her office, shutting her door with a little more force than necessary.

She collapsed against the cushions, her strong exterior completely dissolving. She had done everything she could to hold back her tears in his presence, but his quick exit allowed her to unleash the torrent she had been suppressing.

She had never felt this horrible before in her life. She would've called in sick if it weren't for the fact that she knew her job was in jeopardy. *It isn't fair*, she thought to herself. *I should have Lynch's job.* For the hundredth time Jennifer went over in her mind the scenario that had taken her completely by surprise.

She had been groomed for the director's position by Meg, long before Meg left to start a family. Jennifer had put in countless hours on different accounts to make sure her and Meg's statistics had been well researched and presented in a polished manner. She had done the bulk of Meg's work, along with her own, as Meg progressed into her third trimester. It simply wasn't fair!

The day corporate brought in Harrison Lynch and announced he would be the new director, instead of her, she was livid. She felt demeaned and unappreciated. Everyone in the office knew she had worked hard for the job and had deserved it. But corporate behaved in their typical chauvinistic manner and took the opportunity to replace Meg with a man instead of another woman. Testosterone was the only asset that Harrison Lynch had that she did not.

While the other women in the office were quick to overlook the injustice of the situation because of Harrison's availability, good looks, and charismatic personality, she only saw him as a thorn in her side.

She would only be fooling herself if she said she didn't see his appeal. He was older than she was—the classic tall, dark, and handsome type. His sparkling brown eyes and wavy brown hair gave him a boyish charm, but his stature and muscular body proved him to be anything but boyish. His enigmatic character made him the kind of man that breezed through life with ease, putting the Midas touch on everything he encountered. But the way he clashed with her, rubbing her the wrong way and always trying to put her in her place, made his good looks less appealing.

Jennifer had butt heads with Harrison ever since he had shown up. She was not afraid to speak out against his proposals or the way in which he supplied information to a client. She had caused him more than one embarrassing moment in important meetings with prospective accounts. She upstaged him with what she called "a more efficient way to gather and record information." She didn't think it beneath her to use her feminine mystique with a client in order to work on a case that Lynch would've preferred to handle by himself. Lynch had put her on the spot on more than one occasion, but somehow she always came out looking professional in front of the clients.

When she had worked with Meg, Jennifer's desk was out front with everyone else's. She liked it that way. She enjoyed working in an environment that buzzed with activity. But Lynch changed all that. He made it very clear that Jennifer was his assistant, and he needed her at his personal disposal. And so he had her move her things into the smaller of the two conference rooms.

Giving Jennifer her own office was not a reward but a sentence. She felt he had isolated her on purpose to break her spirit. It had taken the wind out of her sails for a short period, but she decided two could play at that game. She promptly ordered custom office furniture and personalized the space. What he had intended on being a lonely, sterile environment, she had turned into a showplace of warmth and femininity.

She had one-upped him again and gloated in the fact that he could do nothing about it. After all, he was the one that gave her her own office and the freedom to decorate it the way she wanted. The fact that she did it with pastels in a style she knew he disliked (even though she disliked it too) was icing on the cake. Harrison had declared that an office should reflect professionalism not personality and initially insisted she get rid of everything. His request was denied when Mrs. Weissler came in and admired what she had done with the old conference room. With Mrs. Weissler on her side, Jennifer had once again thwarted Lynch's authority.

Lynch had finally had enough. He called her into his office a week earlier and lowered the boom. "I'm giving you two weeks notice."

"You're firing me?" Jennifer was floored. Though she knew that he disliked her as much as she disliked him, he would have to explain to corporate why he was letting such a valuable employee go.

"No, I'm not firing you . . . yet." He was cool and calm as he sat behind his solid oak desk. "I'm giving you two weeks to change your attitude. I'm tired of the mind games, the flirting with clients, and the way you insist on making proposals before discussing them with me. Weissler and Schuler should present a united front to all our clients, not a sense of division and indecisiveness. You have two weeks to get on board, assume your position as my assistant, and change your 'I can top that' attitude. If you choose not to, you will give me no alternative than to let you go."

Now, it was just a week later, and Jennifer had given Lynch the perfect opportunity to show corporate that she was not the team player that they had assumed her to be. Corporate was breathing down everyone's neck about the Yomahama account. It meant millions to them if they could seal the deal. If they felt she hadn't given it her all, they would allow Lynch to have his way, no questions asked.

Jennifer sobbed into the arm of the floral couch that she despised. She thought about all the ways she had tried to make work uncomfortable for Harrison Lynch but knew she had failed. On occasion, he had tried joking with her and having innocuous conversations, but she would have none of it. She wouldn't accept the olive branch that he tried to extend to her. Now he would have the last laugh, and it would be her own fault.

The door swung open once again. Harrison was poised and ready to battle with her, only to find her hunched over, her head in her hands and tears falling onto her charcoal colored slacks.

He felt uncomfortable finding her in such a vulnerable position. The all-business exterior he had resolved to use with her now took a back seat to the compassionate Harrison that others had seen. He stood for a moment before taking a seat on the couch alongside her and waited for her to gather her composure. It took several minutes before she could speak.

"I know what you're going to say, so I'll save you the energy." She rubbed at her aching brows and sniffled. "You'll have the files for the Yomahama account on your desk by the end of the day, and I'll clean out my things. You can do what you want with the furniture. I don't want it." She held her head like she was afraid it was going to snap off her neck.

Harrison just sat there, not saying a thing. Jennifer wished he would just leave. She felt defeated and humiliated. He'd gotten his way; he'd won. With the experience she'd gained at Weissler and Schuler, she'd have no problem getting a job elsewhere, so she resolved to give up without a fight. Her only desire right then was to get home before her head exploded.

It seemed like an eternity before he spoke again. "What have you taken for it?"

"What?" She was confused. There was no smugness to his tone. In fact, if she wasn't mistaken, he actually sounded concerned. She didn't dare look at him. Just lifting her head would hurt too much.

"Is it a cold or the flu?"

"A cold," she answered, wondering why he was being so nice. It was a trait she didn't think he was capable of, at least not with her. He got up and left the room without saying another word.

She glanced at his receding steps, totally confused. She grabbed a tissue from her purse and tried to wipe away the salty tears and runny nose that was moistening her lips. She gently rolled her head back against the couch and sighed heavily, thankful for the solitude. It didn't last long; within minutes, Harrison was back.

He sat down alongside her, causing her head to sway and a small moan to escape her lips. He handed her a glass that was fizzing, along with several pills. "Here's something for your headache, a decongestant, and a bi-carbonate. They should do the trick."

"No thanks," she said through closed eyes. "I can't take pills. They knock me out and make my head swim. Besides, I still have too much work to do. I don't have time to pass out."

"The way I see it, you're already wasted. You're no good to me like this. Take these, and in an hour you'll feel a lot better. I guarantee it. We'll work on the Yomahama account then."

"I should have known you wouldn't let me die quietly," Jennifer retorted, looking at the pills he was still holding. "And if I don't take your concoction?"

"Then I'll have to assume the Yomahama account isn't as important to you as I gave you credit for, and I'll get Jerry to work on it with me instead."

"Jerry!" She sat up, her head throbbing with disapproval. She slowly lowered herself back to the comfort of the couch, covering her eyes with the palms of her hands. "There's no way I'm going to let Jerry take all my research and screw it up."

"Okay, then. I guess you'll have to do it my way," he said. "Take these, dim the lights, and allow yourself some sleep. Don't worry about watching the clock. I'll come and get you in about an hour."

Jennifer realized it was no longer a suggestion. Harrison put the pills in her hand and waited for her to drink them down with the bi-carbonate.

She tossed them to the back of her throat and held her breath as she drank the fizzy water. She knew she had to do it in one swig, or it would never stay down. Her shoulders shuddered in protest, and she thought she saw the hint of a smile form on Harrison's lips. He pressed the button for the automatic shades to cover her office windows and dimmed the lights. "I'll check on you in an hour." With that, he closed the door and left her with her thoughts.

What just happened? she thought to herself. *He had the perfect opportunity to fire me, and instead he helped me.* Jennifer couldn't concentrate on figuring out the answer to that one. Her head was throbbing so hard, it was making it impossible for her to reason.

She pulled her feet up under her and allowed her head to rest on the padded arm of the couch. *An hour's sleep, then I'll be able to push through the rest of the day.* She drifted off quickly. She was a lightweight when it came to tolerating medicine, and with the mixture she had just taken, she knew that she would finally get some rest.

Harrison walked back to his office and closed the door. He stood before the expansive window and watched the falling snow blanket the Chicago streets. Jumbled emotions crowded his mind. He was afraid that he'd allowed Jennifer's weakened state to play on his sympathy, but it wasn't unlike him. He really was a nice guy. It's just that since he'd arrived at Weissler and Schuler, he and Jennifer had clashed . . . no, more like collided.

He found out soon enough that she had thought she was a lock for his job because of the work she had done with the previous director. He tried to talk to her about it and let her know he understood her disappointment. When he told her he was excited to be working with such a talented analyst, she only stiffened at his attempt at civility. Her spitefulness and malice made her look so unattractive—nothing like the vulnerable woman he had just left in the darkened office. He finally saw in her what some of the men in the office already had seen. She was a lot more appealing when she wasn't being conniving or manipulative. With her defenses down, he actually found himself drawn to her, but he was wary that would change as soon as she had her strength back.

HARRISON HAD BEEN WORKING TIRELESSLY at his computer when he glanced at his watch. He realized it had been more than an hour since he had left Jennifer in her office. He quietly opened her door and leaned in to see how she was doing. She was curled up on the couch, her face flushed and moist. He moved to her side, leaned down, and carefully placed the back of his hand to her forehead. She was feverish. She stirred under his touch, but her eyes had a difficult time focusing. She looked at Harrison and tried to figure out why she was lying down and why he was hovering over her. She closed her eyes and vaguely remembered being late to work and taking a handful of medicine.

"What time is it?" Her voice was barely above a whisper.

"Almost 3:00 p.m."

"Oh, my gosh." She tried sitting up as her head spun out of control. "I've got to get working. We have the Yomahama meeting tomorrow. We can't waste any more time."

Harrison pressed his hands against her shoulders and gently pushed her back against the couch cushions. "You need to rest. Your body is obviously trying to fight something. You have a fever."

"We don't have time for this, Mr. Lynch."

She again moved to a sitting position. She wiped at the perspiration on her forehead and scooped her long blonde hair up into a handful on top of her head. She started pulling at the pink cashmere sweater she was wearing, bellowing it to get some cool air up against her skin. "I feel like I'm suffocating."

"That's the fever."

Before Harrison realized what she was doing, Jennifer reached for the hem of her sweater and began to pull it over her head.

He turned away and sputtered, "What are you doing?"

"If you have a fever, you're supposed to keep at least one foot and one shoulder exposed to cool air."

"Where did you hear that?"

"I'm not sure, but it's worked before."

She continued to remove her sweater. Harrison was relieved to see that she was wearing a silky, pink shell underneath the soft sweater. She pulled her black, high heeled boots from her feet and curled up into a fetal position once again.

"You look miserable; you need to go home. This is ridiculous. There's no way you're going to be able to get any work done under these conditions," Harrison added as she tried to get comfortable.

"I'd be fine if my head would just stop pounding, and I wasn't so hot."

"Let me call you a cab. You need to go home."

"No! I can beat this. Let me just rest a little bit longer. If I could just get rid of this headache, I know I could finish our proposal. Please give me another hour." She was determined to finish what she had started, especially since it could quite possibly be her last account. Harrison was being uncharacteristically nice to her at the moment, but if the Yomahama meeting didn't go well, she knew she would be the proverbial scapegoat.

Harrison stood with his arms firmly crossed against his chest and doubt in his eyes. He knew from past experience there was no sense arguing with her. Of course, there was nothing that said he was obligated to wake her up either.

"Fine, I'll see you in about an hour." He left her office with no intention of disturbing her again. If she had the strength to wake up, she would have to do it on her own.

Although Harrison knew he needed to spend every minute on the Yomahama proposal, he found himself thinking about Jennifer. Why hadn't he noticed her crystal blue eyes or the delicate curve of her jaw before? Maybe because whenever he talked to her, her eyes were glaring and her jaw was set.

He wandered back into Jennifer's office around 4:30 p.m. He watched her as she slept. Her breathing was even and her complexion no longer looked flush. His eyes followed the tip of her chin to where it rested near her exposed shoulder. He felt his thoughts wandering in a direction that was far from work related. He had always been cautious to keep his professional life separate from his personal life, but somehow seeing Jennifer in such a vulnerable state also exposed a side of her that was quite beautiful.

He left her office and drifted down the hall. People were beginning to shut down their computers and straighten up their workstations. The talk was all about the snow that had continued to fall throughout the day. The weather report was predicting another foot before morning. Harrison waved goodnight to them as they left and headed back to his office.

Doris followed him down the hall, worry etched on her kind face.

"Mr. Lynch, I'm concerned about Miss Patterson. I know she was awfully sick this morning when she came in, and she didn't look any better when she returned from lunch. I haven't seen her since you . . . well, since you spoke with her this afternoon."

Harrison knew what Doris was alluding to. The way he had barked at Jennifer when she returned from lunch had obviously been heard throughout the office.

"I gave her some medicine earlier today, and it made her pretty sleepy. That's why you haven't seen her."

"Will she be okay to drive herself home? The road conditions have gotten pretty bad."

"Don't worry, Doris, I'll make sure she's okay before she leaves."

"Okay, I was just concerned. She really is a sweet girl; she just comes off a bit harsh sometimes."

"Harsh? That's an understatement!"

Doris just smiled. "Well, good night, Mr. Lynch."

"Good night, Doris, and thank you for your concern."

CHAPTER TWO

The office was shrouded in shadows when Jennifer woke up. The only illumination in her office came from the dimmed overhead lights and the screen saver on her computer monitor. She slowly lowered her feet to the floor and waited for a negative reaction from her body. Nothing. She felt a bit chilled, but other than that, she felt better than she had earlier in the day. She stood up and paused, making sure she had her balance before moving to her desk.

She pressed the spacebar to bring her computer out of sleep mode. When her eyes focused on the time in the bottom corner of the screen, she gasped out loud. *There must be a mistake!* The clock read 7:03 p.m. She threw open her door and walked hurriedly down the hall. Harrison caught a flash out of the corner of his eye as Jennifer rushed by.

She looked in the main office and saw nothing. Everyone was gone; the huge florescent lights were off, and the room was dim. She shuddered at the thought of being all alone in the huge office building. She spun around to race back to her office and ran right into Harrison. His arms automatically reached out to brace her as she let out a small scream.

"Why did you let me sleep so long? Are you crazy? Now we'll never get done in time!" She pushed away from him and marched to her office.

"Well, so much for beauty and vulnerability," Harrison mumbled as he followed the old Jennifer back to her office.

"What did you say?" she snapped.

"Look, it was obvious you needed your rest. So I let you sleep. I guess I can assume by your attitude that you're feeling better?"

"Feeling . . . I'm feeling like an idiot. It's 7:00 at night and I'm still at work." Jennifer threw her arms in the air with a flourish.

"Then let's get the proposal wrapped up before you hyperventilate!" The look on his face was just short of a grin.

"You think this is funny, don't you?" She whirled around and looked at him in disgust. She plopped onto the couch and started pulling on her boots. "Then you can just finish the proposal yourself. I'm out of here."

"Come on, Jennifer. You're in no condition to go out in this weather. There's three feet of snow out there." He gestured towards the shaded windows.

Jennifer looked at him with steely eyes before jumping up from the couch and hitting the button that retracted her window shades. She was shocked. He was right; the snow had piled up and was continuing to fall.

9

"What were you thinking? There's no way we're going to get out of here."

"I came to that conclusion about an hour ago," he said casually as if it were no big deal. "And since there's nothing we can do about the snow, we might as well get some work done."

Jennifer could not believe the cavalier attitude he had taken. She was stunned. "You might not want to do anything about it, but I'm leaving." She reached for her sweater, jacket, purse, and briefcase before she marched past him and down the hall.

She only got as far as the elevator banks in the reception area when suddenly the room went completely black. A familiar terror from her childhood seized her. Her hands reached out in front of her, struggling to feel anything solid. Her fingers scratched the surface of Doris' desk. She slumped alongside of it, cowering in the darkness.

"Jennifer?" Harrison raised his voice against the darkness. "Jennifer, where are you?" Harrison could hear her timid cries, but the cubicle walls were making it difficult for him to figure out where they were coming from.

Jennifer could hear Harrison calling after her, but could do little about it. She was terrified to move, her mind playing horrible tricks on her.

Harrison was finally able to maneuver around the office maze and reached out toward her cries. It startled her, causing her to jump.

"Jennifer, it's me."

She cowered further underneath Doris' desk.

Harrison thought her behavior was rather bizarre. Of course she was afraid, but she seemed to be over-reacting. "Either take my hand or sit in the dark by yourself. It's your choice." Harrison's words were firm and laced with frustration.

She reached out her hand to him, grasping at the darkness. He grabbed it and pulled her up from where she had taken cover. He could feel her trembling as they carefully made their way down the hall and back to her office. The lights were still out, but the battery backup on her computer allowed her monitor to be a beacon in the darkness.

She sat on her couch, whimpering and rocking back and forth. Harrison watched her, not sure what he was seeing. Her fear of the darkness ran deeper than what he would consider normal. It almost seemed to paralyze her.

He sat alongside her and impulsively put his arm around her, trying to comfort her. She didn't pull away, but neither did she speak. It was a while before she was able to stop rocking and even longer before she was able to say anything.

"This has to be the most embarrassing day in my life," she said with a slightly nervous laugh.

"There's nothing to be embarrassed about. You're sick. So you over-reacted a little, so what!" He was trying to act casual, hoping to put her at ease.

Her spine straightened and her shoulders became rigid. She didn't want him to think she was some kind of drama queen, but to explain the reason for her fear would be opening wounds that she had tried so hard to ignore. "I didn't

10

mean to go schizo on you; it's just that I had a bad experience when I was younger, and it kind of stuck with me."

"Hey, I know all about that. I have an older brother that used to shove me in the toy box all the time."

Jennifer wished it was only a childhood prank that had made her so fearful of the dark. Then maybe she'd be able to put it behind her.

They sat for a few moments in silence, Jennifer realizing Harrison's arm was still draped across her shoulder. She could feel the warmth of his hand against her skin and the awkwardness of being so close to him. She wasn't sure what to do or say. It was easy to know how to act when he was being arrogant or domineering, but his concern and what seemed to be genuine compassion was harder for her to respond to.

She moved to the edge of the couch, causing Harrison's arm to fall away. She wrapped her arms around herself, feeling a chill without her sweater. She had dropped it somewhere in the hallway during her earlier meltdown.

"You're cold. Let me go look for your sweater." He moved to get up.

"No! That's okay," she answered abruptly. The thought of being alone again was worse than the chill that was raising bumps on her flesh.

"Don't be ridiculous. I can see that you're cold. Let me just go look for your sweater and jacket." He got up and was out the door before she could protest any further.

She murmured silently to herself. *You're fine. It's not completely dark, and you're not completely alone. Harrison will be back in just a moment. Don't make a bigger fool of yourself than you already have.* She was rocking again—a mechanism she had come up with as a child to help her bear the silence. Her rocking would cause the floorboards to creak and somehow that brought her comfort and helped to distract her from what was really going on.

Harrison watched her from the doorway and saw her rocking again with tears running down her face and her eyes tightly squeezed shut. He slowly lowered himself onto the couch, trying not to startle her. He handed her the sweater and accepted her thanks. While he watched as she lifted it over her head, his heart raced. Her body moved as the form-fitting sweater slid over her petite form. Unbeknownst to her, her movements were sensual and captivating to him. Harrison felt guilty for what he was thinking, especially when he again caught the glistening tears on her cheeks as she freed her head from the sweater's confines. He looked away, sure his eyes would give away what he was feeling.

"I know what you must be thinking."

Did she really? Was he really that transparent?

"I'm not usually like this. I'm sure the medicine has just made me more jittery than usual. I'm sorry for making you so uncomfortable."

If she only knew.

Silence filled the room. They sat side by side, but they were alone in their own thoughts.

"Well . . . I think we better get that proposal finalized before we have to turn off the computers."

"Why would we have to do that?" she questioned nervously, knowing their only light was the bluish haze from the monitor.

"Battery backups only last so long. They really aren't intended for continual work. They're only a safety net to give you time to finish a project and shut it down."

There it was again, he thought to himself. A panic look seized Jennifer, causing her body to sway back and forth again. "Don't worry," he tried to assure her. "We'll probably have power back by then."

She swallowed hard, pushed her silky blond hair behind her ears, and stood. She smoothed non-existent wrinkles from her wool slacks and nervously tugged at her sweater. "Okay then, let's get this done." She moved around her desk to her computer and started rattling manicured nails across the keyboard.

Harrison hovered over her shoulder as she went through the many different files she had prepared for the Yomahama account. He added his suggestions and listened as she explained her reasoning and some of her theories. They were working together smoother than ever before. They were on the same wavelength on many points and listened intently to each other's suggestions on others.

They changed positions so that Harrison could work at her keyboard. He used his passcode to open up the files he had been working on, and they again worked in tandem to accomplish the joint venture.

Before they knew it, a battery warning flashed on the screen. They had been working for two hours straight and had not noticed that time was slipping past them.

"Okay, let's save what we have and shut this puppy down. I'm going to send it all to my computer and then go shut mine down, too. Then we'll both have a complete copy of the proposal." He went through the steps of sending the documents through the corporate network to his computer.

Jennifer scurried around her office, gathering every candle she had ever been given as an office gift and set them on the edge of her desk.

"What are you doing?" Harrison watched as she moved about furiously.

"Well . . . if we have to turn the computers off and the power doesn't come back on right away, I want to be prepared. These candles will prevent us from having to sit in complete darkness." She looked through her desk drawers for matchbooks and matchboxes that she had picked up at different restaurants, and quickly a small stack took shape.

Harrison couldn't help but laugh.

"I think that's plenty. You have enough matches there to start a small bonfire."

She looked at the pile she had created and smiled sheepishly.

When Harrison left for his office, Jennifer was tempted to follow him, not wanting to be alone, but she controlled the urge and sat down on the couch.

Now that their work was completed, she was suddenly aware that the medication she had taken earlier was beginning to wear off. Her sinuses were feeling blocked again, and a dull ache was forming across her eyebrows. She was massaging her temples when Harrison returned.

"Headache back?" he asked as he put an armful of items on her desk.

She nodded slowly.

"Then it's time for your medicine." He twisted the tops off two medicine bottles and poured her some water. He plopped two tablets into the glass and watched it as it fizzed. As soon as she heard the sizzling of water she moaned.

"I don't think I can stomach that stuff again."

"Oh, come on. I know it tastes bad but remember how much better you felt after taking it." He squatted down in front of her and held the glass within inches of her mouth. The jumping water tickled her nose and made her giggle.

She glanced up and was instantly caught in Harrison's stare. She felt as if he were looking right through her.

"That was nice."

"What?"

She took the glass from his hand.

"You laughed."

Jennifer could feel color heating her cheeks, and it wasn't from the fever. She held out her hand for the tablets that Harrison had been holding. As much as she hated taking medicine, she did it so she could break the mesmerizing hold his gaze had on her at the moment. She allowed her head to swing back and hastily swigged down the bubbly water. Her body quaked once again. She handed the glass back to Harrison and wiped at her lips.

"Are you going to be okay if I turn off the computer now? I promise to light the candles first." He was trying to be sensitive to her obvious phobia of the dark.

She slid her boots from her feet and tucked her legs up on the couch. She shook her head in approval just before closing her eyes. *Stay calm*, she kept repeating in her head.

After Harrison lit the multitude of candles, he turned off the computer and decided to stay with Jennifer. She could feel him brush against her feet and the sofa cushion shift under his weight as he sat down. A mixture of citrus, vanilla and a floral scent filled the air. She cautiously opened her eyes, preparing herself for the darkness she would see, but instead, the room glowed in reds and golds.

It was dark, but she could still see the outline of her office furniture and Harrison stretched out next to her. He sat with his arms crossed behind his head and his legs extended out in front of him. His eyes were closed, and he seemed to be resting. It was now almost 10:00 p.m. If she knew Harrison, he had probably been at work since 6:00 a.m. He had to be exhausted. She closed her eyes and was beginning to feel the effects of the medicine again. She was about to drift off when he whispered a question.

"So why are you so afraid of the dark?"

She opened her eyes. His were still closed so she pretended not to hear him. He glanced in her direction and saw her head nestled in her curled up arms.

"I know you're not asleep."

He saw her lip twitch. She was trying to ignore him.

"Come on. I told you what my brother did to me. It can't be any worse than that. Look, I'll even promise not to laugh."

She continued to ignore him. He had no idea what he was asking her to do. Her situation had not been a laughing matter.

"So that's your solution. You're just going to ignore me? And after everything I've done for you today." He was being antagonistic. "I guess you don't feel the least sense of obligation. Well, good. Then I won't feel any obligation to include you in the presentation with Yomahama."

"That's not fair," she snapped back.

"See . . . you were awake." He suppressed a laugh but not a grin. He was feeling pretty proud of himself. He had tricked her into admitting she was awake.

"Look, I've done a lot of work on that account, and you know it. I even stuck it out today when I felt horrible. There's no way you're going to keep me from that presentation."

"But you're forgetting one thing . . . I'm the director. What I say goes." He was only teasing her, but it was enough to put her over the edge.

She leapt from the couch, losing her balance slightly, and braced herself on her desk. She turned to face Harrison.

"You are the biggest jerk I know, and I don't care if I have to walk home in a blizzard, I'm not going to sit here one more minute and be badgered by you. I knew it was too good to be true. One minute you're acting like a real person as though you care, and the next minute you're the same jerk that walked in here months ago, thinking you're God's gift to Weissler and Schuler."

She took a candle from her desk. Harrison realized she was going to leave, using the candle as her only light so he blocked the doorway.

"Look, I was only kidding. Why is it that you get so bent out of shape when people try to get to know you?"

"What are you talking about?" she asked, wanting nothing more than to leave.

"Nobody knows anything about you; I've asked. You've been at Weissler and Schuler for three years and nobody knows where you live, where you grew up, if you have siblings . . . parents . . . a pet. It's like you don't exist outside these walls."

"Maybe because my personal life is nobody's business and has nothing to do with my job, unlike you." She glared at him, while making her point. "I know the reason you got this job is because your father was a college buddy of Frank Schuler. I, on the other hand, have had to work hard all my life to try and get ahead."

Jennifer was feeling weakened by the medication. Her body began to shake and tears filled her eyes, but she continued on.

"You want to know why I have such a problem with the dark? You want to know something personal about me? Fine, I'll tell you. My father used to lock me in a closet for hours, sometimes days. There . . . are you happy? Now you know. And about my personal life—I have no siblings, my father died when I was thirteen, my mother when I was nineteen. So, now you know why I've kept my personal life to myself. I don't have memories; I have nightmares."

Jennifer was trembling, and the wax from the candle was ready to drip on her hand. Harrison carefully took the candle from her and led her back to the sofa. She covered her face with her hands and sobbed. He placed the candle back on the desk and rubbed his face. He felt as if all the air in the room had just been sucked out. He had pushed and she pushed right back. The only difference was—he was kidding, and she was being gut level honest.

He knelt in front of her and gently placed his hands on her knees. His touch wasn't meant to be intimate but compassionate. He could feel her shaking, and it made him feel worse than he already did. He wanted to hold her, to comfort her, to show her how genuinely sorry he was. Words seemed so hollow, but he had to try.

"I'm so sorry, Jennifer. I had no idea."

"Forget it." She kept her face buried in her hands.

"Look at me, Jennifer."

She could feel his breath as he spoke, aware of his closeness. She didn't want to look at him.

"I said to forget it."

"How can I? You were right. I was acting like an idiot, and now I feel like a real jerk."

Jennifer slowly raised her eyes.

"Just please don't tell anyone. I've tried so hard to keep my private life just that."

He stared into her eyes. They spoke of the pain he had just forced her to reveal. He stammered for something to say, feeling at a complete loss.

Jennifer saw that Harrison was struggling to say something, but she didn't want to hear it. She moved further back into the comfort of the cushions. "I just need some sleep. My head is swimming again, and it's obvious we're going to be here until morning. I think I'll just try and get some rest."

"I understand," he said softly.

He moved from her office so fast, she wasn't sure what to make of it. When he returned with his 3/4 length cashmere coat and draped it over her, she gave him a conciliatory smile and pulled it close to her chin. He went back to his office and came back with the cushions from his own couch. She watched as he put them on the floor in front of her and laid down on top of them.

Both perplexed and irritated by his actions, she blurted out, "Now what are you doing?"

"If the candles go out, I don't want you to panic. I'll be here all night. You won't be alone."

She didn't know what to say. She was fighting to keep her eyes open, but the medication was acting like a heavy weight, pulling down her lids. She finally offered him a timid thanks before she allowed herself to drift off to sleep.

Harrison lay awake for some time, hoping his imagination was worse than what Jennifer had actually experienced as a child. After bouncing from one scenario to another, each one getting more violent and maniacal, he tried to push his runaway thoughts out of his head. He thought instead about something else Jennifer had said during her meltdown. She knew something of his background, his father's connection to Frank Schuler. That must have meant that she was curious enough to ask. The thought made him smile. He glanced at her one last time before falling asleep.

CHAPTER THREE

It was 5:00 a.m. when Harrison was awakened by a blood-curdling scream. He was so disoriented, it took him a few seconds to make sense of his surroundings. Candles, vanilla, Jennifer. He scrambled to the edge of the couch.

"Jennifer . . . it's okay." Instinctively he reached for her and was shocked when she fought back. Her hands slapped at him and for a minute he was stunned. He realized she wasn't coherent but was in the middle of a nightmare.

"Jennifer, you need to wake up."

She lunged forward at him, but he was able to still her hand as she struggled with an unseen force. She cried out against her attacker, and it made Harrison's stomach retch. He pushed in behind her on the sofa and grabbed her other hand. He held her against his chest while trying to calm her. Jennifer tried to wrestle herself free, but Harrison held her even tighter. As she lashed about, she threw her head back, slamming it against his nose. He could feel the blood trickling down his lip, but he didn't let go of her.

"Jennifer, wake up!" He shook her, trying to bring her out of the nightmare that ensnared her.

She gasped. She couldn't figure out where she was. She pleaded incoherently, before snapping out of her nightmare. She knew she was awake, but where was she? She felt a man's arms around her, and it terrified her. The smell of vanilla and flowers was confusing her even more.

"Jennifer . . . it's Harrison. I'm not trying to hurt you. You need to relax. You're okay. Nobody's going to hurt you."

It was like cold water washing over her. In an instant, she knew where she was and who she was with. She relaxed, causing Harrison to loosen his hold on her. Immediately, she began rocking.

"What happened to you, Jennifer? What did he do to you?" Harrison's words tumbled from his mouth in horror.

She moved away from him. "Please go."

"What?"

"Please. I just want to be alone."

"But Jennifer . . ."

"Please. Please just go."

Harrison didn't know what to say. He could hear the desperation in her tone—the terror, the humiliation. He didn't want to leave her alone, but he knew he couldn't argue either. He backed out of her office and quietly closed the door. In his private restroom, he washed his face and ran his fingers through his hair. He wasn't sure how long he stood at the basin, trying to piece together the bizarre events of the last several hours when all of a sudden, lights began to flicker on in the bathroom and throughout his office. The power was back just as the dawn began to chase away the darkness outside.

HARRISON KEPT GLANCING DOWN THE HALL, waiting to see when Jennifer would open her door. It had been more than an hour since he had witnessed her breakdown, and he was beginning to worry about her. He'd already changed his clothes and gotten ready for the Yomahama presentation. He had tried rescheduling it, calling Yomahama's private number and waking him at an early hour. He used the power outage and the snowstorm as an excuse, but to no avail. Mr. Yomahama would be flying back to Tokyo later that day. The meeting would have to go on as scheduled.

Harrison spent the next few hours fine-tuning the reports he and Jennifer had finished the night before. He looked at his watch and realized it was only two hours before the presentation, and he still hadn't seen Jennifer. He decided to check in on her and see if she would feel up to sitting in on the meeting. The roads had already been cleared and he thought he had enough time to drive her home, let her change, and still get back for the meeting.

He knocked gently on her door, but his knock went unanswered. He tried again, but the room was still silent. Finally, he pushed open the door.

"Jennifer?" He looked around. She was gone. His coat and the cushions from the night before were in a stack against the wall and the aromatic candles still lined her desk, but she was gone. There was a sealed envelope on her desk with his name on the front. Quickly tearing it open, he read:

Dear Mr. Lynch:
Please accept my resignation, effective immediately. I am sorry that I was unable to give the proper two weeks notice, but an emergency has presented itself at this time, and I must leave. Please thank all my co-workers at Weissler and Schuler. The experience I have received here is invaluable.
Respectfully,
Jennifer Patterson

"No! No!" Harrison tossed the letter down on the desk and dashed to the reception area. "Doris, did you see when Jennifer left?"

"Well, yes. About 20 minutes ago. I reminded her about the Yomahama presentation, and she told me not to worry about it, that you had everything under control."

Harrison hung his head.

"I knew something was wrong when she left." Doris shook her head in disappointment. "I've never seen Jennifer look so sad. I told myself it was just the fact that she'd not been feeling well, but somehow I got the feeling it was more than that."

Harrison thought for a moment before responding. "Look, Doris, get Jennifer's personal file. I'll need her address." He quickly turned and walked away before Doris could ask him any questions.

THE MEETING COULDN'T BE OVER FAST ENOUGH for Harrison. The deal had been signed, thanks in large part to Jennifer's pointed statistics and exhaustive research. Frank Schuler shook Hideo Yomahama's hand while giving Harrison an awkward glance. He had been annoyed by the distraction he saw in Harrison's manner, but in the end, was pleased by the outcome of the presentation.

"Harrison, could I speak with you for a moment?" Frank moved back inside the conference room and closed the door while Harrison was gathering up his paperwork. He gave Harrison a stern look. "I'm sure you have a very good reason for your behavior today, but I must tell you, even though the outcome was a success, I am very disappointed with your obvious distraction." Harrison made eye contact with his superior and braced himself for the reprimand he deserved.

Harrison headed for Doris' desk as soon as his impromptu dressing-down by Frank Schuler was over.

"Doris, did you get that address?"

"Yes, Mr. Lynch." She handed him a slip of paper.

Harrison was surprised by the location. He wondered how Jennifer had been able to travel back and forth on her lunch break since the address was a good 25 minutes away. He grabbed his coat and impatiently headed down to the company parking garage. Intent on his goal, he jogged to his car and quickly drove out the exit, looking nowhere but straight ahead.

Meanwhile Jennifer sat in her car, hoping that Harrison might leave as soon as the meeting with the Yomahama people was over. She saw him across the garage and as soon as he left, she slipped back into the office building.

HARRISON PULLED UP TO THE CURB in front of a quaint two-story apartment building. He glanced down at the address again: Apartment 2B. He headed upstairs, located the correct door, and knocked. After a moment, an elderly lady answered the door.

"Yes?"

Harrison was puzzled. "I'm looking for Jennifer Patterson."

"I'm sorry, dear, there's no Jennifer here. Are you sure you have the right building?"

"2724?"

"Yes, that's correct, but I'm afraid I don't know anyone by that name."

The older woman gave Harrison a sympathetic look before closing the door.

Lost in thought, Harrison made his way slowly down the stairs. He stopped at the first apartment he had passed as he had entered the building and knocked.

"Are you by any chance the manager of the building?" Harrison asked the middle-aged housewife.

"Yes, well, my husband is."

"Did a Jennifer Patterson ever live here?"

"Yes."

Harrison's heart beat faster.

"But that was more than two years ago."

"Did she leave a forwarding address?" Harrison questioned.

"Yes, I believe she did. Just a minute."

The woman returned quickly and extended a piece of paper to him. Harrison looked at it and sighed.

"This is a post office box."

"Yes, I know. If I remember right, she said something about her job sending her out of the country and that she would be getting reestablished when she returned. That was the only address she gave us."

"Well, thank you, anyway."

Harrison walked to his car feeling his frustration mounting. At least that explained how it was that Jennifer could go home on her lunch break. Obviously, she had moved closer to the office some time in the last two years. *Why hadn't her personnel file been updated?* he thought to himself. His gut told him it had not been an oversight.

JENNIFER SLIPPED FROM THE ELEVATOR and was immediately greeted by an exuberant Doris. "How are you feeling, dear? I was so worried about you."

"I'm doing okay, Doris," she said with a sniffle. "Is Mr. Lynch in?" Jennifer asked, knowing full well he wasn't.

"No, he stepped out for a moment." Doris didn't know why, but she didn't think she should tell Jennifer that Harrison had asked for her personal address.

"I'm sorry I missed him." Jennifer coughed for a few moments longer than necessary, not wanting to do what she knew she had to. "Doris, I think you should know . . . I'm resigning."

"You're what?" Doris cried in dismay.

"Yes . . . you see I've gotten an incredible offer with another company." Jennifer waited a moment for her announcement to sink in. "Doris, you know as well as I do that Mr. Lynch and I haven't really meshed. I didn't like working with so much tension, so I put out some applications a few weeks ago. Well, I got a great offer and decided to take it."

"But Jennifer . . . this is all so sudden. Are you sure this is what you want to do? You haven't been feeling well. I don't think this is a good time to be making such an important decision."

"I'm sure, Doris." Jennifer extended an envelope to the disheartened receptionist. "My resignation is effective immediately, so I've included an account number where you can deposit my last check."

"Immediately!" Doris nearly shouted. "But Jennifer, you know the girls and I would love to give you a going away party or take you to lunch . . . something."

"I know, Doris, but my new employer was anxious for me to get started. The company's out of state, and I have a lot of packing to do."

"What about your stuff . . . your office furniture?"

"I'm going to grab a few things now, but the rest I'm leaving. If Weissler and Schuler doesn't have a use for it, you can have it." Jennifer knew that Doris had always loved the flowery couch.

With nothing left to say, Doris rose from her chair and moved to hug Jennifer. Jennifer held onto Doris for an extended moment. She was going to miss her.

HARRISON WAS APPROACHING THE COMPANY GARAGE when he saw Jennifer pull into traffic. His first reaction was to speed up, force her to pull over, and demand an explanation, but he decided to follow her instead to see where it was she was going.

She stopped at a pharmacy before turning into a small residential section just north of downtown Chicago. Harrison waited for her to go into her apartment, so he would know exactly where she lived.

His phone rang, causing him to flinch. "This is Lynch."

"Mr. Lynch, I have Mr. Schuler on the line. He says it's urgent."

Harrison debated what he should do. Schuler was calling him back to the office to discuss one point of the Yomahama account. Harrison wanted to see Jennifer, but didn't want to be hurried. He decided he would get work out of the way first and use that time to formulate what he would say to Jennifer when he showed up on her doorstep.

JENNIFER PUT ON HER FAVORITE oversized t-shirt and took another dose of medicine. She had stopped by the drug store on her way home and bought the three medications that made up the concoction that Harrison had given her. As much as she hated to admit it, he had been right. The mixture had been working—she wasn't feeling nearly as sick as she had yesterday. She crawled under her down comforter and flicked the television off, knowing she would soon be dead to the world.

Later that afternoon, Jennifer thought she heard someone knocking at her door, but she decided to ignore it, figuring that it was probably a solicitor and they would go away when she didn't answer.

But the knocking continued and was beginning to irritate her. *Maybe it's the landlord,* she thought to herself.

She dragged herself out of bed and padded barefoot across the hardwood floors of the living room. She spied through the peephole and was shocked. There stood Harrison Lynch—at her apartment! An apartment no one knew about. *How did he find out where I live? No one knows—I made sure of it.*

His knock grew more insistent, and it was obvious to her he wasn't going to give up. Jennifer slowly opened the door and brought her eyes up to meet Harrison's, but only for a moment. She settled her eyes on the tile entryway and demanded, "What are you doing here?"

"I came to talk some sense into you." He pressed against the door and breezed past her, not even waiting to be invited in.

"Harrison, I'm not exactly dressed for visitors."

He glanced at the t-shirt that barely covered her thighs. "That's too bad because I'm not leaving without an explanation," he said insistently.

She walked to her bedroom and grabbed the silk robe laying at the foot of her bed. She quickly wrapped it around her and yanked on the sash before starting in on him.

"Listen, Harrison. I'm not even going to ask how you found out where I live. I'm just going to ask you to leave."

"Why? Why are you acting this way?"

"Why am I acting this way?" She looked at him but only for a moment. There was something in his eyes that tugged at her emotions. "You have to ask?"

He just stared at her.

"You just don't get it, do you?"

"I get it," he said quietly. "You've obviously had a very traumatic past. But look at you—you've risen above it. You're a brilliant analyst. Why would you want to throw all that away and give up?"

"I'm not giving up, Harrison. I just don't have a future at Weissler and Schuler. I've taken a job elsewhere."

"Because of me, right?"

"As a matter of fact, yes."

He should have known she'd be blunt.

She decided to take charge of the conversation and put him on the defense, deflecting the question away from herself. "Tell me why all of a sudden, you want to have me around?" She stood with her arms crossed and her chin raised. "Up until last night, you were ready to fire me. So what's changed?"

Harrison searched for a reason. What could he say—that he was attracted to her, intrigued by her . . . that he had finally seen another side to her and he found it captivating?

"I will not work for someone who pities me. I've got too much talent for that." She turned to walk away.

He gently reached for her elbow and stopped her. He turned her around and waited for her to look at him. "I don't pity you, Jennifer, I admire you."

She rolled her eyes and brushed his cavalier answer aside along with his arm. "I don't need admirers." She headed to her front door, opened it, and stood waiting for him to leave. He walked slowly to the door, feeling as if he had no recourse but to go. He turned to make one last plea, but she cut him off. "If you admire me as much as you say, then you realize I'm wasting my talents at Weissler and Schuler. They don't need me as long as they have you." The door closed the minute he stepped into the hallway.

CHAPTER FOUR

I t had been a week since Harrison had last seen Jennifer. He found himself driving home each day by way of her small apartment. Each day he had to convince himself not to stop but to respect her privacy, and each day it got harder. He didn't understand his preoccupation with her. They had done nothing but argue and butt heads his entire time at Weissler and Schuler. But after spending one bizarre night with her, he found himself understanding more about her tough exterior which caused him to have even more questions about her past.

It was Friday when he drove by Jennifer's apartment and was shocked at what he saw. In her front window was a "For Rent" sign. He pulled to the curb just as a young couple and a smartly dressed woman stepped from the apartment. He got out of his car and jogged across the street. The couple had moved down the steps, but the older woman was still locking the front door.

"Excuse me. Is this apartment really for rent?" He tried to ask in a casual tone.

"Not anymore. That couple just rented it." She turned the key in the lock and started to walk away.

"But what about the other tenant?"

"You mean, Amanda? She moved out yesterday, said she'd be starting a new job on Monday."

Harrison had to think fast. "Well, I was hoping to catch her before she left. She had some important papers of mine, and I came by to pick them up."

The realtor looked suspicious. "I didn't see any papers in the house."

"She had a special place where she kept her important papers. Would you mind if I went in and took a look to see if they're still there?"

He could tell the realtor was having a hard time believing his flimsy story.

"Excuse me." The young couple was headed back up the steps. "We were wondering if there was anyway we could change the move-in date? The furniture and the apartment are in fine shape, and we don't see any need to wait for them to be cleaned."

The realtor went to answer their question when Harrison asked again about having a look inside. The realtor looked back and forth between Harrison and the couple. She turned the key and pushed open the door.

"Go ahead and look around, but I don't have all day." She scowled at Harrison but then turned a charming smile on the young couple.

Harrison moved inside the still perfectly furnished apartment. What was he looking for? He had no idea. He looked around at the immaculate apartment, knowing Jennifer wouldn't have been careless enough to leave any of her personal belongings around. He leaned on the counter by the kitchen, wondering why the realtor called Jennifer, "Amanda." He noticed there was a notepad and pen on the counter. It was all that remained of hers.

"Did you find what you were looking for?" the realtor asked through the open door, interrupting his thoughts.

"Aah, no. She must have taken them with her after all." Harrison casually slipped the notepad into his jacket pocket and headed for the door. "Thanks for your help."

Harrison pulled out his phone as soon as he got into his car.

"Dave Glazer." The voice on the line was upbeat.

"Dave, it's Harrison. You still at work?"

"Just calling it a day, why?"

"I have a favor to ask."

"Yeah?" he asked suspiciously.

"If I were to give you a social security number, would you be able to find out that person's current place of employment?"

"Why would I want to do that?" he asked questionably.

"Well, there's this girl . . ."

"I should have known. Come on, Harrison. You could have almost any woman you want. Why concentrate on the hard-to-get ones?"

"No, no, this is strictly business."

"How so?" It was obvious in Dave's tone he was not convinced.

"I think she's been lying to my company."

"So what do you want me to do about it?"

"I think she was moonlighting while working for me. It could be a conflict of interest. I want to know the name of that company and where they're located."

"You realize I could lose my job for giving out that kind of information?"

"I wouldn't ask if it weren't important."

There was a long pause across the phone lines.

"Okay. Give me the number, and I'll see what I can do. But I'm not making any promises."

"Thanks, Dave. I'll call you on Monday with the number."

When Harrison got back to the office, he pulled the notepad he had found at Jennifer's from his pocket. The page appeared blank, but he could see the small indentations made from a previous note. Harrison brushed the side of a pencil across the pad. He felt a little stupid doing what he had seen T.V. detectives do, but it did reveal a set of initials—WBP.

Harrison couldn't help but laugh at himself. The rookie detective had three initials that could have a million possibilities. He balled up the piece of paper and tossed it in the trash. He spent the rest of the day sulking, trying to piece together the events of the last week.

THE WEEKEND PROVED TO BE A LONG ONE for Harrison. He spent the majority of if with his family. Along with his father and his brother Robert, he had celebrated their mother's birthday with dinner on Saturday evening. Though Robert was nowhere to be found on Sunday morning, Harrison had agreed to accompany his mother to church. Worship had always been important to her, even if his father didn't share her interest.

Harrison was shooting pool with his brother late Sunday night when Robert finally asked what was on his mind.

"It's obvious that something is bothering you, Harry, and I can only assume that it's a woman."

Harrison didn't answer; he just casually ran the table and then offered to re-rack.

"Am I right?" Robert persisted.

"Yeah, but it's not what you think." He explained to his brother about his attraction to Jennifer, but not all the details that had led to her exposing her vulnerable side.

"Wait a minute. Is this the same 'Jennifer' broad that you were ranting about last month?"

"Yes, but that was before."

"Before what?" Robert affixed a wily look to his face. "You slept with her, didn't you?" He grinned with sly approval.

"No, Robert. I didn't sleep with her. Let's just say I was able to see her in a different light."

"Okay, so what's the problem—she playing hard to get?" Robert smoked a shot into the corner pocket.

"I get the feeling she's not who she says she is."

"I don't get it." Robert said before sinking a string of balls. "If she's such a pain, why are you obsessing over her? Move on, Harry. I know plenty of women that would love to show you a good time."

The two brothers' characters had always been polar opposites. While Harrison had had his share of flings in college and a few office romances early in his career, Robert was the typical impress them, bed them, and get over them kind of guy. He and Harrison rarely agreed on women.

Harrison spent the last few hours of the evening explaining to his brother some of the things that were bothering him about Jennifer—different names, different addresses, and her abrupt resignation. He never spoke about her suspected abuse or the fact that her nightmare indicted her father. That information was too personal to bring up in conversation.

Robert agreed with him how strange it was that she would leave for no apparent reason. Of course he didn't know the whole story, but what he did know intrigued him.

Robert and Harrison talked long into the night. Robert wasn't really much help—his answers to everything involved sex and money—but Harrison was at least able to process out loud some of the feelings he had for Jennifer.

FIRST THING MONDAY MORNING, Harrison called Dave with Jennifer's social security number. He told him that he was led to believe that she had taken a job out of state. Dave told Harrison he probably wouldn't have any answers for another week or so, not until new contributions were made to the account. But he assured Harrison he would watch her account and notify him the minute there was activity.

Harrison went about his work, knowing one of the priorities of the week would be to find someone to replace Jennifer as his assistant. His phone rang before lunch. It was Dave and he already had some news to pass on to Harrison.

"You're not going to believe what I found out."

Harrison sat poised and ready, pen in hand to write down the information.

"Jennifer Patterson died over three years ago in a car accident." Dave waited for a response and thought that maybe they had been disconnected. "Harrison, did you hear me?"

"Yeah, I heard you but that's impossible. She's been working at Weissler and Schuler for over three years. There must be some kind of mistake. Maybe your computer pulled up a different Jennifer Patterson."

"That's just it, Harrison. I didn't use her name; I used the social that you gave me. All the information's there, Harrison. She's had contributions made by Weissler and Schuler since January of 2002. Is that right?"

"Yeah, that's right." Harrison answered; confusion in his tone. "So how is it that your information says she's dead?"

"Her file shows that she was reported killed in an auto accident in Tyler, Texas, in September 2001."

"Then how is it that contributions were still made in her name?"

"It was an oversight, I guess. I mean the social security number does belong to a Jennifer Patterson, so according to the computer there isn't a discrepancy. That is until you open up the account and see that she's deceased."

"Thanks, Dave. I'll talk to you later." Harrison hung up the phone while his head swam in a fog. *What's going on?* he kept asking himself, but he had no idea where to go for answers. Not only had she vanished off the face of the earth, but now it appears as if she never even existed.

JENNIFER HAD BEEN RESEARCHING ONLINE NEWSPAPERS of small Midwestern towns when she finally found what she was looking for. She saw that a woman in her late twenties had died in a house fire the previous week. The picture next to the article showed a woman with light colored hair and what looked to be green eyes. *Easy enough,* she thought to herself. The woman was described as a very private person who worked from her home. Her neighbors said she was very kind, often passing out candy to the neighborhood kids. No one knew much about her but everyone was saddened by her sudden death.

Jennifer wrote down the woman's name and then watched for her obituary to appear in subsequent editions. It took only a few days for Jennifer to find out that Samantha Wilder had no family. *Samantha Wilder . . . I like it.*

SAMANTHA WILDER APPROACHED the property management offices of West Beach Properties. She took a seat across from the secretary's desk and waited to be seen.

"Mr. Holmes is ready to see you now," the secretary offered with a smile.

Samantha tugged at her tailored suit and smoothed her neatly coifed hair as she got to her feet.

The reception area reminded her of Weissler and Schuler. She choked back the heaviness in her throat and moved through the large paneled doors. She was Samantha Wilder now. There would be no looking back.

She had done this before, and each time it grew easier—until now. This was the first time that she felt as if she had left something behind. The evening she had spent with Harrison had been difficult to put out of her head. Her internal autopilot had told her she needed to move on. He would have too many questions for her. But there was a part of her that was tired of running, tired of hiding. She wondered what it would be like to finally be honest with someone. But it didn't matter now. She had instinctively made the decision to leave Chicago, and now she had to make the best of it.

She shook hands with Mr. Holmes, thanking him for the opportunity to work with his company. She would have to earn any promotions, but that was okay. Hard work had never been a problem for her; in fact, it was all she ever knew. She exited the offices, and immediately the salty sea air washed over her.

The offices of West Beach Properties were just a few blocks from the famous Santa Monica Pier and the park that overlooked it. She took a deep breath and inhaled her new life. This would be it. This would be the last move, the last name change, the last time she would run. California would be home. Her home.

CHAPTER FIVE

Three Years Later . . .

"Come on, Robert, you said we were coming to California to get you settled. You never told me I would have to play babysitter. If I had known that, I would have stayed in Chicago."

"That's why I didn't tell you." Robert laughed openly. "Come on, Harry, she's not that bad. Besides, you don't have to spend all your time with her. It's just that if Kelly and I hope to have time together alone, I'll need you to run interference once in a while. And face it—you need a little fun in your life. Believe me, Maris is just the woman to give it to you." Robert laughed again, knowing that his approach to life was completely different from his brother's.

Harrison had already been out with Maris twice. She was not his type at all. She was clingy and forward. Most men would have overlooked her behavior because of her incredibly good looks, but not Harrison. He found women with Maris' personality to be far too wild for his taste. There was something to be said about the man leading the relationship. Maris had already propositioned him and saw his refusal as a challenge.

Harrison walked out on the balcony that overlooked the pier. The Pacific Ocean crashed against the pillars and washed over the sand. Robert had invited him on a two-month long vacation as a way to spend time with him before his impending marriage. Robert had dated long distance for seven months before popping the question to Kelly, and now with his brother in tow, Robert had decided to spend the last months before the wedding in California, getting acquainted with what would be his new home.

Harrison was happy for Robert. His brother had gotten himself in and out of trouble over the last few years. His business dealings had proven to be anything but upstanding. He'd always been able to elude prison time, but the path he'd been traveling had been both shady and dangerous. Harrison was hoping that the change he saw in Robert since he'd been dating Kelly would be enough to keep him on the straight and narrow.

Harrison was looking forward to spending this time with him before Robert plunged into marriage. What Robert hadn't told Harrison was that Kelly's best friend and roommate, Maris, would need some company if Robert hoped to spend any time with his fiancée alone.

Harrison went back into the suite where Robert was sprawled out across one of the couches. Robert could still see disapproval in Harrison's eye.

"Come on, Harry, so she's a bit of a flirt. It's not like you're involved with anyone. Loosen up."

Robert and Harrison had grown apart over the last few years mostly because of Robert's business choices and the gratuitous lifestyle he chose to lead. Robert didn't know the meaning of making an honest dollar. Get-rich-quick schemes had always clouded Robert's judgment. And the womanizing he'd done over the years had saddened their mother and put a strain on the family relationship. That's why Robert chose to relocate to the west coast. New girl, new life, new start, that's what he told Harrison. Harrison could only pray that Robert meant it. It had been difficult for Harrison to watch the pain that Robert had caused his parents over the years, especially his mother.

Vivian Lynch was a very conservative woman with a close relationship with God. Though her husband, Robert Sr., a powerful businessman, had never shared her interest in things of God, he hadn't stood in the way of her raising their boys in the church. As Robert and Harrison got older, she witnessed their waning in and out of fellowship with the Lord. Through prayer, she had always kept her boys before the Lord.

Though Robert's life had continued to spiral out of control over the last few years, she'd begun to see a change in Harrison. She wasn't sure what had happened to make him reach out for a deeper relationship with God, but she was pleased nonetheless with the transformation. He continued to succeed at Weissler and Schuler and was made a full partner the previous year. The Yomahama account had proven to be the cornerstone for worldwide contacts that had catapulted Weissler, Schuler, and Lynch into becoming a Fortune 500 company.

Harrison was content—he had his career, his family, and his faith. It was only when the vision of a certain petite blond would cross his mind or infuse his thoughts that he had thoughts of "I wonder what would have happened if . . ."

Jennifer Patterson had fallen off the map the day she left Weissler and Schuler. He had been determined to find Jennifer no matter what and had tried for months to locate her. He periodically called his friend Dave to see where her social security number would lead, but she never re-materialized. Jennifer Patterson had simply vanished.

"So what's on the agenda for today?" Harrison asked, giving his brother a conciliatory smile.

"The beach," Robert said with a dancing eyebrow. "Nothing like a beach full of bikinis to let you know what's missing in your life."

SAMANTHA HAD A GRUELING WEEK, which made the weekend all the more appetizing. She had slept in, pushing back her early morning jog to noon. The afternoon sun would make it a harder run, but then she could relax in the warmth of the rays until late afternoon.

She gathered her beach towel, swimsuit, sunscreen, water bottle, and a package of crackers to munch on for lunch. She pulled on a yellow tank top and white shorts, slid on her sunglasses and a ball cap, and grabbed her iPod before heading to the beach. It was an easy walk. Her quaint, little house was just two blocks from the stairs leading down the cliffs of Santa Monica and across the highway to the beachfront. It was the walk back that always proved to be the most challenging.

ROBERT AND HARRISON HAD PICKED UP KELLY AND MARIS and made their way to the beach. The ladies had packed a picnic lunch for the four of them and led them to a spot close to the pier. They trudged along, carrying their beach paraphernalia across the hot sand, finally finding an area big enough for them to off-load all their stuff. The women spread out a large blanket, and the men dropped towels, baskets, and the large ice chest on it.

The water was calling Harrison. He had been in California for a week, and this was the closest he had been to the water. "I don't know about you guys," he said as he grabbed at the back of his shirt and pulled it over his head. "but I'm heading for the water."

Maris did nothing to hide her sigh of approval when Harrison exposed his sculpted abs and muscular arms. "Wait for me. I'll go with you." Maris kicked off her sandals and slowly slid out of her skimpy shorts to expose an even more revealing bikini. She adjusted the strings on her hips and then gave Harrison an inviting smile. "I'm ready when you are."

Harrison maneuvered around the many beachgoers basking in the sun and made his way to the water. Maris was clutching his arm as he waded into the shallow waves that were lapping onto the sand. Maris squealed as the water licked at her ankles. The cool water felt great, making Harrison want to venture further out, but not with Maris hanging onto him.

"Look, Maris. I want to go out a little further. Why don't you wait here?"

"Oh no, you don't. You're not going to get rid of me that easy," she said as she moved closer to his side.

"It's not that. I just want to be able to do some swimming. The waves can be pretty unpredictable, and I don't want you to get in over your head."

Maris quickly wrapped her arms around Harrison's neck and pulled herself up against his wet chest. "I can be unpredictable, too."

Before he could say anything, she had pressed her lips to his and given him a very demanding kiss. He took her laced fingers and unwrapped them from around him. "Look, Maris, I don't know what Robert told you, but I'm not interested."

Maris bobbed in the water next to him, shocked that he continued to ignore her availability, but her disappointment didn't last long. She smiled at him and let out a seductive laugh. "Robert said you wouldn't be easy, but that's okay. I like a challenge."

Harrison did not handle the forwardness of women well. Instead of saying something he might later regret, he decided to swim away from Maris and venture out deeper into the breaking waves.

She didn't follow him; she chose to wade where the water was just rising and falling around her bikini top.

Harrison took in the sights on the shore. There were toddlers with shovels and pails playing in the wet sand, a boy throwing a Frisbee for a dog that would faithfully retrieve it, and teenagers tossing discs on the ground and riding them on the slick, smooth sand. Several people waded in the shallow water, bending down to splash themselves but not willing to commit to deeper water. Joggers passed back and forth, some sprinting, others barely shuffling their feet.

Harrison enjoyed everything about this, everything that is, except for Maris and the way she insisted on pushing herself on him. He saw her out of the corner of his eye watching him, but he ignored it and chose to look the other way. He continued to scan the shore, when all of a sudden he saw something that made his eyes squint for clarification.

"Jennifer?" he blurted out loud.

It's her! He floated for a moment stunned by her appearance before he feverishly started swimming for shore. He kept her in sight, the jogger in the yellow tank top and white shorts. He was riding a wave in when he heard a shrill voice from behind him.

"Harrison! Harrison!"

He turned. Maris was grabbing for her side, hunched over in the water. She was cramping up. He did a double take towards the shore, looking at the jogger and then back at Maris who was whimpering in the water.

"Dang it!" he yelled angrily.

He was mad. He was furious. He hadn't even wanted Maris to go out in the water, and now because of her, he was losing sight of someone who was a dead ringer for Jennifer. He quickly swam over to Maris and held her as he made his way towards shore. He helped her out of the water and tried to see where the jogger had gone. "Are you all right?" he asked as Maris continued to lean against him, panting for breath.

"Yes, I guess so, but I don't think I can walk back to the blanket. I feel so faint."

Harrison swallowed his anger and lifted her into his arms. He made a quick dash to the blanket, avoiding children that ran across his path and passing people on blankets enjoying the beach. Maris lay in his arms, her head resting on his chest. Her chest heaved from what appeared to be exhaustion, but Harrison suspected her little emergency was staged.

He approached the blanket where Robert and Kelly were caressing each other with oil. They didn't even see Harrison coming until he almost dropped Maris onto the corner of the blanket.

"You okay?" Harrison asked Maris impatiently. When she took too long to answer, he asked again with a tick of belligerence in his tone. "Are you okay?"

"Harrison, what happened?" Kelly looked from Maris to Harrison and then moved forward to comfort Maris.

"She cramped up in the water. Look . . . I'll be right back." He didn't have time to explain; he just got up from the blanket and started down the beach in the direction the jogger had been heading. He jogged along the shore, his eyes darting from the shoreline ahead of him to the swarm of people sitting on the beach. He ran all the way to the pier and then slowly walked back scanning the crowd. He passed where Robert, Kelly, and Maris were sitting on their blanket as he continued his search. He was walking aimlessly when Robert came up behind him and grabbed his shoulder.

"What the heck do you think you're doing?"

Harrison looked at Robert with a stunned expression on his face. "I saw her. I saw Jennifer."

"You what?"

"I saw her. I'm sure of it. She was jogging down the beach when I was out in the water. I would have caught up to her if it hadn't been for Maris."

Robert looked at Harrison like he had lost his mind. "Harry, listen to yourself. You have completely insulted a gorgeous woman so you could run after a figment of your imagination."

"It was her, Robert. I know it was." He was being insistent, his fist clutched in aggravation.

"What are the odds, Harry? Let's see: Three years and 2000 miles away from where you last saw her, both of you in the exact spot, on the exact day, at the exact time. You do the math, Mr. Statistician. It's impossible!"

Robert waited for his words to sink in. *I was sure it was her,* Harrison thought. *But Robert's probably right—the odds are a million to one.*

"Is Maris okay?" Harrison asked, trying to appease his brother.

"Yeah, she's okay. Her feelings are hurt and she's a little shaken up, but she's fine." Robert tossed his arm around his brother's shoulder. "If I were you, I'd take this opportunity to show her what a caring guy you can be. I'm sure she'd appreciate a little coddling, you know, to show your concern."

Harrison knew exactly what his brother meant, but unlike him, Harrison wasn't about to take advantage of the situation, especially since he felt Maris set the whole thing up. He walked back with Robert to where the women were waiting for them on the blanket.

"What happened? Where did you go?" Kelly was asking Harrison, while Maris lay on the blanket, holding her side.

"I thought I saw someone I knew."

Maris didn't even look at him. She looked as if she were resting, her eyes closed.

"Maris, are you all right?" Harrison bent down and asked.

She opened her eyes only slightly and nodded her head.

"I'm sorry. I shouldn't have left you like that."

"That's okay . . . but I think I'd feel better if I went home."

Harrison looked at Kelly to see what she wanted to do. Robert spoke on her behalf.

"Look, why don't you take the car and get Maris home. Kelly and I will take a taxi when we're ready to go." Robert winked at Harrison, but Harrison ignored him.

Harrison realized what was probably a trick on Maris' part could still have turned into a tragic accident. He went ahead and gathered up some of the stuff they had brought so Robert wouldn't have to shoulder it all when he and Kelly left. He helped Maris to her feet and watched as she slowly pulled her street clothes on. The walk to the car was quiet. While Harrison was deep in thought, knowing he hadn't been mistaken about Jennifer, Maris was planning her next move.

Harrison noticed that Maris still seemed shaken up when they got back to the condo she shared with Kelly.

"If you don't mind, I think I'd like to take a nice hot bath," she said in a timid voice.

"No, I completely understand," Harrison said with a smile. "I'll just see my way out."

"Please . . . don't go." She reached out for his arm. "I won't be long. If you could just stay until I got out." She studied him with hazel eyes that were almost doe-like. "I would prefer not to be alone. I still feel a little shaky." She moved to her bedroom and gathered up some things and then crossed to the bathroom. "I'll be right out."

Harrison wandered around Kelly and Maris' spacious condo looking at the mementos that were scattered around. He couldn't help but notice that Maris was with a different guy in every picture.

He finally took a seat on the couch and thought back to the jogger he had seen on the beach. He closed his eyes and replayed the scene in his mind. She was the same height and had the same beautiful, silky blonde hair. When she had glanced over her shoulder towards the water, for an instant he saw her face. It was her, he just knew it, but how was he going to find her? Maybe he could go to the beach tomorrow, at the same time, and see if she showed up again. It would be a long shot, a one-in-a-million chance, but he had to give it a try.

Harrison pondered a few more ideas when he heard the bathroom door opening. Maris stepped out in a breezy halter-style sundress. She crossed the living room to the large picture window that looked out over the water. The light cascading through the window caused the sheer dress to become even more transparent. Harrison could see every curve of her body. Nothing was left to his imagination. He tried to hide his awkwardness by moving to the kitchen and opening wide the refrigerator. "Do you mind if I have something to drink?"

"No . . . not at all." Maris realized her attempt at being a seductress was going to have to be a little more subtle for it to work on Harrison. If she wasn't careful he would leave before Kelly and Robert got back. No, she would have to soften her tactics.

She waited until Harrison was looking her way, and then she reached for the wall and allowed her feet to stumble slightly. Just as she knew he would, Harrison was instantly at her side and placed his arm gently around her for support. "You'd better sit down. You don't look so good."

Maris allowed Harrison to walk her to the couch as she held onto his arm. "Would you mind staying until Kelly gets home? I mean I would understand if you want to go . . . I just . . . I mean . . . I feel . . ." Her eyes fluttered as she played with her hands in her lap and lowered her head. She acted as if she were going to cry.

"It's okay, Maris. I'll stay."

She grinned inwardly as she relaxed beside Harrison, allowing her head to rest on his shoulder. She curled her feet up under her and sighed.

Harrison wanted to move away from Maris. He felt trapped. She was taking advantage of her accident to get closer to him. He looked at his watch and wondered how much longer Robert and Kelly would be. Harrison allowed his head to fall back on the cushions of the couch and closed his eyes. He felt a small shudder from Maris and realized that as much as he didn't appreciate her forwardness, her accident had to have been scary for her. He thought back to her lashing about in the water, but instantly his mind traveled to the jogger on the beach.

It was Jennifer. He just knew it was. He sensed it. Then, as if transported back in time, he thought about the night they had spent together in her office, how he had wanted to hold her close and comfort her. His desire to kiss her that night had almost been more than he could handle.

He visualized them together and fantasized about the kiss that never was. He allowed himself to get lost in his daydream, one that he'd had hundreds of times since Jennifer had disappeared. He wasn't sure how long he and Maris had been sitting on the couch, or how he'd allowed his subconscious to use Maris as a substitute for Jennifer, but an abrupt noise brought Harrison back to the present.

Robert and Kelly, loaded down with beach accessories, stumbled through the door. Maris was pressed against Harrison, leaning into his embrace, her face dangerously close to his. In the midst of his fantasy, he had almost used Maris as a surrogate for Jennifer.

"Well, I see you two are getting to know each other," Robert said as he put down the beach chairs and towels and gave Harrison a devilish grin.

Harrison looked at Maris, embarrassed by what had almost happened. He got up from where he was sitting and crossed the living room. "What are you guys doing back so soon?"

"Kelly was worried about Maris. The beach is no fun if you can't relax."

"Well, now that you guys are here, I think I'll be going."

"What's your hurry, Harry?" Robert said with a sideways glance at Maris.

Harrison gave him a stare that said that he had endured enough of his matchmaking. Robert followed Harrison to the front door and out onto the landing.

"Come on, Harry, you can't leave now," he whispered so as not to be heard by Kelly and Maris, but his frustration was evident.

"Look, Robert. I've done enough babysitting today."

"Well, what I saw didn't look like babysitting. In fact, if we hadn't come in when we did, I think you'd be singing a whole different tune."

"That was a mistake. I wasn't thinking straight." Harrison was embarrassed.

"Maris didn't seem to mind."

"Yeah, well, I don't think there's much that Maris would mind." Harrison was upset with himself and with Robert. "I'll see you back at the hotel." Harrison turned away while Robert was still trying to convince him to stay.

The hotel was only a mile away, so Harrison decided to walk. He inhaled the fresh air and decided to consult his closest friend. He had gotten in the habit of talking to God with an inward voice over the last few years, beginning right after Jennifer had disappeared.

Lord, I don't understand. Did I see Jennifer or not? Why after all this time? Did I imagine it? But if so, what does it mean? Lord, help me to understand what I'm feeling. Why, after so much time? I still have a longing to find her, Lord, even if she doesn't want to be found.

Harrison continued to the hotel, deep in thought. He went out onto the balcony that overlooked the incredible coastline. Maybe jogging was part of her routine. Maybe he could go back to the beach tomorrow and see if he spotted her again. He knew it was a shot in the dark, but at least it gave him something to look forward to.

CHAPTER SIX

Harrison positioned himself once again by one of the lifeguard stands and waited. He'd gone to the beach every day for a week after seeing the jogger he thought was Jennifer. He arrived at noon, giving himself plenty of time in case she showed up early. This time he stayed until 4:00 p.m., never once seeing the blond jogger.

He slowly walked back to the bridge that crossed the highway and scaled the numerous steps to the city streets above. He was dejected and chastised himself for being so optimistic when he knew the odds had been a statistical nightmare.

When Harrison got back to the hotel room, there was a note waiting for him that read, "Went to look at property with Kelly. Won't be back until later tonight."

Good. Harrison thought to himself. At least with Robert gone, he would get a reprieve from having to entertain Maris.

"SAMANTHA, THIS IS MY FIANCÉ, Robert. Robert, this is Samantha, our realtor."

Samantha had to catch her breath. The man leaning against Kelly's car looked like an older Harrison Lynch. He stood and extended his hand to Samantha with a polite smile. It was uncanny.

Samantha caught herself staring and had to shake off the feeling of déjà vu. Robert returned her stare with a smile that was a little too friendly for Samantha's taste, especially since he was there with his fiancée to buy a house. Samantha addressed them as a couple as she launched into her proposal, ignoring what she was sure was an overactive imagination.

"I know Kelly has probably told you everything about this house, but let me go over some of the pertinent details with you. The house is three levels, totaling 5,000 square feet."

Robert and Kelly listened to Samantha explain their dream home in detail.

"The floors are inlaid Italian marble from Milan, and the fresco on the wall was painted by Philippe Arturo almost ten years ago. His work of late has become quite renowned in the art world, making this piece even more valuable."

Kelly simply gushed as she clutched Robert's arm. "Isn't it beautiful, Robert? I think it's just perfect."

Samantha stepped down into a massive room, its sweeping views taking in the coastlines from Marina Del Rey to Malibu. The Italian villa that was perched atop the cliffs of the Pacific Palisades was exactly the house that Kelly was looking for. And why not? She had spent several years in Italy with her family and then again on her own during her college years. Kelly's father was a very wealthy businessman that had lavished an extravagant lifestyle on his family, one that had obviously rubbed off onto his daughter. Kelly would never settle for the ordinary. And this house was far from ordinary.

They toured the rest of the villa from the wine cellar to the private theater. There was an Olympic-sized swimming pool in the side garden, and an impressive, professional-looking kitchen. Robert thought it was a lot more house than they needed, but since Kelly's father was footing the bill, Kelly insisted on getting exactly what she wanted.

"So, what do you think, Robert?" Kelly asked excitedly.

"It's awfully big, Kelly. Are you sure you want this much house to keep up with?"

She looked at him like he was speaking a foreign language. "We'll be hiring a staff, Robert. It's not like I'm going to have to do the cleaning myself."

A *staff*. Robert thought to himself and sighed. He knew Kelly had never lifted a finger in her life, and though the idea of domestic help wasn't completely foreign to him, he hadn't given much thought to having a staff of his own. His mother always had someone in their home helping with the cooking and the cleaning, but when Kelly used the word "staff," Robert knew she meant more than a cook and a cleaning lady. She was talking about full-time, live-in help.

"How much staff are we talking about, Kelly?"

She turned to him, his look letting her know that he was not too thrilled with the idea. "We'll need at least four people, maybe six."

"Six? Why so many?" Robert did nothing to hide his irritation.

Kelly smiled at Samantha and politely excused herself, dragging Robert with her. Samantha tried to appear unaware of their little disagreement. Kelly pulled Robert into the large entryway, and in a whispered voice, scolded Robert for embarrassing her in front of their realtor.

"Robert, what has gotten into you? This is not the time nor the place to discuss our personal situation." Kelly looked at him with a steely stare.

He tried to cover his faux pas with a touch of romanticism. He pulled her close to his chest and raised his eyebrow. "I just want to know when I come home at night that I'll have you all to myself. You know, so we'll have no interruptions." His voice was deep and sultry.

Kelly couldn't help giggling as color crept into her complexion. "I'm sure we'll be able to work something out so that we'll have our privacy."

He'd escaped Kelly's wrath, at least for the moment.

They rejoined Samantha in the massive living room. "We'd like to make an offer," Kelly said with authority and renewed confidence.

Robert was quiet on the way back to the real estate office. Cold feet were beginning to cement themselves inside his designer shoes, but he felt he was in too deep to do anything about it. If he gave Kelly even the slightest hint that he was having second thoughts, she would walk out of his life for good. He was going to have to ride this one out and hope that it wouldn't be the mistake of his life.

HARRISON WORKED ON SOME FILES and e-mailed them back to the office in Chicago. Even though he was now a partner, he still did much of the statistical reports for the larger accounts himself. He closed up his computer and walked out onto the balcony. It was quickly becoming his favorite place because of the relaxing effect it had on him, so much so that he was beginning to entertain the idea of moving to California himself. With computers and video conferencing, he could easily continue to work for the firm but reside on the west coast. Maybe he would do some property scouting of his own.

"I UNDERSTAND WHAT YOU'RE SAYING, but this property is worth every penny the owner is asking." Samantha was polite but direct. "I'm afraid I would not recommend Miss Andrews making an offer lower than the asking price. This house will not be on the market long."

Kelly was losing her patience with Robert. She wanted that house, and at any cost. She angrily muttered under her breath, "Robert, you're being ridiculous. Daddy said he wanted to buy us the perfect house, and I don't want to do anything to lose it."

Samantha shuffled papers on her desk, pretending not to hear the argument that was going on in front of her.

"I just think that if we're meant to have that house, then the sellers will accept our offer."

Kelly's look was one of pure irritation. "What kind of line is that? This is real estate, Robert, not petal pulling. What is your problem?"

Robert got up and started pacing as he pulled his hand through hair that he was sure was turning gray prematurely. "I'm just not sure, Kelly."

She stood with her hands firmly planted on her hips. "About the house, Robert . . . or us?"

When Robert didn't answer fast enough, Kelly snatched up her purse and stalked to Robert's side.

"When you decide what you want, Robert, give me a call. But I wouldn't wait. I won't be on the market long." With that, she stormed from the office and left Robert to figure out his next move.

He glanced at Samantha, embarrassed that she had witnessed Kelly's angry ranting. He knew he should go after her, but he didn't. She was too upset to listen to him. She would need time to cool down. Besides, he wasn't even sure what he wanted any more.

"I'm sorry," Samantha said from behind her desk. "I can't help but think some of this is my fault. I should have just submitted your offer and let it go at that." Samantha crossed her office to file papers in a beautiful antique file cabinet.

"It's not your fault." Robert looked at her, giving her a reassuring grin. He liked what he was seeing. Samantha was a petite blond with a beautiful smile. Robert's pulse tightened. "In fact, I should be apologizing to you. Kelly isn't one to hide her feelings. Sometimes her discretion is not what it should be."

Robert decided that Kelly needed some time to cool off, and he needed a distraction. He slowly allowed his eyes to travel from Samantha's cream-colored camisole to her form-fitting black skirt. The stiletto heels that she was wearing made it look as if her shapely legs went on forever. His eyes finally came back up to her face. She tried to avoid his gaze, already feeling uncomfortable with the attention he was showing her.

"You know, it's already 2:00 p.m., what would you say to lunch? It will be my way of apologizing for making you a witness to our little misunderstanding."

Samantha did everything she could to keep her composure. The commission on this property would be huge, but the look she was getting from Robert was anything but business-like. "I'm going to have to pass" was all she said.

Robert stepped around her desk, closing the distance between them. "Why? You have to eat," Robert persisted.

"You have a fiancée, a very angry one at the moment, I might add." Samantha tried to keep her composure as she stepped away from Robert. She'd avoided many passes over the years, so she just smiled and chose her words carefully. "I don't think it would be in your best interest to go to lunch with me. Besides, you're not exactly my type, and I would hate for you to throw away what you have with Kelly because your testosterone levels are in high gear. If you were smart, you'd go find Kelly and apologize."

"Apologize? You think this is my fault?"

Samantha tossed papers into her leather satchel. "Yes, I do."

"How do you figure? If you haven't noticed, Kelly is extremely spoiled and a little high strung."

"And I'd venture to say you knew that long before today." Samantha snapped shut her bag. "Kelly and I have looked at dozens of houses and none of them compare to this one. This is exactly what she wants."

"Yes, what she wants. She hasn't even considered what I want."

"That's not fair. She could have bought the house last week, without you ever seeing it, but she didn't. She wanted to make sure you were involved with the decision."

Samantha caught herself arguing over something that was not her fight. "I need to go. I have other clients that I need to meet with. Here's my card. After you've had a chance to talk to Kelly, you can give me a call and let me know how you would like me to proceed. I'll ask the owners to give us two days before they entertain other offers. I'm sure you can find your way out." Samantha picked up her bag, along with her purse and blazer, and walked past the reception area and out to her car.

Robert pulled out his cell phone and dialed Harrison's number.

"Hey, what are you doing?" Robert asked Harrison as he watched Samantha pull away.

"Nothing at the moment, why?"

"I need a ride."

Harrison heard something in Robert's voice. "Where's Kelly?"

"We had a small disagreement."

"Where are you?" He groaned.

"West Beach Properties. 416 Crest Road. It's just a couple of blocks from the hotel. Think you can find it?"

"Yeah, I'll be right there."

This doesn't sound good, Harrison thought as he grabbed the car keys and made his way to the lobby. Harrison had gotten the feeling that Robert wasn't ready for marriage, and this might be the first crack before the whole dam broke loose.

Harrison asked at the front desk for directions and then made his way to Crest Road. He was looking for a sign that said West Beach Properties, but instead, was struck by an art deco sign with the simple initials WBP. He screeched to a halt, not even seeing Robert standing at the curb. Robert pulled open the passenger door and slid into the black leather interior of his Mercedes. Harrison sat trance-like, staring at the sign.

Robert waited for him to pull away from the curb, but there he sat, staring at the sign. "What's with you?"

Harrison looked at Robert and then back as the sign. "The sign, the initials—WBP. Those were the initials scribbled on the notepad I found at Jennifer's apartment the day she left."

Robert waited for Harrison to say something that made sense. "Yeah . . . so?"

"Don't you find that strange? First the jogger on the beach, now this?"

"No, I see it as a man grasping at straws. Now, come on, I'm starving and I need a drink. Let's go get something to eat."

It was a moment before Harrison pulled away from the curb and merged into traffic. He wanted to explore this latest find, but knew that Robert's situation required his attention at the moment. It was too early for any of the finer restaurants to be open, so Harrison settled on a small deli across from the Santa Monica Park.

They gave their order to the man behind the counter and then helped themselves to something cold to drink from the cooler alongside the counter. Harrison grabbed a soda while Robert reached for a bottle of beer. When they got their sandwiches, they brought them to a table next to the window. Harrison prayed silently and then with a sigh asked Robert, "So are you going to tell me what happened?"

Robert bit into his sandwich and took a swig from his bottle of imported beer before answering. "I'm not sure. One minute we were talking about the

41

house, and the next minute, it was like we were talking about our relationship, but not really. I wasn't sure if Kelly was trying to pick a fight, or if she was afraid that I was ready to back out."

"Of the house?" Harrison asked between bites.

"Of the whole thing." Robert took another swallow, trying to wash away the tension in his voice. "I thought for sure I was ready to get married, but maybe I'm not ready for that level of commitment."

Harrison gave Robert a few minutes to dwell on what he had just said before asking, "And now?"

"Now I don't know." Robert paused. "I mean, look at me, Harry. I'm a very successful businessman. I just assumed when I got married, I would provide for my family, have a few kids, you know, do the whole family thing. But with Kelly, I see that it's going to be different. She doesn't need me to provide for her. She has her father wrapped around her little finger."

Robert allowed his mind to wander back to when he had first met Kelly. "I thought it was great when we first started dating and I found out that she was independently wealthy. I felt secure knowing she wasn't after me just for my money. But now . . ."

"Now it's that same independence that bothers you." Harrison's words weren't meant to sound harsh, just realistic.

"Yeah, I guess so. Is that stupid of me? I mean, I was the one who thought I'd scored big. Not only is Kelly beautiful, but she's rich. I thought that might be a nice asset to fall back on, but now I'm thinking maybe I was wrong. With everything her father can give her, what does she need me for?"

"What do you need her for?" Harrison's question was blunt and took Robert by surprise.

"I love being with her. She's gorgeous and sexy, and she's got all the right moves. I love holding her, knowing she doesn't have any ulterior motives. I mean, we've never once argued until now. I thought for sure that she was the one . . . now I'm not so sure."

Harrison finished his sandwich and tossed his gingham colored paper into the wastebasket. "Well, maybe it's not a question of love, maybe it's a question of ego."

"What?" Robert retorted.

"You don't like the idea of not being able to control her."

"What's that suppose to mean?"

"Come on, Robert, nothing has happened in your life that you haven't had control over. Even with the scrapes you've gotten yourself into, you've always bounced back better than before. But Kelly's different. She's got her own money, her own circle of friends, and her own opinion on things. She's not going to be like some of the women that you've dated who've hung on your every word, agreed with everything you said, and gushed when you lavished them with expensive dinners or weekends in the tropics. With Kelly, you're going to have to invest more into the relationship. You're going to have to give her yourself, not just things. Are you ready for that kind of commitment?"

Robert didn't answer. He took some time to think about what Harrison had said, and he realized his brother was right. Kelly was accustomed to the lifestyle that he usually used to wow other women. That wasn't what Kelly was after. She wanted a relationship, but Robert wanted to know that their relationship would not include her father. Robert knew they were close and that wasn't what he was worried about. He just didn't want her father nosing around in Robert's business. Robert wasn't sure if he was ready for a power struggle with him. He had enough of that to deal with in his world of creative finance.

"So what happened next?" Harrison took a swig of his soda, not liking the look he saw on Robert's face. "Robert . . . what did you do?"

Robert rapped his fingers on the table before admitting to his stupidity. "I hit on the realtor."

"You what?" Harrison's raised voice got the attention of the shop owner.

Robert kept his voice more controlled. "Look, I was ticked off. Kelly had just shut me down in front of her. I mean, here's this incredible looking woman, and Kelly made me look like an idiot. It was a knee jerk reaction."

"Your knee had nothing to do with it, but I won't argue with the jerk part." Harrison shook his head in disappointment. "What did she say . . . the broker, I mean?"

"She blew me off."

"Smart girl!"

"Yeah, well, it wasn't her smarts that attracted me." Robert had a smirk on his face that irritated Harrison.

"When are you going to grow up, Robert?" Harrison was getting angry. "You've got to stop playing games. Kelly is not the kind of woman you toy with."

"I know, I know. I don't know how it happened."

"Yeah, well, I wouldn't take too much time figuring it out if I were you. I don't see Kelly as the patient type."

Robert thought back to Kelly's warning. She wouldn't be on the market long. He had some damage control to do, and he had better do it quick. He didn't want to lose Kelly or the lucrative deals he'd be able to finance once he had Kelly's assets as part of his portfolio.

"Look, Harry, I need to find Kelly." Robert got up from his chair.

Harrison handed Robert the keys to his Mercedes and waived him away. It was only a couple of blocks back to the hotel, and the walk would do him good.

Harrison strolled back down Santa Monica Boulevard, taking in the sights that he was getting more and more attached to. He was giving serious thought to the idea of moving. Southern California was definitely agreeing with him; he only hoped things would work out for Robert.

CHAPTER SEVEN

Harrison woke just long enough to look at the clock. It was 2:00 in the morning, and Robert was just getting home. That meant one of two things—either he and Kelly had made up, or Robert had spent the night out getting plastered. Harrison rolled over and stared into the darkness. His mind was playing with his senses. He saw Jennifer asleep on the couch at Weissler and Schuler, and then suddenly he saw the jogger from the other day. The two scenes flashed back and forth before his eyes.

He began to think his fixation on Jennifer wasn't healthy. Even if it were her, and he did find her, where would that get him? She had left three years ago, not wanting to be found, not even interested in him. What did he hope to accomplish by finding her now?

No, he needed to let it go. He needed to move on; he needed a change. And his first step would be looking into some property of his own.

ROBERT FINALLY AWOKE to the smell of coffee brewing.

"Well, it's about time you got up," Harrison teased.

Harrison tried to read Robert's expression as he staggered from his bedroom.

"So, what happened last night? Did you and Kelly straighten things out?" Harrison asked as he pushed a cup of coffee in front of his brother.

Robert took a swig of his coffee, followed by a smile.

"I guess from that grin, I can assume that you were able to talk with Kelly?"

"Among other things," Robert volunteered.

Harrison put up his hand. "I don't need the details. I'm just glad you were able to work things out." Harrison sipped his own coffee and sighed. "Are you sure this is what you want, Robert? I mean, I think Kelly is great, but are you certain you're ready to settle down?"

Robert walked over to the couch and stretched out. "I know I don't want to lose her, if that's what you mean."

It wasn't the solid answer Harrison was looking for. He joined his brother in the living room and looked at him intently. "Robert, why don't you and Kelly postpone the wedding, take a little more time to figure out what you want?"

Robert shook his head. "Oh no, if I do that, Kelly will call it quits for sure. No, this is what I want. I want Kelly. Like you said, it's time I grow up."

Harrison heard something different in Robert's voice, a seriousness that proved he was determined to make his commitment to Kelly work. Harrison finished his cup of coffee and moved back to the kitchen. "So what are your plans for today?"

Robert joined him. "We make an offer on the house."

"Mind if I tag along?"

"What for? Of course, I certainly don't mind if you come, but why?"

"I was thinking about looking at some property myself. I thought your realtor might be able to help me."

"You're kidding!" Robert was shocked. "When did you decide this?"

"Well, I haven't decided anything yet, but I've been giving it some thought."

"What about your company?"

"I can work long distance, maybe even pick up some more clients on the west coast."

Robert laughed out loud. "I can't believe it. Mr. Planned, Detailed, and Organized is thinking about doing something completely spontaneous and out-of-the-blue?"

Harrison could only smile. It was true. He was never one to do something impulsively or without a great deal of planning. Maybe the west coast would be good for him.

"So, should I plan on coming with you and Kelly, or should I make an appointment with your realtor for another time?"

"No, come with us. Kelly can introduce you to Samantha. I'm sure she'd be more than willing to make room in her schedule to talk with you."

The look in Robert's eyes told Harrison he was in trouble. "No matchmaking, Robert. I'm not interested, okay?"

"You say that now. Wait until you see Samantha."

HARRISON HAD A CONFERENCE CALL set for 1:00 that afternoon and planned on meeting Kelly and Robert at the offices of West Beach Properties at 2:30 p.m.

The conference call with Frank Schuler went as planned. Harrison had e-mailed his entire presentation on the Haufmeister account to Schuler who had made the presentation himself. Harrison looked at his watch, realizing he didn't have much time, but knowing he wanted to talk with Frank Schuler while he had the opportunity.

"Frank, I have an idea. . . ."

KELLY WAS GIDDY WITH EXCITEMENT when she and Robert entered Samantha's office. Samantha was standoffish with Robert, remembering their last encounter. She decided instead to direct her conversation to Kelly.

Everyone took a seat as Samantha pulled out the papers for the agreement she had previously written up. The three of them went over the paperwork for the full asking price offer. Just then, Robert's phone vibrated, distracting him for the moment.

"I'm sure that will be fine. I'll ask."

Robert looked at Samantha. "Harry is running a little bit late. He wanted to know if it would be a problem if he rescheduled for 3:00."

"No problem," Samantha said and smiled.

Robert relayed the message to Harrison as he watched Kelly sign next to every highlighted arrow on every page of the contract. The house would be in Kelly's name only, a stipulation from her father.

HARRISON PULLED UP IN FRONT OF WEST BEACH PROPERTIES at 2:45 p.m. His talk with Frank Schuler had gone even better than expected, making him even more excited to talk to Samantha Wilder.

He entered the stylish office building and approached the receptionist desk. "I have a 3:00 p.m. appointment with Ms. Samantha Wilder."

The receptionist tapped at her computer. "Harry?"

Harrison chuckled. "Actually the name is Harrison." Robert had nicknamed him Harry when they were kids. He'd had a problem with his 's' as a little boy and somehow through the years it had stuck.

She smiled warmly at him and replied, "I'll tell Ms. Wilder you're here."

The receptionist reached for her phone, but before she could dial, someone called her from down the hall. "Julie, I'm going to grab a bite to eat before my next appointment shows up."

Harrison looked up the minute he heard her voice. He was shocked. Jennifer Patterson was walking towards him! She was juggling an armful of files as she approached and didn't see Harrison until she was almost standing next to him.

Harrison's heart nearly pulsed out of his chest as he dared to whisper her name, "Jennifer?"

Her head snapped up and her arms gave way as the files she was holding tumbled to the floor. Jennifer's eyes were fixed on Harrison, and she was absolutely powerless to move.

"It *is* you!" Harrison stammered.

Jennifer shook off the shock she was feeling and bent to pick up the files. "I'm sorry; you must have me confused with someone else. My name is Samantha Wilder."

Harrison bent down to help her as she tried to gather the files from where they had fanned out on the floor. "But, Jennifer . . ."

She cut him off abruptly. "I'm sorry, but like I said, you must have me mistaken for someone else."

She looked at Harrison, her eyes almost pleading with him. He didn't understand, but he was determined to find out what this was all about. He wasn't going to leave until he knew what had happened to her three years before.

They both stood as Jennifer continued to straighten the disheveled files in her arms. "Well, mistaken or not, I still have a 3:00 p.m. appointment with you." Harrison's voice was firm.

"Uh, I'm sorry, Mr. Lynch, but I'm afraid there has been a mix-up with my schedule. I have another appointment that I need to keep, and I just don't have time for any new clients. If you'll excuse me, I'm sure Julie can reschedule you with another realtor."

Jennifer turned to retreat down the hall, but Harrison quickly grabbed her arm, almost sending the files she was holding to the floor for a second time.

"Don't do this, Jennifer," Harrison pleaded.

She gave him an icy stare until he let her go.

"Like I said, the name is Samantha, and I'm not accepting any new clients. If you have a problem with that, I'm going to have to ask you to leave."

"Ask all you want but I'm not leaving without some answers." Harrison's abruptness startled Julie. She quickly reached for the phone and dialed security.

While Julie was busy on the phone, Jennifer whispered, "Please leave, Harrison. You'll ruin everything."

Her eyes held the same vulnerability he remembered seeing the night he spent with her three years earlier. Except instead of pools of blue, they were now the color of emeralds. When Harrison saw two men in security uniforms approaching him from the far side of the building, he backed away towards the door. "Sorry. My mistake. I guess you're not who I thought you were. After all, she died over six years ago."

The guards watched as Harrison pushed through the glass door and exited the building. Harrison's words chilled Jennifer. *He knew.* Somehow he found out that Jennifer Patterson was an imposter.

"Are you all right, Ms. Wilder?" one of the guards asked her.

"Yes, I'm fine." She forced a smile to her face, though she could feel her arms trembling under the stack of files. "He thought I was someone else. Once I made it clear to him that he was mistaken, he apologized and left. Everything's fine."

Jennifer quickly walked back to her office, dumped the files on one of the tapestry chairs, and began to pace. Her heart was speeding out of control, and her mind was racing between the past and the present. She couldn't believe it. *Harrison is here, here in California.*

Harrison had no sooner left the office building when his instincts told him to rush back in. The last time he left Jennifer to herself, she disappeared. It took all the composure he had not to barge back through the glass doors and demand to see her. Instead, he waited. He would wait until she left and see where she went. Then he would talk to her. Once he had some answers, maybe then he could finally put her out of his mind.

Jennifer took slow deep breaths, trying to regain her composure. As she did, she began to piece things together. She thought back to when she had first met Robert, and how her heart had nearly stopped because of his strong resemblance to Harrison. Then, when Robert made an appointment for his brother "Harry," she should have been able to put the two together. *Why didn't I see this coming? I wasn't paying attention. I let my guard down and now everything's a mess.*

Jennifer's thoughts immediately went into high gear. *I have to leave. I can't stay here. I'll go south, maybe Texas or Mexico. No!* she reprimanded herself. *You promised. No more running. No more lying. You have to deal with this.*

Harrison's actions were sure to raise questions. She began to formulate what she would tell her broker, Mr. Holmes, if he got wind of the small skirmish. *And what if Harrison comes back around?* She chided herself. She was sure he wasn't going to give up that easily. After all, he had already dug deep enough to find out that the real Jennifer Patterson had died in a car accident.

The thought of talking to Harrison made her heart start racing again. What would she tell him? How could she explain to him her need to be someone she wasn't? Her mind drifted back to that snowy night in Chicago. She had seen a different side of Harrison Lynch that night. The compassion in his eyes had taken her by surprise. That was why she ran. The feelings she had for Harrison that night had scared her. She knew he had felt it too, but instead of giving in to them, she ran. She always ran when people got too close.

But now . . . now she didn't know what to do. She had told herself when she moved to California that she wasn't going to run any longer. Of course, she hadn't expected Harrison Lynch to walk through the door of her new life either.

Jennifer didn't leave her office again until it was time to go home. She hadn't accomplished a single thing the rest of the day. Her eyes glanced at the files piled on her chair. They would have to wait until tomorrow. Right then, all she wanted to do was go home and figure out what to do next.

HARRISON SAT IN THE PARKING LOT across the street. When he saw Jennifer step through the office doors a little after 5:00 p.m., he jumped up in his seat and then quickly hunched back down so she couldn't see him.

He watched her as she cautiously looked around. She'd expected him to be waiting for her. When she didn't spot him anywhere, she trotted across the street to the same parking lot where he was waiting.

He reached for the handle of the door, impulsively wanting to jump out of the car and talk to her, but he thought better of it. Another public altercation would only cause more problems. No, he would wait until he found out where she lived. He would make sure she talked to him if she liked it or not.

Jennifer pulled away from the parking lot in a little black Fiat. Harrison maneuvered around as quickly as he could to follow her. She didn't drive far; in fact, she was only a block or so away from his hotel when she pulled into a small driveway that ran alongside an ivy-covered house. Harrison slowly pulled to the curb across the street and watched her open the garage door. She drove her car in, closed the doors, and then walked back to the front porch. She fiddled with her keys and then disappeared behind a large arched door.

Harrison sat, not sure what he should do next. He was afraid if he went to her door immediately, she might get suspicious. He decided to wait until it got dark.

JENNIFER HAD A LOT OF NERVOUS ENERGY that she needed to expend. She changed into her jogging shorts and a tank top, throwing her work clothes on her bed. She jumped onto the treadmill she had set up in the spare bedroom, pushing the start button to bring the machine to life. She would have preferred to jog outside, but it would be dark soon, and she felt it wasn't safe.

She put on a DVD of one of her favorite movies and slowly warmed up to a steady pace. She tried to concentrate on the movie, but all she could see was the look on Harrison's face: first, shock; then excitement; and finally sadness when she refused to see him.

How did he find me? How did he even begin to know where to look? It had to be a huge coincidence. There's no way he could have made the connection between me and Samantha Wilder. She peppered herself with questions the entire time she ran. The more unanswered questions she had, the faster she ran. After an hour of torturing herself with the unknown, she turned off the machine and headed for the shower.

Harrison slowly walked across the street. He had waited more than an hour for the sun to finally lose some of its brilliance. Quietly he approached the charming house and saw that the stucco building was obviously from an era gone by. The arched windows and red tile roof hinted at its old world roots. Ivy nearly covered the entire façade of the house and draped around the rails of the small wooden porch. Deep seated brick formed the curved walkway that led to the house from the sidewalk, and bougainvillaea burst with color along the far side of the small front yard.

When Harrison got to the front door, he wasn't sure what he was going to do. Surely Jennifer wasn't going to just let him waltz into her home and sit himself down like an old friend. He would have to be ready for her rejection, but no matter what, he wouldn't leave without some answers.

A burst of light from the front room brought him back to his senses. He peered cautiously into the large picture window but could see nothing more than the glow from a light through the embroidered sheers.

He took a deep breath and said a quick prayer. *God, don't let me do anything stupid. I just want some answers.* He steadied himself and knocked on the door, quickly moving out of view of the miniature wrought-iron opening that served as a peephole.

Jennifer went to the door and peeked out. When she saw nothing, she figured she had only imagined hearing the knock. Her nerves were twisted so tight, she was sure her mind was just playing tricks on her. She walked slowly towards the kitchen, her black, velour jogging pants dragging on the floor, her hair still wet from her shower.

Harrison waited for her to open the large wooden door out of curiosity. When it was obvious that she wasn't going to do so, he knocked again.

Jennifer was sure she heard the knock this time. Now she was on alert; something obviously wasn't right. She crept up to the front window and carefully peered out from behind the sheers. She craned her neck to see who was standing at the front door, but still she saw no one. With her heart pounding against her chest, she slowly walked to the front door and pressed her ear against it. She heard nothing. *Maybe a solicitor threw one of those coupon bundles against the door,* she thought to herself. She waited another moment and then opened the door slowly.

Harrison was crouched in the yard, down against the railing of the porch, the ivy-draped spindles hiding him from sight. He heard the door creak open but knew he had to wait for the right moment.

Jennifer looked through the crack in the door to see if the bundle she had imagined was there. When she didn't see it, she opened the door wider, looking from side to side.

When Harrison heard the door creak further, he stepped from his hiding place and drew himself up to his full 6'4" frame.

"Hello, Jennifer," he said quietly, the light from the distant fading sun casting a shadow on his figure.

She instantly froze, and then, just as quick, jumped inside the house and tried to shut the door. Harrison moved swiftly, placing his foot on the threshold before she could shut the door completely. She tried slamming it several times, but to no avail.

"Jennifer, I just want to talk to you," Harrison pled as she did what she could to shut him out of her life once again.

She was frantic for her privacy. She would have to explain too much if she let him in. Now she knew why running had always been her only option.

She looked around behind her. Seeing the umbrella that hung on the hall tree, she grabbed for it and jabbed it into his foot wedged in the doorway. He let out a yell, and with it, his anger was only heightened. He gave a violent shove to the door that stood between them, sending Jennifer falling backwards against the tile entryway. She scrambled to regain her composure, but it was too late. Harrison stepped through the entry and slammed the door shut behind him.

She rushed to her feet, pushing her eschewed hair behind her ears. "What do you think you're doing? I'm going to call the cops." She tried to shove past him, but he grabbed her as she moved.

"Good." Harrison yelled, whipping her around so that she had to look at him. "I'd love to tell them how you impersonated a dead person and stole her identity. There are laws against that, you know."

She looked into his raging eyes. Gone was compassion and feeling, replaced instead with anger and hostility.

She yanked her arm free of his hold and returned his chilling stare. "Why are you doing this? I did nothing to deserve this."

"You lied to me; you lied to Weissler and Schuler; in fact, you lied to the federal government. I want to know why."

"Why?" she demanded. "I didn't hurt Weissler and Schuler; in fact, I helped put them on the map. You got all the glory for the Yomahama account—the account that led to Weissler and Schuler going international. You got a partnership out of it, too, I've heard. So why come after me and ruin what's taken me three years to build up?" Jennifer's voice cracked. She realized she was pleading for her life. It wouldn't be hard for Harrison to find out that Samantha Wilder was just another alias. Harrison could, in fact, turn her over to the government, and then she'd be exposed forever. Seventeen years of hiding and running would be for nothing. She would have to go back—back to a life that would imprison her forever.

Harrison heard the emotion in her voice. It pulled at him. He could see the hurt in her eyes. He wasn't trying to hurt her. He was only trying to understand why she was doing this. He wanted to know who she really was.

Jennifer inhaled her resolve and brought composure back to her voice. "Please, Harrison, I am asking you to leave. Please just allow me to live my life."

"I can't do that, Jennifer. Not without answers."

She walked over to the velvety cushions of her antique Moroccan couch. She slumped down into it, her forehead against her knees, her shoulders shaking with uncontrolled tears.

Harrison felt his defiance wane. As much as he wanted answers, it crushed him to see Jennifer so upset. He walked over and stood next to her. When she refused to look at him, he sunk to the couch beside her. Instinctively, he laid his arm across her shoulders, trying to provide her with some sort of comfort.

Déjà vu was setting in. Harrison's thoughts traveled back again to the night that she was so weak, and he wanted nothing more than to give her strength. He didn't know what it was about her, but just being with her again, feeling her beside him, made his heart rush to that moment three years ago when all he wanted to do was kiss her.

Jennifer didn't shrug off the comfort he was volunteering. She had no energy left to fight. She felt as if her world was closing in around her. Her house of cards was finally crumbling.

"Why can't you just tell me the truth?" Harrison whispered, his face not far from hers.

She turned her tear-stained face to him. "You don't know what you're asking me, Harrison."

He brushed his finger across her cheek, catching a tear trailing down her face. His hand lingered, and for a moment, he felt himself experiencing a scenario that until now had only existed in his mind. With his eyes locked on hers, he allowed his touch to trace the slope of her jaw, his fingers to sweep across the outline of her lips. He felt his body slowly lean in closer to hers, electrified by being this close to her once again. It was as if time had stood still. He was with Jennifer again, and the fantasy that he'd built in his mind was playing out before him.

Jennifer knew what was happening, but did nothing to stop it. She wanted this moment as much as he did. He'd cast a spell on her years before, making her fearful, making her run. But this time, she didn't want to run. She wanted to know what it would be like to be with the man she'd only been able to dream about.

She watched as he moved closer. She felt his lips as they gently brushed up against hers. They were warm and tender, not at all forceful or demanding. She had fantasized about this moment many times over the last three years. She had always wondered what it would've been like to allow Harrison to get close to her.

He kissed her again. This time, she felt herself respond with a kiss of her own. She pressed herself closer to Harrison, closing what distance was left between them. The intensity of the moment was too overpowering to fight off. She was ready to give into her desires, not caring about the consequences, when she felt Harrison pull away from her. Her questioning eyes caught his.

"This is not what I came for, Jennifer."

Though his words were whisper soft, to Jennifer, they rang in her ears like a clashing symbol.

She quickly jumped from the couch, humiliation coloring her face. Anger raged inside her. What was it about Harrison Lynch that totally obliterated her senses? Again, he had broken through her barriers, only to cause her more embarrassment and shame.

"Okay, so you've played your little game." Jennifer paced across the room. "I guess that was something you wanted to do three years ago, but I left before you had the chance. Well, you came, you saw, you conquered; now you can notch your bedpost. Just get out of here and leave me alone."

Harrison hung his head between his shoulders. "I didn't mean for that to happen, Jennifer, but I'd be lying if I said I hadn't felt the same way that night we spent together at the office."

"So, I guess the Boy Scout doesn't lie. Is that why you're here? You feel compelled to turn me in because of my lies?"

"I don't want to turn you in, Jennifer. I just want to know the truth."

Jennifer knew she was in the midst of a vicious circle. Harrison wanted the truth, and he wasn't going to leave until he had it. If she refused, he would turn her in and her life would be taken away from her.

The face of her father filled her consciousness. What would life be like if she had to go back? Would he love her and accept her back, a miracle to be treasured, or would he loathe her because of the hoax she'd carried out all these years? Her breathing accelerated and all color was beginning to seep from her pores. Harrison watched as Jennifer's demeanor changed into panic and fear. Her eyes began to flutter and in an instant, he knew what was happening. He got to her just before she collapsed.

Harrison scooped Jennifer up in his arms and quickly carried her down the hall. He peered into the first room but saw only exercise equipment. When he stuck his head into the other room, he found a massive, four-poster bed. Ornate woodwork framed the bed, elevating it far above the floor.

He slid Jennifer onto the silky comforter and moved to what he hoped was an adjoining bathroom. He flicked on the light, grabbed for a nearby towel, and held it under running water. He rung out the cloth and rushed back to Jennifer's side. He pressed the cold cloth to her forehead and spoke to her in a soothing tone.

"Jennifer? Jennifer, you need to wake up."

He brushed the towel across her forehead and cheeks. With a hand to her shoulder, he shook her gently.

"Jennifer . . . Jennifer, open your eyes."

He saw her lids flutter, and then her lashes began to part. She closed her eyes tight and then tried to open them again.

Her vision was blurry . . . or was it her mind? Harrison Lynch was hovering over her. She was dreaming. She had to be. She was in California; Harrison was in Chicago.

"Jennifer . . . can you hear me?"

The voice, it had to be Harrison's.

Jennifer tried to take her thoughts captive. When she pieced everything together, she realized it was indeed Harrison that was hovering over her. Somehow he had traced her to California. He was going to turn her in, and then her father would know the truth.

Tears began to stream from her eyes. She clasped onto Harrison's arms urgent to get his attention. "Please don't. You can't turn me in. My father will kill me; I know he will. I can't go back. Please don't do this to me."

Harrison sat in horror, only now beginning to realize the nightmare he had stepped into. He did his best to calm Jennifer. She was hysterical with fear, thinking that Harrison had hunted her down just so he could expose her.

Clutching her against his chest, he held her tight, trying to convince her he would never do anything to hurt her. He rocked her back and forth, stroking her damp hair, repeating words of assurance and trust. He felt her beginning to calm down. She was no longer holding onto him out of fear; her exhaustion had caused her body to fall limp against his chest.

Harrison closed his eyes and rested his head atop hers. Silently, he was praying. He could only repeat himself, asking God for guidance and help over and over again.

Jennifer pulled her hands in close to her chest. Her breathing had returned to normal and when she felt as if she had control of her emotions, she gently pushed away from Harrison's embrace. She looked at him. She saw his red eyes and realized he must have been crying. It caused her heart to clench even tighter.

She took a deep breath, closing her eyes, before speaking. "I don't know what to say, Harrison. I'm sorry that I fell apart on you like that. I'm sorry that I lied, and I'm sorry that you've wasted all this time trying to find me."

Harrison smiled. "Jennifer, I didn't hunt you down, if that's what you're thinking. The fact that Kelly used you as a realtor is an incredible coincidence."

Harrison knew it was not a coincidence, but he wasn't ready to talk about the power of God and how He could intercede in someone's life. He saw the expression on her face fall.

"So, how many more ways can I embarrass myself in your presence?" She got up from the bed and crossed to the other side of the room. She walked through the rickety glass door that led to a pergola blanketed with flowers. An automatic light went on, washing the small garden area with warmth.

She heard Harrison step through the doorway. She leaned on a splintered beam, crossing her arms against her chest.

"Jennifer . . ."

"The name's Samantha," she corrected him.

"Jennifer, who are you?"

Jennifer looked out into the backyard that she had tenderly planted, cultivated, and enjoyed. She glanced back at the house that had become her home, the home that she swore to herself she would never run away from.

"You can't keep running, Jennifer."

She looked at him squarely. "I know, but I can't go back either."

"Go back to what? You told me your father died when you were thirteen. He can't hurt you any longer."

"He's not dead, Harrison. My father's not dead."

"I don't understand."

"My father didn't die when I was 13; I did."

CHAPTER EIGHT

Jennifer brought two cups of coffee into the living room where Harrison was pacing the floor. She sat down on the couch and set the mugs on the coffee table. Harrison took a seat next to her, swallowed some coffee, and waited for her to begin.

"This is very difficult for me, Harrison. You've got to know that I've never told anyone what I'm about to tell you. And if you were to tell anyone else, I would be in danger all over again."

Harrison felt a twinge of guilt. What right did he have prying into Jennifer's personal life? He had convinced himself it was his right to know; now he wasn't so sure.

"I'm not even sure where to start." Jennifer sighed. Her life was made up of one lie after another, for as long as she could remember.

"What's your real name?" Harrison asked the question he had wanted to know all along.

"Angelica Calderon." Jennifer waited to see if Harrison recognized her name. Harrison was older than she was, and there had been a lot of publicity surrounding her and her mother's death.

"What did you mean when you said that you died, not your father?" Harrison asked.

Jennifer sat, twisting her fingers. "My father was a very violent man. When I was 13, my mother staged our deaths to get away from him."

"She what?" Harrison was completely confused. "Why didn't she just get a divorce or a court order or file charges?"

"You don't understand. You don't divorce a Calderon."

Recognition crossed Harrison's face. "When you say Calderon, you mean Calderon, as in the crime family Calderon?"

Jennifer nodded her head. Harrison was beginning to see the bigger picture.

"Harrison, when my mother met my father, she didn't know what he did for a living. She was young and naïve. He swept her off her feet. She came from a broken home and didn't have much. Her father had left her and her mom when she was five, and her mother was an alcoholic. My father was fascinated with her. She was beautiful and vivacious. He lavished her with gifts, trips, things she never had. But the Calderon family didn't like her. They didn't feel she was one of them. My father didn't care. He told her he didn't want to live without her.

Before she knew it, she was married and pregnant. By the time she realized who he was and what he did, it was too late. She was part of the family."

Harrison sat in disbelief. Jennifer was related to one of the most notorious crime families in the country. She continued, trying to explain to Harrison how things had gone so bad.

"At first, when my mother asked questions about his work, my father brushed it aside or changed the subject. He told her that he didn't want to discuss business at home; his house was his castle, and she was his princess. My mother tried to let it go, a part of her not wanting to know the truth. But when she started hearing things like smuggling and murder, she couldn't ignore it any longer.

"The more she questioned him, the more abusive he got. First, it was just yelling and arguing, then he started hitting her. Things were not going well within the Calderon family, and her many questions were adding to my father's problems. The family kept telling him it was his own fault and he got what he deserved for marrying outside of 'his kind.' They didn't appreciate the fact that she was a blond-haired, blue-eyed woman, instead of someone the family had picked for him."

"Was this before or after you were born?"

"Before. In fact, it was one of my father's rages that caused my mother to go into pre-mature labor. I was born two months early."

"And that didn't make him want to change his ways?" Harrison clenched his fist. He was quickly developing a hatred for a man he didn't even know.

Jennifer felt chilled. It had been a long time since she had revisited the past. She pulled her feet up under her on the couch and rested her chin against her knees.

"My father sat in vigil with me at the hospital. He promised my mother he would change. After we were released, my father stopped drinking and told his family he needed more time at home with his own family. My mother said it was the best years of her life. She told me what a wonderful father he was when I was a baby, how he would just stare at me or hold me for hours. He named me Angelica, because he said I was his little angel."

Harrison saw tears glistening in Jennifer's eyes. He couldn't tell if they were from happy memories or sadness because they hadn't lasted.

"My mother thought things had changed for good. I was about six when I remember my father coming home in a rage, and men swarmed the house with guns."

"What happened?"

"His brother had been killed. It was a hit by a family that was trying to push in on Calderon territory. That started a war and the family looked to my father to take up where his brother left off.

"Everything changed from that moment on. We became prisoners in our own home. My father was sure the Barbera family was going to make a hit on him or us. My father often came home in a rage. He was drinking again, and things were not going well with the family business. Other families were making their presence known and swaying in their allegiance." Jennifer let out a nervous chuckle. "It's funny, he was protecting us from people he thought could hurt us, but he hurt us deeper than anyone ever could."

Jennifer sipped her coffee and groaned at the fact that it was cold. She got up from the couch and reached out for Harrison's cup. He handed it to her and watched as she moved back into the kitchen. He let out a heavy sigh and raked his hands through his hair. He felt like he was listening to a 20/20 news report on someone worlds away, not the woman that had stood toe-to-toe with him in board meetings and conference rooms.

Jennifer came back with their cups filled with steaming coffee. She looked exhausted. He waited until she got comfortable before he asked, "When did your mother decide to leave?"

"When I was ten, things began to get even worse. The abuse was happening more regularly. I could hear my father yelling at my mother late at night. He would come home angry and drunk, and he would take his frustrations and fears out on her. I would sit in my bed and pull the covers over my head. I could hear my mother crying, but I was terrified to do anything about it.

"One night, my mother cried out in such anguish, I couldn't stand it any longer. I ran to her room and pushed open the door. She was on the floor clutching her side, my father hovering over her, his hand raised to hit her.

"I ran to my father, begging him to stop. He pushed me away, causing me to fall. I was stunned and my mother was terrified. He had never raised a hand to me, and now it looked as if he weren't going to stop. He grabbed me and dragged me down the hall to my own room. I could hear my mother crying, but she was powerless to help me.

"When we got to my room, he shook me so hard I thought I was going to be sick. He yelled at me, accusing my mother of turning me against him, and warned me never to come into his bedroom again. He pushed me into my closet and locked the door. He told me that I couldn't come out until he said so; and the longer I cried, the longer I would be there."

"How long were you there?"

"All night," Jennifer said with a monotone voice. "My father had to take my mother to the hospital, and they didn't come home until the following morning."

"You must have been terrified!"

"I was. It was so dark and silent. I sat on the floor and cried silently, trying to make sure I wasn't heard. When I would rock on the floor, the pine boards would creak. The noise helped to break the silence, so I continued. Those creaking boards were my only companions on many nights."

Harrison remembered the way Jennifer had rocked the night they spent together in Chicago. It was a protection mechanism, protection from her own father. "Was your father ever sorry for his actions?"

"No. He showered and changed that morning before leaving for work. It was my mother who came and got me. She cried and apologized, promising me she would do everything she could to keep me safe. It was then that she started devising a plan."

"You were 10 when that happened, but you said that you were 13 when your mother planned your death. What happened in the meantime?"

"More violence and abuse."

"What about your teachers and housekeepers—didn't they witness these rages or see the results of your father's abuse?"

"Yes, but they all worked for the Calderon family. They knew what would happen to them if they tried to interfere."

Harrison and Jennifer sat in silence for a moment. She closed her eyes and leaned back. He saw the goose bumps on her arms and reached for the blanket folded at the end of the couch. When he draped it over her, she jumped, but then nestled further into its warmth.

Harrison knew there was more to tell, but Jennifer looked as if she were falling asleep, clearly exhausted from remembering her tortured past. He waited for her to continue, but when her breathing took on a slow, deliberate rhythm, he let her sleep. She deserved it.

He allowed his head to rest on the back of the couch. *Why, Lord? Why would you allow such abuse?* He watched Jennifer, her breathing slow and steady, her face beautiful. He glanced at his watch; it was after 9:00 p.m. Harrison needed to contact Robert, but he had left his phone in the car, not wanting it as a distraction when he talked with Jennifer. Now he needed to let Robert know that he wasn't sure when he would be home.

Harrison glanced around the room looking for a phone but didn't see one. He slowly moved off the couch, trying not to disturb Jennifer, but it didn't work. Her eyes slowly opened.

"Where are you going?"

"I need to get my phone. I left it in the car."

"Who are you calling?" Jennifer began to panic.

"It's okay, Jennifer; I'm just calling Robert."

"What are you going to tell him?" She sat up, completely alert.

"I'm not sure yet."

"What do you mean, you're not sure yet? You're not going to tell him about me are you?"

"No. I promise." Harrison's look assured Jennifer she could trust him.

Unlocking his car, he grabbed his phone from the passenger seat. He saw that he had several incoming messages and listened to four of Robert's before walking back into the house. He shut the door and looked where Jennifer had been sitting, but she wasn't there. He heard noises in the kitchen and found her there making sandwiches.

She looked up when she saw him. "So, what did you tell him?"

"I haven't called him yet. I wanted you to hear the conversation so that you knew exactly what I had to say."

Jennifer went back to making the sandwiches as Harrison dialed Robert.

"Robert . . . yeah, I know . . . I'm with . . . Jen. . ." She shook her head violently. Harrison quickly corrected himself. "I'm with Samantha. Yeah." Harrison looked at Jennifer who was listening intently. "You were right; we hit it off and decided to grab a bite to eat. I don't know . . . okay, then I guess I'll see you tomorrow."

Harrison saw Jennifer give him an icy look as he put his phone back in his pocket. "What was that for?"

"What makes you think you're staying here tonight?"

"I didn't say I was. Robert told me not to expect him home tonight."

Jennifer flushed with embarrassment. She felt like she was always putting her foot in her mouth around Harrison. She placed the sandwiches on plates and grabbed a bag of chips from the pantry.

"There's soda in the fridge." Jennifer walked past him and sat back down on the couch. Harrison joined her with two sodas and thanked her for the sandwich.

He bowed in prayer, catching Jennifer completely off guard. They ate together quietly. Jennifer picked at her sandwich while Harrison finished his quickly.

"So, what's the story behind Samantha Wilder?" Harrison asked quietly.

"She died in a house fire in Sioux City, Iowa. She was in her late twenties, blond with green eyes, kept to herself, and most importantly, she had no family."

"How do you know all that?"

"An obituary."

"So that's what you do. When you decide to move on, you just become somebody else?"

"It's not that simple, Harrison." Jennifer's tone was short.

"Then why did you run from Chicago?"

"I got scared. That night . . . I said too much. I knew you would continue to ask questions, and I didn't think I could handle it."

"What happened to your mom?"

Jennifer took a while to answer. She was struggling with her emotions. Her mother's death had been the most difficult and the loneliest period in her life.

"She was diagnosed with breast cancer too late. She died within three months of us finding out she was sick."

"Where is she?"

"She's buried in Albuquerque under the name 'Mary Bellamy.'"

"How old were you when she died?"

"Nineteen."

"That had to be hard on you. What did you do?"

"I did what I watched my mother do for six years. I looked on the computer for an I.D. that I could pull off and moved to another state."

"How many identities have you had?"

"Seven."

"Why did you keep running after your mother died? Did you really think your father would hurt you?"

Jennifer stood up abruptly and cleared their dishes. Harrison got a sinking feeling in his stomach. He had a sense that her father's abuse didn't stop with being locked in the closet.

Harrison waited for Jennifer to come back from the kitchen. "Harrison, it's late. I need to know what you're going to do."

"What do you mean?"

Jennifer was switching gears, and Harrison wasn't following her.

"Are you going to expose me? Are you going to turn me in for fraud?"

"Do you really think I could do that, Jennifer?"

"Isn't that what you told me when you got here?"

"I needed some way to get you to talk to me. I had to understand why you ran."

"So, now you do."

Jennifer was shutting him out again. He could feel it.

"What was the final straw? What finally made your mother run?"

"Who says there was a final straw?"

"Something had to make her react. She waited three years after all."

Harrison watched Jennifer's composure get more strained. He finally blurted out what he felt he already knew. "He went after you, didn't he?"

"Harrison, I have a lot of work to do in the morning. I don't want to talk about this anymore."

"That's it, isn't it?"

"Harrison, please. I told you what you wanted to know. I'm Samantha Wilder now, and I have no intentions of ever seeing my father again."

Jennifer moved to the front door and opened it for Harrison.

"Why are you shutting me out?" Harrison yelled out of frustration.

"Why do you care?" she shouted right back.

Harrison moved to the door and slammed it shut. "Because I do care, okay? I cared three years ago, and I've thought about you a thousand times since that night." Harrison tried to calm his raised voice. "I care, Jennifer. Is that so hard for you to accept?"

"Yes, it is," she said defiantly. "I'm an enigma to you, that's what you find so intriguing, nothing more."

Harrison moved in closer to her. "Is that what you really think?" He stood within inches of her. "I wasn't kissing an enigma earlier this evening; I was kissing a woman. A beautiful woman. An intelligent woman. A woman who's talented, captivating, and strong. Why wouldn't I be interested in a woman like that?"

Jennifer hung her head, not having an answer. Harrison placed his finger under her chin, forcing her to look at him. "Can I see you tomorrow?"

"I don't know if that's such a good idea." She diverted her eyes.

"I'll call you." Harrison offered, not taking no for an answer. He bent to place a soft kiss on her cheek before leaving.

CHAPTER NINE

Jennifer stumbled from bed at 5:00 a.m. She had gotten no sleep, thinking only of Harrison and the amount of information she'd divulged to him. She panicked several times during the night, fighting the urge to pack up everything and move far away from California.

She went for a jog, weeded her backyard, and straightened her dresser drawers. She was working at a fitful pace, trying to ignore the feelings that were consuming her. She finally got ready and left for the office, her thoughts on everything but her work . . . or the traffic.

IT WAS 10:00 A.M., and Robert still wasn't back at the hotel. Harrison had already showered, dressed, had breakfast, and checked in with Chicago. He decided not to waste any more time waiting for Robert. He headed to the offices of West Beach Properties, anxious to see Jennifer.

He strolled into the entry, encountering the receptionist that had called security on him the day before. When she looked at him with a slight annoyance in her stare, Harrison rushed to explain. But before he could say anything, Julie cut him off.

"If you're looking for Ms. Wilder, she's not here."

Harrison remembered Jennifer specifically saying that she had a lot of work in the morning. Harrison thought he was being lied to by the receptionist.

"Look, I know that things looked pretty weird yesterday, but Jen—" Harrison nearly slipped. To Harrison she would always be Jennifer. "Samantha and I have talked things out. You don't need to run interference for her."

"I'm not running interference for her. Ms. Wilder called in sick over an hour ago."

Harrison bolted from the building, panicked that Jennifer had run in the middle of the night. He quickly drove to her home, pulled into the driveway, and almost ran to the door. When he got no answer to his pounding, he thought the worst. *She did it again. Why did I trust her, Lord? I should have known she'd do this again.*

Harrison thought of Robert and Kelly. They had to have Jennifer's cell phone number. Harrison grabbed his phone from his pocket and speed dialed Robert.

"Robert, give me Jennifer's cell phone number."

"Who?"

"Samantha, I mean Samantha. I don't have time to explain, just give it to me."

Robert rattled off the number, Harrison barely hearing the last digit before disconnecting with his brother. He dialed Samantha's number but only got her voice mail.

"Jennifer, why are you doing this again? Please don't run, not because of me. I'll leave you alone if that's what you want, but I don't want you to run again. I didn't mean to mess things up for you. Please call me when you get this message. I just want to know you're okay."

Harrison snapped shut his cell phone, feeling even more dejected than the first time Jennifer disappeared. This time he understood why she ran. Furthermore, he knew for the second time, he was to blame. He felt helpless to do anything but pray that she would return his call.

"DO YOU FEEL ANY NAUSEA?" the emergency room doctor asked as he flashed his penlight into Jennifer's eyes.

"No."

"Dizziness?"

"I don't know. I've been lying down since I got out of the car." Jennifer had to be extricated from her crumpled sports car and was immediately put on a stretcher.

The doctor continued examining Jennifer. Her ankle had swelled to twice its size, but he was more concerned with her head and chest area. He ordered numerous x-rays, leaving Jennifer in the hands of a technician.

HARRISON CALLED WEST BEACH PROPERTIES to see if they had heard anything further from Jennifer.

"I don't expect to hear from her the rest of the day, Mr. Lynch. If you'd like, you can leave a message on her voice mail."

"Is this regular behavior for Ms. Wilder? I was under the impression that she had a lot of work to accomplish today."

"Look, Mr. Lynch, Ms. Wilder is entitled to her privacy. If you'd like, I can make an appointment for you with one of our other realtors."

"That won't be necessary." Harrison ended the call and walked to the balcony that overlooked the ocean and leaned on the rail. He was at a total loss.

Robert and Kelly entered the hotel room with exuberant laughter. But when they closed the door and embraced each other, their mood turned passionate. They were oblivious to Harrison's presence on the balcony. Only when he cleared his throat and walked into the room did Kelly nervously compose herself and Robert allow her to slip from his embrace.

"Harry, I didn't see you there."

"I kind of got that."

Robert moved to the kitchen and grabbed himself a wine cooler.

"So, what was that urgent phone call about?"

"Ahh . . . I was expecting to see Samantha Wilder this morning. I had a few questions for her and realized I didn't have her number."

Robert moved back into the living room where Kelly had taken a seat on the couch. "Well, you sounded pretty ticked. Did she stand you up?"

"I'm not sure yet."

Harrison moved towards the door, not wanting to answer any more questions.

"What do you mean, you're not sure?"

"Her office said she called in sick."

Robert and Kelly looked at each other surprised.

"Look, I have to go out for a while. You mind if I borrow your car again today?"

"No, I don't mind, but if you're really thinking about staying in California, you might want to get some wheels of your own."

Harrison nodded in agreement before leaving.

HARRISON CASUALLY STROLLED UP JENNIFER'S WALK, but when he was sure no one was looking, he darted down the driveway and hopped the fence of the back yard.

At first he just stared. He had never seen such an intricate garden. He hadn't looked much beyond the patio the night before, but now he could see flowers of every color and lush greenery draping over the walls and creeping up the large elm tree that shaded the yard.

He walked slowly across the yard to the glass door that led to the house. He stood close, almost pressing his face against the pane and saw the kitchen counter that he had stood at less than 24 hours before. His eyes traveled the frame of the door; he looked intently, knowing that Jennifer would have some sort of alarm system. He craned his neck and saw a blinking light on a control panel just to the side of a wall-mounted phone by the door.

He sighed and backed away. He turned toward the garage. He pulled at the heavy barn doors, the hasp and lock moving slightly. Through the slightest crack, he was able to see the empty garage. He shoved the doors back in place and kicked at them out of frustration.

He had only taken a few steps when he saw a taxi pull up to the curb. The stocky driver got out of the car and opened the door behind him. The passenger handed the cabbie a set of crutches, and Harrison watched as the man carefully helped Jennifer from the backseat of the car.

Harrison sprinted down the driveway, alarming both Jennifer and the cabbie.

"Harrison, what are you doing here?" Jennifer's voice was raised and annoyed. She winced slightly as she positioned the crutches under her arms.

"What happened?" Harrison's eyes traveled up and down her body, seeing the blood on her blouse and the cuts on her face.

She tried to manage her crutches and move around him. The cabbie looked at Harrison with a sneer.

"Is this guy bothering you, lady?" The driver stepped in front of Harrison, while Jennifer hobbled up the brick walk.

"No, I'm not bothering her; I'm a friend of hers." Harrison moved around him.

The cabbie pulled Jennifer's belongings from the back of the cab and followed her and Harrison up the walk. "Just say the word, lady, and I'll call the cops."

Jennifer looked at Harrison and then at the burly man who was waiting for her reply.

"It's all right. He's a friend."

Jennifer fumbled with her keys and pushed the door open.

"How much is her fare?" Harrison asked the cabbie.

"Thirty-seven fifty."

Harrison pulled out a fifty dollar bill and told the cabbie to keep the change. The gruff man gave Harrison a more considerate look as he handed him Jennifer's purse, briefcase, and a clear plastic bag with a pair of high heel shoes, some medicine bottles, and a bunch of papers in it.

Jennifer disarmed the alarm before shuffling to the couch. She carefully lowered herself to the cushions while Harrison put her things down and took a seat next to her.

"Jennifer, what happened?"

"I wrapped my car around a bus bench."

Harrison scrutinized her. One foot was in a brace while the other one wore a flimsy hospital-issued slipper. She had several small cuts on her face and a bandage just above her left eyebrow. When she pushed her crutches aside, she winced and brought her hand up to her chest. It was obvious she was in a considerable amount of pain.

"Are you going to be okay?"

"I think so."

"You think so? What do you mean you think so? You went to the hospital, didn't you?" Harrison hadn't meant to raise his voice. He was just concerned that Jennifer might not have gotten the proper medical treatment.

"Yes, I went to the hospital."

"And?" Harrison continued.

"And the doctor said I was extremely lucky and should consider myself fortunate."

"But he said it was okay for you to be home, right?"

"Yes, Harrison, other than a badly sprained ankle and some cuts and bruises, I'm fine." Jennifer closed her eyes and tried to get comfortable. Each time she moved, she held her arm against her chest.

"What's wrong with your chest?"

"I hit it on the steering wheel."

"Weren't you wearing your seatbelt?"

"Yes, but when the steering wheel gets pushed into your chest, it doesn't do much good."

Harrison just sat there, not knowing what else to say. After a few minutes of Jennifer moving and shifting, trying to find a comfortable position, she looked at Harrison.

"I think there's some medicine in that plastic bag. Can you get it for me and see what it says?"

Harrison reached for the bag that was sitting on the coffee table and pulled three different bottles from inside. He read each label, the instructions, and the accompanying paperwork. He looked at his watch and then moved to the kitchen for a glass of water.

When he came back, he sat alongside of her and waited for her to open her eyes. "Here, this is for the pain."

Jennifer hated to take medicine because of the effects it had on her, but she had no choice—the pain was too great. She took the large pill from him and put it on the tip of her tongue. She quickly washed it down with the water he'd brought her and convulsed. Things hadn't changed. She still had an aversion to medicine.

Harrison got up from the couch. "Would you be more comfortable in bed? I can help you to your room."

"No, I'm fine."

Harrison left the room momentary and returned with a pillow from her bed. "Here, scoot down, so you can put your feet up."

Harrison held her pillow at one end of the couch while she slowly maneuvered her injured ankle from the coffee table to the cushions. Jennifer pulled her lips in, biting on them, trying to silence the pain she was feeling.

"Could you put a pillow under my knee?"

Jennifer was holding onto her right knee, not letting it go until Harrison gently pushed one of her decorative pillows beneath it. She finally laid her head back and sighed. She laid completely still, waiting for the pain medication to kick in. Harrison pulled up an armchair from across the room and sat near her feet.

He wanted to ask Jennifer what happened. He stared at her, sure her accident was his fault. She was running from him, so desperate to get away that she ended up in the hospital. Harrison bowed his head, resting his elbows on his knees.

Lord, help me. Now that I found Jennifer, I don't want to have to let her go, at least not yet. But I can't stay if she's going to self-destruct. It's my fault that she's laying here. Help me to know what to do.

Jennifer heard whispers, but she didn't feel as if they were directed at her. She opened her heavy eyes to see Harrison, his head hanging between his shoulders, talking to himself. No . . . he was praying.

Jennifer didn't know what to make of it. She had never taken Harrison for the religious sort, but she was sure he was praying. Jennifer tried to analyze the situation, but she felt her mind begin to go fuzzy. She would have to figure it out later. Now, all she wanted was sleep.

Harrison was startled by the sound of his phone. He quickly flipped it open and then hurried to the far side of the room so he wouldn't disturb Jennifer.

"Harrison, where are you?" Robert's voice boomed.

"I'm busy at the moment, what's up?" His voice was low.

"Kelly and I decided to go to Catalina for the weekend. I figured you'd enjoy the time to yourself, but if you want to tag along, you can."

Harrison could tell from Robert's tone, it really wasn't an invitation.

"No, you two go ahead." Harrison tried to keep his voice soft, but not so soft that Robert would question him. "I'm sure I'll find something to do while you're gone." He flipped his phone closed and stared at Jennifer as she slept on the couch. The pillow she held against her chest slowly rose and fell with every breath.

Harrison moved around the room slowly, taking in all the beautiful details. It looked nothing like the apartment that Jennifer had when she was in Chicago. That one had been sleek and bright, very contemporary, but the home he wandered around now was decorated to fit the period of the house. Everything had a Spanish feel to it. From the wrought-iron sconces that flanked the fireplace to the velvety red tapestries that hung on either side of the windows. Jennifer's home looked like a hacienda from a period long ago.

Harrison drifted throughout the house, admiring the attention to detail. There was only one thing lacking—warmth. Even with all its rich colors and intricate details, there was no life to the house. There were no pictures or personal mementos, the things that made a house a home. It tore at Harrison when he thought of the life or the lack of one that Jennifer had led.

He sat back down across from her, studying her features. He was praying again when he felt himself begin to relax. Once again, like so many times in the past, she was the last thing he was thinking of before he fell asleep.

CHAPTER TEN

Jennifer woke up to see Harrison scrunched down in the chair. He was asleep, and she could only wonder how he could have gotten comfortable in such an awkward position. His large frame filled the chair, his head crooked to one side, his long legs stretched out in front of him.

Her eyes focused on his face. He was still as handsome as she remembered him, but something had changed. There was something different about him, but she couldn't quite put her finger on it.

Before she could analyze him further, he stirred. Harrison opened his eyes to see Jennifer staring at him. She asked him what she had wondered since he had confronted her at her office.

"What are you doing here, Harrison?" Her words were simple and her voice soft.

He stretched and rolled his neck before answering. "I didn't think you should be alone."

"No, I mean here, in California?"

"Robert. He and Kelly are getting married in June. They've dated long distance for seven months, and Robert decided to come out before the wedding to get acclimated. He asked me to come along. He said he wanted to spend some time with me before he was married, but I think that was just a line."

Jennifer adjusted the pillows around her and carefully pulled herself up to a sitting position.

"Then why did you want to look at property if you were just visiting?"

"California is growing on me—the mild temperatures, the beach, the change in scenery. It's relaxing; I thought I might give it a try."

"It has nothing to do with me?" she asked with a raised brow.

Harrison grinned. "Robert told me that Samantha Wilder was incredibly gorgeous, but no, you had nothing to do with my decision."

She looked at him wondering what else Robert had told him. Harrison didn't miss the look.

"Robert told me what he did."

"Brave man considering the short leash Kelly has him on," Jennifer snapped back.

"He also told me that you turned him down cold."

"Men with roving eyes aren't my style. Besides, he reminded me too much of someone I'd been trying to forget."

Harrison knew that Jennifer had meant to hurt him with her words, but she'd only revealed that she too had not forgotten him.

"So, where do we go from here?"

Jennifer steadied herself. "I thank you for your help, continue on as Samantha Wilder, and you be the gentleman that you are and honor my wishes and my privacy."

"You give me more credit than I deserve," Harrison retorted.

Jennifer closed her eyes in defeat. She didn't have the energy to debate with Harrison. She was aching from head to toe and still had to call work and explain why she would be absent indefinitely.

Harrison moved to the kitchen and decided to put together a late lunch.

When Jennifer woke up again, she saw that Harrison was gone. She sat up slowly and listened for any sign of him. The house was silent, and her feelings of disappointment surprised her. For as much as she had pleaded with him to leave her alone, a part of her had wanted him to stay.

It took a painful few moments for her to get to her feet. She placed the crutches under her arms, feeling the strain in her chest. She hobbled to the bathroom and looked at herself for the first time. She looked like she'd gotten in a fight with a cat. She had tiny cuts all over her face and a rectangular bandage over her left eye. She unbuttoned her blouse and slowly pulled it from her waistband. When she allowed it to fall open, she pressed her fingers to her chest where the discoloration was already visible.

"Are you all right?" Harrison's concerned voice reached out to her while he tried to avoid looking at her revealing reflection in the mirror.

Jennifer quickly gathered her blouse together, the sudden movement causing her more pain. "I thought you had left," she explained as she fumbled with each of her buttons.

"I just stepped outside for some fresh air." Harrison had a hard time knowing where to rest his eyes. "I made you a sandwich about an hour ago. Are you hungry?"

"No, I just hurt."

He moved back from the doorway, giving her room to maneuver. Each step she took looked so painful, he wished there was something he could do to help. She got as far as her bedside and realized for the first time that the height of the large antique bed was going to be difficult for her to scale.

"Let me help you." Harrison read her mind and was instantly at her side. He cradled her gently with one arm around her and the other one behind her knees. He lifted her slowly and lowered her to the bed but paused for a moment before letting her go. Jennifer felt the hesitation and looked at him for an explanation. His eyes told her all she needed to know.

He helped her position pillows behind her head, under her knee, and placed one next to her so she could use it on her chest. Once she was situated, he went to the kitchen and returned with several items.

Harrison handed her two different pills and a glass of water. "The brown one is for inflammation, and the pink one is an antibiotic." She swallowed them slowly.

Next he handed her a plate with a sandwich, some chips, and a few slices of orange on it.

"I'm not hungry."

"But you need to eat something with all the medication you're going to be taking."

"Okay, but not right now. I need to call the office and explain to them that I won't be in for a few days."

"Is that going to be a problem?"

"Only for me. Most of my clients are not the patient type. I'll probably lose them. Can you get me my cell phone? It's in my purse."

Harrison moved to the other room to retrieve her purse. When he handed it to her, he explained, "My mother always told me it wasn't polite for a gentleman to look through a woman's purse."

Jennifer smiled at his bit of chivalry. She dug around for her phone, the small amount of exertion tiring her. She punched in the numbers and held the phone to her ear as she let her head fall back into the down of her pillow.

"Hi Julie, it's Samantha. Could you put me through to Mr. Holmes please? Thank you." She waited with her eyes closed. "Mr. Holmes, hi, it's Samantha Wilder. Mr. Holmes, I have some rather bad news. . . "

When Jennifer ended the call, Harrison couldn't help but comment, "He seemed to take that pretty well."

"I'm his highest earning employee. I've never taken a vacation or a sick day in three years, so what could he say?"

Harrison pushed the plate of food back in front of her, only to be met with a scowl. "Look, you're going to be sorry if you don't eat something."

She didn't answer.

"Okay, but don't say I didn't warn you." Harrison set the plate down and moved to the door in Jennifer's bedroom that led to the garden.

Gazing outside, Harrison was impressed with the lush plantings.

"Jennifer, your yard is beautiful!"

"Thank you."

"Did you do it all by yourself?"

"Uh huh."

"Let me guess . . . in one of your former lives you were a gardener?"

Harrison's joke was met with a sharp look. He realized a moment too late that it was in bad taste.

Jennifer turned away from him and closed her eyes. He decided to let her sleep. He wandered back into the living room and opened what appeared to be an old wine cabinet. Sure enough, it housed a small television. He looked around for the remote and made himself comfortable on the couch. He watched the last 15 minutes of a sports program and was flipping through the channels when he heard his name being called urgently from the other room.

He jumped from the sofa and ran down the hall. One look at Jennifer's face told him all he needed to know. All color was gone from her complexion and she was holding her hand against her mouth. She had gotten herself to the edge of the bed but was unable to reach far enough to get her crutches from where they were leaning against the wall.

Harrison hurriedly put an arm around her waist and pressed her against his side. Her feet barely touched the floor as he whisked her to the bathroom as quickly as he could. She lowered herself to the side of the toilet, her right knee protesting, but her stomach overruling the pain. With the first lurch of her stomach, her hand went up to her chest. The pain was excruciating. She cried and heaved at the same time as Harrison stood by, powerless to do anything.

Her fragile body retched violently as one hand clung to the side of the tub for balance and the other braced her chest against the pain. She quickly tried to push back her hair as it slipped down from her shoulders. Another contraction brought her hand back to her chest, leaving her hair dangling unrestrained.

Harrison moved in behind her and gently scooped her hair back from her face. He sat on the edge of the tub, holding her hair, stroking her back, trying to bring her what comfort he could.

The scene lasted only a few moments, but to Jennifer it was an eternity. She wasn't sure which ran deeper—the pain or the degradation. When she felt her body give up its vicious protest, she crumpled against the side of the tub. Harrison shifted out of the way, making room for her and letting her hair fall from his hands. He grabbed a towel that hung on a nearby rack and offered it to her. She wiped her face of both salvia and perspiration before allowing her head to come to rest against Harrison's knee. She sat there, too weak to talk, or move, or care about how she looked.

Her body began to shiver as her breathing returned to normal. Harrison leaned over and ran his hand up and down her arm, trying to warm her. He was the first to break the silence.

"Let me run you a nice, hot bath to ward off the chill. Do you think you can handle that?"

Jennifer sat with her eyes closed, not wanting to move. Anything right now, seemed like a task too daunting to tackle.

"Come on, it will make you feel better."

It took a moment for Jennifer to begin to move. She lowered the toilet seat and pulled herself up on top of it. She waited a moment, making sure that her stomach wasn't going to rage against the movement. When nothing happened, she tried to stand, her body wavering slightly.

Harrison reached out to brace her and gently sat her back down.

"I need to get a few things," she whispered.

"I'll get them for you; just tell me where they are."

"They're personal," she said awkwardly.

"Jennifer," he spoke in a low tone. "I know what lingerie looks like. Just tell me what you need."

She refused. She would hold onto what little dignity she had left. Her silky robe and her favorite nightie were hanging on the back of the bathroom door. It wasn't exactly appropriate, but with her robe wrapped around her, it would have to do.

"Never mind, I've got what I need here."

"You're not going to want to put that blouse and those slacks back on. Let me get you something else to wear."

"My robe and nightgown are hanging on the back of the door. I'll be fine. If you could just run the water, I think I can manage everything else."

The nausea left Jennifer as quickly as it came, but the dizziness remained. She knew it was because she'd taken medicine without food, a point she was sure Harrison would make soon enough.

It had taken her a little time to get undressed and carefully climb into the tub. Once she sank into the warmth of the water, she could feel the aching ease from her muscles.

The doctor had warned her that she would be sore for several days. Her body had been banged up quite severely; he expressed over and over again how incredibly lucky she was. Her car had nearly collapsed around her, as if some shield of protection had pocketed the area she occupied. She wasn't ready to call it a miracle, as the doctor had, but she was glad she hadn't been hospitalized.

The real Samantha Wilder had lived and died in Iowa, but hospitals always posed a danger of exposing her. Jennifer could fake her hair color, her eye color, and her age, but she would never be able to fake a blood type, or any medical history that could be brought up on a hospital computer. With the way hospitals and police stations networked their information these days, a run in with either always had the potential of trouble.

Jennifer soaked in her bath until the water turned tepid. She had looped her braced foot over the edge of the tub and now needed to maneuver carefully to get back on her feet. The hardest part was being able to balance herself on her one good foot. She bobbled only slightly, letting out a painful breath once she was safely out of the tub.

Harrison had moved her robe and nightie from the hook on the back of the door to the countertop of the vanity. After drying herself off, Jennifer slipped on her gown and wrapped her robe snugly around her body. She got to her feet and limped to the door.

Harrison hurried to the bathroom when he saw the billow of steam escape the open door. He put a firm hand around her waist as her arm involuntarily held onto him for balance. He walked her to the edge of the bed where he had turned down the comforter. He lifted her up and helped her slide between the covers. He propped her right foot up on a pillow and put another pillow under her knee. Her head fell back against the headboard, perspiration above her lip. She couldn't believe the ten paces from the bathroom to her bed had completely exhausted her.

Harrison allowed her a few moments of silence before saying anything.

"I know you don't feel like it, but you are going to have to eat something to help the medicine settle in your stomach."

When Jennifer's lips parted to say something, Harrison braced himself for a rebuttal. He was pleasantly surprised.

"Peanut butter toast. It's what I always have when I don't feel good."

Harrison jumped right on it, wanting her to eat before she changed her mind. He worked around her kitchen, opening cupboards and drawers until he found everything he needed. He shoved two pieces of sourdough bread in the toaster and waited.

When he returned to Jennifer's room, her eyes were open and she was staring off into some unknown world. He approached her slowly and took a seat on the edge of the bed. The shift in the mattress turned her attention towards him.

"What were you thinking?" he asked as he extended the tray with toast and water on it.

"A bunch of things." She didn't know how to explain the thoughts that were going through her head. They were pretty obscure; even she wasn't sure where they had come from.

He didn't press her. The important thing now was to get some food into her. "All you had was sourdough bread."

"I know. It's my favorite. And as odd as it sounds, it tastes really good with peanut butter."

Jennifer took small bites of her toast and little sips of water. It took her over 20 minutes to finish the small meal. She was pacing herself, waiting for her stomach to refuse the nourishment, but thankfully, everything stayed down and soon she was sound asleep.

Harrison found himself wandering again, looking at Jennifer's things, trying to understand the life that she'd led or the part that she'd played. Right now, he wasn't sure which one it was.

He checked on her periodically, glad that she was finally getting some uninterrupted sleep. After a while he took a seat on the couch and began to flip through the T.V. channels again. When he glanced up at the large antique clock on the mantel and saw that it was nearing 5:00 p.m., he decided to see what he could find for dinner.

When Jennifer awoke, her room was dark except for the light from the bathroom. She squinted her eyes to focus in on her alarm clock and realized it was already evening. She could hear noises coming from the other room and decided to see what Harrison was up to.

The pressure of the crutches under her arms pulled at the muscles in her chest. If there was any way to sprain your chest, she was sure that was exactly what she'd done. She made sure her robe was cinched up tightly before steadily moving down the hall.

Harrison was working intently over the stove when he turned to get something. He hadn't heard Jennifer creep up behind him and jumped when he saw her.

The look of shock on his face made her laugh painfully.

"Dang it, Jennifer, you nearly gave me a heart attack."

"Well, I guess that's one for me. Imagine, me startling you."

The playfulness in her tone almost made Harrison forget what he was doing. When he caught a whiff of burning bread, he remembered.

He reached for pot holders and yanked open the broiler. One piece of cheese bread was history, but the other two looked like they could be salvaged. Harrison removed the cookie sheet and dropped it on the stove.

Jennifer stepped closer to the stove to see what was in the large pot.

"Is that chicken soup?" Jennifer asked as she inhaled the aromatic scent.

"Yes, but it's not quite done yet." He shut off the broiler, checked the soup, and then turned his attention to her.

"How are you doing?" He looked at the way she was perched on her crutches.

"I still feel like a bus hit me, but at least I don't feel as sick as I did." She shuffled over to the small dining room set that looked out into the garden and slowly lowered herself into a chair, leaning her crutches within reach.

"Good. And this time when you take your medicine, you'll make sure to have something to eat with it."

She rolled her eyes. Harrison, always the competitor, didn't waste any time telling her I told you so, even if it was in a casual, non-confrontational way.

She watched him as he worked around her kitchen. Her mind fantasized how it would be to share her life with someone. Since her mother had died, she'd had no one to come home to or share a meal with. Her paranoia had made her never let anyone into her house or her life.

She'd had a brief relationship with a man before moving to Chicago, but it was far from what she would consider normal. It was a couple years after her mother had died, and she was going through an extremely dark period. She'd turned to drinking because it helped her forget the fear and the anxieties that caged her in like an animal.

She had stumbled into a bar one night when she was feeling extremely depressed and lonely. That's where she'd met Brad. He sat next to her at the bar and began to make small talk with her. He was attractive, a great dancer, a good listener, and a smooth talker.

Before she knew it, they were back at his place with Brad telling her how beautiful she was, and for once, her not wanting to go home alone at the end of the night.

She'd stayed the night, one of many. But she could tell Brad was as disconnected from her emotionally as she was from him. Their relationship continued for several months—always meeting at the bar, always ending up back at his place. She never felt safe enough to confide in him. Their relationship wasn't really based on trust, only on the physical. They were using each other to fill a need. When his girlfriend, who had previously relocated because of her job, decided to move back in with him, Jennifer was out the door, Brad no longer needing her affection.

It had been an eye opener for Jennifer. Devastated and feeling completely alone again, she went to another bar. When she was hit on within minutes, something inside her went off like a warning bell. She realized what she was doing and how disappointed her mother would be with her.

That night she quit drinking cold turkey, moved to Chicago, and got the job at Weissler and Schuler. She'd never allowed her vulnerabilities to get the better of her since. That is, until Harrison ended up back in her life.

Harrison set down a plate in front of her, pulling her from her thoughts. She looked at the steaming bowl of soup on the plate and the slice of slightly overdone bread slipped in beside it. She inhaled the rich smell, glad that it wasn't doing battle with her stomach. Harrison brought a plate for himself, two glasses of soda, and napkins for both of them, along with the salt and pepper before taking a seat.

"I guess I didn't have the noodles you were looking for," she quipped.

Harrison looked into his own bowl of soup, seeing the mixture of bow tie and egg noodles. "No, but it makes it interesting, doesn't it?" His smile was enchanting and drew Jennifer to him.

"Would you mind if I prayed before we ate?" Harrison asked as he reached across the table to hold her hand.

She shook her head and followed his lead. When he said "Amen," he started immediately in on his soup.

Jennifer sipped the steaming broth and slurped on a couple of noodles. "This is really good. Where did you learn to cook?"

"Making soup isn't exactly cooking. It's throwing things into a pot and seasoning them."

"Okay, where did you learn to season so well?"

Harrison laughed. "We had the most wonderful cook when I was growing up. Robert and I would sit in the kitchen while Marta came up with the most amazing dishes. I guess she taught us an appreciation for fine food."

Jennifer smiled at his reply.

The rest of the meal was eaten in relative silence. When they were finished, Harrison got up and placed two small pills next to her plate. She looked at them with apprehension.

"You should do okay now."

Jennifer took the pills with the last sip of her soda. She moved around, trying to get comfortable in the straight-backed chair.

"Here, I'll help you back to bed." Harrison got up and walked over to her chair.

"No, I can do it."

Jennifer steadied herself on her crutches, but instead of going down the hall, she headed for the living room. She made herself as comfortable as possible while Harrison cleaned up the kitchen. Soon he joined her and sat in the arm-chair, trying to anticipate what she would say next.

Finally she could contain her curiosity no longer. "I never knew you were a praying man."

Her comment came out of nowhere, but he was more than willing to talk about the change in his life.

"I wasn't before, but over the last few years I've come to realize how impor-tant it is to have faith in something. My mother raised both me and Robert in the church. I wandered from it while I was growing up, but I feel like I'm back on track now."

"So, you believe in God?"

"Yes, very much so. In fact, I don't feel it's at all a coincidence that I found you."

"Oh, I get it. You prayed about it, and poof, you found me." There was sar-casm in her tone, but Harrison didn't let it bother him.

"Actually, you're right. I had prayed about it a lot, but I had given up trying to find you until a couple weeks ago when I was on the beach. I saw a jogger that I thought for sure was you. I tried to find her, but I lost her in the crowd. Then, I saw the sign at West Beach Properties with the same initials that I found scrib-bled on a notepad you left behind when you moved."

"You were in my apartment?" she interrupted.

"I was. I drove by your place every day after you left Weissler and Schuler, trying to work up the nerve to talk to you again. Then one day, there's a 'For Rent' sign in the window of your apartment and a realtor showing a couple around. I convinced her to let me in. There was nothing there but a notepad left on the counter. WBP was pressed into the paper. When I saw the sign outside your office, I knew it wasn't a coincidence."

Jennifer thought for a moment before asking, "How did you know that Jennifer Patterson had died?"

"I have a friend that works in the Social Security office. I gave him the number we had on file for you. I was hoping to find out where you were working, so I could talk to you. Imagine my surprise when he called me back and told me you were dead, and that you'd been dead for three years."

"Not what you were expecting, I guess."

"I couldn't believe it. I knew there had to be a mistake somewhere, but Dave convinced me that the information was right, and that it was you who had lied."

"Did he report it?"

"No. It would have caused problems for him to try and explain what he was doing looking into your records, so he dropped it. Anyway, I knew there was no point in trying to find someone who didn't want to be found. I started spending more time at home, with my folks, and slowly got back into the routine of going to church with my mom."

"And you found that it helped?"

"Yeah, I think it helped me to become a person of perspective. I'm not as driven as I used to be."

"But just as successful," Jennifer interjected, knowing Harrison's reputation and his rise in the business world.

"Things have gone well for me, but like you said, you're responsible for some of that success. Your work on the Yomahama account was pivotal for Weissler and Schuler."

"You mean Weissler, Schuler, and Lynch." She corrected him. "I've followed your career, Harrison. The work you did after Yomahama is what catapulted your company into the Fortune 500. That's not the work of a docile, apathetic businessman."

"I didn't say I wasn't focused; I just didn't make every move and every decision like it was life and death."

A broad smile crossed his face, piquing Jennifer's curiosity.

"What's that for?" she asked, sounding slightly irritated.

"So, you weren't as uninterested as you tried to make me believe."

"What?"

"You brushed me off, saying you didn't need admirers, but you must have felt something between us. I mean the info you found on me after you left wasn't exactly front page of the business section. You had to go looking for it."

Jennifer realized she had said more than she had intended. She turned her eyes from Harrison, feeling like she was on the hot seat again.

Harrison got up from his chair and moved to sit on the coffee table next to her. He looked at Jennifer intently, not allowing her to look away.

"Admit it, Jennifer, we connected that night. You felt it as much as I did." His eyes were boring a hole in her, waiting for her to say something.

"Okay!" she blurted out. "So maybe I did, but that was three years ago. A lot has changed since then."

"You really think so?"

"Of course it has."

"Well, I haven't changed how I feel about you."

"Come on, Harrison, you're telling me that you're not angry, or disappointed in me?"

"No, I'm not. I just find myself wanting to get to know you all over again."

"But you can't. I'm not Jennifer Patterson anymore."

"Then fine, I'll get to know Samantha Wilder."

"And how are you going to explain that to people?"

"What's there to explain? I was vacationing in California, met a wonderful girl, and we're spending time getting to know each other. What's so hard about that?"

"So you're not going to tell Robert that I'm Jennifer?"

"I don't need to right now, no."

"Right now," she reiterated. "So when?"

"Why do we need to worry about that now?"

"Because one thing always leads to another."

Harrison acted like she was overreacting, so she decided to explain what she knew all too well.

"Say we keep it from Robert and Kelly, and we just go along with the whole Samantha persona. When do we tell them the truth?"

"Who says we have to?"

"Okay, so we allow them to believe we met for the first time here in California and hit it off. What if we really hit it off, Harrison? What if our relationship grows deeper? You can't take me back to Chicago to introduce me to your business partners. They know me as Jennifer. How are we going to explain that?"

Harrison was hit for the first time with the reality that Jennifer lived with everyday. Once she moved on, there was no going back.

CHAPTER ELEVEN

Jennifer and Harrison ignored the obvious question the rest of the evening. She tried to send him home, assuring him that she was okay, but he was just as stubborn as she was.

Of course, she wasn't very convincing with the way she hobbled from room to room, or how her mood would turn quiet and short when her pain medication wore down.

When it got to be 9:00 p.m. and Jennifer was ready for some more medicine, he made a suggestion.

"How about if I go back to my room, shower, get some fresh clothes on, and come back for the rest of the evening?"

"How about you go back to your room and call me in the morning?" she snapped. Every muscle in her body had continued to stiffen as the night wore on, making her more and more irritable.

"No dice. I'm here for the duration." He turned his attention to the television, ignoring the tight expression on her face.

"And what will Robert say? He'll think that I just rolled over for you."

Harrison chuckled slightly. "That would sure kill his ego. He considers himself such a ladies man, and you turned him down flat."

Jennifer shot him a look of disgust. "And you would let him believe that about me? That I was yours for the taking?"

"Relax. Robert and Kelly went to Catalina for the weekend. He doesn't even know I'm here."

Jennifer backed down a little, glad that Harrison wouldn't have questions waiting for him once he got home. She shifted against the couch cushions, feeling tired, short-tempered, and hurting from head to toe.

Harrison continued playing nursemaid, bringing Jennifer the next round of her medication, encouraging her to get some rest.

Finally, her demeanor weak, she limped to the bathroom, needing some privacy. She could no longer hold back her emotions. She couldn't remember the last time she'd felt so bad. As she moved across the room, she tried to stifle her tears, but Harrison had seen her composure begin to break down before she had even made it to the hallway. He was leaning against the doorframe of her bedroom when she finally emerged from the bathroom.

"It's all right to cry, you know."

He startled her, causing her to gasp, then moan. He moved closer, standing within inches of her. She lifted her face up to meet his, tears streaming down her cheeks.

"I have never felt so horrible in all my life."

With that said, he wrapped his arms around her and pressed her face to his chest, being careful not to hurt her. He held her for some time, enjoying the way it felt having her in his arms, wanting to be the one that encouraged her and gave her strength.

"Jennifer, it's time that you let someone take care of you for a change. You don't have to go through this on your own."

"But it's not fair."

"What's not fair?"

"Complicating your life like this. You're a great guy, Harrison. You deserve someone who will complement your life, not confuse it."

Harrison framed her face with his hands, and waited for her to look at him. Her eyes were a mixture of hope and fear.

"Jennifer, my life has been out of balance for three years now. I'm not confused; in fact, I have never been so sure about something in my whole life. God brought us together for a reason. Let Him help you."

"But I've lied and broken the law, and I've done other things, Harrison, things that I'm not proud of. How can God help me when He condemns those things?"

"Because He's a God of second chances."

Jennifer rested her forehead against his chest, trying to make sense of the situation she was in. She had lived in fear her entire life: running, hiding, terrified of everyone and everything. She had run from Harrison once, afraid that her delirious rantings had exposed her, and he would find out the truth about who she was. But now he was here, knowing most everything about her, and instead of turning away in disgust, he wanted to stay. Jennifer was still afraid, but she no longer had the will or the strength to argue.

She sunk deeper into the comfort and protection that Harrison was offering her. Her determination to make him understand and push him away was gone. Though she knew she could be making a very serious mistake, she didn't care. For once, she didn't listen to what her mind was telling her; instead she chose to listen to her heart.

Harrison felt her resistance melt away. He held her close, silently thanking God for the way He had brought them together. Harrison didn't think about the obstacles that still surrounded them. He knew, in time, they would be able to work things out. At the moment, all he wanted to do was to hold Jennifer and assure her that he would never let anyone hurt her again.

When she looked up into his rich, brown eyes, she didn't see doubt or uncertainty; instead she saw strength and a hint of Harrison's own vulnerabilities.

He slowly bent his face towards her, watching Jennifer, waiting to see if she would pull away. When she didn't, he allowed himself an indulgent kiss, a kiss she accepted willingly. She wanted to be held; she wanted to be comforted; she wanted to be loved. His kiss was full but not demanding. Jennifer allowed herself to enjoy the feeling of intimacy with him, something she had daydreamed about more than once in the last three years.

Jennifer felt uncertain about what to do next. She wanted Harrison to stay with her, all night. She wanted to be able to feel him next to her, draw from his strength when her nightmares weakened her, but Harrison had resisted her before. She was sure it had to do with his relationship with God.

He gently pulled away from her, resting his forehead against hers. "I need to go home, and get showered and changed before it gets too late."

"You could shower here," Jennifer offered, her eyes hinting at something more.

Harrison kept his words gentle. "I don't think that would be such a good idea." He kissed her forehead and then urged her nearer to the bed. "I'll be back in less than an hour." He helped her get comfortable, pulling the covers over her weary body. "Why don't you give me your keys and your security code, and I'll let myself in when I get back?"

Instinctively she refused, saying she would listen for him and let him in when he got back.

Harrison sat on the side of the bed and brushed a loose strand of her hair behind her ear. "Jennifer, you need to trust me."

Trust was such an unfamiliar emotion to her. She wasn't sure she was ready to give it to anyone. Harrison tipped her chin up so he could see into her downcast eyes.

Trust wasn't the only thing that she was struggling with. To give Harrison her security code would reveal to him the extent of the impact he'd made on her long before he had re-entered her life.

"Jennifer?"

"My keys are in my purse." She pointed to where it was still laying on the bedside table. "And the code for the alarm is . . . look, I'm wide awake. I'll listen for you. You said you wouldn't be long. I'll just stay up and listen for you."

"Jennifer, stop being so stubborn. If you don't trust me, you can always change your code tomorrow, but for now, you need to stay in bed."

Jennifer's skin flushed. She didn't think there was any way she could tell him her code. It would be too humiliating, too revealing. But the look on his face was saying he wouldn't take no for an answer.

"Okay, but you've got to know the reason I chose my code was because there was no way anyone would be able to relate it to Samantha Wilder."

He waited.

She stuttered as she spelled it out. "L-Y-N-C-H."

He smiled widely, and she cringed. When she tried to explain herself, he placed a quick kiss to her forehead and moved from the bed, not allowing her to give him any further explanation.

"I'll be back as soon as I can. In the meantime, try to get some sleep."

She heard the front door close, and instantly felt the weight of being alone.

It was funny; she'd been alone for the last 11 years. Not since her mom died had she talked so openly about herself to someone else. Now that she had, she felt the anxiety of being alone. She wasn't sure if it was because of the company she craved or the fear that Harrison could take what information he had and turn her into the police.

She tried to quiet the doubt that was assaulting her. *Harrison wouldn't do that, would he?*

Jennifer allowed her imagination to wander to the extreme. She felt the debate going on inside her mind between her heart and the cynical side of her psyche. Had Harrison felt so slighted by her disappearance in Chicago that he decided to get even with her? Was the compassionate, caring attitude that he'd shown her just a cover for his anger and resentment?

No! She stopped herself. *He wouldn't do that.* His feelings for her were genuine; she felt it. *If he had wanted to get even with me and turn me in, he would have done it yesterday,* she chided herself. But what if that was why he was at her house when she came home from the hospital? Maybe he was there to set her up, to get more information from her before going to the police.

Jennifer was agitated and felt a cold sweat cover her body. She fought with the medication that was beginning to make her feel drowsy. She didn't want to sleep. She didn't want to be startled awake by a sea of police officers, reading her her rights while taking them away.

Her head became too heavy to lift, and her eyes closed without her permission. *Maybe it's for the best. I'm tired of running. I don't want to live like this anymore.* With that, sleep overtook her. It was so strong; she didn't hear Harrison when he came back 40 minutes later.

HARRISON WAS SURPRISED when he let himself into the house, and Jennifer didn't call to him. He smiled when he saw her fast asleep. He approached her bed and brushed his hand against her cheek. She stirred under her covers but didn't open her eyes.

Harrison turned off the bedroom's overhead light but left the light on in the bathroom, pulling the door almost completely shut. The minimal light shining through the crack in the door illuminated the room enough for him to see the outline of the bed and Jennifer's form sleeping in it.

He moved to the other side of the bed and carefully lowered himself on top of the quilt, trying not to disturb Jennifer from her much needed sleep. He kicked off his shoes, brought his feet up on top of the covers, and stretched out. He made himself comfortable, realizing for the first time how tired he was.

With his head resting in the palms of his laced fingers, he stared at the ceiling, thinking about the question he had refused to answer earlier. What would happen if this time he and Jennifer were able to have a relationship, a serious relationship? How would he explain the reason for Jennifer's disappearance and still keep her secret? He could handle Robert. Robert had some of his own "don't ask don't tell" situations. But what would he say to the people in

Chicago? He had to admit that it would be a huge obstacle in their relationship, but he wasn't going to let it deter him.

Harrison took a deep breath and closed his eyes. There would always be tomorrow to figure out the difficulties of their situation. Right now, he needed some rest of his own.

Jennifer was awakened by the pain in her chest. It was still dark so she had no idea what time it was. Her mind did a quick recap of the events that happened earlier that day: the accident, Harrison, and the fact that she had told him almost everything. She closed her eyes and shifted, no longer knowing if the pain in her chest was from her injuries or her feelings for Harrison. She had never felt more confused in her life. She tried to get comfortable shifting from side to side but nothing helped.

"Are you all right?"

Jennifer gasped, startled by Harrison's soft voice.

"I'm sorry; I didn't mean to frighten you." Harrison turned toward her, resting on his elbow, the outline of his body visible in the shadows.

"What are you doing here?" Jennifer asked, feeling awkward at his closeness.

"I told you I would come back."

"I know, but what are you doing . . . here?"

"I wanted to stay close to you in case you needed something."

Jennifer looked at him, wondering if he knew what she was thinking—how she wished they were lying next to each other under different circumstances.

Harrison's feelings were beginning to stir inside him. He wanted to reach out to Jennifer, to show her how he felt about her, but he knew he couldn't. It wouldn't be right. She was hurting, and he had made a commitment.

Harrison moved to the edge of the bed and got to his feet. "It's time for your medication; I'll go get it."

Harrison went into the kitchen, leaned against the counter, and let out the breath he was holding. *Lord, you've got to help me. I've thought about her for three years and now being with her, holding her, it's harder than I expected. Help me, God. Don't let me mess things up.*

He stood there, the sun just beginning to rise and thought again about what he could do to help Jennifer. He hung his head, knowing the obstacles ahead of them seemed insurmountable. Harrison grabbed the medicine bottle from the counter and a bottle of water from the refrigerator. He walked back into her room. Her eyes were closed, and he thought she'd gone back to sleep. He moved to the bedside table and set the bottle of pills down. Jennifer's eyes fluttered, and she reached her hand out to his.

"Where did you go?" Her voice was soft and feathery.

He squeezed her hand. "I got your medicine."

"What's it for?"

"Inflammation."

"Okay, but no more pain medicine. I don't like feeling so soft headed."

"We'll see," he said with a smile as he handed her the small tablet.

Harrison watched as she carefully tipped her head back to wash the medication down with water.

The morning rays cast a brightness across Jennifer's bed, basking her in light. Harrison saw for the first time the bruises that covered her chest. Her thin-strapped nightie was modest enough, but it didn't cover the blue and purple discoloration that crept all the way up to her collarbone. He sat alongside of her, took the bottle of water from her hand, and set it on the nightstand.

"You never told me what happened."

"You mean the accident?"

He nodded. "Were you running?"

"No."

She could tell that he didn't believe her.

"I thought about it. In fact, I was up most of the night weighing my choices, but I promise I wasn't running. I just wasn't paying attention."

"How bad is your car?"

"Totaled. They had to cut me out of it."

Jennifer saw the color disappear from his complexion.

"You could have been killed!"

"I know." Her words were solemn.

"But you didn't try to . . ." He couldn't bring himself to say it.

"No. I didn't do it on purpose." Jennifer was bothered by Harrison's question and fired back at him. "I've fought too long and too hard to stay alive to try and kill myself, but thanks for the vote of confidence."

"Jennifer, I'm sorry, I didn't mean . . . "

"Forget it." Her words were clipped and stopped him before he could finish. She refused to look at him, angry at his assumption.

He moved from her beside, realizing he had insulted her with his worries. "I'm going to fix us some breakfast. Does anything sound good to you?"

"No."

"Then I guess I'll just have to see what I can find." Harrison walked to the kitchen, feeling miserable. It was not the way he had hoped to start the day.

Jennifer wanted to stay angry with Harrison. His unasked question had hurt her. He didn't understand that her whole life had been spent in survival mode. When she felt like giving up, she didn't think about taking her life, she thought only of what it would be like to turn herself in. That was enough to make her more resilient and to endure whatever she needed to in order to keep up the charade that had become second nature to her.

Harrison fumbled over the stove, wishing he could take back the last few moments. He knew he'd insulted Jennifer, accusing her of something he shouldn't have. He pushed the eggs around in the pan and talked to God at the same time.

Jennifer needed to go to the bathroom. The minute her feet hit the floor and she felt the pressure of the crutches under her arms, tears welled in her eyes. She didn't think it was possible, but she felt as if the pain she was feeling was even stronger than it had been the day before. She braced herself for the few steps it would take to cross the room. She hobbled and whimpered at the same time, feeling a sense of accomplishment when she made it to the sink. Her feeling of pride only lasted a moment.

When she looked at herself in the mirror she gasped. The cut that was bandaged over her eye had bruised, and her eyelid was purple and swollen. The thin strap of her nightie exposed the bruises that covered her arms and chest. She flinched each time her fingertips pushed against her discolored skin. It frightened her to see the visible evidence of what she'd endured at the moment of impact.

For the first time she felt thankful. Though she was overwhelmed with pain, discomfort, and a sense of uncertainty, she realized that she was fortunate just to be alive. When she heard Harrison come into the bedroom, she pushed the bathroom door closed for privacy.

He waited for her to emerge from the bathroom. When he saw the discomfort on her face, he realized that she was in for another long day.

"I have breakfast in the dining room, but I can bring it in here if . . ."

"No, I need to walk around, or I'll just get stiffer."

Jennifer hobbled past Harrison and to the dining room. Scrambled eggs, toast, and orange juice were set out for both of them at the table. Harrison waited for her to take a seat before he sat down. When he extended his hand to her, she ignored him. He quietly bowed his head and prayed silently to himself.

Harrison ate his meal, glancing at Jennifer who was just pushing hers around.

"Your other pill is by your plate, but you're going to have to eat something if you expect to keep it down."

She ignored him, drinking her orange juice instead.

Harrison rubbed at his brow. "Jennifer, I'm sorry. I didn't mean to upset you."

"Well, you did."

"Okay, then take it out on me, not yourself. You need to eat, and you need to keep taking your medicine."

Jennifer turned her attention back to her plate. After a few bites, she took the pill sitting on the table and washed it down with her juice. She didn't finish her breakfast, but Harrison was glad that she'd at least eaten something.

There was still a huge silence hanging between them when Jennifer got up and made her way back to her room. Frustrated, Harrison took their plates to the kitchen and ran some water in the sink. He could feel himself getting heated up. He realized that Jennifer was hurt and confused, but he wanted her to stop looking at him as the enemy. When he'd finished with the dishes, he walked firmly to Jennifer's bedroom, only to find the door closed.

He tried the knob, realizing it was locked. "Jennifer, I want to talk to you."

"I'm getting dressed."

Harrison moved to the living room and with exasperation sank into the side chair. His thoughts bounced between Jennifer's condition, all that he'd learned about her, what it was he still didn't know, and if she was ever going to allow him to be a part of her future.

She struggled to get dressed. Between the brace on her foot and the pains across her chest, it took almost every ounce of energy she had just to make herself look presentable. She tried to brush her hair, but had to stop after just a few strokes. It was too hard, and she was too weak.

She stepped from the bathroom, knowing she would feel better if she just didn't have to use her crutches. So, she leaned them against the wall and decided to see if she could support her own weight without them. Her steps were small and jerky, but not nearly as painful as when she used the crutches.

When Harrison saw Jennifer approaching without her crutches, he rushed to give her a hand.

"I'm all right, Harrison. Just let me do it myself." She used the wall and the furniture for counterbalance as she limped to the couch. Harrison watched, ready to help if she lost her balance. She lowered herself to the couch, took a breath, and then pulled her right leg up onto the cushions. Harrison quickly grabbed a pillow and pushed it under her knee.

"Thank you," she said as she allowed her head to sink back to the armrest.

Harrison waited for Jennifer's breathing to settle down before saying anything.

"I was thinking I could go get some groceries. You're running pretty low. Is there anything special you'd like or need?"

"No."

Harrison waited for a further reply. When he didn't get one, he moved toward the front door.

"Harrison . . ." Jennifer stopped him. ". . . we need to talk."

From the ominous tone of her voice, he was sure it wasn't going to be what he wanted to hear. He moved to the edge of the coffee table and waited for her to say something.

"Harrison, we need to figure out where we go from here."

"What is there to figure out? I want to help you. I want to be with you. I know we're going to have obstacles, but every relationship has obstacles."

"Relationship? Is that what you think we have?" she asked. "Harrison, we shared a difficult evening three years ago and now . . . it's happened all over again. That's not the basis for a relationship. That's being thrown together under difficult circumstances."

"Okay, so maybe it's not a relationship yet, but you're here and I'm here; and I have feelings for you, and I don't think you can deny you have feelings for me. You're just afraid, Jennifer, and I don't blame you. But don't push me away, not this time."

He moved closer to her and reached for her hand. He held it between his and leaned nearer still. "I'm not going anywhere, and in your condition, you can't go far." He chanced a smile. "So please, let's just take things one day at a time and see what happens."

"But that's what worries me . . . what might happen." She allowed her eyes to meet his. "Harrison, I'm afraid. I'm afraid if we get involved, it will only mess up your life."

"Well, I'm not." He brushed his hand across her cheek before pressing a kiss to her lips. His kiss was sweet and tender. She was glad it was one of the few places on her body that didn't hurt.

CHAPTER TWELVE

Jennifer was sitting up when Harrison returned from the market. She had a little more color in her face, and if Harrison wasn't mistaken, she even hinted at a smile. She watched as he made a second trip to carry in more bags and sat bemused when he went out the door for the third time.

"What on earth did you buy? You're not moving in, you know."

Her words were immediately silenced when Harrison walked through the door with a huge bouquet of daisies. They were a mixture of vibrant orange, sunshine yellow, and delicate white. When a look of astonishment filled her face, Harrison smiled. It was exactly the reaction he'd hoped for. He moved to her side and knelt down, handing her the bundle. She allowed the bouquet to sit just under her nose, taking in the wonderful scent of the flowers.

"Harrison, they're beautiful! Thank you."

"No, thank you. I was thinking I might not ever get to see that smile again." He kissed her on the forehead. "I'll put them in water. Do you have a vase somewhere?"

"Over the stove."

He pulled out a couple different vases from the cabinet, all of them too small. Jennifer heard him searching and limped to the kitchen. She watched as he tried to arrange the flowers in two small vases. She had to hold back a giggle as he struggled with the long stems of the flowers and the small, squatty vase. When the vase tipped, causing water to run down the front of the counter to the floor, she couldn't suppress her laughter any longer. Harrison heard her giggling as he righted the vase. It tipped once again, sending more water down the side of the cabinets. In frustration, he set the vase in the sink and squatted to mop up the water pooling on the floor.

"What are you laughing at?"

"I'm not laughing," Jennifer said through the hand that was muffling her amusement.

"You are too laughing." Harrison looked over his shoulder and threw the wet dish towel at her. His shot was right on, catching Jennifer right in the face.

Jennifer gasped as the towel dropped to the floor. When she raised her hand to touch her bandage and stumbled back against the wall, Harrison realized with horror that he'd hurt her.

"Jennifer, I'm sorry. I don't know what I was thinking." He gently held her forearms and craned his head to see into her closed eyes. "I was playing with you. I didn't mean to hurt you."

She stood still, not commenting or opening her eyes.

"Jennifer, are you all right? Please, tell me you're all right."

Harrison brushed her hair back from her face. Just then, he felt her shoulders shake slightly and then a giggle escaped her lips.

"You're laughing!" A stunned Harrison let go of her. Her giggling becoming more pronounced. "You let me stand here thinking I'd hurt you." Harrison backed away, putting his hands on his hips in defiance. "I can't believe you."

She looked at him, her eyes sparkling with playfulness. "Well, that's what you get for throwing something at me. I'm fragile you know."

"Fragile? You're manipulating, that's what you are."

"Oh . . . tell me how you really feel." She raised her brow playfully.

"Really?" He stepped closer. "You really want me to tell you how I feel?" He took a few more steps so that he was standing breathlessly close to her.

"I was only teasing, Harrison." His eyes were locked on hers, and she felt powerless to break his stare. "I think I need to sit down."

He pressed his hands to the wall, framing her face with his closeness. "Afraid to hear the truth?"

"No. I just feel a little weak."

"Then I guess you don't have the energy to ward off my advances."

"Is that what you're going to do . . . take advantage of me?"

"You bet."

Harrison's lips were warm and tender. Jennifer's first reaction was to stop him because of his overconfident attitude, but her senses weakened her resistance.

She knew the desire she felt for Harrison was being fueled by her longing to have a normal life with a normal relationship, but she knew that wasn't all. She had daydreamed and fantasized about Harrison for years. She knew from the first time he showed her compassion and put his antagonistic attitude aside that there was more to him than she had first thought. She had seen a kink in his all-business persona and found his nurturing spirit charming.

Harrison felt Jennifer's hesitation melt away. He wrapped her in his arms and held her gently, careful not to clutch her too tight. His heart raced, and he felt hopeful that this time things were going to turn out differently for them.

Enjoying his touch and his warmth, Jennifer nestled her head in the crook of his neck. He felt so real and for once, she felt real . . . not the made-up, make-believe person that she'd been her entire adult life.

Harrison whispered, his lips brushing against her hair, "As much as I'm enjoying this, I think you need to sit down. I can feel you shaking."

Jennifer wasn't even aware that she was trembling. Her thoughts were completely focused on him.

He helped her to the dining room, and with a peck of a kiss on the top of her head, he turned his attention back to the daisies in the sink and the bags of groceries on the counter. He cut down the awkward stems of the flowers and made two small arrangements. He carried one to the living room and put the other one on Jennifer's bedside table. He returned to the kitchen where Jennifer watched as he pulled out packages of meat, bags of vegetables, canned goods, and a variety of cartons and boxes.

"Harrison, what all did you buy?"

"A little of everything. I hope you like Italian because that's what I do best."

"It really doesn't matter because you won't be here to cook it."

Harrison swung around and looked at her in bewilderment. "Why are you being so stubborn?"

"Because you have a job to do and a brother to baby-sit, and I have a job that I have to get back to."

"I can do my job from anywhere, Robert is not going to be a problem, and there's no way you can go back to work for at least a few more days. So stop playing macho woman. You're stuck with me."

Harrison loaded up the refrigerator while ignoring the stubborn look on Jennifer's face. When he was done in the kitchen, he moved to her side.

"How about we sit outside for a little while? The fresh air will do you good."

Jennifer took a seat on the swing that overlooked the yard. Harrison sat down next to her, allowing his arm to drape around her shoulders. The rocking motion was soothing to Jennifer and the light mid-morning breeze played with the wisps of hair that lingered around her face.

"Why aren't you married?"

"Whoa, where did that come from?" Jennifer's question took Harrison completely by surprise.

"I just don't get it. You're successful, handsome, and you've obviously learned how to temper the competitive side of your personality that I found so unappealing. So why haven't you found some debutante or socialite to marry?"

"Handsome, huh?" Harrison teased her. She put her elbow into his ribs causing him to jump. "What was that for?"

"Come on, Harrison, don't try to be coy. You know you're handsome."

"Well, yes, but it's nice to know that you think I am."

Jennifer rolled her eyes at his cockiness. Harrison laughed, enjoying their lighthearted bantering.

"What about you?" Harrison asked.

"Me?" Jennifer retorted. "You didn't answer my question."

"I've had my turn at socialites, daughters of my mother's friends, and set-ups with every airhead that Robert ever tricked me into dating. But I never found anyone that challenged me."

"So, that's what I am to you, a challenge?" Jennifer eyed him over her shoulder.

"That's for sure. Remember when I was working on the Sinclair account? I asked you to get me specific statistics to back up my presentation. Then you waltz into the meeting right as it started with stats that had nothing to do with my pitch but worked brilliantly with yours. You did everything you could to make me look bad those first few weeks. You were such a pain in my side. I couldn't believe the lengths you went to, to make me look bad."

"Do you blame me?" Jennifer asked defensively. "That job was supposed to have been mine. I worked my tail off, and everyone knew it. It was humiliating to have corporate parade you around like a boy genius and completely disregard my talents and accomplishments."

"That's not how it was, Jennifer." Harrison's tone was soft but serious. "Corporate knew very well that you were extremely talented and a valuable employee, but you sabotaged yourself. Instead of doing your job, you obsessed about my job. You were a time bomb waiting to go off."

"Then I guess I saved you a lot of hassle by leaving." Jennifer didn't appreciate him critiquing her work performance.

"Hey, now don't get all riled up." Harrison stroked her shoulder trying to soothe her irritation. After a few moments of silence he asked, "So what are you going to do about your car?"

Jennifer noticed the sharp change in subject. Her first instinct was to ignore it and continue to defend the stand she took while at Weissler and Shuler, but reconsidered. She didn't have the energy to fight.

"The police at the scene told me to call the Santa Monica station to find out where it was taken, and then I have to call my insurance company so they can go out and inspect it. I guess the fact that its front end is completely gone doesn't count as totaled until an insurance inspector says so."

"Did the police question you about the accident?"

"Yeah. I mean the basics. But I wasn't much help. It happened so fast. "

"What did happen?"

"I was coming up on traffic. I didn't think I was going that fast, but all of a sudden, this sedan was in front of me, and I swerved to miss it. I went right up the curb and hit the concrete bus bench. I'm just glad that no one was sitting there."

"Were there any witnesses?"

"Witnesses to what? I wasn't paying attention. It was my fault, Harrison." Jennifer's tone was abrupt, knowing she had no one to blame but herself.

"You know . . . I was going to have to go looking for a car of my own. Sharing Robert's just isn't working out. Maybe we could go car shopping together."

"Maybe." Jennifer wasn't going to make any plans. She would be kidding herself to say she wasn't enjoying having Harrison around, but she wasn't going to get her heart set on anything.

They enjoyed the peace and quiet of the outdoors for a little while longer. Harrison was satisfied with just being with Jennifer, and she was too afraid to face the questions that were vying for attention in the recesses of her mind.

Harrison felt the weight of Jennifer's head fall back against his arm, and he realized she was drifting off to sleep. His arm was going numb and his fingers were tingling, but it was worth it to have Jennifer trust him and to have her so near. He closed his eyes and talked to God about his feelings for Jennifer and his determination not to let her go this time.

A small gust of wind rattled the fallen elm leaves. Jennifer sighed. Pulling her head up, she forced her eyes open. "I'm sorry, I must have fallen asleep."

"Don't be sorry. You need whatever rest you can get."

"What time is it?"

"It's only 11:00 a.m."

She moved to the edge of the swing. "I really need to be up and walking. I'm not going to get any better if I keep sitting around."

"You're not planning on going to work tomorrow, are you?"

"I've got to try."

"Jennifer, you're in no condition to go to work. You can't drive, let alone try to show property to clients."

"I know, but I have some files I need to work on and some properties to research—that much I can do in my office."

"Why do you push yourself so hard?"

"Why shouldn't I?" Jennifer got up and hobbled to the door leading to the kitchen. Harrison followed behind, waiting for more of an answer.

When Jennifer saw the perplexed look on his face, she continued. "What? Look, Harrison, I don't have a family to show off or past accomplishments to fall back on. My work is the only thing that defines who I am."

He followed her to the living room. She smiled when she saw the daisies grinning back at her, but her agitation wouldn't allow her to sit down. She stood by the front window, rolling her head, rotating her left arm, trying to loosen up the soreness across her chest."

"Want to go for a drive?"

"Why?"

"Because you're acting like a caged animal. Come on, let's go for a drive. We can head up the coast and stop for lunch somewhere along the way."

"I can't go out looking like this." Jennifer reflexively felt the bandage over her eye."

"Oh, but you can go to work tomorrow?" Harrison asked sarcastically.

Jennifer hadn't remembered her appearance when she thought about going back to work. All she could think about was the pressure of not falling behind, of not failing.

"Come on, Jennifer, you don't look so bad."

"Gee thanks. You have such a way with words."

"You know what I mean." He came up behind her and turned her around so he could see her. She hung her head, feeling insecure about the way she looked. Harrison nudged her chin so he could see her. "Jennifer, you look fine. If you wear a pair of sunglasses no one will even see the bruising."

"But I ache all over. I don't know how comfortable it will be to sit in a car."

"Well, let's give it a try. Robert's car is pretty luxurious. If you get too uncomfortable, we can always turn around and come back."

Jennifer pondered the idea. She was feeling restless and pent-up. Maybe a nice Sunday drive would help distract her from her worries.

"Okay. Let me get something decent on."

"You look fine." Harrison's eye traveled over the yoga pants and tank top she was wearing. "Just grab a jacket in case it gets cooler."

Jennifer pulled the jacket that matched her pants from her closet. She again struggled to try and brush her hair. She wasn't sure if it was her own pride or because she wanted to look good for Harrison. Either way, the effort brought tears to her eyes.

"Why are you crying?" Harrison's reflection appeared behind Jennifer in the bathroom mirror.

"I'm not crying," she insisted as she swiped at the moisture under her eyes. "I'm just having a hard time brushing my hair."

"Here, let me do it."

Harrison took the brush from her hand before she could protest. Slowly, methodically he ran the brush down the length of her silky blond hair. He carefully worked out a few tangles but soon found himself caressing her hair for his own pleasure.

Jennifer closed her eyes, the stroking of the brush and Harrison's hands felt hypnotically therapeutic. He watched Jennifer in the mirror. He saw her shoulders relax, her head tip back, and a tranquil look cross her face. He couldn't resist the desires that rose inside him. He brushed her hair away from her shoulder and pressed a kiss to the nape of her neck.

His touch startled her and she flinched, but she didn't pull away. She allowed herself to enjoy the intimate moment. She leaned back into his broad, sturdy chest as he continued. Jennifer's instincts told her to put a stop to this, but she ignored them. She turned her face to his and allowed his lips to find hers.

Soon she was in his arms, each of them exchanging passions of their own. Harrison had never experienced such heat, such longing. Jennifer never knew her desires could run so deep. She was terrified by her feelings. They were darting ahead of her so fast; she wasn't able to rein them in. One thing she was sure of, it wasn't merely a physical attraction with Harrison.

Her mind whirled to the time she had spent with Brad. Their relationship had been solely physical. She was angry after her mother died. She hated the way she felt so lonely and afraid. She tried filling that emptiness with someone else. She'd experimented with her sexuality, and Brad had been more than willing to fill her needs and feed his cravings at the same time.

But this was different. Strangely different. Fearfully different. Her analytical mind refused to call what she was feeling for Harrison love. That would be ludicrous. But her heart was telling her different. She had never experienced anything like this before. But how could she be in love with someone who had only been in her life for fleeting moments at a time?

Questions assaulted her, heightening her fear. She pulled away from Harrison, dropping her head, embracing herself for support. "I'm not ready for this." Her words were abrupt as she dragged herself from the bathroom.

Harrison took a few deep breaths, trying to restore some balance to his brain. He had never meant to overwhelm Jennifer. Of course, he'd never meant to fall in love either.

He walked from the bathroom and sat on the edge of the bed. He pulled his fingers through his hair and took another deep breath.

"I didn't mean for that to happen. I'm sorry. The last thing I want to do is overwhelm you."

"Good. Then I shouldn't have to worry about it happening again." Jennifer grabbed the jacket she had laying on her dresser and headed for the living room.

Harrison had to push down the tinge of frustration he was feeling. Jennifer had made it sound like she held no fault in what had just happened. While he would admit that he started things, she did nothing to stop him. In fact, her own actions had only intensified the situation.

Harrison met her at the front door, set the alarm, and then helped her across the street to Robert's car. She left her crutches at home, feeling as if she maneuvered better without them. She slid into the rich interior of Robert's Mercedes-Benz. The soft, supple upholstery welcomed her aching muscles. Harrison slid behind the wheel and revved the engine to life. He pushed the button to lower the top before steering through the sleepy neighborhood and headed for Pacific Coast Highway.

Jennifer sat with her head back, enjoying the sun, the breeze, and the salt air. Conversation wasn't needed for Harrison to know how much she was enjoying it. He continued to maneuver around the weathered cliffs and sweeping turns that made up the California coast.

They cruised through Malibu and into Ventura before Jennifer fell asleep. When she opened her eyes and read the highway signs, she turned to Harrison.

"How long were you going to let me sleep?"

"I figured I would stop in Santa Barbara."

She didn't comment; she just turned her attention back to the scenery as it unfolded.

"Are you hungry yet? I could stop now."

"No, I'm all right."

Harrison continued to drive. They had gone less than 20 miles when Jennifer blurted out a question that took Harrison completely by surprise.

"Have you ever had a serious relationship?"

"What do you mean by serious?"

"Serious . . . potential for marriage . . . sexual."

"Yes, no, and yes." Harrison continued to stare at the road in front of him. He could see Jennifer out of the corner of his eye, and it was obvious by her expression that she wanted him to elaborate. He let her squirm for a few seconds before continuing.

"I dated while I was in college, but I was only 19 at the time. I wasn't thinking about marriage, I was thinking about frat parties, sorority girls, and having fun. I dated one girl for a while but she was taking things more seriously than I was. I even told her so, but she continued to stick around, and I took advantage of her availability."

Jennifer wasn't sure why she was so surprised by Harrison's explanation. It described 90% of college males. But somehow, she had expected more from him.

"You look surprised." Harrison chanced a glance in her direction. "Sorry to disappoint you."

"Who said I was disappointed? I am hardly in a position to judge someone over past deeds."

Harrison was amused by her attempt at aloofness. "For someone who's spent most of her life in hiding, you're not very good at disguising your feelings."

Jennifer just shrugged her shoulders and turned away from Harrison. She shifted in her seat a little, her muscles beginning to get tight. "So, when do we stop?"

"You hungry?"

"No, but my leg is stiffening up on me."

Harrison took the next exit and cruised through a picturesque seaside town. He stopped at a diner that was perched on the edge of a small bluff and helped Jennifer from the car. She took a minute to stretch her stiff muscles and then with Harrison's help, made her way into the old-time eatery.

It was as if they had stepped back in time. From the spinning chrome barstools to the shiny red booths, the diner looked as if it had never left the '50s.

Jennifer's eyes wandered as Harrison led her to a booth. He waited as she slid her stiff leg under the formica tabletop that was pressed up against a large picture window and slipped in opposite her. In a few minutes a flouncy waitress, complete with bouffant hairdo and a crisp white uniform approached them.

"What can I get you two to drink?"

"I'll take a Coke," Harrison replied and then looked to Jennifer.

"I'll have the same."

"Did you want to add a flavor to that? We have lemon, vanilla, or cherry."

Jennifer's eyes lit up. "I'll take cherry."

The waitress looked at Harrison. "I'm fine, thanks," he said.

She laid two menus on the table and went to get their drinks.

Harrison picked up one of the menus while Jennifer took in all the quaint details of the small diner.

There were only eight booths and less than a dozen barstools. Metal signs advertising Coca-Cola decorated the walls while Elvis played on the old juke box in the corner.

"Are you going to eat?" Harrison asked as he peered over the top of his menu.

"Sure." Jennifer stopped her musing and picked up the other menu.

The waitress returned with their drinks, pulled a pencil from behind her ear, and waited with pad in hand to take their order. "So, what can I getcha?"

Jennifer grinned when the waitress walked away yelling their orders to the cook behind the grill. "I feel like I just stepped back in time."

Harrison nodded in agreement.

They enjoyed their burgers and fries before heading back to Santa Monica. Once they were on the road, Harrison decided to test the waters with a few questions of his own.

"Jennifer, what do you think would happen if your father found out you were still alive?"

She snapped a look of contempt at him. "He's not going to." Her words were exact, leaving no room for misunderstanding.

"But what if . . ." Harrison couldn't even finish his sentence before she cut him off.

"What are you saying? Are you crazy, Harrison? This isn't about a family that was separated and is waiting to be reunited. This is about a dangerous man who will stop at nothing to have his way. I'm not a daughter to him, Harrison. I'm a possession—a possession he lost 17 years ago and would do anything to get back. I don't want to see him, Harrison . . . ever again."

Emotion crept into Jennifer's words, and Harrison could see her hands trembling.

"He hurt you, didn't he?"

"Of course he did. He ruined our family."

"That's not what I mean." Harrison looked at her but she quickly looked away. "He can't hurt you anymore, Jennifer. You're an adult now."

"And you think that matters?" Her voice cracked and got louder with every sentence. "You just don't get it, Harrison. He was outsmarted. Do you really think he's going to let that go? No one makes a fool out of Carlos Calderon."

"And no one should be able to abuse their daughter and get away with it." Harrison hadn't meant to raise his voice, but he couldn't control his own indignation. He drove, his hands clutching the wheel. He had to concentrate to make sure he didn't take his frustration out on the accelerator. "You're not going to tell me, are you?"

"What . . . you want all the gory details, is that it? Fine, I'll tell you. I fell in love . . . or at least it seemed like love to a 13-year-old." Jennifer closed her eyes, trying to pretend what happened was just a bad dream, but she knew the truth. It was her fault that Jesse was dead.

"Jesse was 15, and his father was our gardener. Sometimes Jesse would come and help his father around the grounds. We became friends. Of course, my father didn't know that. He would have never allowed me to see him. The hired help was exactly that. He didn't allow me or my mother to strike up friendships with the people that worked for us. That was unacceptable in his mind.

"On my 13th birthday, my father threw a huge party for me. It was supposed to be for me, but it was mostly his friends, and our family, of course." Jennifer stared out the windshield, not looking at anything in particular. "Everyone was so busy talking and playing and eating that no one even noticed when I slipped out the back door and crossed the yard, or so I thought.

"I was meeting Jesse in the pool house because he had something for my birthday that he wanted to give to me. There he stood, in the dark, with a small red box in his hand." Jennifer smiled at the memory. "It was a little silver locket with roses etched on it. I knew it didn't cost much, but I also knew that it had probably cost him more than he could afford. Jesse put the necklace on me and then he kissed me." Tears ran down Jennifer's face as she remembered the innocence of the moment.

"It was my first kiss, and Jesse was so sweet, so gentle. We were only kids, and the feelings I was experiencing were new for me. We got a little carried away, and I lost track of time. Before I knew what happened, my father burst through the door. He grabbed Jesse and literally threw him across the room. My father was so enraged; I thought he was going to kill him right then and there. I got between him and Jesse and begged for him to stop, but he only pushed me aside and continued assaulting Jesse.

"Finally, Frank, one of the men who worked for my father, came in and saw what was happening. He pulled my father off Jesse and told Jesse to get out of there. He was afraid to leave me, but I pushed him towards the door. I knew if he didn't leave then, my father would beat him to death.

"I had never liked Frank. He was assigned to the house, and I'd always catch him staring at me. I told my mother once, and she made me promise her I would never put myself in a situation where I was alone with Frank. I think she knew he was a creep but was powerless to do anything about it. But that night, when Frank came to Jesse's defense, I thought I might have misjudged him. I soon found out I was wrong."

Jennifer twisted her hands in her lap, perspiration mingled with the tears streaking her face. Harrison wanted her to stop. To see the anguish in her face was more than he could handle. He could feel tears stinging his own eyes.

"Jennifer, you don't need to tell me. I'm sorry I pushed you into talking about it."

Jennifer continued anyway, her voice so monotone it was as if she were trying to separate herself from the events from her past.

"When my father looked at me that night, I saw hatred in his eyes. I had disappointed him, humiliated him. He came at me yelling at the top of his lungs, shaking me, telling me I was an embarrassment to him. He said I was no better than the women he paid to entertain his men.

"I tried to get away from him, but he grabbed me, tore at my dress, and called me trash. He insisted that Jesse was taking advantage of me. He accused us of having sex and slapped my face each time I tried to refute him. He wouldn't believe me. He was out of control.

"Frank stepped in to protect me. When he did, I thought my father was going to kill him. But instead he got a twisted look on his face and made Frank a proposition."

Jennifer's shoulders shook with the sobbing that racked her body. "He told Frank to kill Jesse. If he did, I would become his reward."

Harrison felt his burger inching its way up his throat. He whispered, feeling as if his words were an intrusion. "Is that when you left?"

"Yes." Jennifer could barely be heard. "The next day my mother said she was taking me shopping to cheer me up. We ran a couple errands and did some shopping. Before I knew it, we ended up in a warehouse, switched cars with a man I'd never seen before, and began to drive. We didn't stop until late that night. When we did stop, we spent hours cutting our hair and changing its color. Before we went to sleep, my mother explained to me that life would be different for us and that we could never go back. I found out the next morning that Monica and Angelica Calderon had died in a tragic car crash."

"It's funny," Jennifer said in a melancholy voice. "My mother warned me that we would have to keep moving and that we had many more changes to make before we could settle in any one place, but somehow I knew she would make everything okay. For the first time in a long time I felt safe, even though we were running. I knew she wasn't going to let anything happen to us."

Jennifer's tone had taken on a calmer, gentler quality. When she talked about her mother, a sense of pride came over her. It was obvious that she admired the woman who had turned her life around.

"Tell me about your mother," Harrison prodded, seeing how at peace Jennifer was when talking about her.

"She was wonderful. You know, she always looked beautiful; my father would have it no other way. She was a trophy to him, but once we were on our own, she became even more beautiful. When she smiled, I could see it in her eyes. I know there were nights that she laid awake wondering if she'd done the right thing, but she never once made me feel afraid. I knew she would never let anything happen to me again. I just wish I could have done the same for her."

Sorrow crept back into Jennifer's words. The loss of her mother was something she would never completely get over.

"You see, Harrison, she gave up everything for me." Jennifer turned to him, making sure he understood the sacrifice her mother had made. "She risked her life so that I could have one without terror or fear. She saved herself in the process, but I don't think she would have run if it hadn't been for me."

"I wish I could've met her."

"You would've liked her. She was strong, stunning, and incredibly smart, but when she smiled or laughed, her real beauty showed through."

"Then I guess you two have a lot in common."

Jennifer smiled at the compliment, proving Harrison was right.

CHAPTER THIRTEEN

"Jennifer, wake up," Harrison whispered with a nudge. Jennifer had slept the rest of the way home. She was emotionally and physically exhausted. By the time Harrison walked around the car to her door, she was awake and pushing aside the cobwebs in her mind.

The rest of the evening was spent in silence. There wasn't anything left for Jennifer to say, and Harrison knew she needed some down time. He made them a simple dinner of grilled chicken and pasta. When they were through, he cleaned up the kitchen while Jennifer went outside to sit on the swing.

She looked up at the sky, closed her eyes, and spoke to her mother. *What should I do, Mom? I never thought I would find someone I could trust. I've told Harrison everything, and I think he really cares and is trying to understand me. Am I wrong to trust him? Is it selfish of me to want someone in my life when it is such a mess? I can already feel my heart falling, and I don't know if I have the strength to catch it.*

"May I join you?" Harrison broke into her thoughts.

She smiled her answer.

He took a seat close to her, his arm pulling her against his side.

"You looked pretty far away," he said as he began to tip the swing back and forth.

"Not really." She relaxed against him, her head resting in the crook of his arm.

"Robert will be coming home this evening. I should probably be there when he does."

"I'll be fine, Harrison. I still ache, but I'll be able to get around on my own."

"What about work?"

"I think I will take one more day off."

Harrison was surprised. Jennifer's attitude seemed so different, so peaceful—calmer than it had been when they started the day.

"I think that's a good idea."

They sat in the still of the night, looking at the stars; each thinking about the other, but not sure if they had a right to.

Harrison stood to leave and Jennifer put out her hand for help. He gently pulled her to her feet but didn't let go of her once she was beside him.

"May I kiss you goodnight?"

She smiled and dropped her head in amusement. "Why are you asking now?"

"Because this time I want to know that you want to kiss me as much as I want to kiss you."

"Then the answer is yes."

WHEN JENNIFER WOKE UP the next day, she felt strangely alone. She laid in bed and thought about what her life would be like to have a constant companion, someone to fall asleep with, to wake-up with, to share her life with.

She reined in her feelings before they turned into dreams. She felt hopeful, but knew she had to be cautious as well. Harrison still hadn't answered the question of how they would be able to have a relationship when so many of his colleagues knew her as Jennifer Patterson. It was an obstacle that couldn't be ignored.

When her phone rang, Jennifer knew immediately that it was Harrison. Her heart began to beat faster, and she could feel herself flush even though she was all alone.

"Hello."

"How are you doing this morning?"

"Good."

"Have you called your office yet?"

"No, I wanted to be able to talk to Mr. Holmes, and he doesn't usually come in until after 9:00 a.m."

"I thought I could come by later and bring you some lunch."

"Okay." Jennifer slowly swung her feet over the side of the bed and smiled at the bouquet of daisies that greeted her.

"Have you talked to Robert yet?"

"No. He got home pretty late. I'll talk to him today, but what exactly is it I'm telling him?"

"What do you mean?" Jennifer wasn't sure she understood what Harrison was asking.

"I mean, am I telling him the whole Jennifer/Samantha thing, or am I just telling him that we're seeing each other?"

"Is that what we're doing, seeing each other?" Jennifer teased.

"Well, I could tell him I slept with you, but I didn't want to give him the wrong impression."

"Harrison! I can't believe you said that. You fell asleep on my bed; we did not sleep together."

"That's just a technicality." He chuckled.

Harrison could hear Jennifer sputtering, trying to gather her wits enough to fire back, but being completely flustered in her attempt.

"Hey, I can tease just as well as you can." His laughter softened the set of Jennifer's jaw when she realized he was only playing with her.

"I'll see you at lunch."

By the time noon rolled around, Jennifer had already had a pretty productive day. She had called the office once again telling Mr. Holmes she would be out one more day, assuring him she'd be back on Tuesday. She called the police station to find out where her car was being impounded and then called her insurance company. She answered numerous questions while they recorded everything. Though there was no question in her mind that she was at fault, she really couldn't remember much, other than the sedan that appeared out of nowhere and the bus bench that landed in her lap. The agent assured her they would wait to get the police report before processing the case.

Feeling as if this was the first morning she could stand without every muscle in her body protesting, Jennifer decided to use what energy she had to take a shower so she could wash her hair. It felt stringy and oily, and she couldn't stand it any longer.

She wrapped her brace in a plastic trash bag and taped it closed. She allowed the water to run over her body for some time before attempting to wash her hair. It hurt her chest to raise her arms over her head, but she took her time. She managed to lather her hair twice and slowly work the shampoo against her scalp. She lingered in the gentle stream of water a little while longer before getting out.

She tidied up the house in an attempt to feel useful, making her bed and plucking a few wilted daisies from their vases. She decided to do some car shopping online. Money was not a huge concern for Jennifer since her mother had left her with a healthy bank account, thanks to her father. Jennifer had found out, when she was 18, that her mother had done some creative money managing in preparation for their disappearance. When her mom was diagnosed with cancer and the doctors told her she was terminal, she put her bank account in Jennifer's name. Jennifer had used it to buy her house, her other car, and to set up a plan to fall back on in case she got in trouble, but rarely did she dip into the account. Her job at WBP had been quite lucrative. The account served as a safety net if the time came when she had to relocate once again.

She perused the different websites for both new and used cars. She'd loved her little sports car, but felt like this time she wanted something a little more substantial. Robert's Mercedes had been incredibly comfortable, and she knew her boss would be pleased if she drove around in something with a little more class, but she couldn't help but think a Mercedes was a bit too extravagant.

She cruised the Lexus and Toyota sites, liking the look of their four-door sedans. She was looking seriously at the Lexus GS-430 when she heard a rattling at her front door.

Harrison smiled when he saw her emerge from the other room. The sparkle in her eyes was mesmerizing, and he hoped he had something to do with it. He put down the fast-food bags on the kitchen counter before turning to her and catching her up in his arms. His lips quickly covered hers, silencing any kind of protest.

She allowed herself to absorb the feel of his touch. This time she wasn't going to refuse herself the thoughts and emotions that another person could bring. She was all but consumed with Harrison and wanted nothing more than to bask in the warmth of his affection. She would no longer put up barriers or keep him at arms length. She was entrusting herself to his care, knowing he would do nothing to hurt her.

"Wow, maybe I should go out and come back in."

She laughed. "Why would you do that?"

"So I could get some more of this." He squeezed her gently.

She blushed, knowing her response to his kiss had been a little too reckless. She pushed away from him and fiddled with the bags of food on the counter. She'd had plenty of practice on how to give a guy the brush-off, but unfortunately, now that she wanted to explore her feelings for Harrison on a deeper level, she wasn't doing such a good job of showing much self-control.

He stood behind her, pressing himself close and wrapping his arms around her shoulders. "I didn't mean to embarrass you," he whispered in her ear. "I was just letting you know I appreciated the welcome."

"I missed you, that's all. I didn't mean to seem so enthusiastic."

"Enthusiasm is good. I like a go-getter." He still had a teasing lilt to his voice, but Jennifer decided to ignore it.

She fixed their burgers and fries on plates and carried them to the table. Harrison noticed that she was walking better.

"You're hardly limping today. You must be feeling good." He took a seat and then reached across the table for her hand. "Mind if I pray?"

Of course she didn't. She'd come to realize over the last few days that it was very much a part of his life and respected him for it; she just didn't understand the need for it.

"So did you call your insurance company today?" he asked before digging into his burger.

"Yeah, they said they would wait for the police report before they make their ruling, but it's only a formality as far as I'm concerned. There was no one else involved."

"I'd liked to help you with the expense of buying a new car. I can't help but feel that I'm partly to blame."

"That's ridiculous, Harrison. It was my fault. You had nothing to do with it."

"Yes, I did. You wouldn't have been so distracted if I hadn't pushed you into a corner."

"It doesn't matter. I can afford my own car. I don't need your help." She hadn't meant for her words to be that blunt. She was just accustomed to taking care of herself. "I didn't mean it like that, Harrison. I just meant that I can handle it."

He accepted her apology, knowing this wouldn't be the last time her pig-headedness got in the way of her pride.

"So did you talk to Robert?"

"Yep."

"What did he say? What did you tell him?" Jennifer was anxious to know what Robert would think of her and Harrison's involvement. The fact that he'd been easily distracted let her know that Robert wasn't cut from the same cloth as Harrison.

"I told him that we'd spent the weekend together and that I thought we'd be seeing a lot of each other in the future."

Jennifer bristled and Harrison quickly explained himself.

"Robert knows I'm not that type, Jennifer. He knows we spent time to-gether, not slept together."

"But you didn't tell him about me and Chicago?"

"No. I mean, I probably will eventually, but it's too complicated right now. He has his own problems with anticipating the wedding, buying the house, and keeping his hormones in line. He doesn't need to be trying to figure out my fu-ture as well."

"So what about him and Kelly—do you think they'll make it? He was aw-fully quick to hit on me when she stormed out of my office. It's obvious that she's a bit high-maintenance. Do you think he's going to be able to make a go of it with her, or do you think the wedding will be called off?"

Harrison pondered the idea for a moment. "If he knows what's good for him, he'll get his act together. But he has an impetuous side that's been known to get him in trouble." Harrison only had to think back to last year when Robert had almost completely bankrupted himself on a shady venture. Miraculously he'd dug himself out. That's when he met Kelly. Harrison wasn't convinced that Robert's scheming was completely behind him. All he could do is pray that his brother would take this opportunity with Kelly and make it a life-long invest-ment.

"What about your parents, are you going to tell them you're seeing someone?"

"Not just yet. I want to be able to spend some time with you without outside complications." He looked at her for a reaction. "Is that selfish of me?"

"Are you afraid to tell them about me?" Jennifer felt defensive, thinking Harrison was feeling somehow embarrassed by her.

"Yes." Harrison dipped his head, confirming Jennifer's fears. "But not be-cause of you. My mother has been trying to set me up for years. Her intentions are good, just a little misguided. If she found out I was seeing someone, she'd be on the next flight out. Believe me, you're going to need all your strength when you meet my parents." Harrison's smile was disarming, assuring Jennifer that he was telling her the truth.

She had nothing to fear with Harrison. She knew he would do nothing to hurt her or expose her. Her heart pulsed with renewed life—life that she'd never felt before.

HARRISON AND JENNIFER JOGGED ALONG THE BEACH in the

early morning mist. She'd finally gotten clearance from her doctor the week before and today was her first day back to her daily routine.

When they reached the pier, Harrison doubled over and rested his hands on his knees. "Give me five before we head back."

Jennifer paced slowly, breathing hard, perspiration glistening on her shoulders. She wasn't back to 100% yet, but she wasn't going to let that get her down.

The last two weeks had been like a dream to her. Though work had been grueling with impatient clients and endless paperwork, her nights had been unforgettable. She and Harrison had spent every evening together, from romantic dinners out to cozy dinners at home. She'd found herself being swept away to a world she'd never experienced before.

"You ready?" Jennifer asked when it seemed as if he'd caught his breath.

"Sure, as long as you take it easy on me on the way back."

Harrison stole glances at Jennifer as they pounded the sand. She looked remarkable with the sun dancing off her hair and a smile behind her eyes. They jogged back to the parking lot where her new Lexus was parked. When they got there, Jennifer was only slightly winded.

"I can't believe you. We just ran five miles, and you look like you took a stroll in the park." Harrison laced his fingers together and rested the palms of his hands on top of his head as he tried to catch his breath.

Jennifer pulled her shoes off and poured the sand on the asphalt. "I've been running all my life." She squinted against the sun and smiled at him, making sure he knew she was joking. "Maybe that partnership of yours has made you a little soft."

"Soft!" Harrison refuted with a surprised chuckle. "You're relentless. You'd make a great drill sergeant."

"Hey, I haven't had a lot of control over the things in my life, so I guess I take my health serious; it's my way of controlling something."

Harrison walked around the hood of the car and put his hands on her exposed waistline. "Well, I'm certainly not complaining. Believe me when I say your hard work is greatly appreciated." He lifted his brows and winked.

"You're such a cad." She slapped at his arm and turned to enter the code on the driver's door.

Harrison playfully pinned her against the door with his body and wagged a scolding finger in her face. "I beg your pardon. I have been nothing but a gentleman in my pursuit of you. I believe if anyone is at fault here, it's you. Anyone who could look that good after running five miles covered in sweat could easily weaken anyone's self-control."

"Is that what I'm doing, weakening your self-control?" Her words were low and sultry.

"If you only knew."

She wrapped her arms around his neck and pulled his head down to hers. She didn't bother to temper her advances. She kissed him passionately, doing nothing to control the fervor that raced through her body. Harrison enjoyed the sensuality he felt in her movements and allowed his hands to trace the well-toned body that she prided herself on.

He felt the seduction of her actions, knowing they were meant to tempt him. He justified his actions knowing they were in a public place and safe from things getting too out of hand.

When she playfully licked at the sweat that trickled down his neck, he felt his senses explode and quickly put a stop to her enticements. "Okay, I think that's enough or else I'm going to have to sentence myself to another five miles."

"Who's the drill sergeant now?" she asked teasingly as she dipped her head to his neck once again.

"Come on, Jennifer, you need to cool it."

Now she was offended. Just seconds before he was enjoying things just fine, but now he was scolding her for wanting more.

"You know, I don't get you. One minute you're feeling your way around just fine, and now you're telling me to cool it. Which is it, Harrison? If it's your faith that tells you this is wrong then fine, but you can't pick and choose when to keep your commitment and when to ignore it. I can't change gears that fast."

Her words couldn't have stung any more if they had been a slap across his face. She unlocked her door, got in, and shoved her key in the ignition. Harrison walked around the car, feeling the weight of her indictment. When he got in, she could see from the set of his jaw that he was agitated. She decided to let him sulk.

They didn't talk at all on the drive home. When Jennifer pulled into her driveway, Harrison didn't move from his seat. Jennifer stormed through the back door and threw her keys on the kitchen counter, angry not only at him but herself as well. She knew Harrison's stand on sex. He'd explained it to her before when they had found themselves in a heated moment, but she had tried to push him. She didn't understand his boundaries. If they truly had feelings for each other, why was he so hesitant to explore them?

Jennifer knew the answer; she just didn't want to accept it. She didn't believe in his God. She had no reason to. Why should she follow the rules of a deity that had done nothing to prove His power or His mercy in her life?

The squeaky door hinges announced Harrison's presence. Jennifer was leaning against the kitchen counter with her back to the door. She reached for the refrigerator handle and grabbed for a bottle of water, trying to look preoccupied.

"I need to apologize to you . . ." Harrison began.

"You . . . you didn't do anything that needs apologizing for, that's the problem."

She walked into the other room, leaving him with her reproof.

"So, would that make you feel better?" He stormed in after her. "If we had sex, would that convince you how much I care for you?"

Jennifer refused to look at him. She sat on the couch, her arms wrapped securely around herself in defiance while he paced up and down.

"I thought the fact that I was here and had done nothing but think about you for the last three years was proof enough that I care about you. You've got my heart twisted so tightly around yours; at times I can barely breathe. I've pleaded with God to show me a way to free you from your terrors and fears and allow me to be in your life forever. But hey, if sex is all you want, then baby let's go." He tossed his hands in the air with a snide look and a cavalier attitude. "I've got a God that forgives."

"That's not fair!" Tears burned her eyes. "You're making it sound like all I care about is the physical. I just want to be with you. I want to feel like you're mine and I'm yours. Is that so wrong?"

Harrison crouched down in front of her, squeezing her knees. "But that's what I'm trying to tell you, Jennifer. I'm not going anywhere."

Harrison's eyes were filled with assurance, letting Jennifer know she had no reason to doubt him. Of course, now she felt like a desperate woman who had just thrown herself at a man so she could hold onto him.

She tried to smile through her embarrassment. "So, is this where I try to salvage a shred of my dignity and leave the room pretending that I just didn't proposition you?"

Harrison smiled broadly and brushed the loose strands of her hair behind her ear. "Actually, I think it was me who propositioned you."

"Yeah, but you didn't mean it."

"How do you know that? I could have been just acting out."

"Not you. You're too stubborn when you're committed to something you believe in."

"Is that so bad?"

"No, not for you."

"But not for you?" His question was more of a statement.

She knew that look. Harrison had already tried on several occasions to talk to her about God.

"Look, Harrison, we've already gone over this." She brushed her hand across the stubble of his cheek. "I know you feel this relationship thing you have with God is important and I'm glad; it seems to have made you more . . . at peace." But it's just not going to work for me. The only reason I've survived this long is because of pure instinct and determination. I can't afford the luxury of leaving my best interests in the hands of some unknown force."

"How do you know that? Maybe God has guarded your steps this far and that's why your father hasn't found you . . . and I have. Maybe it's God's hand that's protected you this long."

She saw the hope in his eyes. He wanted so badly for her to understand his commitment, his faith, his need to believe in something bigger than himself. But she just couldn't relinquish that kind of control to someone or something. She'd held it too tight for too long. Faith in herself was the only thing that had kept her alive.

CHAPTER FOURTEEN

Jennifer flipped on the light while Harrison stretched out on the couch. He patted the seat next to him, and Jennifer willingly snuggled up close to his side.

"Is it just me or was Robert acting strange tonight?" Jennifer mused.

"No, you're right. He was definitely on edge about something."

Harrison and Jennifer had just returned from one of many evenings out with Robert and Kelly. The four of them had been spending a lot of time together. In fact, Kelly had even begun to ask Jennifer's opinion on decisions regarding the wedding. They only had a month to go before the big day . . . and a big day it was going to be, for everyone.

The guest list was 500 strong and the arrangements resembled what Jennifer felt were plans worthy of royalty. Kelly had thought through each detail and every facet of the event, from the pattern of the china at the reception to the seating arrangements and the orchestra's play list, down to the individually wrapped gifts that would decorate each place setting.

Jennifer was nervous, not only for Kelly but for herself. Soon she would be meeting Harrison's parents, and the very thought of it made her heart race. She quickly put the thought out of her mind and turned her attention back to her original question.

"Do you think he's getting cold feet?" Jennifer asked, still wondering what it could be that had made Robert so distant and preoccupied during dinner.

"I don't know. He's been acting that way a lot lately." Harrison didn't want to say anything to Jennifer, but he had his own ideas why Robert was so distracted. He'd overheard a business conversation between Robert and an obviously unsatisfied associate. The exchange that had taken place over the phone ended short of an all out shouting match. When Harrison had question Robert about it, he had been vague with his answer and brushed it aside as a minor setback.

Harrison was concerned. Robert had been drinking heavily and had major mood swings ever since that conference call. He had tried to talk to Robert more than once, but Robert was being secretive about exactly what kind of business situation it was. If Harrison had to guess, his gut reaction was that it had nothing to do with business. His instincts told him Robert was gambling again, and the thought of it made him cringe.

"Hey," Jennifer nudged Harrison, "where'd you go?"

He had drifted off in his thoughts about his brother and had missed Jennifer's end of the conversation.

"I'm sorry. What did you say?" He turned a smile to her.

"The wedding . . . do you think it's too much pressure on Robert?"

"I think that has something to do with it."

Jennifer sighed and allowed her head to fall back against Harrison's outstretched arm.

"What was that for?" he asked her.

"When are we going to tell them? I wanted to do it before your parents get here, but if Robert's going to be this uptight all the way up to the wedding day, I don't want to add more stress to his world. Maybe we should just wait until after the wedding. We could tell your parents before they fly back to Chicago, and then tell Robert and Kelly when they get back from their honeymoon."

Jennifer perked up, feeling she'd found an answer that would allow them to put off the conversation she'd been dreading for weeks. It made her stomach knot just thinking about letting anyone else know who she really was. Going from ignoring the reality of her situation for years to trusting people with her life-long secret was going to be a huge step—a step that she wasn't sure she was ready to take.

"No, we need to let them know before the wedding. You and Kelly have gotten too close. If we're going to impress upon her how important it is that you not be photographed, she needs to know the reason why."

"Maybe I just won't go." Jennifer sighed out of frustration.

"Come on, Jennifer, you know you want to be there."

He was right. Jennifer couldn't wait to witness the event unfold after seeing all the preparations that went into it. But knowing she would be introduced as Kelly's realtor, not as a special person in Harrison's life, disheartened her.

"But what am I going to do? You're going to be all wrapped up with best man duties while I wander around, trying to blend in."

"But I want you there, and Kelly's going to want you there. That's why we need to explain things to them before the wedding."

Jennifer's second thoughts filled the room with silence but Harrison didn't allow her to sulk long. He nuzzled up to her neck, rousing a restrained giggle from her. She tried to ward off his advances but put very little effort into it.

When their actions turned from affectionate to something deeper and more physical, Jennifer put on the brakes.

"It's getting late. You should probably go." She scooted away from Harrison and got to her feet.

Harrison was surprised that Jennifer was the one who realized they were crossing the line and put a stop to it. He was disappointed in himself, because he could feel his self-will waning but was impressed with Jennifer as well.

"Don't look so surprised, Harrison. I know the boundaries you've set for yourself."

"Yeah, but this is the first time that it was you that made sure we didn't cross them."

"I know it's important to you and believe it or not, I'm not trying to make you break your code of ethics. Even if I don't believe the way you do doesn't mean I would want you to compromise your beliefs for me."

"Jennifer," Harrison's tone turned serious. "Can we talk about that?"

"Harrison, I agreed to go to church with you tomorrow, can we just leave it at that for now?"

Harrison's smile was consolatory, though he was disappointed inside. "Sure." He moved from the couch and stretched. "How about if I come over a little early, and we can have breakfast together?"

They walked to the front door hand-in-hand. "That sounds good." Jennifer turned to him, resting her head against his chest. He wrapped his arms around her, and they swayed in each other's embrace. Harrison's heart was aching, aching both from love and from disappointment. He loved Jennifer; there was no question about it. But he'd made a commitment to God and for the first time was feeling the anguish of wanting something that God clearly spoke against.

At night, he found himself debating with God about the rules of being un-equally yoked. He knew, in time, he would be able to show Jennifer her need for a Savior. But the thought of having to do it outside the bounds of marriage, having to wait until she understood what real love was, was hard for Harrison to comprehend. His inability to make a complete commitment to Jennifer was dif-ficult for her to understand. He knew she was judging his restraint as the possi-bility of him not being wholly committed to her. Her capacity to trust was continually being tested.

He gave her a kiss laced with sweetness before leaving.

It was late but Jennifer's mind was unable to let her rest. Instead of heading to bed, she changed into some shorts and got on the treadmill.

She had promised Harrison that she would go to church with him. She thought it was her way of showing him she was trying to understand this belief he had in a deity of grace, protection, and mercy.

She turned up the treadmill, trying to outrace her thoughts. She was having a hard time comprehending what salvation was. If God was so willing to save people who sinned, why wouldn't he protect people from the sins of others? She had been an innocent victim in the lifestyle that was her father's world. She had been abused physically, emotionally, and psychologically. She had lived in fear her entire life and still hid from the man that terrorized her nightmares and memories. If God had wanted to show her protection and mercy, why hadn't he punished the man who deserved to be penalized for his sins instead of letting him take them out on his little girl?

She was sweating and panting by the time she turned off the machine and stepped from her self-imposed torture. Her mind was now as exhausted as her body. In desperation she cried out, "I don't understand who you are, God, or if you're even there, but if you do exist, You have a lot of explaining to do."

She wrestled with the idea of going to church and listening about the glories of God. As far as she was concerned, he was a crutch for people who had no depth or determination to make it in the world on their own. The only anomaly to that thinking was the fact that God had played such an obvious role in Harrison's life. She would never view him as weak or dependent. He was strong and intelligent. He exuded confidence and self-sufficiency. She listened to him as he described his dependence on God and the level of commitment and desire he had to serve him, but it was difficult for Jennifer to comprehend.

HARRISON HAD FOUND a small church when he'd arrived in Santa Monica. The people had been friendly and welcoming his first time there, and he'd been back most every Sunday since.

He pulled into the church parking lot as Jennifer continued to fiddle with the strap of her purse. Harrison reached over, clutched her hand, and smiled.

"You're going to church, not before a firing squad. Relax."

"I'm trying," she snapped back, feeling completely out of her element.

"Harrison . . ."

Jennifer heard someone call out to Harrison as he got out of the car. She felt like sinking further into the upholstery of his leased Chrysler 300. The next hour was going to feel like an eternity.

Harrison stepped around to her side of the car to help her out, while carrying on a polite conversation with a man in Dockers and a polo shirt. Harrison had told her the dress code was pretty casual. She wished she had listened. She would've been a lot more comfortable in a simple sundress, instead of the power suit she had chosen. She had brought her A-game, thinking it would make her feel more in control, but now she looked even more out of place.

"Samantha, this is Pastor Carter. Pastor, this is Samantha Wilder."

Harrison was careful to introduce Jennifer properly. He was getting good with it since whenever they hung out with Robert and Kelly, she reverted back to being the real estate agent that Robert had fixed him up with.

"Nice to meet you, Samantha." The pastor's smile was genuine as he extended his hand. Jennifer shook it politely, noticing he couldn't have been much older than Harrison. "Well, I guess I'll see you two inside." He nodded to Harrison and walked away.

"He wasn't at all like I expected."

"What did you expect?"

"Someone older for starters. You know, silver hair, black suit, with a 10 pound Bible in his hand and a booming voice that could raise the dead."

Harrison laughed as they climbed the steps. "You've been watching too many late-night televangelists."

The feel of the sanctuary was just as welcoming as the pastor's handshake. Harrison was greeted several more times before they took a seat near the back of the small chapel.

Jennifer continued to jitter and fuss in her seat, pulling at the hem of her skirt, playing with the buttons on her silk blouse. Harrison leaned over and whispered in her ear.

"You won't get any dessert with your lunch if you don't sit still in church."

She had just heard the little boy in front of them get scolded for the same thing with the same outcome. When she looked up at Harrison, he had a smile and a wink for her. He grabbed her hand and held it in his lap, along with his open Bible. The congregation was reading a scripture passage along with the pastor, so Harrison turned his attention back to his Bible. They closed in prayer and then another man who also had to be in his thirties approached the pulpit. He welcomed everyone, visitors included. When he asked for visitors to slip up their hand so they could be given a card to fill out, Harrison slipped his up for Jennifer to help alleviate the awkwardness that he knew she was feeling.

Samantha filled out the card and put it in the offering plate as it was passed around. They sang a few more worship songs and spent a short time getting to know the people seated around them before the youthful pastor began to deliver the morning message. Jennifer was impressed with how friendly everyone was— not friendly in a pious, holier-than-thou way, but with a genuine kindness in their faces.

Jennifer listened as the preacher told the story of David and how a delusional king sought out to destroy David, hunting him down like an animal when he had done nothing but be obedient. She listened as he told of David fleeing from the king, hiding in caves, scavenging for his food. Jennifer shook her head in disbelief. Even the Bible spoke of the unfairness of God.

Jennifer's mind wandered to her own situation. It wasn't often that she allowed herself to think of the "what ifs" of her future. What if her father found out after all these years that he'd been fooled and she was alive? What if he wanted to have a relationship with her? What if he demanded retribution because he had been lied to and Jennifer had perpetuated the lie? Would he accept her back like a child that was lost and was now found, or would he treat her like a problem that needed to be silenced?

Jennifer had followed the New York newspapers and read everything that was written about her father. She knew that he'd remarried only a year after her and her mother's supposed death and immediately had a son. She also knew her father's son was only three years younger than herself. He'd been having an affair the entire time he was married to her mother. His mistress was now his wife.

She had seen a piece on him in the news last year when he'd been up on trafficking charges and was walking into court, surrounded by lawyers. Now 60, his hair was gray and his gait a little slower, but he still had the piercing eyes that had terrorized her as a child. She shuddered involuntarily.

Jennifer felt Harrison put a hand to her knee while his head was bowed in prayer. She realized her thoughts had pulled her away from the service, and she had missed the rest of the pastor's message.

The congregation said "amen" in unison and stood up. Harrison looked at Jennifer, a question in his eyes.

"You okay?" he whispered.

"Yes, I just got distracted."

Harrison and Jennifer walked into the lobby where they were once again greeted by the pastor as they headed for the door.

"It was nice having you, Samantha."

"Thank you. It was very interesting and everyone was quite friendly."

"Well then, I hope we see you again sometime soon."

Jennifer only smiled. She wasn't sure if she would be back.

Harrison started the car and pulled from the parking lot before turning to Jennifer and asking what she really thought.

"It was interesting, but it only proved my point."

"Which is . . . ?"

"That I don't understand why people believe God is so merciful. That character, David, the pastor spoke about is a perfect example. He did nothing but what he was told and look where it got him. He was treated like a criminal, forced into a life on the run."

Harrison shook his head. "You stopped listening, didn't you?"

"No. I mean, I didn't mean to. I just got distracted."

"Well, while you were distracted, the pastor went on to explain that because of David's faithfulness, he ended up being king." Harrison's tone belied his agitation. "If you're going to judge something, Jennifer, you need to make sure you have all the facts."

"Don't get upset, Harrison, I just have a hard time with the whole 'serve thing.' So, David became king. It paid off for him. But I bet he lived in fear of messing up or getting on the bad side of God the rest of his life. He was probably afraid to breathe in case he did it wrong."

Harrison's disappointment was growing. Jennifer was being petty and derogatory. She wasn't even trying to be fair in her assessment.

"It's called respect, Jennifer, honor. People don't serve God out of fear or at least they shouldn't. I serve God because I respect God. I worship God because of who he is. I've accepted Christ into my life because he loved me so much he was willing to die for me and the sins that are so much a part of my life. He made the ultimate sacrifice with his life and all he asks of me is to believe in who he is and what he did with my heart. The fact that I want to be found faithful comes from respect. Because you know what, if I screwed-up tomorrow and allowed my life to get completely out of control, God would still love me. He wouldn't remove his love from me out of disappointment, or shame, or even anger. God is faithful, even when I'm not."

Jennifer could hear the hurt in Harrison's voice. He was taking her lack of respect personally. "Harrison, I'm sorry I upset you. I'm trying to understand. "

That was a lie and she knew it. She hadn't tried to understand. She didn't want to see God as fair and just. The way she saw it, if God was who Harrison said he was, then he was the only one who'd had the power to step in and intervene on behalf of an innocent little girl. The fact that he didn't was all the proof she needed.

CHAPTER FIFTEEN

arrison and Jennifer were going to finally do it. They were going to have Kelly and Robert over to her house and explain the puzzle that was her life.

Jennifer worked side-by-side with Harrison in the kitchen preparing a salad that would go with the steaks he was grilling.

It had been a couple days since their heated debate over God, and Jennifer had really expected it to be the first hit that would chisel away at their relationship, but she was wrong. Harrison was still as kind and as loving as ever. She was grateful for his willingness to let it go, at least for now.

She glanced at her watch, her anxieties mounting, when she heard the doorbell. Her stomach felt like a vice, strangling her from within. All color raced from her face, leaving her looking like she was going to be ill.

"It's okay, Jennifer. Everything's going to be okay."

Harrison gave her a squeeze and pressed a kiss to her cheek before heading for the door.

Dinner was the same as usual when the four of them got together. Kelly talked non-stop about wedding plans, explaining to Jennifer what new details had been taken care of while Robert and Harrison talked business. Their meal was interrupted twice when Robert was pulled away from their outdoor dining area to answer important business calls. With each call, he became more distant and closed off. When Harrison asked him about it, Robert would just shrug it off as a minor setback or a lack of communication between business partners. But when Harrison tried to find out exactly what kind of business he was talking about, Robert would casually change the subject and pretend to be an attentive fiancé and listen to what Kelly and Jennifer were talking about.

Harrison was concerned. He knew Robert too well. He could tell by the redness in his eyes and the fact that he was drinking his scotch straight, that he was in over his head.

Dinner concluded and Kelly and Jennifer cleared the table while Robert and Harrison lounged outside.

"You're gambling again, aren't you?" Harrison was tired of skirting the issue and decided to be direct.

"Come on, Harry, don't start on me." Robert's defenses were up.

"I'm not starting anything. Answer the question, and I'll get off your back."

"No you won't. You'll start lecturing and nagging."

"So I take that as a yes."

"Drop it, Harry. I'm a big boy. I can take care of myself." But Robert knew nothing could be further from the truth. If things didn't turn around soon, he would lose everything.

Jennifer looked at Harrison nervously as he walked in from the outdoors. He caught the anxiousness in her eyes and moved across the room to reassure her everything was going to be okay.

"Here, Kelly, why don't you take Robert some pie and relax. We'll be right in."

Jennifer watched as Kelly rounded the corner to the living room and then nervously began wiping down the countertop.

"Jennifer, it's going to be all right."

"I'm a freak show," she huffed. "A walking, breathing freak show."

"Stop it. You are not." Harrison tried to pull her close, but she rebuffed his advances and started shoving dishes in the dishwasher.

"Yes, I am. I remember seeing the look on your face when I told you who I really was. You looked at me like I had a third eye."

Harrison laughed. "You almost did. If you remember, you were bruised from head to toe and had a bandage over your eye. I wasn't staring at you out of shock; I was more concerned with the pain you were in."

"Whatever!"

This time Harrison would not be brushed aside. He grabbed Jennifer gently by the elbows and pulled her close. "Everything is going to be fine. It might take them a little time to digest the extent of your cover-up, but when they do, they'll understand how important discretion is."

Jennifer moved forward to rest her head against his chest and try to let his strength and reassurance rub off on her.

"I'll tell them, okay?" Harrison looked at her with confidence. "They don't need all the details, just how important it is that you not be found out."

"I don't want them to know my real name, or who my father is. I just want them to know how important it is that I stay anonymous."

Harrison understood, hugging her before she took a final deep breath and walked into the living room with him.

"What, no dessert for you?" Kelly quipped to Jennifer.

"No, I'm pretty full from dinner." Jennifer couldn't even imagine trying to eat with her stomach so tied up.

"Oh yeah, those few bites of steak you ate must have been real filling." Kelly had been watching Jennifer's behavior, knowing that something was wrong.

"Jennifer and I need to talk to you guys about something," Harrison said as he sat down on the edge of the chair.

"I knew it; something's wrong." Kelly was quick to react.

"Not wrong," Harrison corrected. "Just a bit complicated."

"What does that mean?" Robert was on the defense, thinking Harrison was going to try to nail him on his gambling in front of Kelly.

"Well, like I said, it's complicated." He looked at Jennifer to make sure she was ready for the questions that were sure to come.

"Remember that day we were on the beach, and I was convinced the jogger I saw was someone I knew?"

It took a minute for Robert to get on the same page. He was expecting this little confrontation to be about him. "Yeah, I remember. You made a fool of yourself, dumping Maris off on the beach blanket and running after a girl you thought you couldn't live without."

Jennifer grinned when she saw Harrison's face flush slightly. It warmed her to know that all that he'd tried to convince her of was true. He really had thought of her through the years and felt a connection that had never dimmed with time.

"Well, allow me to introduce you to Jennifer Patterson." Harrison turned a sweeping hand in her direction, trying to keep the mood light.

Robert did a double take while Kelly sat with a perplexed look on her face. Harrison waited for his announcement to sink in and then continued.

"It was Jennifer I saw on the beach that day and my meeting with Samantha Wilder confirmed it."

"Wait a minute." Robert scooted to the edge of the sofa and started flailing his hands. "Are you telling me that the Jennifer that you ranted and raved about for being a royal pain in your . . ." Harrison raised an eyebrow causing Robert to clean up his language before continuing. "The Jennifer that you said simply disappeared off the face of the earth . . . the Jennifer that you became obsessed with, is really Samantha Wilder and I'm the one that hooked you up?" He flung himself back in the cushions of the sofa. "That's incredible!"

"Wait a minute, you lost me," Kelly said befuddled. "Why are you going by the name Samantha if your real name is Jennifer?"

Harrison interrupted. "Actually, that isn't her real name either."

"Then what is?" Both Robert and Kelly questioned.

"Look, guys," Jennifer said with a strained look on her face. "I know this sounds like some ridiculous comedy routine, but that couldn't be further from the truth. The fact of the matter is I've been hiding from my father since I was thirteen. He's a very powerful man in New York, a very corrupt man. I was reported killed in a car accident, along with my mother, and have been living under assumed names ever since. I live in terror of being discovered and have done everything I can to lead a quiet existence." She let out the breath she was holding during her rushed explanation. *There, I did it. I presented my horrible life in a nice, neat package.* She took another breath and continued. "The reason I'm telling you all this is because it is imperative that I remain in the background at your wedding. I won't be there as Harrison's date. I will merely be there as another well-wisher that blends in with the rest of the guests."

Jennifer's eyes were like ice as she locked stares with both Kelly and Robert. She had to make it clear to them how serious she was. To her, it meant life or death.

Kelly and Robert sat in stunned silence while Jennifer fought the instinct to run, to hide, to disappear. Harrison could see the discomfort she was feeling and moved to sit next to her. He wrapped his arm around her shoulders and tried to offer her comfort and strength.

"So . . . Jennifer, I don't get it." Robert said with a perplexed look. "How is it that you knew, even before Harrison did, that he would be looking for a house in California? Wait a minute, how did you know that . . ."

Jennifer realized Robert thought she'd set the whole thing up. "Robert, I didn't orchestrate this. It was just some bizarre twist of fate."

Her words were like a punch in the gut to Harrison, and he sunk back into his own dejection. With all they'd talked about God and prayer, she still believed their meeting was by chance.

"Do you really think you're in danger?" Kelly asked timidly.

"Not as long as no one finds out who I am."

"You said you were reported killed when you were younger, was that because your father tried to have you killed?"

"No, my mother took me and ran. She staged an accident so we could get out from under my father's power."

"Where's your mother now?"

"She died a little over ten years ago."

Kelly knew she was pushing, but she was trying to understand. "But if your mother was responsible for taking you and she's gone, couldn't you have returned and explained that it wasn't your fault?"

"Kelly, the reason my mother ran was to protect me. You see, my father is not like your father. He's a cruel, violent, and controlling man. If I'd gone back, I would have become a prisoner, a possession. He wouldn't want me back because he loved me or because I was the daughter that he thought he'd lost. He'd want me back out of principle, to prove to other people that no one could get out from under his control."

Kelly's mouth hung open in sheer astonishment. She was having a hard time grasping the macabre picture Jennifer was painting.

"So, do you think people are after you?" Robert chimed in.

"No. I know my father investigated the accident and probably had his doubts at first, but after all this time, I'm sure he's forgotten all about us."

"Then why the theatrics?"

"Robert!" Harrison snapped.

"Well, come on, she said it herself. He's probably forgotten all about her."

"But that doesn't mean I can let my guard down, Robert." Jennifer got up and began to pace. She knew this had been a bad idea. How could anyone understand the bizarre life that she'd led? It sounded like the fallout from a bad B movie. "The reason Harrison thought we should tell you is because of the attention your wedding is getting. It's going to be a who's-who in society circles, and I need to make sure I'm not in any of the pictures you release for publication."

"So, after all these years, you think your father would recognize you?"

"Yes. The resemblance to my mother is what he would notice. When we first ran, we cut our hair and dyed it a lot, trying to change our appearance. But after all this time, I've gotten lax about that. I've allowed my hair to grow back to its natural color. The only thing different about me now is the contacts. I really have blue eyes, not green."

The four of them sat in silence, not really knowing what else to say. Harrison was frustrated by Robert's less than compassionate attitude and was disappointed with Jennifer's unwillingness to recognize God in their equation. Jennifer was still pacing the room, feeling more caged-in than she had in a long time.

Kelly got up from where she was sitting and went to Jennifer, embracing her. "I'm sorry. I'm not even sure what to say."

"I know. And I didn't mean to be such a downer, especially with the wedding so close. But I knew I needed to say something, either that or stay home from the wedding."

Kelly held Jennifer at arms length. "You are coming, though, right?"

"Yes, now that you understand why I won't be there with Harrison."

"The place settings! This will definitely affect the place settings. I have you sitting with Robert's parents, figuring they would want the time to get to know you. Are you going to tell them?"

Harrison answered. "We're going to have to. I've already told Mom I was seeing someone special. But you'll still have to change the settings. There would be no reason for your realtor to be sitting with family."

"Wait a minute." Robert began shaking his finger. "The people at Weissler and Schuler already know you as Jennifer, how are you going to explain yourself as Samantha Wilder? I mean, if you and Harry decide to make this a more permanent relationship, isn't that going to be a little hard to explain?"

Harrison wanted nothing more than to have Jennifer as a permanent part of his life, but there were still many obstacles preventing that from happening. "We haven't quite figured that part out yet. Right now, we're just trying to get through your wedding."

The solemn voice with which he spoke caught Jennifer's attention. She looked at him and saw the signs of defeat, like he was beginning to lose hope. Jennifer wished Kelly and Robert were gone. She wanted to talk to Harrison alone. She needed to know if he was beginning to think the odds were too insurmountable. Up until now, it had been his insistence that they could work through anything that had given her hope. She wouldn't be able to fight the negative feelings that bombarded her at night if she knew his determination was wavering.

When Kelly and Robert finally left, they offered their assurance to Harrison and Jennifer that they understood the gravity of the situation and would protect Jennifer's identity. Kelly would make it clear to the photographers that had been hired for the wedding and reception that absolutely no pictures were to be given to the press or media without her expressed consent.

Harrison walked them to the door while Jennifer collected up the dessert plates and moved to the kitchen. She began to wash them by hand in order to work off some of her nervous energy. Harrison was soon at her side, hand drying the dishes she laid on the drying rack. She glanced at him and could still see the solemn expression that had clouded his features earlier in the evening.

"It's finally hit you, hasn't it? You're beginning to see what we're up against." Jennifer questioned as she dried her hands and leaned against the counter.

"No, the way I see it, we have a fifty-fifty shot at making this work, but our odds have nothing to do with your father or your past. It's the present that's going to make or break us."

"I don't get it—what are you trying to say?"

Harrison dried his hands and flung the towel on the counter, showing his clear frustration. "You still think our whole relationship is some huge coincidence. You're not even willing to give God credit for that much."

Now she knew what was bothering him. He was taking offense at her crediting fate with bringing them together. He had taken it as a disregard for his feeling that God had given them a second chance.

"Harrison, I'm sorry; I didn't mean to upset you. I was just trying to get Robert to understand this wasn't some grand set-up. That it just happened."

"That's what I mean, Jennifer, how can you say it 'just happened'? If you were to run the figures for us finding each other after three years, you being someone completely different, in a different line of work, the odds would be astronomical. And you would still rather believe in those odds than the idea of there being a God who loves you and wants to have a relationship with you."

Jennifer rubbed her eyes from exhaustion. They continued to debate this subject over and over again. God was so real to Harrison, but to Jennifer it was like trying to believe in someone from a fairy tale. She just couldn't grasp the idea of a Supreme Being. And when she did, it only angered her. If God wanted to be her anchor, why did he wait until she was an adult? Where was he when she really needed to be saved?

"It's just hard for me, Harrison, you know that." Jennifer gave him a sexy look and moved to him, brushing her hand against his cheek. She didn't want to fight. She just wanted to be able to curl up with him and enjoy what was left of the evening, not spend it discussing God.

"But you're not giving God a chance."

"I can't afford chances." Her voice bristled, but she placed a playful kiss on his neck anyway, doing what she could to change his mood.

He cupped her face in his hands and looked her directly in the eye. "You're right—you can't afford chances; you need to believe in something that is real."

"I believe in you. I know you would never do anything to hurt me."

"But I can't save you. I can love you and protect you with every ounce of my being, but I can't save you from the power of death, only Christ can."

The watery pools in Harrison's eyes caused Jennifer's chest to ache. Once again she was causing him pain. She didn't mean to, and she wished she could alleviate it, but she just wasn't ready to. She wasn't ready to open up her life to a God that had ignored her so many years ago.

Their evening ended with a pall of coolness hanging between them. Jennifer closed the heavy wooden front door as Harrison left, feeling weak and emotional. She wouldn't play games with Harrison and pretend that she was ready to accept his God when she wasn't, and he would see right through any subterfuge, even if she tried.

A melancholic feeling hung on her shoulders like a heavy, wool shawl. She wandered to her closet and saw the packed suitcase she always had ready in case the time came when she had to leave quickly. She reached for it and carried it to her bed.

She sat alongside of it and pulled at the rugged metal zipper. She threw back the cover of the suitcase and stared at the things that made up her existence. Her mother had kept mementos from each identity in her life, even things from her childhood. Though many of the things were silly and would look insignificant to anyone else, each item had been chosen carefully and now it was her only connection to her mother.

It was as if she could feel her mother sitting with her each time she looked through her precious treasures. Jennifer fingered the frilly barrettes she had worn as a child and the long polka dot ribbon that her mother would always tie her curls back with. She laughed at the snapshot of her and her mother dressed up for a small town Halloween party they had gone to when they had lived in Nebraska. It was the only picture she had of her mother, other than the pictures in her mind. They had worn Raggedy Ann and Andy costumes, complete with heavy white make-up and red wigs. The only reason she'd been able to keep the picture was because it looked nothing like them, but it didn't matter to Jennifer. She knew it was her mom under the costume, and she loved looking at the smile on her face.

Jennifer brushed a tear from her cheek. Her mother had done everything she could to make up for the dark years, and on days like these, Jennifer missed her incredibly. *Why didn't you save her, God? If you had wanted to prove yourself real to me, you would have saved the only person who had ever loved me.*

Jennifer forced herself to push aside her anger and continued her reminiscing. It wasn't until she reached for the sealed manila envelope that the smile slid from her face. She pulled it from where it was laying in the bottom of the suitcase and brushed her hand across the written words—Mary Bellamy. It was what she'd been given at the hospital when her mother had passed away. It was filled with paperwork and her mother's personal belongings.

Jennifer had never opened it. In fact, the day her mother died, Jennifer packed up what she could carry and left the small but bright apartment they had shared. There was no service for her mother, no formal burial. Jennifer left an envelope of cash and instructions at the hospital requesting that her mother be cremated and buried in the cemetery she drove by every day on her way to the hospital.

She fingered the envelope, knowing it contained the diamond stud earrings that her mother had always worn and the inexpensive diminutive sapphire necklace she had bought for her the Mother's Day before her death.

Jennifer looked at the envelope for some time before she finally ran her finger under the flap. The envelope opened easily, the seal weakened with time. It took another few minutes before she tipped the envelope and allowed the papers and the three small pieces of jewelry to trickle out onto the bed. She closed her eyes. Looking at the necklace was too painful. Jennifer's face fell into her hands as uncontrolled sobs shook her shoulders. The only other noise in the room was the splat of her tears on the paperwork in front of her.

It took Jennifer quite some time to control the emotions she kept locked away. She sniffed, wiped at the moisture above her lip, and dried her eyes. When she looked down at the stack in front of her, her eyes were immediately drawn to a small folded piece of paper with a business card poking out of it. As she slowly unfolded the paper, she was startled to see her mother's frail handwriting.

Jennifer's hands began to shake, realizing her mother had used what little energy she'd had left to leave her a note, a note Jennifer had never read, had never even known existed.

Jennifer swallowed the knot that she was sure would tighten around her heart as she began to read.

My precious Angel,
I had a visitor today, after you left . . .

Jennifer immediately thought back to the day when the doctors had informed her there was nothing more that could be done for her mother, and it was only a matter of time. Her mother had slept most of the day, and it was difficult for Jennifer to sit by and watch her slip away. Jennifer had stepped out of her room for not more than an hour, and when she came back, she was told her mother had passed away.

Jennifer let her mind drift back to the events of that evening. Her mother had been so weak. How could she have had a visitor? Jennifer continued to read her mother's scrawled handwriting.

. . . A minister came to visit me and asked to have prayer with me. I explained to him that I didn't have a relationship with God, and he told me it wasn't too late. We talked and he was right. I prayed with him and felt a peace I can't explain. You need to talk to him, Angel. You need to listen to what he has to say. He has something for you. I love you, Angel. Don't be sad. I'll always be with you.

Jennifer glanced at the business card that she could barely read through her tears. It listed a Pastor Walt Allen from Albuquerque.

An urgency rose up in Jennifer to talk to the man who had been the last one to speak with her mother before she died, but that was over ten years ago. Would the man even remember her mother after all these years? She had to find out. She had to try.

CHAPTER SIXTEEN

Jennifer had a hard time keeping her concentration at work the following day. She flipped the business card around in her hand, waiting for her lunch break to make the call. She was shuffling the files for her next few appointments around on her desk when the phone rang. She cradled it against her shoulder and answered. "Samantha Wilder."

"Hey." Harrison's tone was reserved. "Are we still on for lunch?"

"Actually, I'm going to have to cancel. I have an important call I have to make during my lunch break."

It was obvious in Jennifer's tone that she was distracted. Harrison felt like he was getting the brush-off.

"Can I come over tonight, or are you going to be busy then as well?"

Jennifer caught the antagonism in his tone.

"Harrison, I really have an important call I have to make. I'll tell you more about it tonight, if you still want to come over."

"Why wouldn't I want to come over?"

"Harrison, I can hear the agitation in your voice. I know you're disappointed with me."

"I'm not disappointed with you, Jennifer. I just wish I could make you see what's missing in your life."

Jennifer thought about the words in her mother's note. She had found peace. Jennifer wondered if it was the same peace she saw when she looked in Harrison's eyes. The thought was perplexing to her. Her mother had never spoken to her about God or faith. Could she have really had what people talked about as a deathbed experience? She hoped talking with the pastor would answer some of those questions.

"Jennifer?" Harrison's abrupt tone broke into her thoughts.

"Sorry, I'm just a little distracted." She played some more with the business card in her hand. "But I really do want to see you tonight."

"Then I'll be by around 6:00 p.m. I'll bring dinner."

"Sounds good." Her tone was a little more centered on Harrison. "I'm sorry. I know I'm a lot to handle. I wish my life didn't complicate things so much."

A smile crossed his face as he pictured the beautiful blond that he knew he'd never be able to live without. "It's okay; you're worth it."

Jennifer went back to work, meeting with two clients before lunch, one to sign the final papers on a counter-offer, the other meeting was to encourage sellers to lower their asking price. They had set an astronomical price, assuming people would buy anything with a view. Three months on the market told them otherwise.

Jennifer ushered her last appointment out the door and glanced at the clock. She moved nervously behind her desk and picked up the business card that hadn't been out of view since she found it yesterday. Her fingers shook as she dialed the long distance number. She nervously waited for someone to pick up on the other end of the line.

"Albuquerque Community Church."

Jennifer took a deep breath before she spoke. "I'm looking for a Pastor Walt Allen."

"Oh, I'm sorry dear, Pastor Allen is no longer here. He retired two years ago."

Jennifer's heart lurched. "Do you have a number where I can reach him?"

"Can I ask what this is regarding?" The secretary's voice was pleasant, but cautious.

"Well, my mother had spoken with him several years ago, and I wanted to talk to him, to see if he remembered their conversation."

"Oh honey, I'm so sorry. You see, Pastor Allen retired after suffering a stroke. Though his recovery has been remarkable, his memory suffered the most."

If Jennifer's heart had been a balloon, the secretary's words acted as the pin that punctured it. She set her jaw, fighting back the defeat she was feeling.

"Would it be possible to get that number anyway?"

"Sure, deary."

Jennifer hung up the phone feeling like she'd let her mother down. If only she'd open the envelope sooner. If only she'd seen her note and been able to speak to the pastor before now. She looked at the number written on the business card and felt the connection to her mother fade.

She went through the motions the rest of the day. She didn't have the energy to call the other number, only to be told again about the pastor's memory loss. She would wait until after she talked to Harrison.

HARRISON HAD GONE OUT FOR A JOG after working on a proposal most of the day. He was still panting when he walked into his hotel room, right in the middle of Robert attacking someone on the phone with one expletive after another. When Robert turned and saw Harrison, he calmed himself and moved to the balcony, sliding the door closed behind him. Harrison could tell by his sharp movements and expressive hands that Robert was near his breaking point. Harrison sat on the couch and waited for Robert to come back in.

"What's wrong?" Harrison asked the minute Robert reentered the room.

"What do you mean, what's wrong? Everything's fine . . . wonderful . . . couldn't be better!" He shouted as he threw his cell phone across the room, taking out a glass that was sitting on the bar. Robert clawed his fingers through his hair, clasping his hands behind his neck in an attempt at self-control. "Sorry, that was stupid of me." He tried to act composed as he crossed the room and picked up his phone. He flipped it open, making sure it was still working before slipping it into his pocket.

"How much?" Harrison asked bluntly.

"What do you mean?" Robert poured himself a Scotch and threw it to the back of his throat.

"How stupid do you think I am? You've been dodging my questions for weeks. This is not a business problem; this is a gambling problem.

"It's nothing I can't handle."

"Oh yeah, I can see you're handling things just fine."

"Get off my back, Harry. I know what I'm doing. I just need a little more time, and I don't need your patronizing attitude.

Robert grabbed his jacket from the back of the chair and stalked out.

Harrison sunk his head to his chest, not knowing what to do. He'd never seen Robert so close to the edge. *God, stop him from self-destructing before it's too late.*

Harrison's drive to Jennifer's seemed long, though it was only blocks away. He'd picked up steaks, figuring they could grill them even if he didn't have much of an appetite. When he got there, it took Jennifer a few minutes to get to the door. Harrison's heart skipped a beat. After her distracted attitude on the phone earlier that day, his first thought was that she had run once again. Even after all this time, there was a part of him that tensed, thinking she could disappear at any moment. Not until he heard the door unlatch and saw her face did he allow himself to begin to breathe again.

He leaned down and placed a kiss on her cheek before walking in. He carried the bag of groceries to the kitchen and set them on the counter.

"How was your day?" she asked, trying to sound upbeat.

"Not great. Robert's bouncing off the walls but won't tell me what's wrong. I know he's gambling again and because of it, he won't confide in me. He knows how I feel about it so he's hiding it instead of trying to get help."

Jennifer snaked her arms around his waist and placed her head to his chest. "I'm sorry. I know I probably didn't make things much better."

He wrapped his arms around her and settled his chin against the top of her head. "Well, your preoccupation did have me a little worried. I know I've been pushing you lately and after our little exchange last night, I was afraid that I'd pushed too far."

"No, it's not that. It's what happened after you left that has me upset."

He craned his neck to look into her eyes. "What happened?"

She took him by the hand and led him to the couch. Sitting down next to him, she began to explain, "I found something of my mother's, a note that I didn't realize she'd left for me." She walked to the mantel, picked up the small piece of paper and handed it to him.

Harrison's eyes strained to read the shaky writing. He couldn't believe what the message revealed. He quickly read it again to make sure he understood it correctly.

"This is incredible." Harrison was beaming. "You know what this means, don't you?"

"I think so, but I wanted to be sure. This was included in the note." She handed him the business card. "I called to talk to the pastor. He's no longer there. He had a stroke and retired."

"But this is great, Jennifer. Your mother came to know the Lord before she passed away. Where did you find this note?"

"It was in an envelope the hospital left for me. It had been sealed. I thought I knew everything that was in it—her earrings, her necklace, her medical papers. I never opened it until last night. That's when I found the note."

"Is that the necklace?" Harrison asked.

Jennifer fingered it. "Yes, I gave it to her for Mother's Day. She died a month later."

Harrison turned his attention back to the note. "Your mother wanted you to know the decision she'd made, the change that she felt. What a wonderful gift she left you!"

"I guess." Jennifer plopped down and pulled her knees up close to her chest. "I just wish I could talk to the preacher that spoke to her. I'd like to know if he remembers her and their conversation."

"But you know what it is she wanted him to tell you." Harrison placed his hand over hers. "She wanted you to know that she'd found peace. She wanted you to find that peace as well." Harrison felt a surge of hope. He prayed silently that this was the nudge Jennifer needed for her to open her heart to what it was he had been trying to show her. "Did you call the other number?"

"No, I figured if the pastor's condition was serious enough that he had to retire, how could I expect him to remember a conversation that happened over ten years ago with a perfect stranger in a hospital bed."

"But if you called, at least you would have your answer."

Jennifer thought about it, glancing at the clock, wondering if she could muster the courage to explain herself to a perfect stranger. "What would I say?"

"Just explain it to whoever answers the phone. Tell them about the note."

Jennifer got up from where she was sitting and paced in front of the coffee table and Harrison's watchful stare. She looked at the clock again, knowing it was an hour later in New Mexico, but thinking it was still early enough to call. She left the room without explanation and returned quickly, her cell phone in her hand. She sat next to Harrison on the couch and punched in the numbers.

Harrison could feel her trembling. He brought his hand up to her neck and began massaging her tightened muscles, hoping to alleviate some of the tension, doing what he could to help her relax.

She jumped when a voice came over the line. Jennifer's voice faltered slightly as she spoke. "Yes, I was wondering if this is the home of Pastor Walt Allen." Jennifer closed her eyes waiting for the response. "Well no, I don't know the pastor but I think he spoke to my mother once when she was ill. I know it was a long time ago and I've been told of the pastor's stroke, but it's very important for me to find out if he remembers my mother and the conversation he had with her. It happened more than ten years ago. She was at Sunrise Hospital and passed away the evening they spoke."

The woman gasped on the other end of the long distance connection. "Christy . . . Christy Bellamy?"

Jennifer struggled to catch her breath unable to respond to the woman.

"Hello? Hello . . . are you still there?"

Jennifer thrust the phone at Harrison, not wanting to lose the connection with the woman who knew who she was or who she'd once been, but not having the words to answer her.

"Yes, we're still here." Harrison replied.

"I can't believe it, after all these years. My husband looked for her for years, but she just disappeared."

He realized the reason for Jennifer's shock. The woman knew who she was. "Could you hold on for just a moment?" Harrison asked politely.

Harrison covered the phone and looked at Jennifer. She was still trying to recover from the shock of hearing the name from her past. "Are you going to be okay?" he whispered.

She took a couple of deep breaths, and then reached for the phone. "I'm sorry. I guess I was just so surprised that you knew my name. I mean, it was so long ago."

"You're right, but Walt spent years looking for you. Your mother, she left something with him to give to you, but he had no way of finding you. He tried to . . . "

"Wait, did you say he had something of my mother's?" Her eyes darted to Harrison's.

"Yes."

"Does he still have it?"

"Well, yes, of course. His prayer was that someday he would find you, or you would find him. You know up until the stroke, he prayed for you every day. Your mother wanted so badly for him to speak to you. He felt he had let her down somehow by never finding you."

Tears rushed down Jennifer's face and the weight of her emotion was evident in her voice. "Do you think I could speak to him?"

"He doesn't talk on the phone anymore. It's too difficult for him."

"What if I was to come and see him?"

There was a pause on the phone that was ominous, a silence that Jennifer didn't want to hear.

"Christy, he hasn't said anything about you or your mother since the stroke. He doesn't remember and quite honestly, I'm thankful. It was so heartbreaking for him to feel as if he'd failed. I don't want him to feel that way again."

"But I'm here now. He wouldn't have to feel bad. He'd know that his prayers were answered." Jennifer's voice raised in desperation. "I just have to know what they talked about!"

"Christy, I'm not sure I can take that chance. It might just confuse him."

Jennifer slumped in resolve. "But you said he had something of my mother's."

"Yes, of course, if you give me your address, I can send it to you."

"Actually, if you wouldn't mind, I'd like to come by and get it. I haven't been back to Albuquerque since my mother died, and I have some things I need to take care of there."

ROBERT WAS SITTING IN THE DARK when Harrison returned. When he flipped on the lights, Robert flinched beneath its harsh glare. He looked horrible and did nothing to hide it. He swirled the ice around in his glass, staring into nothingness.

"I've really screwed up this time, little brother. I'm in over my head."

Harrison took the seat opposite him. "What happened?"

"I thought I could let things play out, that I'd recover, but if I don't come up with $50,000 right away, I'm history."

Harrison looked into his brother's bloodshot eyes, knowing that the stakes this time had been too high. The people Robert had a tendency to gravitate to were anything but forgiving. He felt physically ill at the seriousness of the situation. Robert was continuing to throw his life away, his gambling addiction spiraling out of control.

Harrison had bailed him out before and sworn he'd never do it again, that Robert would have to learn from his mistakes. But the gravity of the situation this time was too dangerous to ignore.

"Tomorrow I'll make some calls, do some liquidating. I should be able to have the money by noon. Is that going to be soon enough?"

"Yeah." Robert let his head fall back in relief. "Thanks, I knew I could count on you."

"Well, when am I going to be able to count on you?" Harrison fired back. "When am I going to be able to believe you when you say you're through with gambling and shady business deals?" Harrison got to his feet, his agitation no longer allowing him to remain seated. "We've been down this road before, Robert, and every time you tell me it's going to be your last. When am I going to be able to trust you? You're a brilliant businessman. Why can't you be satisfied with honest business? Why do you always turn to gambling and get-rich-quick schemes?"

"Maybe because I'm fed up with everyone comparing me to you!" Robert shouted back. "Everything you touch turns to gold. You've never had a business deal go bad on you, or poured yourself into something that didn't go your way. You've gotten everything you've ever wanted in life—everything!" Robert took another hard swig and wiped his mouth with the backside of his hand. "You've had everything handed to you in high school, in college, right down to Dad getting you in with Weissler and Schuler. You got the corner office, the partnership—everything. And now even the one thing you thought would never be attainable—the girl of your dreams, the only one for you, your precious Jennifer—waltzes back into your life. Poof . . . another prized commodity just handed to you. I'm tired of it, and I'm tired of you. I'm tired of your sanctimonious life and your holier-than-thou attitude."

Robert got up with a swagger and stumbled towards his bedroom door. "Keep your freakin' money. I don't want it. I'd rather lose everything than have to be indebted to you and have to listen to your 'what you need is God' speech just one more time."

Robert slammed his door, leaving Harrison angry, frustrated, and heartbroken. He loved his brother, down deep he knew he did. But he hated the man he'd become. He had hoped that Robert's relationship with Kelly would have changed him, made him more centered. He had also hoped this little trip of theirs would give them the time they needed to talk out issues and mend their fences. Harrison knew that Robert felt resentment towards him. They'd talked about it before . . . actually more like had skirmishes and knocked down fights about it. Harrison tried to show Robert what was missing from his life was the Lord, but Robert would have none of it. His plan was to prove to everyone he could make it on his own, but all he'd managed to do was spiral deeper and deeper into debt and a dysfunctional lifestyle.

Harrison pulled out his computer and reviewed his accounts and investments late into the night. He wanted to know what calls he had to make in the morning and which funds would be easy enough to liquidate on such short notice. He and Jennifer had flight reservations for three in the afternoon, and he wanted to make sure that nothing interfered with their schedule. She had enough on her mind, and he didn't want to trouble her with Robert's activities.

Harrison took a shower before turning in for the night. He leaned his hands on either side of the shower head, needing the hot, pulsating water to work on his tight shoulder muscles. He was feeling the strain of being pulled in different directions. He wanted to be there for Robert but his belligerence was only causing things to get worse between them. And then there was Jennifer.

Harrison wasn't sure what to expect from this trip to Albuquerque. He knew it was going to be emotional for Jennifer, that's why he'd insisted on going. She would have to deal with the memory of her mother's death, but he prayed that it might be a new beginning for her as well.

He laid awake, talking with God about the upheaval he was feeling. He wanted to be solid for Jennifer. He wanted to be able to give her the support she needed, but he wanted her to find the way on her own. He wanted her to feel the need to have God in her life, not as some sort of connection to her mother, but because she was ready to acknowledge her need for a Savior.

ROBERT LAID AWAKE, fueled with resentment. Once again he'd had to turn to Harrison for help. And once again, he'd had to sit under the lecturing of his perfect brother.

He had convinced Harrison to come to California with him to see if they could find some equal ground after all these years. In actuality, Robert hadn't hoped to level the playing field; he had hoped he would be able to show Harrison some of the fun that was missing from his life. He had thought the California lifestyle would have loosened Harrison up and shown him there was more to life than God and self-righteousness. Robert had once again underestimated the commitment level of his brother. He had come to realize they were polar opposites, and there was no amount of swaying or cajoling Robert could do to get Harrison to see life from his prospective.

He swigged his scotch and decided there was no use in trying. He mumbled to himself. "Go ahead and live your life of control and perfection, little brother. I don't care anymore as long as I get my money."

Robert's glazed-over eyes glared into the night. He knew Harrison would get him the money; he always had. The problem was, where would he come up with the rest of it? The $50,000 was only a retainer to buy him more time. If he didn't do something fast, he wouldn't make it home from his honeymoon.

CHAPTER SEVENTEEN

J ennifer had been up to watch the sunrise. Actually, she'd never really gone to sleep. Her thoughts had traveled over her lifetime, where she'd come from, and where she was going. As traumatic as her childhood was and as difficult a life she had led, she had managed to have a simple though lonely adulthood. Not until her encounter with Harrison over three years ago did her life start to get complicated again.

A breeze played with her bangs as she sat in the swing in her backyard looking out onto the beautiful streaks of gold and oranges as the sun announced a new day. Harrison's face continued to drift threw her thoughts, playing with her emotions. She knew how she felt about him, of that she was certain. But how fair was it for her to expect him to become a part of the masquerade she called her life? He was a successful businessman and was gaining prominence in the corporate world. As much as he liked to keep a low profile, his growing notoriety would force him to spend time being seen in certain social circles. There would be no way for them to maintain a quiet existence.

Jennifer pulled herself from the swing and pushed her thoughts aside. She needed to pack for their trip and get ready for work. She tried to busy her mind with everything except what was waiting for her in Albuquerque. She would put off dealing with those emotions until she absolutely had to.

Jennifer rushed into the lobby of WBP, talking as she went. Julie, the receptionist had no choice but to follow her, paper in hand, so she could write down the instructions Jennifer was rattling off as she headed for her office.

"Okay, so I need to reschedule your afternoon meetings until Monday. What else did you want me to do?" Julie held her note pad trying to keep up with Jennifer.

"I need you to transfer any new clients that are on my schedule to someone else."

"You mean for today?"

"For today and any I have scheduled for next week. I have too many other things going on right now to take on any new clients."

"It has to do with that man who was here, doesn't it?" Julie inquired.

Jennifer quickly looked up from the mound of papers on her desk. "What man?" Her pulse instantly began to race, her mind immediately thinking about her father and the possibility that he'd found her.

"The one that I called security on. That hunk of a man that came looking for you the day of your accident."

Jennifer exhaled with relief and then a small smile filled out her lips. "His name's Harrison Lynch."

"So," Julie squealed with delight. "This is about a man. Good for you."

"Excuse me?" Jennifer couldn't help but giggle at Julie's enthusiasm.

"It's about time, girl. All you've done since you got here is work, work, work. It's about time you found yourself a man. And I must say he looks like he was well worth the wait." Julie lifted her pencil-thin brows and allowed a mischievous smile to form on her ruby-red lips. "So why all the rushing around this morning?"

"Harrison's picking me up at noon. We have a 3:00 p.m. flight we need to catch, and I need to make sure I have all this paperwork done by then."

"Ooh, a trip together . . . do tell. Where are you going? Let me see, you're only going to be gone for the weekend." Julie tapped her chin with her well-manicured fingernail. "Hawaii . . . no, Mexico. A little salsa, a little fiesta, a little romantico."

Julie made Jennifer laugh out loud, followed by a heavy sigh. Inwardly she wondered what it would be like to be on a romantic getaway with Harrison, just the two of them. No Robert. No Kelly. No work. No rules. Just the two of them and uninterrupted time.

After a moment of wishful thinking, Jennifer snapped back from her daydream and shooed Julie from her office so she could get a stack of work done before Harrison arrived.

HARRISON PICKED UP THE ENVELOPE from the franchise broker's office and headed back to the room. He packed while he waited for Robert to show up. He'd been asleep when Harrison left, and now his room was empty. He kept his eye on the clock, watching as time ticked away. He called his cell phone but only got Robert's pre-recorded message. He had no choice but to leave without talking to him. He sat down and wrote a quick note to go with the bundle of cash.

Robert—
I had to go out of town. I hope this helps. All I want to do is help. I hope we can talk when I get back.
—Harry

Harrison grabbed his bag and left. He pulled up in front of West Beach Properties and jumped out of his black Chrysler. When he walked into the reception area, Julie was all smiles. "Good afternoon, Mr. Lynch. Ms. Wilder is expecting you."

Harrison was surprised by the changed demeanor of the receptionist but glad he wasn't going to have to go through security to explain why he was there.

"You must have made a huge impression on Samantha," Julie mused while giving Harrison a flirtatious smile.

"Excuse me?"

She smiled bigger. "Samantha hadn't missed a day of work, no sick days, no vacation days, nothing . . . that is until she met you. I don't know who you are or how you caught her eye because believe me, there have been quite a few fine looking men who have tried. But I'm glad you did. Samantha's a wonderful person and deserves to have a little fun."

She pressed her intercom button, announcing his arrival, and then directed him to the third door around the corner. Harrison walked slowly, smiling at what the receptionist had said before knocking lightly on the solid door.

"Come in." Jennifer raised her voice. She was rushing around her desk as he stepped in. "I'm almost ready. Just let me leave this note for Julie."

Jennifer hunched over her desk, writing frantically while Harrison took the chance to look around. Her office was beautifully decorated, greeting everyone who entered with comfort and warmth.

She turned off her computer, pulled her jacket from her chair, and grabbed up her purse and the last remaining file before walking around the corner of her desk. "Ready."

"Yes, you are." Harrison said with a pleased tone and an admiring eye. "You look great."

"Well, I feel horrible. I didn't sleep at all last night, I have all this work I should be doing, I spilled coffee on my pants, and I'm not sure if I packed my toothbrush." Jennifer's tone raised with every detriment she listed. Harrison pulled her close and waited for her to look up at him.

"It's going to be okay, Jennifer, just relax. You look wonderful, and we can buy you a toothbrush at the hotel." He brushed back her hair and bent to place a gentle kiss on her lips. It wasn't long or lingering, but she still felt the affection behind it.

He reached for her carry-on bag sitting by the door and with his hand to the small of her back, walked with her to the front lobby.

"Here, Julie. Would you mind taking care of this one for me?"

Julie didn't take her eyes off Harrison. Her stare was so intense, he could feel his skin begin to heat up.

"Julie?" Jennifer tried to get her attention.

"Sure, Samantha, I'll take care of it. You two just go and have a good time."

"It's not like that, Julie. I have some business to take care of, and Harrison agreed to go with me."

"Sure . . . of course . . . business."

Jennifer ignored Julie's playful sarcasm and stepped toward the door.

"Have a good time. I hope you remembered your sunscreen."

Jennifer could hear Julie's giggling as the door swung shut.

The drive to the airport was quiet. Jennifer stared apprehensively out the passenger window while Harrison was pre-occupied with Robert's situation.

They picked up their reserved tickets at the counter and worked their way over to the security line. Jennifer still hadn't said much. She was jittery, fumbling with anything she could get her hands on, pushing her hair behind her ears, fingering the tiny sapphire necklace that hung around her neck. And now, Harrison noticed her pale complexion.

"Jennifer, what's wrong?"

"Nothing!" Her tone was sharp and completely unbelievable. She wrapped her arms around herself, trying to still the nerves that were rising inside her.

Harrison let it go as they made it through security and found their gate. They still had 45 minutes until their flight took off. Harrison set down his bag and took a seat facing the windows. He waited for Jennifer to take the seat next to him, but she just put her bag down and moved to the large pane of glass.

She stared at the tarmac, watching planes taxiing and workers rushing about.

"You're afraid of flying, aren't you?" Harrison spoke over her shoulder.

"That obvious, huh?" she answered while gazing out across the runways.

"Just a hunch." He wrapped his arm around her, stroking her arm, trying to relieve her tension. "Come on, sit down and relax."

He led her over to the connected chairs and sat down with her, drawing her close to his side. She closed her eyes, resting her head on his chest, gulping back her anxieties.

"So, why are you afraid of flying?"

Jennifer debated telling him, tired of explaining the ordeals that made up her pitiful existence. "One time my mother and I were on a plane, and she thought we'd been found out. There was nothing we could do. We had to sit through the remainder of the flight, cowering in our seats. It was terrifying."

"But Jennifer, that's not going to happen."

"I know. It just gives me such a claustrophobic feeling to be somewhere and not be able to get out."

Harrison knew her fears ran deep. He didn't blame her; he just wished there was something he could do to drive away those fears. He would like nothing better than to be able to take Jennifer somewhere far away and give her the peaceful existence she deserved.

"So, if you could live anywhere in the world, where would that be?"

Jennifer looked up at him, a puzzled look on her face. "That's a pretty random question."

"I'm distracting you. So play along."

She couldn't help but laugh. Harrison was the most charming man she'd ever met. The range of his qualities was never ending.

"You didn't answer the question," he said playfully.

"What was the question again?"

After repeating himself, Jennifer closed her eyes and tried to imagine the perfect setting. "A lighthouse."

"A what?" He laughed, amused.

"A lighthouse."

"Why a lighthouse?"

"Why not?" Jennifer pictured the setting in her head. "Just imagine, the magnificence of the ocean laid out before you; the waves rolling like thunder, crashing on rocks; the foamy mist shooting to the sky. But at the same time, there's a peacefulness that fills the air. It's a paradox."

"And do you see someone there with you?"

His question hit her like a ton of bricks.

"I don't know," she said guardedly as she moved away from him and scooted back in her chair.

Harrison could have kicked himself. He had only meant to tease her, to lighten the mood. He didn't understand why she'd turned so cold so quickly.

Jennifer sat with her hands clutched tightly in her lap, carrying on an angry debate with her conscience. Harrison's playful question had been the wake up call she needed. She had no business dragging him to New Mexico or dragging out this so-called relationship of theirs. She was only fooling herself, imagining what a normal life could be like. Harrison was an honest, upstanding man who believed in God. She was a deceptive fugitive who had only herself to count on for survival. They were only kidding themselves if they thought they would be able to overcome such surmountable obstacles.

"This is ridiculous, Harrison. You don't need to go with me. I can go to Albuquerque by myself."

"Hey, where did that come from?"

"I'm a big girl. I don't need a babysitter." Her words were biting.

"Whoa, whoa, whoa." Harrison turned in his chair to look directly at her. "I am not babysitting you. I was coming along for emotional support."

"Well, I've gotten used to handling things on my own." She stared straight ahead, avoiding eye contact with him.

"Why are you doing this?" His words were gritty and spoken under his breath.

"No! The question is, why are *we* doing this?" She turned quickly, her tone razor-sharp, her eyes piercing.

"What are you talking about?"

"What are we doing here, Harrison? There is no way we're going to be able to make this work." Jennifer lowered her voice when she noticed a woman at the end of the row of chairs staring at them. "Like you so aptly pointed out before, impersonating someone is against the law and since you know that I'm not Samantha Wilder that means you're aiding a criminal. Don't you get it, just by being with me, you're putting yourself and your reputation at risk; and there's nothing you or I can do about that. I can't change, Harrison. Not even for you."

He sat in a stunned silence, replaying her stabbing words. He wanted to refute them but knew he couldn't.

Just then, the overhead speakers announced the boarding call for their flight. Jennifer bent over, picked up her bag and turned towards the gate's entrance. Harrison grabbed his carry-on and tried to step around her.

"Where are you going?"

"I'm going to New Mexico," he said confidently, trying again to step around her. She reached out for his forearm and pulled him to a stop.

"But I don't want you to."

"Well, I'm sorry you feel that way because I'm going anyway."

Harrison strode to the awaiting flight attendant, handed her his ticket and headed down the tunnel that led to the plane. Jennifer stood dumfounded. She pulled her carry-on further up on her shoulder and headed towards the gate. The attendant that greeted her on the plane pointed out her seat, but Jennifer didn't need any help. She saw Harrison stowing his carry-on and knew she had the seat next to him. She walked down the narrow aisle and caught the smile he was trying to hold back. He took her carry-on out of her hand, heaved it over his head, and put it in the compartment next to his. They each took their seats.

"This is ridiculous, Harrison."

"I don't think so."

"Didn't you hear anything I said back there? I am a criminal." She whispered. "I will always be a criminal. You can't tell me that you're willing to turn your back on that as if it doesn't matter."

"I'm not saying it doesn't matter. I just think we can work it out."

"How?"

Before he could answer, the attendant began to give the in-flight instructions. Jennifer's phobia came back with a vengeance. The other passengers went about what they were doing, casually whispering among themselves, not really paying attention. Jennifer listened to each and every instruction while feverishly looking around as if someone from her past was going to jump out at her. Harrison reached over and put his strong, comforting hand over hers.

"Relax, Jennifer. The only person who knows you on this plane is me." He squeezed her hand for reassurance.

Her resilience crumbled, and she clutched his hand in return. She was glad his stubbornness would not allow him to leave when she had asked him to, but she hated the fact that she was becoming so dependent on him.

She pressed her head to the back of the seat as the plane positioned itself for take-off. Harrison stroked her hand with his thumb, trying to soothe away the tension and anxieties that were consuming her.

She squeezed his hand, and her eyes tightly shut as the plane sped down the runway. She didn't allow herself to breathe or relax until she felt the plane leveling off. Opening her eyes, she loosened her grip on his hand, but he didn't allow her to pull away.

She looked at his hand that was still covering hers and then up to meet warm, assuring eyes. "In case there's turbulence" was his flimsy excuse. She turned back in her seat and closed her eyes.

What am I going to do? There's no way I can live without this man. God, if you're out there, and if you really care about me the way Harrison says you do, then do something. Help us figure out a plan. I know what I've done is wrong, but I had no choice, and you never stepped in to offer any help. Here's your chance to make it up to me and show me that you really care. Figure out how we can make this work, and I'll believe in you.

Harrison glanced at Jennifer. Her eyes were closed, but she didn't look restful. He turned to look out the window. *God, what am I going to do? I love her, but the obstacles seem so overwhelming. Show her you're real. Help her to see that she needs you in her heart and life.*

They both sat quietly as they struggled with their own inner conversations. Jennifer wanted proof that God was the powerful provider that Harrison claimed him to be, and Harrison cried out to that same God, confident his Redeemer would make himself known to her.

The seatbelt sign was finally turned off. A few passengers got up to stretch, while others reached for their carry-on bags from the overhead compartments. The flight attendants started their slow procession up the aisle with their beverage cart, offering the passengers drinks and snacks.

"What can I get for you?" The stunning brunette smiled broadly at Harrison before noticing the way he was holding Jennifer's hand. She looked at Jennifer and gave her a curt smile.

"I'll have a Coke." Harrison offered with a smile, oblivious to the eye contact that was going on.

"And for you, ma'am?" the attendant asked coldly.

It was the way she stretched out the "ma'am" that let Jennifer know she was being insulted. The youthful attendant realized Harrison was not alone on the flight and was obviously trying to get under Jennifer's skin.

"I'll have a Diet Coke," Jennifer answered tightly.

The woman never even acknowledged her reply. She just poured a Coke for Harrison and leaned completely over Jennifer in order to set it on his tray. She hovered there for a moment, her blouse puckering against her buttons. "And what would you like to snack on?" she asked Harrison next. It was then that he realized she was flirting with him.

A flush came over him as he fooled with his napkin, trying to keep his eyes anywhere but where she intended them to linger. "I'm not hungry, thank you." He smiled quickly and took a sip of his soda.

The woman stood up slowly. "Well, just let me know if you get hungry. I'm sure I could find something for you to nibble on."

Jennifer was ready to call the woman out. Her behavior was completely inappropriate, especially when she could see that Harrison was with someone.

The attendant flashed him a sultry smile before going on with what she was doing. She poured Jennifer's drink, haphazardly setting it on her tray, causing it to spill. "Sorry about that," she said in a completely unbelievable tone. She tossed a couple of napkins down on the tray and then began to push the cart forward.

"Wait a second. Aren't you going to offer me a snack?" Jennifer asked with irritation in her tone.

"Of course," she answered as if she didn't want to be bothered. "I just thought that the gentleman was speaking for both of you."

"Well, I don't think what you were offering the gentleman was for both of us." Jennifer met the attendant's piercing eyes, letting her know she was on to her little game.

"I don't know what you're talking about." The attendant flung her hair over her shoulder and planted her hand on her hip.

"Really . . . do you always offer passengers a view to go with their drink?" The attendant was ready to interrupt, but Jennifer would not allow it. "Look, I don't appreciate your behavior, and I don't think your supervisors would either."

Harrison squeezed her hand, signaling her to calm down. She flashed him a look and then turned back to the attendant. "I would like some pretzels, in fact, make that a bag for each of us. I don't want you to have any reason to come back and disturb us again because if you do, I will talk to someone in charge."

The attendant placed two bags of pretzels on Jennifer's tray and with one backward glanced, moved on.

"What was that all about?" Harrison spoke under his breath.

"Come on, Harrison, if you'd had an aisle seat she would have offered you a lap dance with your soda."

Harrison grinned.

"What's that smirk for? Are you going to tell me you didn't know she was flirting with you?"

"You're jealous." His grin grew wider.

"No, more like irritated. Her behavior was completely unprofessional."

"You made that abundantly clear. In fact, I'm sure the people across the aisle are clear on how you feel as well." His teasing only served to make her more agitated.

"Well, excuse me if I embarrassed you. Next time a woman decides to throw herself at you, I will gladly step aside."

A low chuckle escaped him as he tried to avoid Jennifer's glare. She bit her lip in frustration and crossed her arms tightly against her chest. He was laughing, and it infuriated her. He reached for her hand, but she quickly pulled it away.

"Come on, Jennifer, don't be mad." He was still having a hard time controlling his laughter.

"You're laughing at me, and I'm not supposed to get mad?"

"I'm not laughing at you; in fact, I think your possessiveness is kind of . . . cute."

"Possessiveness? I'm not being possessive." She huffed.

"Don't be so defensive." He clutched her hand and brought it up to his lips. His kiss was warm and sent chills throughout her body. "It just proves to me that you're not willing to give up on us." He leaned across the seat, placing a kiss on her cheek. "We're going to make it, Jennifer. Just hang in there."

She felt her heart wrap around the hope she saw in Harrison's eyes.

JENNIFER WAS SITTING STIFFLY IN HER SEAT, Harrison holding her hand as the plane made its descent. It taxied to the gate, cutting into the heat that drifted through the stillness of the desert air.

Harrison got their bags out of the overhead storage and made his way to the front of the plane, while she followed behind him. She caught the eye of the offending flight attendant and dared her to say anything to them. As they made their way forward, the sassy brunette turned towards the galley and busied herself at the counter. Jennifer grinned in satisfaction.

They stepped from the airport terminal out into the desert heat. After getting shuttled to the rental car pick-up area, they headed for their hotel. Harrison had gotten directions from the rental agency and easily maneuvered through the streets of Albuquerque. Jennifer, consumed with her thoughts, stared blankly out the window. When they pulled into the circular driveway of a posh hotel, she turned to Harrison for an explanation.

"I thought I said to book something economical."

"No, you said to get us a good deal, and I did. These rooms usually cost a fortune."

"Oh, so what are we paying, half a fortune?" she commented as a valet helped her out of the car. Harrison walked around the trunk and met her at the curb. With a hand to her waist, they entered the lobby, and he whispered.

"You're not paying anything. We said we'd split the expenses. So, you can pay for the rental car, and I'll pay for the hotel rooms."

Jennifer arched a defiant eyebrow. "I have the money, Harrison. I don't need a handout."

"Yeah, and if you had booked the rooms, we would've ended up in some economy lodge somewhere with a vending machine right outside our door and children running up and down the hallways. I thought we deserved something a little more tranquil then that."

"Harrison, this is not a pleasure trip."

"Nothing says it can't be." He smiled his charismatic smile and approached the front desk.

HARRISON PUSHED OPEN the door to Jennifer's room and let her step through ahead of him. She was greeted by rich shades of cool tans and warm browns. Though the massive bed, covered in an elegant velour throw, dominated the room, the quaint sitting area next to the French doors was just as inviting.

Jennifer stepped out onto the balcony and gazed out over the tropical pool setting. She closed her eyes and listened as the waterfall splashed into the crystal blue water.

"So, what do you think?" Harrison stepped outside and joined her.

"I think it's beautiful," she said softly.

"So, you're not mad at me?"

She turned to look at him. "No. I'm not mad."

He stepped forward, allowing his hands to slip around her waist. "You thinking about tomorrow?"

She looked up at him, voicing her biggest fear. "What if she won't let me see him?"

"What did she say?"

"She said I was welcome to come and pick up what my mother had left with him, but she wasn't sure if it was a good idea for me to talk to her husband. She's afraid it might upset him."

Harrison pressed her head to his chest and wrapped her up tighter. He inhaled the enchanting scent that was exclusively Jennifer's as she looped her arms around him, trying to draw from his strength. He held her, stroking her back, trying to calm the unsettling feelings that were fighting for her attention.

"Tell you what," he pulled back just far enough so he could look at her as he spoke, "why don't you let me go put my things into my room? That will give you a minute to freshen up and then we can go have ourselves a nice dinner."

"I really don't feel like going out. Why don't we just eat in?"

"Because you need to go out. You need to do something other than sit here and think about tomorrow."

She wrinkled her nose. "Do I have to?"

"Yes." He quickly planted a kiss on her forehead before letting her go. "My room's right next door." He motioned towards the adjoining door as he left. "Knock when you're ready."

Jennifer's eyes wandered around the room again, taking in all the little extras. She leaned into the bathroom and flipped on the light. She smiled when she saw the spa tub in the corner, surrounded by marble and polished brass. She fingered the luxurious bathrobe hanging alongside the tub and wished above all else that she could enjoy the extravagance that Harrison was showering on her without the uncertainty that was hanging over her.

She caught a glimpse of herself in the mirror and leaned closer. She brushed her bangs to one side and scrutinized her complexion. She grabbed her bag from the other room and dug out her overnight case to touch up her make-up. She didn't normally wear a lot, but her complexion was pale and if she was going to go out, she figured she might as well look nice.

She brushed her hair into an upswept style that would look a little nicer for evening and applied a hint of perfume to her wrist. She pulled the clothes from her bag and looked at what she had to work with. She really hadn't been thinking about anything other than meeting the Allens, but her nervousness had made her pack more outfits than she needed.

She moved her clothes around on her bed, making new combinations and trying to take the conservative items she had brought and make them look a little special. She finally decided on a long, full skirt in a soft shade of green which she paired with an ivory top made of linen. She fiddled with the delicate silk ribbon woven into the bodice, appreciating the feminine touch it added. She picked up the sandals she had thrown into her bag at the last minute and slipped them on her feet.

She took one last look at herself in the full-length mirror and sighed. "It's going to have to do."

She tapped on the door to Harrison's room and waited for him to answer. When he did, Jennifer's heart skipped a beat. Harrison looked incredible. He wore khaki slacks and a white linen shirt, uncharacteristically untucked. He looked as if he'd just stepped from the pages of *Gentlemen's Quarterly*. Jennifer was so taken by him that she didn't notice him drinking her in.

"Wow . . . all that for me?" His words hung between a whisper and a heavy sigh.

"No," she said abruptly, trying to shake off the overwhelming feelings she continued to try and deny herself. But she realized that was exactly what she'd done, dressed with him in mind. She quickly tried to diffuse his comment. "I just wanted to wear something not so business-like. I wear suits and blazers all day long."

"Lucky me," he said as he stepped closer to her and bent to place a kiss on her neck.

His touch was electrifying, causing her to exhale slowly. She leaned against him, wanting to absorb his energy, his strength, his confidence. He was everything she wasn't.

Harrison held Jennifer, enjoying the closeness and the way she felt in his arms—her skin, soft and smooth against his lips and the warmth of her body pressed against his. He loved it. He loved everything about Jennifer . . . except for the deception. There had to be a way for Jennifer to go on in life without living a life made up of lies and fears.

Jennifer pulled herself from her daydream and from Harrison. "Did you say something about dinner?"

"Yeah." The spell broken, Harrison led Jennifer out into the hallway with a gently placed hand.

They passed the hotel's main dining area and continued outdoors. Soft, twinkling lights lit their way as they crossed an arched bridge that spanned the hotel pool and spa. The arid breeze played with Jennifer's hair, and the warmth of the air tickled her senses. She reached for Harrison's hand and decided to enjoy the beautiful night and push away the real reason she was in New Mexico at least until tomorrow.

Harrison and Jennifer were met with the soothing rhythm of a single guitarist as they entered the dimly lit dining room. An older gentleman in a white dinner jacket escorted them to a table that was tucked away in a private corner.

"I feel like I'm underdressed," Jennifer whispered as Harrison held her chair for her and then took a seat himself.

"Are you kidding me, you look beautiful."

"You don't look so bad yourself."

They shared a satisfying smile.

The maître d' slipped away quietly, leaving them to enjoy each other and their privacy. A small, ornate frame displayed a selection of vintage wines and the evening's menu, with a select choice of main courses. No prices were displayed, another clue to Jennifer how exclusive and prestigious the resort was.

"Okay, Harrison, this is obviously not your run-of-the-mill hotel that you call up one day and have reservations the next. How did you arrange all this on such short notice?"

"I have my connections." His roguish grin was intoxicating.

"In New Mexico?" She questioned playfully.

"You'd be surprised."

"I thought that was my department . . . surprises I mean."

He reached across the table and took her hand in his. "I'm not as predictable as you think I am."

"Really?" She couldn't contain a slight giggle. "And what is it that's unpredictable about you?" Her tone was filled with amusement. The thought of Harrison being anything but the stable and predictable person that he was drew a laugh from her.

He caressed her fingers with his, never taking his eyes off of her. "How about the fact that I'm a very accomplished dancer?"

She dipped her head to hide her laughter.

"You don't believe me?" he challenged.

She tried to regain her composure. "I didn't say that."

He got to his feet and extended his hand to her. "Try me."

She looked at him stunned, smiling at his insistence. When he continued to stand, waiting for her to join him, seriousness filled her countenance. "You're serious?"

"Dance with me, Jennifer."

The soft strumming of a flamenco guitar, the dim ambient lighting, and Harrison looking incredible was an irresistible combination.

Jennifer took Harrison's hand and stood. He led her just a few steps from their table out onto a small patio that shimmered in the moonlight. He slipped his arm snugly around her waist and pressed her close to his chest. They swayed not only to the music that flowed over them but to the rhythm of their own hearts. As Jennifer rested her head against Harrison's chest, enjoying the scent of his cologne, she began imagining what life would be like if they could live every day in the comfort of each other's arms.

Harrison relaxed his chin atop her head, caressing her back, wishing he could change her world as easily as he had changed her mood.

She turned her eyes upwards and looked at the man who'd stolen her heart. No words were necessary for them to communicate what they both were feeling. He only needed to lower his lips to hers to get the affirmation he was looking for. They indulgently embraced the moment and each other.

CHAPTER EIGHTEEN

Jennifer was up before the break of dawn. Sleep had eluded her most the night, and she found herself huddled on a patio chair, watching the colors of the morning erupt in the desert sky.

She closed her eyes and relived the magic of the night before. The intimacy between them had reached a level that both thrilled and terrified her. Her heart soared when she closed her eyes and thought about what they had shared: gentle kisses, caressing touches, and the promise to each other that they would work out the obstacles before them.

For the first time, Jennifer had felt as if maybe God was bigger and more powerful than the evils of her father. Harrison explained to her the steps they could take to ensure her safety while going to the authorities and getting her life straightened out.

Her heart quaked with terror when she thought about finally coming out of hiding after all these years. But there was a bigger part of her that wanted to cling to the glimmer of hope that Harrison was offering her. It would be the most pivotal decision she'd ever have to make. Once she was exposed, there would be no going back. If her father viewed her years of deception as a defiance to his power, he would stop at nothing to control her and show her the depths of his retribution.

Jennifer looked toward the sky, knowing that if there was a God, he could see her struggles. She just found it hard to believe after all these years he would be willing to offer her any answers.

"Not for me, God, but for Harrison. If you care about him, offer us some kind of solution. Then maybe I'll understand better why it is he's so willing to trust you with everything."

Jennifer moved back inside and quickly got dressed. It was still early but she had somewhere to go before they left to meet with Mrs. Allen.

She slipped from the hotel and met the taxi at the curb. Clouds formed overhead, changing the sky to a dreary gray. There would be no rain, but the overcast expanse matched the gloom in her soul. She asked the cabbie to wait for her as she stepped to the grassy curb.

Jennifer looked out over the hillside of the small cemetery. Headstones of different sizes and shapes dotted the landscape, bringing a coldness to the tranquil setting. She looked from right to left, trying to get her bearings. She had only been there once before when she knew the inevitable was coming, and she had to make arrangements for her mother. But she had chosen a special place and was sure she'd be able to find it.

She spotted the oak tree on the far corner of the property and slowly walked towards it. She glanced at headstones made of marble, reading the inscriptions of loved ones dating back generations. As she neared the foot of the tree, her heart tightened in sorrow. There in the shadow of the outreaching branches was a stone that bore the simple inscription: *A most beloved mother and friend.*

Jennifer slowly dropped to her knees, instinctively brushing her hand across the engraved image of a whimsical angel. It was the only thing that identified her with the unnamed grave. Records showed Mary Bellamy was buried there, but Jennifer hadn't been able to bring herself to put the false identity on her mother's final resting place.

Tears spilled unrestrained from her eyes as she pulled at a few weeds that bordered the ivory-colored marble.

"I miss you, Mom. I miss you more now than I thought was even possible. I need your help, and I wish you were here to talk to me. I have an important decision to make, and I'm not sure what to do. I met a man . . . a wonderful man, but if I hope to have a future with him, I need to stop living a life of deception. I just don't think I'm strong enough to go back."

Jennifer spent some time alone with her mother. She explained to her the amazing qualities that Harrison had and how wonderful she felt whenever she was with him. She carried on both sides of a conversation when she talked about the struggles and fears she had with finally coming out of hiding, wondering if her father would accept her or torment her. The thought of becoming a prisoner once again in the Calderon house sent chills down her spine. She questioned her mother about the peace she had talked about in her note. Jennifer found it hard to believe that the short visit with the pastor could have made such a change in her mother.

She thought back to the bouts of depression her mother had suffered because of the sacrifices and decisions she'd made to ensure their safety. She never told Jennifer who it was that had helped them, or how the accident had been so convincing. She never explained to her the details, she would only say that she wasn't proud of what it was she'd done, but there had been no other way.

Jennifer was glad her mother had finally been released from her guilt. She just had difficulty understanding how the brief visit from the preacher had made such a difference.

After a long silence, Jennifer got up from her knees and brushed the grass from her slacks. Her melancholic mood followed her all the way back to her hotel room. When she pushed open her door, Harrison was sitting on her couch waiting for her. He had gotten the note she'd left, explaining why she needed the time alone.

Harrison waited a moment before saying anything. Jennifer took a seat on the couch next to him and rested her head on his shoulder. He wrapped his arm around her and pulled her close.

"You all right?"

"Yeah."

Harrison didn't bother her with conversation. He felt the time she'd spent with her mother was too personal for questions. He just held her and prayed that she'd get the answers she was searching for.

JENNIFER LOOKED PALE as Harrison drove to the small suburban neighborhood on the other side of town. Her biggest fear was that she would not be given the opportunity to talk to the pastor. His wife had never agreed to a meeting, but it had been the chance she'd been willing to take.

Harrison turned the corner and slowed in front of a sprawling ranch-style house. He double-checked the address before turning off the car. He squeezed Jennifer's hand.

"Ready?"

She glanced at the house and then back to him. "As I'll ever be."

He got out of the car and went to open Jennifer's door. She got out and stood beside the car, staring at the house. She steadied herself, preparing for what could be a very short visit. Harrison walked with her to the door, Jennifer clutching his hand. He knocked and stood back.

An elderly woman answered the door and immediately knew who Jennifer was.

"You must be Christy."

"Yes." She tried to smile to loosen the tension she was feeling. "Thank you for seeing me."

The women glanced at Harrison so he took the chance to introduce himself.

"Hi, I'm Harrison, Christy's friend." He extended his hand, and she shook it politely and then moved to shake Jennifer's hand as well.

She stalled for a moment, and Jennifer was sure she wasn't even going to make it past the threshold. Then the older woman stepped back away from the door and invited them in. Jennifer and Harrison followed her into a modestly decorated living room and took a seat on the gold floral couch.

The pastor's wife introduced herself as Ellen. She made polite conversation, asking them where they had traveled from and how their trip had gone so far. Hope was growing in Jennifer that she was going to be able to meet with the pastor. Ellen was so welcoming, so personable, she was sure it was only a matter of time. Harrison conversed with the elderly lady while Jennifer allowed her eyes to roam around the room. When the conversation reached a lull, Ellen picked up a manila envelope from the end table and crossed the room to hand it to Jennifer.

"This is for you."

Jennifer reached for the envelope, a plea in her eyes. "I thought . . . maybe, I mean . . . if I could just talk to your husband. Just for a few moments. Maybe he would remember something, anything at all." She tried to control the emotion in her voice, but it was there right below the surface.

The look on Ellen's face was bleak, giving Jennifer her answer.

Harrison and Jennifer stood in the awkward silence. Harrison could almost feel the desperation in Jennifer's touch when he took her hand in his. They walked slowly to the door, Jennifer feeling weighed down by every step.

"I'm sorry. I know you're disappointed but I have to do what I think is best for my husband," the fragile woman tried to explain. "You don't understand how hard it was on him, all those years, unable to find you. God has graciously allowed him to leave those memories in the past, and I think it's best that we leave them there as well. I'm thankful you contacted us and finally got what it was you mother left for you, but that is all I can offer you. I'm truly sorry."

Jennifer nodded her head in polite understanding even though everything inside her was screaming for just a moment of the man's time. They stood at the front door when a rustling behind them caught their attention. They turned to see an aged man standing in the doorway of the kitchen.

"Mary?" he gasped.

Ellen turned to her husband, trying to usher him out of the room, but he didn't move, never allowing his eyes to move from Jennifer.

"Mr. Allen? Mary was my mother. I'm Christy," Jennifer blurted out.

The glassiness in his eyes was almost more than his wife could bear. She realized the protection she had wanted to provide for him was not to be.

His hand quivered as he clutched the walking stick in his hand, and his wife quickly helped him to a chair in the entryway. He stared at Jennifer with astonishment, hoping what he was seeing was real.

"You came! After all these years, you came."

"Yes, Mr. Allen." Jennifer knelt in front of the man. "I found a note from my mother. She told me that you had something for me, but more importantly, she told me about the conversation you had with her. Her note said she'd finally found peace. I was wondering if you remember what it was you talked about."

He stared at Jennifer silently, and she was afraid the shock of seeing her had been too much for him to handle. With a shaky hand, he reached for Jennifer's and gave it a light squeeze.

"She loved you very much." He smiled timidly.

"Yes, I know. She sacrificed everything for me." Jennifer stroked his frail hand. "Do you remember anything you talked about that night?"

He closed his eyes as if he needed to travel back to that moment in time. "Your mother struggled with some very painful decisions she had made, decisions she said she had never shared with you because of the shame and guilt she felt. She didn't want to disappoint you. She was afraid if she told you what she had done, you wouldn't be able to forgive her because she had never been able to forgive herself."

"Her note said you two had talked and that she finally felt at peace."

Jennifer paused, waiting for him to look at her. She saw something in his eyes. "She told you what it was, didn't she?"

He sighed and slumped as if a weight had settled on his shoulders.

"This is too much for him." Ellen chimed in. "I'm afraid I'm going to have to ask you to leave."

"No!" The pastor's words were firm and strong. "I have carried this weight far too long." He turned his eyes back to Jennifer. "Your mother wanted you to know the truth, as difficult as it might be for you to hear it. But the reason she wanted you to know what it was she wrestled with for so many years is so you would understand how great a peace it is she found. You see, she finally understood the power of forgiveness. Your mother realized she needed a Savior, a Savior that died for her sins and loved her unconditionally, a Savior that was ready to receive her unto himself."

To Harrison, it was a moment of triumph. To Jennifer, it only caused confusion and raised more questions. "But I don't understand. My mother was never religious. She never talked about God. We never went to church, or prayed, or anything."

"It was her guilt. She never felt as if she had a right to God."

"Did she tell you about the life we led?" Jennifer asked cautiously.

"Yes. She told me how you ran and hid. She told me how she had learned to assume other peoples identities."

"Okay, so we ran, and lied, and hid, but she did it because we had to. She was protecting me. Why did she feel so guilty about that? She did what she had to do to keep me safe. What is so wrong about that?"

Harrison laid a hand on Jennifer's shoulder to try and get her to calm down. Her words were getting defensive and her tone sharp.

"Christy," the pastor began, "your mother was responsible for the death of several people involved in the accident that covered up your disappearance."

Jennifer couldn't focus. She couldn't feel her feet beneath her. The room began to wave in front of her like a mirror in a carnival funhouse. Harrison knew she was losing it. He wrapped his arm around her and led her to the couch in the other room.

"Jennifer," he whispered close to her ear as Ellen quickly brought him a glass of water. Jennifer sipped it as she tried to calm her breathing.

The pastor shuffled into the room, trying to catch up with the commotion and turmoil that he had initiated. He sat in the chair at the foot of the couch, wanting to make sure that Jennifer was going to be okay.

She took a moment to regain her composure. Once she was sure her words would be able to move around the racing pulse she felt in her neck, she turned to the pastor with empty eyes.

"I'm sorry, Christy. I wish I didn't have to be the one to tell you such tragic news, but your mother wanted you to know."

"Why? Why would she want me to know? If she'd wanted me to know she would have told me herself." Jennifer bolted to her feet. "You're lying!"

He shook his head with such sympathy that Jennifer sunk to the couch, somehow knowing deep down he was telling the truth. She thought about the midnight tears she had witnessed her mother shedding and the somberness in which she would sit for entire afternoons. She'd always known there was something more that her mother struggled with, but she had always been too hesitant to ask.

She shoved the heels of her hands against her eyes, trying to stop the tears that were beginning to swell.

"She loved you so much, Christy, she was willing to take the chance of you hating her for her sins, rather than letting you die in your own. The peace she found is called forgiveness. It rushed over her the moment she prayed for Christ to come into her heart. She wants that for you, Christy. That's what she wanted me to tell you. She wanted to be able to see you again. She wanted you to know that you're not alone in the world, that there is someone who loves you and wants to protect you even more than she did. She wants you to know the love of God.

JENNIFER HADN'T SPOKEN since leaving the pastor's house. What Harrison had thought for sure would be an incredible breakthrough had turned into a glacier of separation between them.

She sat with her arms tightly folded against her chest, her jaw set, her eyes cold. She tightly clenched the still unopened manila envelope in her hand, her knuckles turning white.

When Harrison pulled into a parking space, Jennifer was out of the car and walking briskly toward the hotel lobby before he could even kill the engine. He almost caught up with her, but not before she stepped onto the elevator and closed the doors without him. By the time he'd made it to their floor, she was already in her room.

Harrison rubbed his eyes and pressed at the bridge of his nose as he slumped on the corner of his hotel room bed. He rested his elbows on his knees and tried to sort out the events of the afternoon. He could see that God was trying to make himself known to Jennifer. The revelation that her mother had come to know the Lord before her death was incredible, but finding out her mother had been somehow involved in someone else's death had completely devastated Jennifer.

Harrison was clueless as to what he should do. Jennifer had closed herself off from him as soon as they'd left the Allens. He wanted to talk to her, to help her assimilate the overwhelming amount of information she'd been given, but she'd asked to be left alone.

He sat in his room, fearful as to how she was going to react to this new information. She'd run in the past when things got to be too much for her, and he was afraid he saw a distance in her eyes that could mean she was ready to run again. He decided not to take any chances. He picked up the room phone and called the front desk.

JENNIFER SAT SHIVERING ON THE BALCONY. Though the air was hot and bone dry, she couldn't seem to ward off the chill that came from within her. She drifted somewhere between physically ill and numb.

She'd known the accident that had reportedly taken her life as a teenager had been staged, and she'd even asked her mother about it on occasion, but her mother never wanted to talk about it. Now, she knew why.

Jennifer felt a sense of betrayal. She was angry at her mother for keeping the secret from her. Knowing it now served no purpose but to cause a wedge to come between Jennifer and the memories she had of her mother.

Jennifer stared at the aged envelope that she had tossed on the small patio table. She was afraid to open it, knowing whatever it held could not be good.

Pastor Allen's memory of that night had been shockingly precise. Though his voice was shaky, and he had to stop to catch his breath several times during their conversation, he'd explained in detail how the envelope had been hidden in the lining of her mother's suitcase.

Her mother had pleaded with him to make sure no one but Christy ever looked at its contents, and he'd been true to his word. Though the envelope was dog-eared, creased, and even had a corner missing from the flap, it was still sealed with yellowed tape and a rusted fastener.

Jennifer wanted to rip it up. She didn't want to know what else her mother had kept from her. She had thought she and her mother had shared everything, and now she knew there was a part of her mother that she hadn't known at all, a darker side that actually knew someone was going to be killed in order for them to live.

Jennifer's thoughts became too much for her to digest. Her heart was breaking, her cries coming from the very core of her being. *Why, Mom? Why didn't you tell me? Why let me find out this way? What else didn't you tell me? What other secrets did you hide from me?*

The envelope lying on the table pierced her thoughts. An anger rose inside her as she grabbed it and ripped it open, shredding the tops of the documents. She yanked out the papers and held them with shaking hands. She recognized her mother's handwriting, but it wasn't the frail writing of her mother's last days. The pink parchment was dated in the beautiful script that was uniquely her mother's. It had been written five years before her death and begun with the words her mother had used so often.

My dearest Angel,
   If you are reading this letter, it means something has happened to me. I hope you are safe and no harm has come to you. It also means I have never been able to gather the courage to tell you what I'm about to explain.
   Please know that I love you, Angel, and what I did, I did for us.

Jennifer shivered and moved from the patio to the couch in her room. She wiped at her moist eyes before continuing.

You have to know that your father would have stopped at nothing to find us if we had just decided to disappear. The lengths I went to, to assure us our freedom were extreme, and something I have struggled with all these years. I knew the woman and girl that died in our place. I arranged it.

Jennifer tossed her head back, trying to control the revulsion rising inside her. *Why, Mom? How could you have done something like that?* It was a moment before she turned back to the letter, bitterness moistening her lips.

It was horrible and I have no defense, but I saw no other way to ensure our escape. I hired someone to help me locate people who could easily be mistaken for us. Two months before the accident, I was introduced to them.

Her mother's letter went on to explain that Sharon was in her early 30s and addicted to crack. Nicole was a prostitute and living on the streets. Her mother befriended them, offering them her help, which equated to financing Sharon's habit and getting Nicole off the streets. Nicole had no intentions of giving up her night job but was thankful for a place of her own to crash.

The day of the accident, it was Sharon and Nicole in the car. They had been picked up by the man that had switched cars with them in the warehouse and told them they were to take the car and meet her mother at a pre-designated location. The car was rigged. When Sharon lost control of the wheel, she ran into a light post, and the car burst into flames, flames aided by explosives.

Jennifer read on, horrified that her mother also admitted to silencing the man that had helped her. Through a string of contacts, no-named people, and seedy underground characters, she'd made sure the man that had aided them in their escape could never tell anyone of her plans or his involvement.

Her mother's letter was both a confession to the crimes she had kept secret for so many years and an apology to her daughter for not having the guts to tell her sooner. She explained that she'd wanted to tell her, trying many times to broach the subject as she had gotten older, but she could never bring herself to tell her and consequently face the disillusionment she was sure she'd see in her daughter's eyes.

Jennifer closed her eyes not wanting to read further, not wanting to believe her mother was capable of the things she was discovering about her. She dropped the stack of papers to the couch in total exhaustion. *What more, God? My life wasn't bad enough as it was? Now I have this to deal with.*

Jennifer paced back and forth, wanting to scream out loud in frustration but somehow not having the strength to do even that. She glanced at where the stack of papers taunted her from the couch. There was more. She knew it. She could sense it. She walked mechanically back and forth, trying to come to grips with the fact that her mother, the only person she'd ever trusted, the person whom she'd admired and put on a pedestal, in some ways was no better than her father. Her innate humanistic need for survival had calloused her to the idea of taking another person's life. The end justified the means, even if it meánt killing three people. Jennifer took a seat back on the couch and turned to the next page of her mother's letter.

> *There will never be an excuse for my behavior, Angel, but I hope deep down inside you will know that what I did was out of love for you. I would have gladly gone to jail or suffered any punishment for my crimes if it meant that you would have a life apart from the fear and control of your father.*
>
> *There is one more thing that I must tell you. To leave your father was the most terrifying thing I ever had to do. And because of that fear, I made sure I had something of value of your father's before we left, a bartering chip in case he found out the accident had been a set-up.*
>
> *I've carried this information around with me all these years, thankful your father never came after us, but never feeling safe enough to destroy it. I feel torn in giving this information to you, but feel that I must. I've seen the look of defiance and determination in you when we've spoken about what we have gone through and what we have missed out on. I know there is a side of you that wants justice and to see your father pay for what he's done. I'm afraid that after I am gone, you will try to expose your father and make him answer for his abuses. But you have to know the power your father holds and the extent of his corruption.*
>
> *The enclosed papers are copies of a ledger your father kept. It lists the names of the people he owned. These people were very influential—congressman, senators, chiefs of police, judges, and attorneys. Though these people might not be in power when you get this, it shows the far reaches of your father's control. You can be assured that he continues to own powerful men, using them as a buffer between him and those who would seek to take him down.*
>
> *Please, Angelica, continue to live life as best as you can, but I beg you not to try to right any wrongs. If anyone found out that you held this information, your life would be in danger and your father would stop at nothing to silence you. I'm telling you these things not to scare you but to impress upon you the need for you to stay anonymous.*
>
> *I know this is a lot for you to absorb, and I'm sorry I never told you these things before. I guess I was too selfish with what we had, and I couldn't bear to see the disappointment in your eyes. I love you, Angelica. Above all else, I love you.*

Jennifer's tear-filled eyes glanced over the information on the faded ledger paper. The recognizable names and the amounts of money were mind boggling, especially since the accounts were almost 20 years old.

This changed everything. Just a few days ago she had entertained the idea of going to the authorities and trying to get her life straightened out so that she could spend it with Harrison. She knew she couldn't do that now. She would never be able to trust the authorities with her life or the information that she now had in her possession. After all these years, nothing had changed. She would continue to be someone she wasn't, live the life of an imposter, and she would do it alone.

CHAPTER NINETEEN

"Mr. Lynch, she just left in a taxi."

"Do you know where she was going?" Harrison asked as he began shoving things into his overnight bag.

"The airport."

Harrison was kicking himself for not insisting on being with Jennifer after leaving the pastor's house. He knew she was struggling and was headed for a meltdown, but there was a part of him that had hoped she would reach out to him and ask for his help. He hoped she would see him as the one person in her life that wouldn't let her down. He had prayed she would turn to him and God. But instead she did what she instinctively knew to do—she ran.

JENNIFER STARED AT THE DIGITAL BOARD listing arrivals and departures that hung over the ticket counter. Her jumbled emotions were making it hard for her to think. She could leave now for anywhere in the states and try to start over, but this time, she'd be leaving someone behind.

The thought of Harrison caused her eyes to sting. She loved him, and she knew he loved her, but what choice did she have? She couldn't go to the authorities now. She wouldn't know whom to trust. And she could never ask Harrison to live in her world of deception. He deserved better than that.

Exhausted. That was how she felt—mentally, physically, and psychologically exhausted. It seemed as if every ounce of her strength had evaporated beneath the New Mexico sun.

"Ma'am?"

The sharp tinny voice got Jennifer's attention. The ticket agent was waiting for her to volunteer her destination. Jennifer stared at the clerk, feeling as if she had no place to go.

HARRISON FINALLY MADE IT through the airport traffic, bypassing the rental return area, pulling the car to the curb next to the sign that said, "No Parking." He knew when airport security ran a check on it, they would see it was a rental. He would pay stiff penalties for ditching the car, but he didn't care. He had to try and catch up with Jennifer before she disappeared forever.

JENNIFER PUSHED HER BAG in the overhead compartment before taking her seat. She stared out the window, ignoring the commotion of the other passengers as they shuffled down the aisle, taking their seats and trying to get situated. Her legs trembled, and she started twisting her hands together. The anxiousness of being on a plane was hitting her full force, especially since this time she was all alone. She closed her eyes, trying to reign in her feelings. She could feel her throat tighten and her breathing become more labored as a passenger took the seat next to her.

Her senses played with her mind and for a moment, she thought she could breathe in the familiarity of Harrison. A flight attendant introduced herself over the overhead speaker and began to give the in-flight instructions. Jennifer kept her head down and her eyes closed. A slight rocking moved her body back and forth.

And then, it happened again. Just as she was sure her mind was teasing her and filling her senses with what she could only hope for, she felt his hand reach for hers.

She turned to see Harrison looking at her. His rich brown eyes were filled with emotion. He pulled her hand up to his racing heart and pressed it against him.

"Do you feel that?" he asked in a whisper.

She nodded, feeling the tremors in his chest.

"Don't do that to me again, Jennifer." His words were stern but compassionate. "I love you and I am in this with you no matter what happens. Please don't run from me. I'm not your father. Don't treat me like the enemy." He was scolding her yet loving her through it.

She buried her head in his chest and sobbed. He held her close, trying to muffle her cries, so as not to bring attention to them. When she thought she had control, she looked at him and tried to explain, but her voice quivered and sputtered. Harrison hushed her with a gently placed finger to her lips. "It's okay. We can talk about this when we get home." He smiled his reassuring smile and swept the loose strands of her hair behind her ear. "You look exhausted. Why don't you try to get some rest."

The roar of the engines signaled their takeoff. Jennifer clutched Harrison's hand, desperate to cling to the only thing in her life that was real, the only thing she didn't have to pretend about, the only thing worth living for.

THEY WALKED TO WHERE HARRISON HAD LEFT HIS CAR in long-term parking, sharing an embrace but keeping their thoughts to themselves. They loaded their things into his car, pulled on their seatbelts, and held each other's hand atop the center console.

Harrison glanced at her a few times while he maneuvered through traffic before saying, "This doesn't change anything, Jennifer. You're not responsible for what your mother did."

Jennifer didn't answer. There was so much more that Harrison didn't know.

Harrison's phone rang, and he quickly pulled it from his pocket and was relieved to see it was Robert. He'd tried several times while he was in Albuquerque to get ahold of him, but only got his voice mail.

"Robert, where have you been?" The minute the brisk words were out of his mouth, he regretted it. He hadn't meant to sound so harsh. He had just been worried that he hadn't talked to his brother since their blow-up and Robert's payoff over his gambling debt.

"Look, if you're going to start in on me . . . "

"I'm sorry. I didn't mean to snap, I was just concerned that I hadn't heard from you. Is everything okay?"

Robert bristled at what he was sure was a pious tone in his brother's voice.

"Things are fine. Where did you wander off to?"

"Jennifer had some business to attend to so I decided to tag along."

"Really?" Robert said in a tawdry tone. "Sounds cozy."

"It wasn't like that, Robert." Harrison said firmly, getting Jennifer's attention.

"Too bad. You could use some loosening up."

"Look, Robert . . ."

"Relax, Harry, I'm just pulling your chain. Jeez . . . you are such a boy scout. You know, maybe if you got yourself a little time between the sheets you wouldn't be so uptight."

"Oh, and you're the one to be giving me advice on how to live my life?"

Robert was ready to fire off another rebuttal, when Harrison put a stop to it.

"Robert, I'm sure you didn't call to give me advice on my love life."

Jennifer looked at Harrison, wondering what it was Robert was saying.

"Did you get everything straightened out while I was gone?" Harrison changed the subject.

"Yeah. Thanks." His words lacked appreciation.

"You and Kelly doing okay?"

"I'm getting more than you are. Does that answer your question?"

The belligerence in Robert's tone gave away the fact that he'd been drinking. Harrison did what he could to control his temper. He couldn't handle an outburst from Robert over the phone so he decided to back off all together.

"Look, Robert, Jennifer and I have some things to take care of tonight. What do you say we do lunch tomorrow?"

"Sure. Where?"

"The deli?" Harrison suggested.

"Okay, I'll see you around 1:00 p.m. I'll call if I can't make it."

Harrison agreed before ending the call.

"That seemed like a pretty strained conversation. Is everything okay?" Jennifer asked.

"I hope so, but somehow I doubt it."

Harrison pulled into Jennifer's driveway, wondering when she was going to break. Her eyes looked like glass, reflecting everything, but not taking anything in.

Jennifer picked up the junk mail that accumulated just behind the front door while Harrison pulled their luggage from the trunk.

"You would have thought that I'd been gone for a week," Jennifer said, bending over to gather the sale flyers, the satellite offers, and the coupons for carpet cleaning and termite control.

Harrison went to her bedroom and dropped her overnight bag by the dresser. When he walked back to the living room, she was standing in front of the picture window, trying to grasp what her future would hold, the envelope tight in her hand.

He took a seat on the couch and waited. Straightening her shoulders, Jennifer moved to the couch and sat on the edge of the cushion. Reading her body language, Harrison could tell he wasn't going to like what it was she was going to say.

"I can tell from that look what you're going to say. And I can already tell you, you're wrong. Nothing's changed."

"Then read it for yourself." She handed him the envelope.

"Are you sure?" he asked.

She nodded her approval and watched as he pulled the papers from the ragged envelope and began to skim them. His face remained expressionless as he shuffled from the letter to the ledger pages. Jennifer knew the exact moment the relevance of the information hit Harrison. He swallowed hard and let out a long breath. He read again the names that stared back at him. Harrison knew the stakes had just gotten higher, but if they played it right, Jennifer would be able to use it to her advantage.

"You realize this is the proof you were looking for," he said, referring to the stack of papers in his hand. "Now when you go to the authorities they will better understand why you've gone to the lengths that you have. It's no longer your word against your father's. This proves he had most of New York's city and some of its state officials on his payroll. You had no choice but to run. This has proven your case."

"It also proves that I can't trust the authorities. I have no idea how many more people he has in his hip pocket. I can't just walk into the D.A.'s office or go to the FBI with this ledger. I could be turning myself into someone who's on the take."

"Then we won't let that happen. I have a friend . . ."

She started shaking her head before he could even finish. "I can't let you get involved in this, Harrison. If something goes wrong, you can't let people know you had anything to do with me. If I have to disappear again, I can't take the chance that someone will go after you to try and get to me."

"Sorry, it's too late for that. I'm already involved. Besides, if any disappearing is going to be done, I'm going to go with you. I'm not going to let you out of my sight until we get this figured out once and for all."

His look was composed, unaffected by the amplified problems they were now facing. He moved closer to her, holding her hand in his. "We are going to make it through this. God knows your heart. He knows the decisions you've made, and the choices you were forced into making were not your doing. He understands, Jennifer. You've got to believe that."

"Well, I don't understand." She got to her feet. "I don't understand his whole reward and punishment system. The more I ask God to prove himself to be who you claim he is, the worse my situation seems to get. So either he's not in control, or he flat out doesn't care."

"What are you talking about?" Harrison was perplexed as he watched her pace. As far as he knew, other than church, Jennifer hadn't given God a chance.

"I challenged God, Harrison. I asked him to prove himself. I figured if he wanted my respect, then he could give me some clear cut answers."

"Are you talking about your meeting with Pastor Allen?"

"Yeah. I wanted some closure, Harrison, some peace. I wanted to know my mother's final thoughts and then figure out how to go on with my life. Instead, I find out my mother arranged the deaths of three people. Why would God do that to me? Why would he take the only thing that I hold so precious, the memory of my mother, and distort it like that?"

As much as Jennifer was hurting, Harrison was not going to allow her to shift the blame. "Jennifer, you're blaming God for something your mother did. Your mother wrote that letter, you're the one that discovered the note, and you're the one that insisted on meeting with the pastor." With every point he made, her shoulders slumped a little more. "I don't say any of this to make you feel worse, but none of this is God's fault."

"So, you're only willing to give God credit for the good things in life, like seeing me on the beach, or finding me at West Beach Properties, but not the bad things like what happened this weekend, or what happened to my mother, or what happened to me for that matter?" His indictment of her mother's character caused her to lash out at him.

"And you're only willing to credit God for the bad and not the good." He could hear his voice intensifying due to her combativeness, but he wasn't going to let her revel in her condemnation. "Look, you had a lot of obstacles ahead of you this weekend, and you were able to push through every one of them. Just because things didn't go the way you wanted, doesn't mean God let you down. You wanted answers. You got them."

She stood insolently, her arms crossed, not willing to look as if any of what he'd said had penetrated her thinking. Harrison matched her posture and stood firm and unyielding.

They stood in an awkward silence, the only sound coming from the ticking clock on the mantel. Jennifer finally dropped her arms and headed out of the room.

"You can't ignore this Jennifer; you just can't walk away because the pressure is getting to be too much," Harrison taunted.

She stopped and turned to look at him, making sure he didn't miss what she had to say. "Then maybe I'm not walking away from the pressure. Maybe I'm walking away from you."

HARRISON STOOD AT THE END OF THE PIER, his thoughts as tumultuous as the waves in front of him. He wasn't sure if the chill he was feeling was from the spray of the ocean or the fact that he kept replaying Jennifer's words in his mind.

She'd left him standing in the living room, the slamming of her bedroom door punctuating her callous words. Leaving Jennifer's had been the hardest thing he'd ever done. He knew when he walked away that there would be no guarantee he'd ever see her again.

The only thing overshadowing his anger was the throbbing in his heart. He had told himself he would never walk away from Jennifer, but he hadn't expected to be hit with such venomous words.

He kicked at the railing, letting out a loud, guttural groan. Passersby looked his way but quickly went back to their conversations and casual strolls. The realization that God was allowing Jennifer to slip away from him was more than Harrison could handle. Though he believed everything he'd just told Jennifer about God, having to accept the good and the bad, it was finally dawning on him that it was a lesson he hadn't fully learned himself. He had been looking for answers too, asking God how they were going to make it, how they would be able to secure Jennifer's safety, and if she was ever going to turn to him. He realized now he had to prepare himself for answers he hadn't expected.

JENNIFER LAID IN BED, FEELING NUMB AND EMPTY. She'd cried herself to sleep after she realized what she'd done. But now, in the light of a new day, she realized it was for the best. She had never meant to lash out at Harrison, to hurt him so deeply, but to take her words back now would only make life more difficult for the both of them.

They were too different, her problems too complicated. She had struggled with the idea of turning herself in, but now she didn't need to. The only reason she'd been willing to go to the authorities was because of Harrison. And now, with him out of her life, she no longer had to struggle with the thought of exposure. She would continue to live the life she had carved out for herself. She would be alone, but she would be safe. The evidence her mother had left her would go into her suitcase of memories, hidden once again.

She knew Harrison expected her to run, but she wouldn't. There would be no reason to, not anymore. She would ask that Harrison respect her decision, and maybe, after time, he would realize she made the only choice that she could. He would go back to Chicago, and she would stay in Santa Monica. He could move forward in life, and she would have the sweet memory of the weeks they'd spent together.

HARRISON WAS ON THE COUCH when Robert got back to the hotel. It was only a formality that Robert shared a hotel room with Harrison; most of his time was spent at Kelly's or at their new home. He tossed his keys on the counter and stared at Harrison.

"What happened to you?" Robert said, first with a smirk on his face, but when he studied Harrison's demeanor, his grin quickly faded.

Harrison exhaled. "Life."

"What?"

"I won't be seeing Jennifer anymore. It's not going to work."

"You blew it, didn't you?" Robert said with disgust. "You tried brainwashing her with that Bible crap until she just couldn't take it anymore. Well, what do you know—for once the golden boy doesn't get his way. How refreshing to see that you're not perfect after all."

"Thanks for the support, Robert. It's good to know when I need someone to talk to, you'll be there for me. Oh, that's right," Harrison said with a mocking voice. "You've never been there for me. The only time you care about me is when you're in debt up to your eyeballs, and you need someone to bail you out. Well that stops tonight. No more. If you can't get your act together before the wedding, you don't deserve to be married. If I've learned one thing through all of this is that opposites might attract, but they seldom change, no matter how hard they try."

Harrison left the room before Robert could say anything. He turned the handle of the shower nozzle, and steam almost immediately filled the room. He took an extra long shower. The pain of the scalding water was nothing compared to the pain ripping at his insides. He dried off and got dressed. When he walked to the kitchenette for a soda, Robert was in the living room waiting for him. Harrison ignored him.

"I'm sorry, Harrison. I know how much she meant to you."

"Whatever. I know you. As far as you're concerned, you probably think I should go pick up a hooker, spend the night having sex and getting drunk, and forget I ever met her."

"True. That would work for me, but I know that's not your style."

Harrison ignored Robert and headed back toward his room. "Come on, Harry. I'm trying here. I don't know what to say. Dang, I can't even keep my own life straight."

Harrison stopped, hearing the effort in his brother's voice. He sat on the couch and put his feet up on the coffee table.

"What happened? Is it because of her past?" Robert asked, moving to take a seat.

"Yeah. She found out a few details on our trip that complicate things even more."

"More? How much more complicated could things get?"

"Let's just say, the information she now holds could blow her father out of the water or get her head blown off if it falls into the wrong hands." Harrison flinched at the thought of it.

"So, does that mean she's going to skip town?"

"I don't know. Right now, she's safe because no one knows she has the information, or that it even exists. But it's enough to keep her quiet and not willing to come out of hiding. I guess you could say we've reached an impasse. I'm not willing to live a life of deception, and she knows nothing else."

"But Harry, with your money, you two could live anywhere in the world. She wouldn't have to come out of hiding. She would just become Mrs. Harrison Lynch. Voila, a new identity."

"It's not that simple, Robert."

He thought a moment, studying Harrison. "So, it is the religious stuff that's coming between you."

"Robert, you don't understand. My commitment is important to me. As much as I love Jennifer, I can't just push it aside. This is my own fault." Harrison stood, feeling frustration rising inside him again. "I should have never allowed myself to get so close to Jennifer. I guess I was just hoping I would be able to show her what was missing in her life."

"I think you did," Robert said will all seriousness. "She wants you."

"Not anymore. I think we both finally realized our differences are too big to ignore."

"So, what are you going to do now?"

"I'll be going back to Chicago after the wedding. It will make it easier if I stay busy and put some distance between me and Jennifer. I don't want to put any more pressure on her. She's made her decision. I just have to figure out how I'm going to live with it."

"And Jennifer?"

"You mean, Samantha?" Harrison corrected him. "I guess she'll keep doing what she's doing. I don't see any reason for her to have to change, at least not now."

There was a knock at the door. A look of hope colored Harrison's eyes. He pulled back on the door, only to see Kelly standing there.

"Hi, Harrison," she said brightly as she walked into the room. "I'm glad you're here. I wanted to invite you and Samantha over to our new home." She gave Robert a quick kiss before continuing. "Nothing formal. I just want her to see the decorating I've been doing. A lot of the ideas are ones I discussed with her, and I thought she might want to see the final product before our dinner with your parents."

Harrison smiled politely. "Sounds like time better spent just the two of you. I'm sure she'd love to see what you've done. You'll have to give her a call."

Kelly glanced back and forth between Robert and Harrison. "Okay, I'm missing something here, aren't I?"

"Things between Harry and Samantha have kind of cooled. I don't think we have to worry about that introductory dinner after all." Robert used buffered words. "Why don't you just invite her over for lunch or something?"

Kelly dropped her hands to her side and then studied Harrison for a moment. "You're sure about this? I mean you two have shared a lot of history. Maybe you've just had a little set back, a misunderstanding?"

"I'm pretty sure we understand each other," Harrison answered politely, though his words were strained. "There are just a few things that we seem to keep running up against. As much as I love her, I don't see these things as debatable. That's just the way it is."

Kelly put her hand to his shoulder and smiled. "To tell you the truth, Harrison, I think it's for the better. With her background, you would never know what you were up against. You deserve better than that."

Harrison bristled at Kelly's armchair psychology. There she stood, acting as if she knew all there was to know about relationships, dispensing advice, when she didn't even realize the sordid details in her soon-to-be husband's background. Harrison decided not to comment. He just walked into his room and closed the door.

Robert looked at her with irritation and whispered. "What was that all about? I thought you liked Samantha?"

She answered back in her own hushed tones. "I do, as a realtor. But after finding out all that stuff about her life the other night, it kind of freaked me out. Look, I did a little checking."

"Checking . . . why?" Robert acted annoyed.

"Come on, she tells us she's from some powerful family with a father so horrible she had to fake her own death, and you aren't the least bit interested?"

Robert gave her a shrug and asked. "So, what did you find out?"

"Well," she said with excitement, wanting to share her discovery. "I researched accidents that happened around the time Samantha would have been in her teens. I searched for anything in New York involving a mother and daughter. There were several of course, but only one that got front page news because of who the family was—the Calderon family."

The notorious name got Robert's attention while Kelly continued.

"If I'm right, he isn't just some low-life criminal. He's dangerous, very dangerous. I don't think Harrison knows the seriousness of his situation. He's let love blind him to the cold, hard facts. She's a danger, bottom line. He's better off without her. I know I'll feel a lot better knowing she's not connected to your family."

Robert chewed on what Kelly was saying and had to agree. He hadn't given much thought to Harrison being in danger because he was more focused on his own mounting problems.

He looked at Kelly and the way she smiled at him with complete naiveté. She didn't know it, but she was worse off than Harrison. At least Harrison had a glimpse of what he was getting into with Jennifer. Kelly, on the other hand, was completely clueless about Robert's situation and the very real danger he was in. If he didn't come up with $500,000 before his wedding, there would be no wedding. In fact, there would be no groom.

Kelly noticed a change in Robert's complexion. "Robert, what's wrong?"

He'd broken out into a cold sweat at the thought of what it was he had to do. "Nothing, I'm fine."

"You're not fine. You're dripping in sweat, and you're white as a sheet."

He quickly pulled the back of his hand across his forehead and around his mouth. "I think I might be coming down with something. Don't worry, it's nothing."

"It better not be. Listen; let's go get you some medicine. The wedding is just a few weeks away, and I don't want to take any chances."

HARRISON CALLED WEST BEACH PROPERTIES first thing Monday morning. He had to know. He had to know if Jennifer was gone.

"West Beach Properties. This is Julie."

Harrison got nervous the minute he heard someone's voice besides Jennifer's. "Samantha Wilder, please."

"One moment please. May I tell her who's calling?" Harrison hung up, feeling a sense of relief. She hadn't run; she was just screening her calls, no doubt so she didn't have to talk to him.

He spent the day pouring over his computer, trying to ignore the hole in his heart. He set up conference calls with his associates, getting brought up to speed on the projects he'd left them in charge of.

Harrison wandered aimlessly around the hotel room between calls, feeling as if its spaciousness was shrinking with every hour. He felt trapped, confined. With every breath he took, he thought of Jennifer.

He picked up the phone numerous times throughout the day. He wanted to hear her voice and give her a chance to take back her rejection. But every time he brought the phone up to his ear or pressed her quick-dial number, he stopped himself. She had made her choice, and he had to be willing to let her go.

JENNIFER SAT STARING AT THE OCEAN through her office window. She had expected to hear from Harrison by now, and for every hour that slipped away, she knew he was respecting the choice she had made. As much as she wanted to take it back, to tell him she was sorry, she knew she couldn't.

Her phone buzzed. She turned sharply, reaching for it like it was a life line.

"Samantha, Kelly Andrews is on the phone. Should I put her through?"

Jennifer sighed. "Go ahead."

"Samantha, I heard about you and Harrison. I'm sorry."

Jennifer tightened her jaw. Kelly's perky voice showed no sign of commiserating at all. "What can I do for you, Kelly?"

"Well, I don't see why your situation with Harrison should interfere with our friendship." Jennifer rolled her eyes. Kelly was being her typical self-centered self as she continued to rattle on. "I've been working hard on the house with designers and decorators, and I wanted to show it to you. I'm not completely done, but between the dinner I'm throwing for Robert's parents, my upcoming wedding showers and luncheons, and the final details for the wedding, I wouldn't get a chance to show it to you until after the honeymoon. And since we're going to be gone for a month, I didn't know if you'd still be around when we got back."

Jennifer wasn't sure what dig hurt more, the fact that the dinner Kelly had been planning once included her, or the reference to her not being around in a month. She was accustomed to Kelly's abruptness, but having it directed at her was a little hard to accept.

"I'm not really in the mood for socializing, Kelly, but thank you for asking." Jennifer tried to be courteous.

"Oh, come on, Samantha. I really want to know what you think. Please?"

Jennifer was torn. She had enjoyed talking, designing, and decorating with Kelly. It would be incredible to see what she'd done with the house, and if, in fact, Kelly had taken any of her suggestions.

"You're not setting me up, are you? I mean, I'm not going to get there and find out Harrison is there, and you're trying to smooth things over between us?"

"No. I promise you. That is not what this is about." Kelly's voice took on a serious tone. "Look, I'm sorry that things didn't work out for you and Harrison, but I'm not going to try and play matchmaker. You two are adults. I think you better know if you have what it takes to weather your differences."

Jennifer was surprised by Kelly's no-nonsense attitude but appreciated her candor. She decided to accept her invitation. She needed to do something besides going home and let loneliness surround her. She arranged to meet Kelly at the house.

Harrison was out for a jog, his way of working out the tension that had his body in knots. Robert was glad to finally have the room to himself and the chance to jump on Harrison's computer. He made sure he had an internet connection and then did some surfing.

Kelly had given him the name of a mob guy in New York that she thought could be Samantha's father. He typed it in and watched as a page of matches unfolded, the first of many. He scrolled the first few pages, and then saw the headline, "Crime Boss' Family Killed in Crash." Robert hit the link, which took him back to a front page story from the *New York Times* archives. The article was 19 years old.

Robert read the details of the fiery crash that took the lives of Monica Calderon and her 13-year-old daughter, Angelica. The article went on to say that the accident had been investigated for foul play due to the notoriety of Carlos Calderon, but that the police had finally ruled the accident an unfortunate tragedy. The photos attached to the article showed a car completely burned out and a grief-stricken Carlos Calderon. It took a couple of cross-references for Robert to finally find a picture of Monica Calderon. She was standing with a group of women at a charity function held a year prior to the accident. Though the picture wasn't very clear, there was no doubt in Robert's mind that it was of Samantha's mother. The strong resemblance was a dead giveaway.

He heard Harrison's key in the door and quickly closed the windows on the laptop. Harrison came in, breathing heavy, perspiration soaking through his t-shirt and across his face. When he saw Robert sitting at his computer, he gave him a puzzled look.

"I needed to check some of my investments. I figured you wouldn't mind if I used your computer. My Blackberry is great, but my head is pounding and I didn't want the strain of looking at the screen."

Harrison went to the fridge and grabbed a bottle of water. By the time he walked back to the living room and peered over Robert's shoulder, the NYSE site filled the screen.

"I'm going to go grab a shower. You going to be here when I get out?"

"Right here."

Robert waited to hear the bathroom door shut and the water running. Then he quickly went to work on Harrison's computer, deleting temporary and history files. As long as Harrison didn't get suspicious and check up on him, he'd never know he'd found out Jennifer's real identity.

He jumped around the internet some more, to put back some files on the history. Then he closed it down, flipped on the T.V. and got involved in a ball-game.

Harrison wandered out from his shower, feeling only a slight improvement in his attitude. He raked his fingers through his wet hair and relaxed on the couch. He reached for his computer and rested it on his lap. He turned it on and waited for his desktop to come up. It took him only a few minutes to know that Robert was hiding something. He glanced at Robert as he watched the ballgame, wondering what he was up to.

CHAPTER TWENTY

Jennifer pulled up to the imposing wrought-iron gates that flanked the long brick driveway. She could see two cars parked in front of the four garage stalls as she stretched to press the intercom button. She recognized Kelly's car, but wondered who the other one belonged to. She waited, thinking that maybe the security system was activated. She pressed the button again, this time Kelly was quick to respond.

"Sorry, Samantha, I'm still getting used to the system."

Jennifer heard a buzz of electricity and watched as the gates slowly opened. She pulled around the slope of the circular driveway and stopped in front of the massive portico. Kelly met her at the door with a look that seemed distant and preoccupied.

"Kelly, are you all right?"

Kelly stepped closer to her and in a whispering tone said, "I'm having a little dispute with one of my decorators."

"Oh, I can come back another time." Jennifer took a step back towards the driveway.

"No!" Kelly's words were abrupt, and she quickly controlled her voice before saying anything more. "I need your opinion." Kelly clutched onto Jennifer's arm and drew her into the tiled entryway. "I wanted to use only linen in our bedroom." Kelly continued as she ushered her down the hall towards the master suite. "I wanted it to be cool and welcoming so Robert would feel comfortable, but Marcus is insisting that I use silks. He feels that linen would ruin the aura of the house. I think he's being ridiculous. It's my house. Besides, its nobody's business what our bedroom looks like. What do you think?"

Before Jennifer could even formulate an opinion, she walked into the master suite and came face-to-face with the disconcerted decorator. He acknowledged her with a full length glance and an air of disinterest.

"Fine, Kelly, do what you want," he said with an exaggerated flair. "You didn't need to bring in reinforcements."

"Marcus, don't get so upset. I didn't call in reinforcements. This is Samantha Wilder, my realtor."

She smiled at him uncomfortably, not liking that she'd been drawn into an obvious stand-off.

"But since you're here, Samantha, what do you think of these fabrics?"

Kelly stepped aside and pointed to a chair that had two different swaths of material tossed over it.

Jennifer stole a quick glance at Kelly and then walked over and touched the fabrics. She ran her thumb across each one, enjoying their luxurious texture.

"If it were me, I would go for the silk. It's absolutely gorgeous."

Kelly looked deflated while Marcus smiled with satisfaction.

"But if I were a newlywed and wanted my new husband to appreciate all my efforts, I would make sure he was as comfortable as possible. I would have to go with the linen. It might not be as indulgent as the silk, but it will still look amazing and put a man more at ease."

Kelly straightened up, realizing what Jennifer was doing. She knew how to handle people. She was smart enough not to walk into a room and insult a designer to his face. She'd made sure to compliment his choice first, even if she didn't agree with him.

Marcus scowled at both of them and threw up his hands. "Fine, Kelly. You win." The designer scooped up the fabrics and draped them over his arm. Kelly moved Jennifer into the master bathroom to show her the latest touches she'd made to the already luxurious space.

When they were done, Marcus was still standing in the bedroom, material in hand.

"What's wrong, Marcus?" Kelly asked.

His eyes wandered the expanse of the room. "I was just thinking, what if we go with a darker color palette? It would complement the living room and add mystery and seduction to the most important room in the house."

He raised his eyebrow at Kelly, trying to make her see the allure of darker tones.

"Marcus, we've already talked about this. Robert does not want to feel as if he's sleeping in a dungeon. We decided on light colors, end of discussion."

With a flamboyant turn, Marcus stormed to the door.

"I'll need the bedroom ensemble completed in the next two weeks. Don't stall just because you didn't get your way." Kelly's attitude was harsh and demanding.

"I am contracted to you until the end of this project. I am at your beck-and-call and will make sure everything is perfect before the wedding day. But believe me, you will pay handsomely for all the long hours I'm putting in."

"You live up to your end of the contract, and I'll live up to mine. Because if you don't, I'll make sure everyone who ever steps into my home knows that Marcus Denali is not a man of his word."

Marcus turned and glared at her, clearly agitated by her threat. But he didn't say anything, he simply walked away.

Kelly took a breath as if to clear her thoughts of all unpleasantness. She turned an excited smile on Samantha. "Come on, I want you to see the living room."

When Jennifer stepped down into the lavish living room, she was without words. The room that had been beautiful but empty just weeks before, now burgeoned with lavish furnishings, ornate accessories, and massive sculptures and artwork.

Jennifer allowed her hand to travel across a Charles X rosewood table with inlaid works of ivy.

"It's an original," Kelly announced. "My mother bought it for me when she was in Italy last year."

Jennifer's eye took in the way Kelly had been able to bring together Italian antiques and modern flair. She noticed the armless chairs with inlaid Italian alabaster, and the classic baroque Lombard bureau, obviously imported from Italy. But it was the way she'd blended them so flawlessly with the traditional chocolate leather sofa and loveseat that lent comfort and ease to the room. There were Italian vases and novelty items on the end tables and mantel, leaving no doubt that the room was inspired by the architecture of the house, but the warmth of the room was soothing and inviting.

"Well, what do you think?" Kelly was bursting with enthusiasm.

Jennifer went over to the floor-to-ceiling French doors that led out onto the terrace. "If I didn't know better, I would think I was in a villa overlooking the Bay of Naples."

"Do you really like it?" Kelly clapped her hands together like a child who'd just won a prize.

"I think it's absolutely beautiful. You've done a wonderful job."

"You really think so?" Kelly wanted to hear more words of affirmation.

"Are you kidding me—it's magnificent! What does Robert think?"

Kelly's smile twisted into a grimace. "He doesn't care as long as it's not costing him a penny, which I keep having to remind him of when he sees the receipts in the study." Kelly smiled again. "Come on, come see the kitchen."

When Kelly and Jennifer walked into the kitchen, Jennifer was sure she heard footsteps. She quickly turned to look at all corners of the room. "Didn't you hear that?" Jennifer asked

"Hear what?" Kelly acted unaware.

"I heard footsteps. Is someone else here?"

"No. Just us."

Jennifer glanced around again. When she didn't hear or see anything, she figured it was her own paranoia edging its way into her senses. She turned back to Kelly and allowed her to elaborate about every detail of the kitchen.

Next they looked at the formal dining room, entertainment room, and exercise room. After two hours of listening in detail about every find and every purchase Kelly had made in the last year, they made their way to the guest rooms. When Jennifer found each one of them finished to perfection, it caused her to wonder.

"What's that look for?" Kelly asked.

"I don't understand something, Kelly. Why is it that your guest rooms are done before the master suite? I would have thought you'd have done it the other way around."

"Well, my bridesmaids fly in next week. They'll be staying with me before the wedding, helping with final details and such. I want their rooms to be perfect when they arrive."

Jennifer had a follow-up question but didn't dare to voice it. She tried to listen as Kelly described how she found the antique headboard for one of the guestrooms at an estate sale a few years back. As Kelly rambled on, Jennifer couldn't help but begin to feel sorry for Robert. It seemed that everything Kelly did was about her, and her family, and her friends. The only time Kelly had spoken about Robert all afternoon was when she talked about his complaining.

"Okay, there's that look again. What is it this time?" Kelly crossed her arms and waited for Jennifer to speak up. Jennifer debated whether to say anything or not. Her irritable side got the better of her and before she knew it, she'd blurted out her question.

"Do you love Robert?"

"What?" Kelly nearly gasped.

"Do you love Robert?"

"What makes you ask that?"

Answering a question with a question was not a good sign.

"It just seems like . . . I don't know . . . like you tolerate him more than you love him. You keep talking about his complaining and how difficult he's been during all you're decorating and the wedding plans. You haven't said one nice thing about him all day."

"Well, maybe because he has been annoying and argumentative and irritating lately."

"Then how do you know you truly love him?"

"Because we're good together. We complement each other." The hint of belligerence in Kelly's tone, revealed her own uncertainties. "I know how to act in his world, with his business contacts, and he knows how to act in mine, around my family and our associates. He knows how to handle businessmen, and I know how to work a room. We complete each other."

"You just described a business partnership, Kelly."

"Then maybe that's what we have." Kelly planted her hands on her hips and got indignant. "Don't start spouting off to me about true, happy-ever-after love. I had that once. I was engaged to the most wonderful guy and then, boom, he was gone, killed in a boating accident. I was numb and never wanted to be touched again, not like that. But eventually I pulled out of my self-imposed prison and started living again, and living is what I did. I enjoy the fast lane, Samantha, and Robert fits into that world. He's exciting and daring. He doesn't mind taking chances. I feel good when his body's up against mine, and I feel alive when I know that I turn him on. Maybe it's not love, maybe it's just sex or passion, but I'm all right with that for now. We both signed a pre-nup, so no one is taking anyone for their money. It could lead to love, then again maybe it won't.

I'm willing to try and see. All I know is right now, I'd do anything for Robert, and I know he'd do anything for me. If things don't work out in the long run, we walk away from each other, glad for the good times we had. End of story."

Jennifer felt as if she'd just been physically assaulted. Kelly's words were filled with emotion, but not the emotion Jennifer was looking for. Kelly was being fueled by apathy not love.

"What, no rebuttal?" Kelly snapped.

"What am I suppose to say, that you're a sorry excuse for a fiancée? That you're a spoiled debutant who is so used to getting her own way she's willing to destroy another person in the process? I'm sorry, Kelly, I guess I gave you more credit then you deserve."

Jennifer turned to walk away, but Kelly stopped her. "Then answer me one question. Who's worse off—me or you?"

"What do you mean by that?" Jennifer was confused and annoyed at the way Kelly was turning the tables on her.

"The way I see it, at least I have a chance at love. Mine and Robert's relationship might not be perfect, but we're willing to make a go at it. What's your excuse? Harrison is everything a woman would want in a man. He worships the ground you walk on, even with your dysfunctional past. And what do you do? You shut him out of your life like he's a stray mutt scratching at your door. So, who's worse off—me or you? At least I'm taking a chance at love, but you're letting it slip away."

Jennifer turned away from the sting of Kelly's words. She was right. Jennifer had no business lecturing anyone on the essence of love. The old adage "Physician heal thyself" jumped into Jennifer's thoughts. When she turned back to Kelly, she saw someone just outside on the patio. She lunged in front of Kelly, reached for the handle of the door and flung it wide open only to find Marcus standing with his back against the wall trying to hide himself.

"What are you doing? Why do you keep watching me?" Jennifer felt Marcus' presence had something to do with her.

"I wasn't watching you; I was listening to Kelly."

"What are you talking about, Marcus?" Kelly jumped in.

He stood taller now, trying to regain some of his composure. He pulled at the collar of his jacket and again at the hem. "I wanted to see what you were saying about me when I wasn't around."

Kelly let out an absurd laugh. "You were spying on me—you insecure little weasel!"

"I refuse to take this abuse any longer!" the designer sputtered. "You can find someone else to finish your house. I quit." He turned on his Italian leather loafers, and for dramatic flair, marched around the side yard to the driveway.

Jennifer felt horrible. "Kelly, I'm sorry. This is all my fault. I shouldn't have talked so rudely to him or to you. It's not my place to judge or analyze your relationship. I'm sorry for what I said."

"Don't worry about it." Kelly was quick to accept her apology, something that surprised Jennifer. She had expected Kelly to be the kind of person to write people off, like she'd just done to her decorator.

"What about Marcus? How will you finish the master suite in time?"

"Don't worry. I'll take care of it myself. He was beginning to get on my nerves anyway. You would think this is his house or something."

Kelly walked Jennifer to the door and out to her car. "You're still coming to the wedding aren't you?" Kelly spoke as if the argument they'd just had never even happened.

"I don't know, Kelly. I don't want to make things difficult for Harrison or his family."

"You won't be. Harrison's a big boy; he can take care of himself. And his parents won't even know who you are. Just a face in the crowd, like you wanted." Kelly smiled a compelling smile.

"Okay, I'll go to the service and make an appearance at the reception, but only so I can see how beautiful you and all your plans turn out."

"Thanks, Samantha, you don't know how much this means to me."

Kelly stood in the driveway and watched as Jennifer exited, smiling at her own art of persuasion.

IT WAS ONLY DAYS BEFORE THE WEDDING and Harrison thought for sure that at any moment Robert was going to jump out of his skin. Robert waited for Harrison to go down to the hotel weight room before making his call. He'd been smart enough to pick up one of those pre-paid phones at a local store, just to be safe. He didn't want the call to be connected to him in any way.

"Hello, Carlos Calderon, please."

"Mr. Calderon is busy." The man's voice was brash and impatient.

"I think he'll want to talk to me, that is if he wants to find out the where-abouts of his daughter Angelica."

CHAPTER TWENTY-ONE

Jennifer sat on the edge of her bed with a heap of dresses piled beside her. She'd tried on each and every one, trying to find the perfect one to wear to Kelly and Robert's wedding.

She knew what she was doing. She wanted to wear something that would catch Harrison's attention just so she could see his beautiful brown eyes gaze at her once more. It was cruel and unfair, but she couldn't help herself. She wasn't going because she wanted to see Kelly's plans played out before her; she was going because she wanted to see Harrison.

Jennifer finally decided on a flowing, yellow camisole-style dress. Its sheer layers and soft colors gave it a Victorian look, and its pale color played off the bronze of her skin.

She scrutinized herself in the mirror, turning from side to side. The ivory heels she'd chosen added to the vintage look. She curled her hair so that it fell softly across her shoulders. She didn't bother with much make-up, knowing the service would probably make her cry. She gave herself one more backward glance before picking up her purse along with the envelope she planned on mailing to Harrison. He wouldn't get it until he returned to Chicago, but the enclosed note would explain why she'd sent it. She locked the door behind her and walked the side path to her car.

The activity in the church parking lot was being directed by a hired security detail. Jennifer had to show her invitation to even be allowed in. Leave it to Kelly to think of everything. Jennifer stepped from her car into the beautiful sunshine. Another typical day in Malibu. Kelly would have it no other way.

As Jennifer crossed the lot, an uneasy feeling came over her. She glanced over her shoulder, only to see more attendees making their way towards the church. Jennifer shook it off, deciding it was just her imagination working over-time. She'd been wakened almost every night that week by a nightmare that wouldn't go away. She couldn't recall any scenes from it; she only remembered the panic she felt every time she sprung up in bed, covered in perspiration.

She pulled some mints from her purse and tossed them in her mouth. She shook away the feeling of dread and slowly walked up the steps of the ornate chapel.

She was escorted to a seat on the bride's side of the sanctuary by a handsomely dressed usher in a black tuxedo. She sat at the end of the pew and admired the large flower arrangements draping the aisle. Hundreds of people filled the room to capacity. Huge cascades of flowers and dramatic candelabras decorated the massive platform. Music floated from the string quartet, filling the grand room with the sounds of romance and love.

Jennifer looked over the program she'd been handed. She brushed her fingers across the raised lettering and felt the gilded and tattered edges of the elegant stationery. She saw Harrison's name listed as best man and thought there was no truer description.

The tempo of the music changed and a hush fell over the room. Everyone's attention turned to the back of the church, waiting for the start of the processional. Jennifer's heart skipped a beat when she turned to see Harrison standing with what could only be his mother. She was beautiful in a matronly way. Small figure, silver hair, and a soft smile, but it was her eyes that stood out to Jennifer. Harrison had his mother's eyes.

Jennifer shrunk back to hide behind the form of a rather large woman, hoping not to be seen. When Harrison glided past where she was sitting, it seemed as if something drew his attention and he turned just in time to get a glimpse of her. She used the moment to take one last look at what she was leaving behind.

She didn't know she was crying until she felt the first teardrop fall on her hands that were folded neatly in her lap. She quickly brushed the tear aside and stood as the music announced the entrance of the bride. Kelly looked exquisite, like the bride in a fairy tale wedding with a huge flowing gown, beautiful flowers, and a small tiara nestled in her upswept hair. She looked perfect. She floated down the aisle on her father's arm until she reached Robert. He stepped forward and pulled her close to his side, and they walked the final steps up the altar together.

Jennifer didn't remember the music or the vows or the triumphant recessional. She only remembered seeing Harrison and the sadness that seemed to be weighing him down. He smiled for his brother's sake, and when he had his mother on his arm. But she could tell he was hurting, and she knew it was because of her.

She debated with herself all the way to the reception. She'd pulled off the mapped path twice and then begrudgingly got back on the right track because she had promised Kelly to be there. She finally decided that the least she could do was stay until the bridal party showed up. Once again she was asked to show her invitation at the valet booth outside the stately mansion of Kelly's parents. Her car keys were taken and she was escorted to a red carpet that led all the way up to the white canopy erected alongside the house.

When she stepped inside the canopy, she was greeted by a tuxedo-clad waiter who took her invitation and then handed it back with a small card, signifying where she'd be sitting. Jennifer's eyes gazed around at the canopy that was anything but run-of-the-mill. One side was held up by large, white, plantation style shutters that served as doors to the gardens and expansive lawns. It gave a very open feeling to the elegant enclosure. Everything was white—the tablecloths, the china, the flowers—everything. A champagne fountain filled one corner of the tent while an enormous eight-tier wedding cake with flowers flowing down its sides filled out the other. Petite crystal chandeliers with votive candles hung low over every table, giving the room a soft glow. The chairs were draped in linen and small boxes of truffles sat at every place setting. To help guests find their assigned seats, ornate sterling silver letters were showcased in bouquets of white lilies and orchids. Jennifer's card said she was sitting at table "RR" in the back row. She'd been put at the back at her request. She told Kelly she would not want to do anything to ruin Harrison's evening. Her hope was that she'd be able to see him, but he wouldn't see her.

Jennifer took her seat and immediately a waiter was at her side asking her what she'd like to drink. Her heart said scotch, wanting to deaden her pain, but her mind was sharp enough to remember she'd be driving home.

"Lemon water, please."

Jennifer watched as people mingled with each other, wandered to find their seats, and awed over the cake and decorations. She was surprised to hear music drifting in through carefully placed speakers. She thought for sure she'd heard Kelly talk about having a live band and a dance floor but they were nowhere to be seen. Jennifer was surprised to see such key elements missing.

A middle-aged couple took two seats across from Jennifer and quickly tried to draw her into conversation. Soon Jennifer knew they were the Dawsons, long-time associates of Kelly's father. They lived in Morro Bay, had two sons, a daughter, and three grandkids. They chattered on about how disappointed they were with their youngest son and the choices he was making, but quickly asked if Jennifer was single because she would be perfect for him.

She wanted to laugh out loud and ask them how exactly was she perfect for their loser son that just got out of rehab for the second time and only had three months left on his probation? But she didn't. She just smiled at their suggestion and politely declined.

People began to fill the tent. Jennifer recognized the mayor, two assemblymen, and several celebrities. The Andrews family was definitely well connected.

Jennifer began to get anxious. She'd already been there an hour and the bridal party still hadn't arrived. She made her way to a table that had cascading white and dark chocolate running down crystal pedestals. Skewers of strawberries, mangos, kiwi, pineapple, and oranges were arranged in bouquets looking almost too beautiful to eat.

She gently pulled a few skewers from the arrangement and allowed the white chocolate to run over them. She placed them on a china plate and made her way back to her table. The canopy was now filled to capacity, as was her table. The other three couples politely introduced themselves to Jennifer. She just quietly took her seat and ate her fruit.

The murmurings of the guests now sounded like a dull roar. She glanced across the room and saw Marcus Denali, the interior decorator. She was surprised to see him after the falling out he'd had with Kelly. He stood glaring at her but glanced away when they made eye contact. He made her feel uneasy.

There was a rise in commotion as the guests saw the wedding party approaching the tent. Robert and Kelly were beaming, clutching each other's hands, and exchanging playful kisses. Even after her confrontation with Kelly where Kelly admitted she wasn't sure what she felt for Robert was love, Jennifer hoped they would survive the odds and truly fall in love with each other.

When Jennifer saw Harrison, she felt a stinging in her eyes. She realized this would probably be the last time she'd ever see him. At that moment, she heard the striking of a band. She turned around to see the entire left side of the canopy pulled back like a curtain, exposing a parquet dance floor, a live band, and several more tables. The table where Kelly and Robert would sit was elevated and centered. There were tables for the bridesmaids and their guests, the groomsmen and their guests, and for extended family. The bandleader announced the arrival of Mr. and Mrs. Robert Lynch, Jr., causing the room to erupt in applause and a standing ovation. Clinking glasses replaced the applause, signifying that the guests wanted the couple to kiss, and Robert was only too happy to oblige them. The bandleader declared that he would be playing a special dedication from the groom to the bride. Robert pulled Kelly close as the band started playing, "The Way You Look Tonight." While all eyes were on the bride and groom, Jennifer's eyes were on Harrison. She watched as he took his seat with the other groomsmen, each of them having a date—all, that is, except for Harrison. He briefly scanned the room, and Jennifer couldn't help but think he was looking for her. A waiter bent down next to Harrison, asking him what he wanted to drink.

Jennifer smiled as the waiter returned with what looked like a glass of water with a lemon on the rim. She continued to watch Harrison as the music played on and others began to fill dance floor. She remembered the way it felt when she'd danced with Harrison in New Mexico, the warmth of his hand at the small of her back, and the feel of his breath on her neck as he held her close. She closed her eyes and allowed herself to experience it all over again.

When she rejoined the present, Jennifer saw photographers canvassing the room, taking pictures of people on the dance floor, those who were mingling, and others seated at their tables. Jennifer slipped from her seat as one photographer approached, making herself unavailable. She wandered along the fringes of the tent, trying to blend in with the decor.

"Good evening, Samantha."

Jennifer didn't have to turn around to know that Harrison was standing close behind her. She slowly turned and looked up to find his eyes sparkling in the glow of the candlelight.

"Good evening, Harrison."

"Beautiful wedding, wasn't it?"

"Breathtaking."

Silence hung between them. Harrison was desperate for her to say she was wrong and that she wanted him back. Jennifer was looking for a way of escape, knowing her resolve was weakening.

"Where's the butterflies?" Jennifer blurted out. "Kelly had said she was going to release butterflies at the reception."

"She found out if they were released after sunset, they would die. She didn't want to take the chance of having hundreds of dead butterflies on the lawn for the remainder of the reception."

"Oh."

The silence between them returned. Even in a room filled with people talking and laughing, and a band playing in the background, all Jennifer could hear was the awkward silence between them. Harrison couldn't take his off her, knowing it might be the last time he'd ever see her.

Harrison leaned in closer. "Jennifer, please, let's go somewhere and talk."

She felt her knees quiver, and her breath grow rapid. She knew it had been a bad idea to come. She should have never thought she could handle seeing Harrison, not like this, not when everything surrounding them spoke of love, commitment, and happily ever after. Her life would never have a fairy tale ending.

She turned to leave, but Harrison gently reached for her arm. "Please, Jennifer, don't do this to us."

She exhaled and looked up into his searching eyes. "There is no us, Harrison. There is no Jennifer. She's just someone you helped one night through a bad winter storm."

Jennifer slipped from his grasp and went directly to the exit. A waiter stood there blocking her path.

"I am sorry, madame. We've been asked to keep the doors closed at this time, while dinner is being served."

Jennifer looked at him like he was crazy, but the lights were quickly extinguished as a parade of waiters walked into the room, holding trays over their heads, with sparklers bursting with excitement. The effect was dramatic, giving the feel of an indoor fireworks display.

"If you'll take your seat, the doors will be opened momentarily."

Jennifer slipped back to her seat where the Dawsons and the other three couples looked on with awe. After a few moments, they went back to their own conversations, the men talking politics, while the women continued on about decorating. They were trying to come up with subtle ways of finagling an introduction with Kelly's decorators. It irritated Jennifer because they were acting as if they were trying to arrange an audience with the queen. They went on and on until finally Jennifer butted into their conversation and said, "Look, her designer's name is Marcus Denali, and he's sitting right over there." She turned to point in Marcus' direction, only to find that he was once again staring at her. He abruptly turned and Jennifer looked back at the women.

Mrs. Dawson huffed. "Well, I don't know where you obtained your information, my dear, but that is not one of Kelly's designers. I was told by her mother that she was working closely with Franco Decicco and Voli direct from Italy. I don't know who this Marcus person is, but I can tell you who he isn't."

Jennifer turned a sharp eye on Marcus. He turned from her and got up from his chair. Jennifer sat stunned and confused, not knowing what to make of it. Why would Kelly introduce him as one of her decorators if he wasn't? Maybe he was an assistant and Jennifer misunderstood her. She replayed the conversation in her head: *"You live up to your end of the contract, and I'll live up to mine. Because if you don't, I'll make sure everyone who ever steps into my home knows that Marcus Denali is not a man of his word."*

There was no mistake. Kelly had led Jennifer to believe the man was her decorator, and if he wasn't, then who was he?

A cold chill ran down Jennifer's spin as she felt the room closing in around her. She needed to get out. She needed to get away. Something wasn't right. She watched as Denali mingled with the other guests and tried to look inconspicuous. Out of the corner of her eye, she could feel him watching her, keeping her in his sights. She knew she could be overreacting, but something was telling her she needed to get out of there. Fast.

She tried to look casual as she pretended to answer her phone. She dialed 4-1-1 as she held the phone close to her ear. She plugged her other ear as if she were having a difficult time hearing. She moved to the edge of the tent and then continued to talk and smile, and laugh, carrying on like nothing was wrong when she was actually calling for a taxi to pick her up outside the Andrew's estate.

She flipped her phone shut and glanced at her watch. She had 20 minutes before the cab arrived; she hoped it was enough time to figure out how to slip out of the tent without Denali seeing her.

She decided to move around and see if she could lose him that way. She wandered around tables, striking up conversations with people she didn't even know. She always had a sense of where he was in the room and waited for the right time to slip out through the now opened plantation doors.

Her time finally came. A man stood between her and Denali and waved a camera at him. He wanted Denali to take a picture of him and his companion. Denali tried to refuse while looking in Jennifer's direction. She acted as if she were deep in conversation with two women standing near the edge of the tent. The minute Denali took the camera and held it up to his face, Jennifer sprinted.

She was out of the tent and running as fast as she could on her high-heels. She ran to the edge of some shrubs, out of sight, and quickly unbuckled the thin straps of her shoes. She held them in her hand and watched the main street, waiting for the taxi to appear. She repeatedly glanced back at the tent, expecting to see Denali bursting from its confines, but she saw nothing. She waited, her head like a pendulum swinging from the tent to the front gate.

Finally, she saw the headlights from a yellow cab. She looked once more towards the tent before moving from her hiding place. Then she heard his voice, but she didn't turn around.

"Miss Wilder. What are you doing out here all alone? Surely you're not leaving the celebration so early."

Jennifer could feel the bile rising in her throat. It was the moment her nightmares were made of—being found, being caught. Though she'd thought of this moment a thousand times and always tried to prime herself for what she would do, nothing could have prepared her for the sheer immobilizing terror that was stiffening her legs, making them unable to move.

"I'm feeling a little sick. I think I might have had too much to drink."

"Lemon water can do that to a person," he answered smoothly, letting Jennifer know that he had indeed been watching her every move.

Jennifer couldn't control it. She felt the lurching in her stomach and the reflex in her throat. Without warning, Jennifer bent over the same shrub she'd been hiding behind and vomited ferociously. She felt Denali creep closer to her, to see if she were really sick or if he were only being suckered in. When Jennifer saw the tips of his shoes on the ground just a foot away from her, she spun around, her shoes still in her hands, and swung them at him violently. She felt the heels of her shoes dig deep into the skin on his face. His hands immediately went up to his face in shock and something thudded on the ground.

She took the opportunity of his panic to kick him in the groin with all the force she could gather. He dropped to his knees, writhing in pain. That's when she saw the gun that had fallen. She snatched it away from Denali's reach. When she tried to run, Denali grabbed at her ankle, knocking her to the ground. He was still in pain, and blood was running down his face as he tried to wrestle the gun away from her but failed. Jennifer pushed the end of the barrel into Denali's chest and pulled the trigger. There was a high-pitched squeal, a look of shock on Denali's face, and a loss of pressure from his grip on her arm. He fell to the grass, a gurgling the only sound he made. Jennifer looked down at the gun in her hand, realizing what she'd done and what she still had to do.

She looked back at the tent in the distance. She could still hear the music, the people, and the sounds of celebration. No one was even aware of what had just happened.

She shoved the gun in her purse and walked towards the front gate. The taxi looked like it was beginning to pull away so she started running. She didn't want to yell and draw attention to herself, especially now that she was wearing no shoes, her hair was in disarray, and there were streaks of blood down the front of her dress. She just ran as fast as she could, past the valet booth, and hit the rear panel of the taxi with a thud.

His brakes chirped as he came to a sudden stop. Jennifer clawed at the door handle and quickly got in.

"What's your problem, lady?"

"Just drive, please. Just drive." Her words couldn't have been more urgent.

The valet attendant was peaking into the windows, trying to find out what the commotion was all about, but when the taxi driver got one look at Jennifer, he put his car in gear and took off.

"Lady, are you bleeding?" The taxi driver tossed a couple of serious looks over his shoulder as he maneuvered down the steep residential street.

"No, I'm fine. I just need to get home." Jennifer was panting and crying at the same time.

"Listen, lady, if someone took advantage of you, you need to report it. Don't let some rich jerk get away with it."

"I'm okay, really." Jennifer's body was shaking so hard, her teeth were beginning to chatter.

"You don't look okay. You look like some guy really did a number on you."

"Please. I don't want to talk about it. I just want to go home."

"Fine." He slammed his hands against the steering wheel. "Suit yourself. You're just letting some slimeball off so he can do it to someone else."

Jennifer gave the cabbie the address of a house two blocks from her own. She paid him, listened to his speech one more time about reporting her assault, and then watched as he pulled away.

She jogged around the block, down the alley and to the back gate of her house. She watched from between the pickets. It took only a moment before she saw movement in the kitchen. She'd been found out!

She backed away from the gate and jogged through two more alleys. She was rounding the corner of a liquor store when a sharp pain radiated from her foot. She looked down to see a piece of glass sticking out of her heel and blood beginning to run down her insole. She reached for it, and with a quick yank, pulled the thick shard of glass from her foot. For a moment she felt faint. She leaned against the building, taking a minute to regain her balance and composure. Hobbling into the liquor store, she made her way to the trashy bathroom at the back. She swung her foot up into the yellow-stained sink and rinsed the blood from her foot. It continued to bleed as she looked around for some paper towels. The dispenser was broken and an empty toilet paper roll was hanging from a bent wire. She gathered the used paper towels out of the trash can and began folding them into squares she could hold against her heel. She allowed herself to put pressure on her heel as she shimmied out of her slip. She ripped at the hem until she had a piece she could tie around her foot to keep the towels in place. It wasn't much, but it would have to do for the moment.

When she was done, she looked into the mirror, and without thinking, cried out to God. "Help me, God. Just keep me safe long enough to get to the bus station."

Harrison flashed through her thoughts. Did he realize she was gone? Did he even know what had just happened? She thought about calling him but knew she couldn't. Her father had found her but maybe he didn't know there was a connection between her and Harrison. She knew she was only fooling herself. If her father had found her and her house, then he had to know everything. He wouldn't rest until he did.

HARRISON'S EYES WANDERED around the room. He was sure that

Jennifer had left after they'd spoken. But he was hoping he was wrong. He watched as someone spoke to Kelly's father. Mr. Andrews' facial expression went from jovial to grim in an instant. Soon, another man was at his side, and then another. Finally, Mr. Andrews stepped out of the tent, so Harrison followed in the same direction. He glanced outside and saw several men huddled with Mr. Andrews, coarse words and bursts of emotion coming from the group. The older man pulled a handkerchief from his breast pocket and wiped it across his forehead. Something was definitely wrong.

Harrison couldn't help himself. He approached the group of men and their conversation came to an abrupt stop.

"Mr. Andrews, I couldn't help but noticed how upset you are. Is something wrong?"

He looked at Harrison, pale and almost in shock. "My security detail just found a dead man on the lawn. Shot. This is a horrible nightmare." The older man just kept rubbing at his brow, beside himself with bewilderment.

"Who is he?" Harrison asked.

"I don't know. There was no I.D. on him. This is preposterous. No one was allowed in without an invitation. He was seen in the tent by some of my other men. The only way he would have been in the tent is if he showed up on the registry."

"What about the staff?" Harrison was trying to be helpful, listing other possibilities of who the man might be. "Maybe he was one of the kitchen or wait staff?"

"He wasn't wearing a uniform; he was dressed as a guest," one of the security guards answered.

"Is there anything else? Did they find an invitation or anything on him? Do you have the gun?"

"No, but the valet said a woman left the party looking very upset," another security agent added. "She didn't have any shoes on, and she'd been crying. She'd called for a taxi and took off before he could find anything out. We found a pair of ladies shoes by the body."

Harrison turned cold but remained calm. "Where are these shoes?"

"We left them by the body. We didn't want to touch anything."

"Can I see the man? If you couldn't recognize him, maybe he's one of Robert's friends, and I could identify him for you." Harrison's excuse was plausible.

Andrews looked at his security agent. He shrugged like they had nothing to lose. "Mr. Andrews, go back inside. You need to be there and look as casual as possible. We will inform you the minute we find out anything." The security agent was trying to keep everything and everyone in order.

Harrison walked with the security agent across the expansive lawn. "Where were you when this happened?" Harrison snapped.

"First of all, we don't even know when it happened." The agent was defensive, knowing that Harrison was insinuating that he and his team had failed. "It must have happened when we were handing out assignments. We weren't prepared for anything like this. We were hired to stop the media from crashing the party and to make sure things didn't get out of hand inside."

They approached a shadowy figure on the lawn. When Harrison saw the petite ivory shoes, his heart nearly pulsed out of his throat. They were Jennifer's. Jennifer was involved in this, and if she was involved, where was she now?

JENNIFER HUNCHED DOWN in the back of a city bus, looking nothing like herself. Gone was her long hair, hacked off with cheap scissors from the liquor store. She had also picked up a pair of flip flops, a package of band-aids, and a bleach pen. She tried to get the bloodstains out of her dress, but it was no use. She now wore a heavy coat she bought from a homeless guy for $50. The pungent smell and filthy wool kept people at arms' length. Now all she thought about was getting to the bus depot safely.

HARRISON LISTENED AS THE VALET EXPLAINED for the umpteenth time what he had seen. "She came running out of nowhere and slammed into the side of the taxi. She was crying, her hair was all messed up, and I think she might have been bleeding."

"Why do you say that?"

"Because there was blood on her dress." The valet's answer was belligerent. He didn't know about the dead body, so he could only assume it was her blood.

"What'd she look like?"

"Small, blond, cute. She was wearing a yellow dress, but no shoes."

"When you say she ran into the taxi, what do you mean by that?"

He rolled his eyes. "She ran smack dab into the side of the taxi. He was ready to pull away, and she ran into him to make him stop."

"Did you talk to her at all?"

"No. As soon as she was in the cab, he took off."

The cabbie had to know something, Harrison thought to himself.

"Do you remember what cab company it was?"

"Speedy Cab—the one with the hourglass on the side of the car. I already told the other guys all the same stuff. Can't you guys just talk to each other?"

Harrison went over to where the security agent was standing with a team of men. "Did you call the cab company to see if the driver remembers the woman?"

"Look, Sergeant Friday," he bellowed at Harrison. "I don't give a rat's you-know-what about that girl right now. That's up to the cops. I have to figure out how I'm going to tell a tent full of people that the police will be here any minute and none of them will be able to leave until they've been questioned."

Robert, Harrison thought. *I need to warn Robert.*

He jogged back to the tent, knowing for the time being that Jennifer had gotten away on her own, not forcibly. He needed to get to her, but he had to talk to Robert first.

Harrison wiped his face of perspiration and straightened his jacket. He casually approached Robert, where he was standing with Kelly and some of their guests. He leaned over his brother's shoulder.

"Can I speak to you for a moment privately?"

Robert chuckled before turning and seeing the seriousness in his brother's eyes. He turned back to Kelly and placed a kiss on her cheek. "I'll be right back." He smiled at her so she wouldn't ask further questions. She smiled back and turned her attention to her guests.

Robert followed Harrison a few feet away from the tent. Harrison stopped and turned to Robert.

"All right, what gives, Harrison? This better be good."

"Okay, I'll make it good—there's a dead man over there on the lawn and Jennifer's involved somehow. How's that for good?"

Robert shook his head, like he was trying to clear water from his ears. "What?"

"That's right, and I want to know if you had anything to do with it?"

"What are you saying, Harrison? I don't know what you're talking about."

It took all the intestinal fortitude that Harrison had not to punch his brother right in the mouth. He clenched his jaw and tensed his fist.

"I saw what you were doing on my computer. You found out who Jennifer really is. What did you do, Robert? What horrible, asinine mistake have you made this time?"

"Okay, I admit it." He threw up his hands. "I called her father."

Harrison had his hands around the lapels of Robert's jacket and drove him back against the trunk of a sturdy palm tree before Robert even knew what hit him. His head thumped against the tree as Harrison shook him violently.

"What were you thinking? How could you do that to me . . . to her? What—was it money you needed? You know I would have given you any amount if I knew you would sink to this."

"I didn't do it, okay." Robert yelled above Harrison's accusations. "I thought about it, but I didn't do it." Robert tried to break Harrison's hold on him, pleading to let him explain. Harrison finally let him go, his own exhaustion the only thing making him stop.

"Look, the 50k was only the tip of the iceberg. I owed half-a-mil and I was being leaned on hard. You're right it was dumb of me, but I was desperate. I figured if this Calderon guy was as bad as you and the papers said he was, he would pay any amount to get information on Sam . . Jen . . .his daughter. So, I called him, but I couldn't go through with it, Harrison." Robert looked at his brother and saw the hurt through his anger. "I knew I could never look at you again if I turned her in. I figured I would have to either ask you for the money or tell Kelly about my gambling problem. So, I decided to be a man and tell Kelly the truth. She was furious with me, absolutely livid. But once she calmed down, she told me she forgave me and that she would work it out."

"So, what happened, next?" Harrison yelled.

"She worked it out. She gave me the money and I paid off my bookie."

"Did you tell Kelly you figured out Jennifer's identity?"

"I didn't have to. She was the one who told me." The brother's eyes met, the same thought hitting both of them. "You don't think Kelly had anything to do with this, do you?" Robert asked, chilled at the possibility.

"All I know is there's an invited guest out there on the lawn dead, and Jennifer's involved. How else would that person have gotten an invitation?"

"Are you sure it's a guest?"

Both Robert and Harrison heard the sound of distant sirens.

"I guess you'll know soon enough." Harrison turned to Robert. "Look, you and Kelly can't expose Jennifer, not yet. As far as you know, she's Samantha Wilder, realtor. I have to go find her. I have to make sure she's all right."

"But what about the police? They'll want to question you."

"Tell them I left early with the flu. Give them my cell phone number and tell them I would be happy to answer any of their questions."

Harrison took off jogging across the lawn and slipped through the gate. He was in his car and heading down the dark street before the red and blue lights came into view. He quickly dialed Jennifer's cell phone but immediately got her voice mail.

Jennifer took her time at the bus depot, making sure she wasn't being followed. Her heel was raging, making her walk with a slight limp. It was quiet for a Saturday night. She had hoped for more of a crowd so she could blend in.

When she felt sure that no one was paying special attention to her, she reached for locker 416 and slid in the key. Inside, she pulled out a large backpack, closed the locker, and headed to the ladies' room.

Less than an hour later, Jennifer emerged with red hair, wearing jeans, a t-shirt, and a pair of tennis shoes. She'd re-bandaged her foot but hadn't been able to stop the bleeding.

Gone was the heavy overcoat, replaced with a run-of-the-mill jean jacket. She looked younger than her years and would use that to her advantage. She slung the backpack over her shoulder, shoved a set of keys in her pocket, and headed for the U-Store-It building on the corner of Sunset Boulevard and Hobart.

Harrison pulled up past Jennifer's house, not seeing any lights on and her car wasn't in the driveway. There were more cars parked on the street than usual, making Harrison feel uneasy. He slid in next to the curb about six houses down from Jennifer's and then dialed her number.

"Jennifer, I got your message, I'll pick you up at Fifth and Broadway in 10 minutes."

Harrison flipped his phone closed fast and looked in his rearview mirror. Sure enough, three very large men walked down Jennifer's driveway to a car parked a few houses down. His ruse had worked. His phone call had served to flush them out. There was no mistaking the fact that Jennifer was in terrible danger.

Harrison waited until they were gone before he started his car and pulled away from the curb. He talked to himself all the way back to his hotel, wondering if Jennifer would call him, wondering if she were hurt. When he saw a police car parked in front of the hotel, he kept going. He couldn't let the police detain him. He was the only one who could help Jennifer. He had to find her before her father did.

CHAPTER TWENTY-TWO

The cab pulled up outside the storage facility. Jennifer paid the driver from her stash of money and used her access card to open the walk-up gate. The 24-hour availability was the reason she'd chosen the facility along with the fact that it was on the other side of town, away from where she lived and the obvious places people would look for her.

She limped a couple rows over and down an aisle that was barely lit. She used her key to open the lock and threw open the sliding metal door. Inside was a nondescript Toyota Corolla, one of the most common vehicles in the United States. She stood for a moment, staring at the car. It was an escape that she had planned for but hoped she'd never have to use.

She opened the trunk and pulled out a large duffle bag. She tossed it in the backseat before getting in and starting up the engine. It turned over immediately. She had been careful to stop by every once in a while, always at night, to run the engine and make sure it would be ready for her. She sat behind the wheel for a moment and stared out across the aisle at the sliding metal of another storage unit. It became a movie screen, playing scenes from her life.

She remembered how it had felt being whisked away by her mother with promises of a better life. She remembered the different apartments and cities they lived in until they'd settled in New Mexico. She remembered her heart breaking when the doctors told her there was nothing more they could do for her mother. A tear slid down her cheek when she relived the pain she felt when she left the hospital that chilly evening, knowing she'd lost her best friend. The reality of being alone in the world had hit her hard, nearly crippling her.

Her mind played snapshots of the run-ins she'd had with Harrison in Chicago before that wintry night that changed everything. From that moment on, he'd never left her thoughts. The scenes of the last few months began to play, making her heart twist and contort. She was sure that whoever said, "It is better to have loved and lost than to have never loved at all" was lying. To have to go on the rest of her life, knowing what she'd lost, what she'd been forced to give up, would be as painful as the moments she'd spent watching her mother slip away from her. *Why God, why have you taken everything from me once again?*

She angrily wiped the tears from her face, pulled the car out, locked up the storage unit, entered a pass code at the gate, and began to drive. She already knew her destination. The maps in the glove compartment had her route all marked out for her. She wouldn't drive far tonight. If the police already had an

APB out on her, the border patrol might take a closer look at a woman traveling alone late at night. Even if she no longer looked like Samantha Wilder, she couldn't take the chance. She would wait until tomorrow and cross the border with the normal throng of traffic.

Jennifer drove through the Sepulveda Pass, using the boulevard instead of the 405 freeway. She thought about Harrison and wondered if he knew what was going on. If he even knew that she was gone. A dead man on the lawn would have definitely put a damper on the wedding festivities, but did Harrison realize she was involved?

Her thoughts drifted to Kelly and what it was she'd done to her. She'd been set-up. The invitation to the house, meeting her "designer," insisting on her being at the wedding—it was all a set-up, but why? Kelly had everything—money, prestige, position—what would she gain from exposing her? Jennifer tried to make sense of it, but there was no way of accounting for Kelly's actions.

She continued to drive. Her fear of being caught made it difficult for her to maintain the speed limit and stick to her out-of-the-way route, but she knew she had to take the time to be cautious.

AFTER DRIVING IN CIRCLES, HARRISON FINALLY PULLED against the curb of a quiet residential area, far from where anyone would be looking for him. He knew what he had to do. It was the only thing he could do if he hoped to help Jennifer. He pulled out his cell phone and dialed.

"Agent Dennison."

"Bill, it's Harrison."

"Harrison, what's up? You fly off to California and I don't hear from you for months—some friend."

Harrison ignored Bill's teasing and got right to the point.

"I need your help."

"Harrison, what's wrong? You sound desperate."

"I am. I need you to meet with me."

"Sure. Are you in town?"

"No. I need you to come to me."

"Okay, Harrison, what's going on?"

"I can trust you, right? I mean, really trust you. This is big, Bill. I need to know that I can trust you completely. You can't involve anyone else."

"Okay, Harrison, enough with the dramatics. What's going on?"

"I'll tell you when you get here."

"Where are you?"

"Santa Monica, California."

"I'll get there as soon as I can." His tone was all business.

"Okay. Call me when you land. I'll arrange to meet you somewhere."

"Harrison . . . "

"I can't tell you anything else, not until we meet. Just call me when you land."

183

Harrison hung up the phone, feeling like he was going to be ill. "Lord, please let this be the right thing to do. I don't know how else to help Jennifer."

Harrison started his car, drove down the quiet tree-lined street, praying Jennifer would call him.

JENNIFER APPROACHED THE FRONT DESK, hoping she looked like a normal tourist, not a woman running from the police.

"Can I help you?" The older man asked from behind the counter.

"I'd like a room for the night, please."

"Sure. I'll just need to see some I.D."

Jennifer pulled her new identity from her backpack and handed it to the clerk. He looked at the picture and tossed a glance at Jennifer.

"I'll need a credit card for incidentals."

Jennifer handed him a credit card with the name Melissa Dower on it. "I'll pay with cash though." She looked at him and smiled.

"No problem." He took an impression of the card anyway.

"I'll go ahead and pay for tonight, if you don't mind. I'd like to get an early start in the morning."

"Sure, sweetie. Let me just get all your information down." Slowly he plucked at the computer keyboard. "How many keys would you like?"

"One would be fine."

"A pretty thing like you traveling all alone, that doesn't seem right." He gave her a fatherly smile.

"Actually, I'm surprising my fiancé," she said in a bubbly voice. "He's been here all month on business, and I've arranged to kidnap him for the day. His boss helped me set it up and everything."

The clerk smiled at Jennifer's convincing story. He handed her an envelope with her key in it, explained to her how to get to her room, and wished her a good evening.

Jennifer pulled her car around the side of the motel and parked in front of the door with the numbers 112. She grabbed her duffle bag and backpack and hobbled inside.

She locked all three devices on the door and turned to take in an average looking motel room. There were two double beds with a nightstand between them, a desk in the corner, a dresser with a small television on top of it, and a small bathroom.

Jennifer set her bags down on one of the beds and collapsed next to it. She looked at her foot and saw that blood had saturated her sock. She limped to the bathroom, sat on the toilet, and gently removed her tennis shoe. Blood had soaked the inside of her shoe, making her feeling momentarily woozy. She carefully removed her sock and hung her foot over the side of the tub. She ran the water until it reached a soothing temperature. It took several attempts before she could allow the water to run over her foot without pulling it away in pain.

When the bleeding seemed to diminish, she turned her foot over and rested it against her thigh. She knew the cut had been deep when she wrapped it at the liquor store and again at the bus depot, but this was the first time she'd actually been able to examine it. It was obvious she needed stitches. Without the pressure of something keeping the wound closed, it would continue to spread open and bleed. She pinched the sides of her heel together and waited for the blood flow to subside. Of course, she knew the minute she let go of it, it would start bleeding again, so she had to come up with something that could keep constant pressure on it.

She unzipped her bag and rifled around until she found her hooded sweatshirt. She pulled the string from around the neck and limped back to the bathroom. She grabbed two washcloths from the towel rack and went to work on her makeshift bandage.

By 1:00 a.m., Jennifer was in bed with her foot propped up on a stack of pillows, her eyes fixed on the ceiling. She tried to rest, but even with her eyes closed, she could do little more than listen for the sound of hurried footsteps or muffled whispers. She imagined what it would be like to open the door to her motel room and see a squad of police officers, pointing their guns at her, telling her to give up. Worst yet was the chilling thought of seeing men sent by her father, not to convince her to give up, but to silence her because of what she knew.

She tried to shake off her morose feelings, convincing herself she would be able to disappear, just like she had every other time. Even with the police looking for her, she would be able to slip across the border and vanish once again.

"HARRISON, I'VE JUST LANDED."

Bill had already let Harrison know he would be flying into LAX. In the meantime Harrison scouted out the surrounding area looking for a place they could meet.

"Okay, grab a cab and have them take you to Barney's in El Segundo. I'll be waiting for you there."

Harrison looked at his watch and continued to pray that he was doing the right thing.

Twenty minutes later, Harrison pulled into the parking lot of the posh hotel. He only had enough time to pull to the back of the lot and turn around before he saw a taxi pull to the curb and stop. He watched Bill step from the backseat and lean forward to pay the driver through the passenger window. When the cab merged back into traffic, Harrison pulled forward and rolled down his window. Bill made immediate eye contact with him, walked around the front of Harrison's car, and got into the passenger side.

Bill looked at Harrison and shook his head. "Man, what happened to you? You look horrible."

"You won't believe it."

"Try me."

Harrison drove across the street and parked in a structure that serviced both a mall and a theatre multi-plex. He pulled into a parking stall where he could blend in with a sea of other vehicles. He killed the engine and slumped over the steering wheel in exhaustion.

"Thanks for coming," Harrison said in a weary voice.

"You're welcome. Now, what's going on?"

"Before I tell you, you've got to promise me if you can't help me, you'll just walk away. You'll forget whatever it is I tell you and go back to Texas like nothing happened."

"Harrison, you know I can't do that, but I'll do everything in my power to help you. You're just going to have to trust me."

Harrison debated his choices, knowing he didn't have any. He felt he was betraying Jennifer, but he didn't see that he had any other options. Jennifer wasn't just hiding from her father, now she was running from the police as a murder suspect. This was the only thing Harrison knew to do.

"I know about what happened at the wedding."

Harrison looked at Bill with a look of surprise.

"I did some investigating while I was on the plane," Bill informed him. "I also know you are wanted by the police for questioning. Are you going to tell me that you're the one that shot that man?"

"No, I didn't shoot the guy. I don't even know who he is. But I think I know who did it."

"Samantha Wilder," Bill volunteered, showing he'd done his homework.

"It's not what you think, Bill. It's much more complicated than a random shooting."

"Then why don't you try to uncomplicate things for me."

JENNIFER WOKE UP THE NEXT MORNING, startled by the sounds of activity outside her door. Her heart raced out of control long after the noises grew faint. She was covered in perspiration and felt like she was burning up. When she tried to move her foot from the stack of pillows it was resting on, fiery pain radiated up her leg. She reached for her ankle, feeling the heat and seeing the blotches that were sure signs of infection. She undid her make-shift bandage, only to see a still open wound, red and inflamed.

Pushing through the pain, she got dressed and changed her bandage, using one of her socks instead of the washcloth. She rinsed the blood out as much as possible and left an apology note for the manager. She slipped on the flip flops she'd bought at the liquor store and walked out to her car.

When she was loading her bags in the front seat, she noticed the gas station across the way and decided to make sure her tank was completely full before crossing the border. She drove across the four lanes of traffic and pulled up next to a pump. She walked past the pay phone outside the mini mart and stopped. She thought a moment before continuing inside. The clerk behind the counter was a large, heavyset woman. She had glasses perched on the edge of her nose and was watching one of the morning shows on the television behind the counter.

Jennifer eyed the calling cards behind the counter. "Fill up on three," she said as she laid a hundred dollar bill on the counter.

"You got to spend at least half of that; otherwise we don't take bills that large."

"I will." Jennifer smiled and walked slowly back to her car.

While she stood with the nozzle in the gas tank, she debated her plan. She knew by now Harrison would be frantic with worry. She had to call him before he did something desperate. If she used the pay phone and a calling card, she would be safe. She would talk quick, just to let him know she was okay.

She walked back inside the market and roamed the aisles. She picked up a couple of bags of chips, a few sodas, a package of mini donuts, and a bottle of orange juice. She looked down the medicine aisle and grabbed a first aid kit from the shelf. She balanced two Ace bandages and a bottle of Tylenol on top of the kit before heading back to the front counter. That's when she saw the headline of the Sunday paper: "Debutante's Wedding Marred by Murder."

She took a breath and forced her heart back down her throat. She set her purchases on the counter, casually adding a newspaper to her stack.

"Could I also get a $20 calling card?" Jennifer said, her voice cracking slightly.

"Sure thing." The woman reached behind her and grabbed the card. She slid each item under her scanner and stuck them in a flimsy plastic bag. When she got to the newspaper, she rolled it up and stuck it in the bag as well.

"What a shame. Can you image planning your wedding and then having someone killed at it?"

"What?"

"That girl on the front page of the paper. She had a beautiful wedding and then they found some man dead on her lawn."

"Oh." Jennifer smiled casually. "I'm just buying the paper to look in the classifieds for an apartment. I didn't even notice the headline."

"One of her guests was shot, right there at the reception."

"Did they catch the person who did it?" Jennifer tried to act interested, even though it was difficult for her to even form the words.

"No, but they have two suspects. Some girl that disappeared, and get this, the best man, but he's disappeared as well."

Jennifer clenched the counter for support, the woman's words hitting her like a ton of bricks.

"That will be $85.73." The woman held the hundred dollar bill up to the light and then slipped it through the slot on the register. She counted back Jennifer's change and handed her the bag of groceries. "Good luck."

"Good luck?"

"Finding that apartment."

"Oh, thank you." Jennifer stuffed her change in her pocket and walked stiff legged to the car, putting the bag on the front seat. She drove around to the side of the market, pulled the newspaper from her bag, and quickly began to scan the front page story. "A yet to be identified man was found shot . . ." Jennifer skipped ahead. "Police are looking for Samantha Wilder, a guest at the wedding, and best man, Harrison Lynch. Neither was present for questioning and while the police are not yet calling them suspects, they are saying they are people of interest."

Jennifer tossed the paper down on the passenger seat, stunned. *Where is Harrison, and what is he thinking?*

She eyed the phone booth, dug the calling card out of the bag, and got out of the car.

Harrison's phone rang, interrupting his conversation with Bill. He eyed it with a strange look on his face. The screen indicated it was an unidentified number.

He no longer feared the police. He and Bill had spent the night tucked away in a non-descript motel room. It had taken hours for Harrison to explain to Bill everything he knew about Jennifer, Carlos Calderon, the proof of her father's corruption, and the danger that Jennifer was in before the shooting. Bill had been on the phone the rest of the night gathering information and enlisting the help of key agents he knew could be trusted. He informed them that the Andrews murder was not a typical homicide and their "person of interest" was not a typical suspect. They were no longer looking for a green-eyed blond. They were now looking for any female traveling alone that matched the general description of Samantha Wilder. Now that Harrison had Bill on his side, he decided it was safe to answer the phone.

Jennifer had almost given up. With each unanswered ring, she struggled not to hang up the phone before hearing Harrison's voice.

"Hello?" Harrison's voice was cautious.

She sighed, relieved to know he was okay. "It's me; I wanted you to know I'm okay."

When Harrison heard her voice, he shot out of the chair he was sitting in, getting Bill's attention. He nodded his head to Bill to let him know it was Jennifer. Bill went to work on his own phone. "Jennifer, where are you?"

"It doesn't matter. I'm okay, but you need to turn yourself in. You can't ruin your life because of me."

"Jennifer, I want to help you."

"There's nothing you can do. I'll be fine. I've done this before, remember?"

"But Jennifer, I can help." Harrison took a deep breath before telling her about Bill. "I have this friend who works for the FBI. I would trust him with my life. He says he can help."

Jennifer's eyes grew big at the reality of what Harrison had just said. "You told him?"

"I had to. It was the only . . ."

"Harrison, how could you?" Her voice shrieked with emotion.

"Listen, Jennifer. He can help. You don't need to run any . . ."

Before Harrison could finish, the disconnection of the phone buzzed in his ear. He ended the call and looked at Bill. "She hung up." Harrison slumped to the chair, his head in his hands. "She's terrified, Bill. I shouldn't have told her about you. I should have done something else, talked about something else, anything to keep her talking."

"Don't beat yourself up over it, Harrison. She's a smart girl. She wasn't going to stay on the phone with you for long anyway." Bill was on his phone talking to someone else while trying to console Harrison. When he hung up, he walked over to Harrison and put a reassuring hand on his shoulder. "She wasn't on long enough to get a trace, but we'll still be able to find out where she made that call from. It will just take a little longer."

Bill pulled the other chair around to face Harrison. He relaxed back against it and folded his hands behind his head. "So, you told me everything you knew about Angelica Calderon. Why don't you tell me a little something about Jennifer?"

"What do you mean?"

"Come on, Harrison, this is a girl you're willing to risk everything for. I mean the Harrison Lynch I knew in college might have done something as foolish as harboring a criminal, but not this Harrison Lynch, not the Harrison Lynch of today."

Harrison was staring off into another world, thanking God that Jennifer was okay, but hating himself for the feeling of betrayal he heard in her voice.

"Come on, Harrison." Bill slapped his knee to get his attention. When Harrison turned towards him, Bill locked eyes with him. "It's going to be okay. We're going to find her. And when we do, I promise I will do everything to ensure her safety."

"What if we don't? What if her father finds her before we do?"

"That's not going to happen. She's been at this too long, and he has nothing to go on. She never went back to her house. She left her car at the scene, and so far Samantha Wilder has disappeared off the grid. She's using another identity now, headed who knows where. Calderon is not going to be able to follow her any closer than we do. Besides, she contacted you. We're one up on the man. In a little while we'll know where she made that call from, and we'll have an idea where she's heading. My guess is the border. I don't think she'd be brave enough to leave the country by plane. It's too risky, too many variables."

Harrison thought about her fear of flying, about feeling trapped with no way out. "No, you're right. She wouldn't fly. I'm sure of it."

"Okay, then." Bill sat back, trying to get Harrison to follow his lead and relax a little bit. "Tell me again about how you ended up finding her in California."

JENNIFER SLOWED DOWN as she reached the back end of the traffic going into Mexico. She quickly looked in her rearview mirror, making sure the blotchiness caused by her crying had gone away. She had to look like a typical tourist when she got to the border patrol. She didn't want to look the least bit suspicious.

She'd cried for an hour, horrified that Harrison had betrayed her, that he would go to the FBI when he knew the extent of her father's corruption. She'd been stupid to call, stupid to trust Kelly, and stupid enough to trust Harrison. Well, she wouldn't make that mistake again.

She pulled sunglasses from her bag and inched towards the border with new determination. Never again. Never again would she allow someone to penetrate her heart and soul.

"Good afternoon. What is your reason for entering Mexico?" the patrol officer asked her as she stopped along side of him.

"Vacation." Jennifer answered with a convincing smile.

"Can I see some ID?" he said while his eyes traveled around the interior of the car. He looked at her I.D. and then handed it back to her. "Can you open the trunk for me, Ms. Mower?"

"That's Dower," she corrected him with a smile and then pulled the small latch that was alongside her seat. Her trunk popped open, and he walked back to take a look. Was he trying to trip her up, stating her name incorrectly? Was he suspicious of her? Jennifer took slow, even breaths, trying to calm the adrenaline that was racing through her body. Out of her side mirror, she saw the officer tip his head and say something into the radio strapped to his shoulder. Her foot hovered over the accelerator. She wanted nothing more than to floor it and try to get as far away from this torture as possible, but she had to let it play out. Her I.D. would check out, her registration would check out. She just had to stay calm and go along with the routine.

"So, Ms. Dower, how long will you be in Mexico?"

"Five glorious days." She threw her head back in a flirtatious way.

Jennifer saw by the look on the officer's face that someone was talking through the earpiece that snaked around his collar. He gave her one final look and said, "Okay then, have a good trip. I recommend you buy car insurance while in Mexico. It will save you a real headache in case you have any mishaps while you're here, and with the way people drive, you can never be too sure."

"Thanks, officer. I'll do that."

He waved her through and when she'd gotten 50 feet away, she finally began to breathe again.

She saw him in her rearview mirror, studying her as she left. She wanted to panic and speed away, but she coaxed herself into acting normal. *Stay calm. He's only doing his job*, she kept telling herself as she drove closer to freedom.

BILL TOSSED A HUGE BAG at Harrison. "Here, I did some shopping for you."

Harrison pulled out a pair of jeans, a polo shirt, a pair of running shoes, socks, and toiletries—everything he needed to get out of the tuxedo he still wore from the night before.

"I guess I won't be getting my security deposit back on this," Harrison said as he pulled the shirt off and tossed it on the bed.

"Take a shower, Harrison. You'll feel better. We should be hearing something soon. I want to be ready to move when we do."

Harrison didn't answer; he just tossed everything back in the bag and closed the bathroom door behind him.

It took him only 15 minutes to shower and brush his teeth. He decided to keep the shadow on his face, just in case he had to go out where he might be seen. After all, his picture had been printed in the local papers as a person of interest regarding the recent murder.

He was sitting on the edge of the bed, pulling on athletic socks when Bill's phone rang. Harrison watched as Bill quickly scribbled something on a piece of paper. "Okay. She's headed for the border. Call the border patrol and tell them to stop every female that's traveling alone. I'll tell you what I find out."

Bill pulled his jacket from the back of his chair and started shutting down his computer.

"What is it? Did they find her?" Harrison was feverishly tying the laces on his new shoes.

Bill slammed his computer shut and slid it into his briefcase. "She has to be headed for Mexico. The call she made to you was placed from a mini mart just outside the border. Come on. We're going to see if anyone remembers seeing a woman using the phone. Maybe we can get a description of her or the vehicle she's driving."

Harrison scooped up everything he'd laid around the room and tossed them in the shopping bag. They opted to use the stairs instead of the elevator and were out of the motel and crossing the parking lot in two minutes flat. *Please God, let it be her, let someone remember something, anything.*

Bill glanced at Harrison as they got in the unmarked car. "Keep praying, Harrison. We're still a long way off."

THE AFTERNOON SUN WAS BEATING DOWN on them as they got out of Bill's car at the gas station and walked into the mini mart. They saw an older lady behind the counter, reading a tabloid newspaper. Bill pulled out his badge and cleared his throat. She looked at him, at his badge, and back to him again.

"Miss, were you working this morning around 8:30?"

"Yeah." She glanced at Harrison and then back to Bill.

"Did you happen to notice a woman using the pay phone outside?"

"Sure, sold her a calling card."

"Can you tell me what she looked like?"

"Well, she was tiny, had short red hair, kind of sassy looking. You know, how the kids all wear their hair today. All chopped up and going every which way."

"What was she wearing?"

"Jeans, red tank top, flip flops."

"Is there anything special you remember about her?"

The woman took a hard look at Harrison before answering the question.

"No. We talked a little about that murder," she said as she pointed to the newspaper.

"What did she say?" Bill asked coolly.

"She really didn't seem to care much. Said she was buying the paper for the classifieds, looking for an apartment."

"Did she buy anything else?"

"Some food, a first aid kit, and some bandages."

Harrison felt his throat go dry as Bill continued his questioning.

"Did she appear hurt?"

The woman thought for a moment. "Now that you mention it, she did have something wrapped around her foot, and she was limping. I guess that's why she was buying the bandages." Again, the woman focused on Harrison.

"Did you see what kind of car she was driving?"

"I did, but I don't know a Honda from a Saturn."

"Do you remember what color it was, maybe how many doors it had?"

"It was a sedan. I can tell you that much, and it was gray or silver, something like that."

"Could you tell if it was older or newer?"

"If I had to guess, I would say it was older. Real boxy looking, not round like the newer cars, but I couldn't say for sure. It just looked like every other car that pulls up to these pumps." She tossed a glance towards the station's island.

"Okay, Ma'am, you've been very helpful. Here's my card. If you remember anything else, anything at all, please call me."

"What'd she do?" the woman asked, her eyes wide with interest.

"She's involved in smuggling illegals across the border."

Her eyes grew with the morsel of information, a piece of her very own gossip to share with her friends.

"Thanks again, Ms. . . . "

"Edith Smith," the woman answered proudly.

"Thank you, Edith. You have a nice day."

She glanced once more at Harrison, squinting her eyes in recollection as they headed for the car.

JENNIFER HAD BEEN DRIVING FOR OVER AN HOUR when she decided she could go no further. The throbbing in her foot was more than she could bear. With each step on the accelerator, pain coursed through her body. She pulled off at a little roadside motel and looked out the window. It was old and a little run down, but she didn't care. She needed to be able to prop her foot up and get some medicine on it.

She limped up to the counter where a little girl with a coloring book was lying on the ground. The girl quickly got up and rushed behind a curtain that hung in the doorway. A moment later, a middle-aged woman came out and smiled at Jennifer.

"Vacancy?" Jennifer asked.

"Si."

"Cuanto cuesta?"

"Viente-dos."

Jennifer dug $22 out of her backpack and gave it to the woman who handed her a key.

"Diez."

Jennifer smiled, nodded, and headed back to her car. She pulled around to the end of the ten unit building. A tall tree shaded the edge of the parking lot, offering the perfect place to park her car, out of plain sight but still close to her room. She grabbed both her bags, not wanting to make two trips. She struggled in the dirt of the unpaved lot. She had only a few steps to go when her duffle bag slipped from her shoulder, throwing her off-balance and causing her to fall.

She sat for a moment in the intense heat, feeling almost too weak to get up. *What now, God, are you going to send vultures to swoop down on me too?* When she looked up, she saw a man walking towards her, directly towards her. A vulture.

"Senorita, you need some help?" the man asked kindly, his accent heavy but his English perfect.

"No, I'm fine, thank you."

"You don't look so fine." The man took her duffle bag and swung it over his shoulder. He picked up the key that had dropped from Jennifer's hand, unlocked the door of the motel room, and carried her bag inside. She rushed to get to her feet, keeping her backpack close to her side. She was covered in dirt, but she didn't care. She kept her eyes on the man as he stepped from her room and walked back to her side.

"Here, let me help you." He reached for her elbow, but she quickly pulled away. "I assure you, my only intentions are to help you. I saw you go down, and I thought you might have fainted."

"I didn't faint; I stumbled." Jennifer spoke in a clipped tone. "Your English is good," Jennifer commented as she took short steps to the front door, insisting she walk without his assistance. He followed her and stood in the doorway, looking at her foot. She turned to him. "Thank you for helping me with my bag, but now, if you don't mind, I'd like to get some rest."

"What's wrong with your foot?" he asked, ignoring her polite way of dismissing him."

"I cut it. It's nothing."

"It doesn't look like nothing. It's red and swollen."

"It'll be fine. I just need to change the bandage and put it up for a little while." Sweat was running down her face, and she began to feel lightheaded. She wasn't sure if it was from heat, hunger, or the pain she'd been trying to ignore. She dropped to the edge of the bed, trying to keep her focus on the man that was still standing in the doorway. "I am . . . I just . . ."

Jennifer couldn't think. She could hear herself mumbling but nothing was making sense. The room began to sway, and she could see the man moving towards her. She shook her head and reached for her backpack, but before she could do anything, the room went black.

CHAPTER TWENTY-THREE

Harrison and Bill sat with a border patrol officer in a room filled with security monitors. Three officers remembered seeing women traveling by themselves. One woman was black, so she was immediately dismissed. Another woman had been too heavy to be confused for Jennifer's 5'4", 125 lb. frame. They were now down to the last tape.

"I know she came through before 10:00 a.m.," the officer said as he rewound surveillance tapes. "We even called her license in, but everything checked out." He continued to fiddle with the monitor. "There! That's her car."

Bill and Harrison stared at the tape of a late model, silver Toyota Corolla. "The vehicle's right." Bill said as he scooted closer to the monitor. "Zoom in on the driver."

"Sure." The officer stilled the video and pushed a couple of buttons, making the picture larger but blurrier.

Harrison squinted to make out the frame of the woman. Her hair was short, just like the mini mart clerk said, but the woman's head was turned away from the camera, making it hard to see her face.

"Let the tape run for a few minutes. Let's see if she shows us a better profile."

"I think it's her." Harrison stated.

"You do?" Bill looked at him for affirmation.

"I can't be sure, but that woman is definitely avoiding being filmed. Jennifer would have known there would be surveillance cameras, so she purposely kept her head down." Just then, the woman in the car threw her head back as if she were laughing. Harrison gasped.

"Now, I'm sure. That's Jennifer!" The officer freeze framed it. Harrison stared for a moment at Jennifer. "So what now?" He turned to Bill, a glimmer of hope in his eyes.

"Don't get too excited. We still have a lot of searching to do."

"But we can get help, right? The Mexican authorities will help us find her, right?"

"We can't involve them, not yet."

"What do you mean we can't involve them?"

Bill turned to the officer and thanked him for his help and then had to practically force Harrison out of the security office.

"I can't believe we are just walking away." Harrison growled under his breath as they continued to walk towards the car. "We know where she is; now all we need to do is find her, and you're just going to walk away? I thought you were going to help? I thought you knew how important this was to me!"

Harrison continued his ranting until they were in the car. Once inside, Bill let him know the score.

"Look, Calderon is already here!" Bill hollered over Harrison's fury. "He's got his finger in everything from trafficking people and drugs to prostitution and gambling. His corruption doesn't stop in the states. He's got Mexican officials in his hip pocket as well." Bill watched as the reality of the situation sunk in for Harrison. He regained his composure before continuing.

"Just let me do this my way, okay? It might take us a little longer, but we'll have a better chance of getting to Angelica without drawing attention to ourselves. She trusted you enough to call once. Maybe she'll do it again."

Harrison relived the shock he heard in Jennifer's voice when he told her he'd involved the FBI. He wasn't expecting another phone call. "Do you think he already knows she's here?"

"Chances are good."

"Then she doesn't have time. We need to get to her before he does."

"I know. Just trust me, Harrison. I'm going to do everything I can to find her."

Harrison rubbed at his face, wanting to scream or yell or do something. "So now what?" he asked calmly, realizing Bill was not the enemy.

"She's less than three hours ahead of us. We're going to Mexico."

JENNIFER WAS JOLTED BACK TO CONSCIOUSNESS by a searing pain.

"Sorry, I know this is painful, but it's necessary."

The voice wasn't familiar, and it took a moment for her eyes to focus. The man who helped her in the parking lot was sitting at the foot of the bed. He had her foot in one hand and something else in the other. Instinctively, she pulled her foot away, causing herself even more pain. "What are you doing to my foot?"

"I'm irrigating the wound. It's infected and needs to be cleaned before I stitch it up."

She pushed herself even further up on the bed. "Are you insane?" she yelled. "I'm not going to let you stitch up my foot. I don't even know who you are."

He got up from the chair he was sitting in, removed a latex glove from his hand, and extended to her. "Then let me introduce myself, my name is Juan Sanchez."

When it was clear she wasn't going to shake his hand, he let it drop to his side.

"How did you get such a nasty cut?" he asked as he moved back to the chair, but left her foot alone. "I'm guessing glass."

She nodded her head. "How did you know?"

"It's a pretty jagged cut, deep too. Did you get it here while you were in Mexico?"

Jennifer stared at him. "Yeah."

"Playing on the beach, I bet."

Jennifer nodded again, not knowing what to make of the man in front of her. He was tall and lean with bronze skin, dark hair, and a reassuring smile. He was nicely dressed and seemed to know what he was talking about. He didn't look like the type of man that would follow a woman back to a seedy motel room and rape her, but then again, what was a good-looking guy like him doing in this shanty of a town?

"What were you doing?"

"Like I said I was trying to get the infection out before I stitched it up." Her skeptical look made him laugh. "Don't worry; I know what I'm doing. I'm a doctor."

"Right and I'm the Queen of England."

"If that's the case, what are you doing here?" He laughed. "You know it's dangerous for a woman to travel alone in a foreign country without her court."

"I could say the same thing to you," she shot back.

"Well, first of all, in case you didn't notice, I'm not a woman and this is my native country." He laughed some more.

She rolled her eyes in exasperation. "I meant, what's a doctor doing in the middle of Ghettoville?"

He stiffened at her indictment of their surroundings. "If you must know," he spoke in a defensive tone, "I come to 'Ghettoville' every week to volunteer at the free clinic across the street. And since they appreciate my help more than you do, I think I'll leave. I hope you enjoy the rest of your stay in Mexico." He bent down at the foot of the bed, picked up his medical bag and left without even a backward glance.

Jennifer sat dumfounded. A *doctor,* she thought to herself. A doctor that was used to asking no questions, one that just volunteered and helped where he could, and she sent him away.

She closed her eyes, worn out and angry at herself. The pulsing in her foot was strong, but not as strong as her exhaustion.

IT WAS 5:30 P.M. AND JUAN WAS FINISHING up at the clinic. His day had been filled with vaccinations, patients with pneumonia, bronchitis, ear infections, and what seemed like a hundred different kinds of cuts, abrasions, sores, and infections.

He was sterilizing his tools and taking inventory of his supplies when he heard the front door swing open. "I'm sorry, but we're closed, unless it's an emergency." His voice dropped off as he rounded the corner and saw the woman from the motel propped against the door jam. She was covered in perspiration and white as a sheet.

He quickly crossed the room and helped her get to a chair while scolding her. "Why didn't you send Maria? She could have come and gotten me."

"Because I didn't want Maria apologizing for me. I wanted to do that my-self."

Her skin was clammy, and he could feel her trembling. "I'm sorry I insulted your town, and I'm sorry I refused your help. Would you still be willing to give me a hand? I can pay. I just need your help."

Her eyes began to pool and she swayed to the right. Without another word, he scooped her up into his arms and carefully carried her through the doorway to one of the exam rooms. She looked around at the crude equipment—the worn cabinetry and the discolored countertops. She was sure it was worse than any clinic in the states, but everything looked clean and sterile, and at the mo-ment, she wasn't in the position to be picky. She stared at Juan's back until he turned around to give her instructions.

"I'm going to give you something for the pain." He stood with a syringe in his hand.

"No." Her hand shot up as he leaned towards her. "I can't take pain medi-cine."

"But, I need to stitch . . . "

"Can't you just do something local, something topical?"

"Yes, but that won't get rid of the pain completely. You'll still feel what I'm doing."

"That's okay." She eased herself back down on the table. "I'll take my chances."

He didn't argue. He figured she'd change her mind once he got started. "Do you know when you had your last tetanus shot?"

"Just a couple of months ago," she answered, remembering being asked the same question after her car accident.

"Good."

He got everything ready that he would need and then removed the flimsy bandage she had wrapped around her foot. She braced herself for the worst. Good thing, because that was exactly what she got.

HARRISON STARED AT THE DMV PHOTO of Melissa Dower. Even with the crazy red hair, all he could see was Jennifer. He looked up at the crush of traffic they were sitting in and wondered how in the world they were going to find her when she didn't want to be found. Especially now, now that she felt be-trayed. He was sure she would never call him again. But he wasn't going to give up. He was convinced that Bill would be able to help Jennifer. He just wished he'd been able to convince her of the same thing.

WHEN JUAN WAS DONE, he rolled his squeaky chair back from the table and snapped the bloodied gloves from his hands. Jennifer laid on the table, her labored breathing slowly returning to normal. He had to hand it to her. She'd clenched, grimaced, and whimpered but never backed down. She let him clean out her cut and stitch it up with nothing more than a local anesthetic.

"So what's your name?" he asked while rinsing off instruments.

"Melissa."

"So, Melissa, why Mexico . . . solo?"

"I just came off of a bad break-up. I was looking for some solitude."

His back was to her as he hovered over the sink. "Where were you heading?"

"What do you mean?"

"Well, certainly you didn't intend on staying at the El Rancho, did you?" he said, referring to the motel across the street.

"No. I just couldn't drive any further." She allowed her eyes to close. "I didn't really have any solid plans. I just got in my car and drove."

"So what do you do for a living?" He pulled some paper towels from a dispenser and turned to her while he was drying her hands.

"Real estate," she said without flinching, though she was beginning to get irritated with his questions.

He turned back to a locked cabinet and pulled a few different bottles out.

Jennifer started shaking her head. "I told you I can't take pain medication."

"This is nothing more than Tylenol and an antibiotic, nothing that's going to make you incoherent."

He continued to measure out the pills, sliding them into a little white pouch. After he was done, he turned to her, his arms crossed against his chest.

"Now, since you weren't planning on staying at the El Rancho, why don't you let me drive you to a nicer hotel? There are better places to stay about 40 minutes up the road."

"That's not necessary. I'm sure the El Rancho will be fine for one night."

"You're sure?"

"Yeah. I'll lock the door and pull a piece of furniture in front of it, if that would make you feel any better."

"It would." He stared at her making her feel awkward. She cast her eyes down to her lap and then looked away. He knew he'd made her feel uncomfortable, so he quickly moved on to the next subject. "Well, let's get you back to that room. You don't want your $20 going to waste."

"Twenty-two." Jennifer corrected jokingly.

"Oh, the price has gone up. That must account for the freshly painted walls."

Jennifer scooted to the edge of the table and carefully let her legs hang over the edge. "Just let me change my shirt, and I'll give you a hand." Juan began to unbutton the short, white medical jacket he'd been wearing.

Even though he wore a thin white t-shirt underneath his official doctor's garb, Jennifer couldn't help but notice his solid muscles. He hung the jacket on a hook in a cupboard and pulled out a fresh t-shirt. When he turned back around, Jennifer quickly looked away, but not before Juan saw that she wasn't completely uninterested.

He pulled on his t-shirt and then positioned himself next to her. "You're not going to hobble across the street again. It's too dangerous. Besides, I don't want you to mess up my fine craftsmanship. Put your arm over my shoulder." He hunkered down to lift her off the table.

"You are not going to carry me. I walked over here just fine."

"Come on, Melissa, indulge me, okay? The highway is not the place for a cripple to be stumbling across in the dark."

"No. That's ridiculous." She pushed away his helping hands.

"I know what it is." He looked at her with a charismatic grin. "You're afraid you can't resist me. You're afraid if we get too close, you won't want to let go of me." His Hispanic accent seemed more suave and pronounced as his smile broadened.

She laughed nervously, knowing he was coming onto her. His tactics were polite and gentleman-like, but he was coming onto her just the same. "Juan, I appreciate your help, but I'm not looking for a fling while I'm here."

"A fling?" he answered back, trying to sound insulted, but his smile gave away his amusement. "A fling sounds so tawdry, so tasteless. I was thinking more along the lines of a nice dinner."

Jennifer smiled at his charm. "I'm sorry, Juan. I appreciate all your help, but I'm not looking for a dinner partner or a partner of any kind right now. My life is a big enough mess as it is. I can't add anything else to it right now, no matter how sincere the offer."

He looked at her with his warm Spanish eyes and smiled. "I understand." He positioned himself again to help her and this time she conceded. They were across the street in no time. Juan unlocked her door and looked around. She stepped carefully into the room and turned once more to the incredible stranger that came out of nowhere. She had thought him a vulture, but it seemed as if she were wrong.

"Thank you, Juan. Thank you so much, for everything."

He pulled her hand up to his lips and kissed it gently. "You're welcome." He let her hand slip to her side as he pulled his business card out of his back pocket. "While you're here, if you change your mind, call me. I would love to show you the enchanting side of Mexico instead of the inside of a free clinic."

She smiled as he handed her the small package of pills and then closed the door behind him. She locked the deadbolt, and then wedged the only chair in the room under the handle. She slid his business card in her pocket and felt the plastic of the calling card she'd used to call Harrison. Forgetting her foot and the time she'd just spent with the young doctor, she relived the short conversation she had with Harrison, hurting at his betrayal all over again. *How could you, Harrison? How could you do that to me?*

She collapsed on the bed, looking for the elusive sleep she needed. The medication that Juan used had taken the edge off the pain, but she knew it wouldn't last for long. She took two pills from the little pouch and swallowed them down with the room temperature can of soda she'd bought earlier. Her stomach growled and she realized she hadn't eaten anything but a package of donuts and a bag of chips all day. She knew she had another bag of chips in her backpack but decided to wait until morning. She turned off the bedside lamp and closed her eyes. She didn't hear another sound the rest of the night.

IT HAD BEEN MORE THAN 48 HOURS, and they still didn't know where Jennifer was. Harrison sat on the edge of his bed praying while Bill was in the bathroom getting dressed. Bill had already given him a pep talk, encouraging him by what they knew instead of dwelling on what they didn't. They knew what Jennifer looked like, what name she was using, and what her car looked like. They just needed to get a break, find someone who'd seen her, figure out in what direction she was headed.

CARLOS CALDERON SAT IN THE DARKNESS OF HIS OFFICE. He was waiting for the latest update on his little Angelica. Since receiving the first mysterious call a few weeks ago, he'd thought of nothing else. He realized that her reappearance could jeopardize the empire that had taken him a lifetime to build. He long suspected that Monica had somehow gotten a look at his private documents, and after the bizarre phone calls and conversations of the last weeks, he was sure of it. Angelica now possessed those documents, and with it, the power to expose him.

Though his man had blown it at the wedding, those who searched the house had found what they were looking for. Angelica's special suitcase had been found buried in the back of her closet. It held all her mementoes she saved growing up, the hospital records of her mother's death, and the copied pages from his ledger. It was those pages that Carlos feared falling into someone else's hands. If Angelica had been smart enough to stay hidden all these years, he was sure that she would have made copies of the documents and stashed them somewhere safe. The only way to find them was to find her.

Frank stepped into Calderon's office. "She's in Mexico. We have our people looking for her."

"Good. I want you down there. I want you to make sure it's handled right. No more mistakes."

"The FBI's involved."

"Really?" Carlos turned in his chair to stare out the window. "And the boyfriend?"

"He's there too."

"Then you know what you have to do. I want a clean house when you leave there."

"We'll take care of it."

Frank left the room and closed the wide double doors. He didn't see the look on Carlos' face; he didn't see the hint of foreboding in his eyes. Everything rode on Angelica and Harrison Lynch being silenced. Without witnesses, the FBI would have no case. Without corroboration, all they could possibly have were a few journal pages, but no proof they belonged to him, or so he hoped.

JENNIFER WOKE UP THE NEXT MORNING feeling as if she'd actually slept. The redness and swelling in her foot had gone down, and she was no longer fighting a fever. Her foot was still tender, but she felt much better than she had the previous day.

She hurried around her room getting ready as quickly as she could. She brushed her teeth and combed hair, wishing she could take the time for a shower, but knowing she'd spent too much time in one place already. She wore the same jeans as the day before, but changed into a black tank top, her red one definitely needing to be rinsed out. She wrapped her ankle in one of the ace bandages she'd picked up to help keep out the dirt. She still couldn't fit her foot in her tennis shoes, so she slipped on her flip-flops before stepping out into the already scorching heat.

She tossed her bags into the car and walked carefully around the side. She saw Maria sweeping the front steps and waved goodbye as she pulled away. She turned to look at the free clinic across the street and smiled. Juan had been kind, helpful, even charming. She silently thanked him for getting her back on her feet.

She cautiously drove away from the little rural town, her eyes darting from side-to-side. Once again, she had to be aware of everything around her, every person and every car. She was all alone, in a country of millions, but her paranoia made her feel claustrophobic.

CHAPTER TWENTY-FOUR

I t was now day four, and Harrison was beginning to think the worst. He sat in a balmy motel room in the middle of Mexico, wondering where Jennifer was and if she was all right. She was smart and she was strong. If she'd been able to elude the FBI contacts Bill had throughout Mexico, then maybe she'd been able to evade Calderon's people as well.

Bill snapped his fingers to get Harrison's attention. He'd been on his phone all night, checking in with his informants, trying to get leads. The expression on Bill's face was hard to read. He looked hopeful but serious as well. Harrison paced until Bill finally hung up the phone.

"She's been spotted in a small town outside of Mazatlan."

"Are you sure?"

"She stopped by a small open-air grocery store. The woman saw both her and her car, and said she was walking with a limp."

"Okay, then," Harrison started grabbing up his things. "Let's go."

"You can't go, Harrison." Bill's tone was calm but stern.

"What?" Harrison stopped what he was doing. "You're crazy if you think I'm just going to sit around here and wait. I've got to be there. She won't trust you. She'll run. I have to convince her that you're on her side."

"You can't go. It's too dangerous."

"I'm going, Bill. There's no way you're going to stop me." Harrison turned his back on him and went back to packing up his things.

"The woman said there had been others asking about the lady in the picture." Bill's tone was ominous.

Harrison stopped what he was doing but didn't turn around. "So Calderon knows. He's ahead of us. So what—you expected that. We just have to work harder."

"There's more. He's also asking about you."

Harrison turned to face his friend.

"His men showed the woman a picture of you and wanted to know if you'd been by asking about the lady." Bill let his words sink in a moment. "So you see Harrison, the stakes have just been raised. It's going to be hard enough to get a step ahead of Calderon and find Jennifer. I can't be worried about you being spotted and someone taking you out as well. Jennifer's no longer the only one in danger. I can't guarantee that I can protect her, but I can protect you. You're just going to have to trust me."

"So, you're just going to leave me here . . . leave me out of it? Bill, please! I need to be there. I need to be close."

Bill debated internally, wanting to protect his friend, but knowing how hard it would be for him to be left in the dark. "You can go as far as Mazatlan. We have a safe house there. But that's it. You'll have to stay put there. No wandering around. My informants blend with the locals. If anyone was to see you as much as passing one of them on the street, their cover would be blown and their lives would be in danger."

Harrison wanted to argue but knew he couldn't. He would take what Bill was offering him for the time being.

They both packed up and headed to a local airstrip. They would be in Mazatlan before midnight.

"SHE'S IN MAZATLAN." Frank's tone was low.

Calderon puffed on his cigar, letting out a slow, deliberate breath. "And the boyfriend?"

"Nothing so far."

"I've changed my mind, Frank. We need to know for sure if Angelica has passed on any information before we silence her. Find her. Then I'll come and have a little talk with her."

"Yes, sir, and the boyfriend?"

"He's dispensable."

"I'll let you know when we have her."

"Oh, and one more thing, Frank."

"Yes, sir."

"Don't forget, she is my daughter. I expect her to be treated with respect until I get there. I haven't forgotten our arrangement, Frank. I promised her to you once, and I'm a man of my word. So, make sure she's well taken care of and after I'm done with her, she'll be yours."

"Yes, sir." Frank closed the doors quietly. As he walked from his private meeting, Frank sneered with delight. He had been promised Angelica when she was just a girl. Now his reward would be so much sweeter.

JENNIFER WAS DRIVING DOWN A DESERTED SECTION of highway when she saw a car pulled off to the side of the road and an older woman swinging her arms violently over her head. Jennifer looked around her, seeing that there was no one else to help the lady. She rolled up all her windows, locked all her doors and cautiously slowed to a stop about 50 yards behind the woman's car, giving herself enough room to pull away if she had to.

The hysterical woman ran up to her window crying and yelling something in Spanish. Jennifer rolled her window down a crack and tried to explain to the woman that she didn't understand.

The woman motioned Jennifer to come with her, but Jennifer didn't budge.

"Esposo . . .esposo!" the woman kept crying, grasping her chest.

Finally, Jennifer was able to decipher that the woman thought her husband was having a heart attack.

Jennifer tried to explain through words and hand signals that she didn't have a phone but would drive to the next town and tell someone.

The woman wailed and begged Jennifer to help her husband. "Agua . . . agua." The woman pointed to the water jug on the seat next to Jennifer. "Por favor," the woman pleaded.

Looking around, and seeing not another car in sight, Jennifer grabbed the jug and opened her car door. Her intentions were to hand it to the woman, but the woman ran back to her car and waved for Jennifer to hurry. Jennifer got out of the car, scanning her surroundings. There was nothing there but the two cars, a small grove of trees, and the open highway.

Jennifer was about halfway to the woman's car when she heard a commotion behind her. She spun around in time to see two kids jump into her car and speed away. When she turned back, the woman was just getting into the driver's seat and roared from the side of the highway.

Jennifer stood, shocked and stunned by what had just happened. She'd been scammed. As careful as she had been, she'd still been scammed. Her car and all her belongings were gone. There she stood in the middle of the highway, in the middle of nowhere, with nothing more than a jug of water.

THE SAFE HOUSE WAS BUZZING with agents. Of course, none of them looked the part. They were dressed like locals and tourists in floral shirts, straw hats, beach sandals, and deep tans. They hovered over a map, each one talking about possible travel routes and out-of-the-way places to hide. Harrison paced the room, feeling like he was going to suffocate.

Bill pulled away from the group and took a seat. Harrison stopped his pacing long enough to ask, "Have you found out anything more?"

"We know she got medical treatment at a free clinic outside of Guaymas."

"Medical treatment?" Harrison's face twisted with worry. "Is she okay?"

"Seems she had some kind of cut on her foot."

"How'd you find that out?"

"She stayed in the motel across from the clinic. The woman who owns the motel said she was hurt and saw her later that night leaving the clinic."

"Did you talk to the doctor?"

"Yeah. He said he stitched her up and gave her some antibiotics, but she refused to take any pain medication."

"This doctor, did he say if anyone else had been around asking questions?"

"No."

"Do you believe him?"

"No reason not to, but we're checking him out just the same."

Harrison started pacing again, massaging and twisting at his neck.

"Harrison, relax. At least we know as of two days ago, she was okay and traveling south. That's more than we knew last night."

JENNIFER HAD BEEN WALKING on and off for three hours. The only thing worse than the burning sun overhead was the heat from the pavement on her feet. Her flimsy flip flops were no protection from the 100° temperatures, and her limping made it difficult for her to move very fast.

She would walk until she saw a cropping of trees, and then she would rest in their shade. The water jug had been a lifesaver, and she sipped at it sparingly, not knowing how much longer she would have to walk before reaching the next town. Even then, she had no idea what she would do once she got there. Her bag, her ID, her money—everything was in her car.

She wandered for another hour, lost in thought, feeling as if this would be the end of the line for her. She felt for the calling card in her pocket and figured she had no choice. She would call Harrison. She would turn herself in to the FBI. She could either die on the streets of Mexico or die at the hands of her father. Either way, she would be out of the misery she was in.

By the time she heard the car behind her it was too late. A police car was pulling off the side of the road, and instinctively she ran. She tried to dart through the tall dried weeds along the highway, but it took only a few minutes for the police officer to overtake her and knock her to the ground. He straddled her, pulling her arms behind her. Then, he cuffed her and pulled her to her feet. He turned her around, but she refused to look at him.

"Look at me." His accent was strong but his words were clear.

She looked up at him, still breathing hard.

"Why'd you run? Why are you out here alone?"

"Someone stole my car."

"Why'd you run then? Why you not ask for help?"

"I was afraid."

"Afraid of what? We are here to help." He walked her back to the patrol car where the other officer was leaning against the hood. He was big and round, and his roving eye let Jennifer know she wasn't wrong to be afraid.

The rotund officer drove while the one who tackled her began to question her. She explained how she was scammed into believing the woman was in trouble and that two teenagers jumped into her car and drove away. He listened intently as they drove back to the small station in the middle of a no-nothing town.

Once they arrived, the officer sat her in an old rickety chair across from his desk and asked her to explain again.

She repeated what happened and how she'd been tricked.

"And you have no ID?"

"No. Everything I had was in the car."

"And you are alone. There is no one in Mexico that can identify you?"

"No." She answered, but then thought of Juan Sanchez' business card. "Wait." She dug her hand in her pocket and grabbed the card. She stood and turned around so the officer could take the card from her hand. "He knows me."

The officer looked at the card. "This Juan Sanchez can identify you?"

"Yes. He treated my foot. He can tell you who I am."

The officer flipped the card around in his hand. "Okay." He smiled. "I will give him a call and see if he'll come down here and identify you."

"Come down? You want him to drive all the way down here? Can't he just do it over the phone?"

"No. I need someone to identify you, not talk to me about you," he explained sternly.

"But it would take him at least a day to drive here. What if he won't come?"

"I would drive a day to help out a friend, wouldn't you?" He smiled as he dialed the number. The officer spoke in Spanish, making it difficult for Jennifer to understand what was being said. Though her heritage was Spanish, her father would not allow it to be spoken in their home. Jennifer had picked up the simplest of words here and there and the cursing that would go on when her father fought with her mother, but bilingual she was not.

After a few moments, he handed the phone to Jennifer. "He wants to talk to you." He helped her cradle the phone against her neck since her hands were still cuffed behind her back. She was relieved to hear the familiar voice of Juan on the other end.

"Melissa, are you okay?"

"Yes. So far. But my car was stolen, with my ID and money and everything." Her voice broke.

"Don't worry. I'm leaving right now. I'll be there as soon as I can."

"You're really going to come all this way, just for me? Why?"

"I can't leave the Queen of England stranded, now can I?" He tried to lighten the mood. "It's going to be okay, Melissa. I'll be there soon."

She dropped the phone into her lap, and the officer retrieved it and put it back on the cradle. "Okay, senorita, it looks like you'll be staying with us for a little while." He walked her into a cell, unlocked the handcuffs that were digging into her wrist, and shut the door behind her. She sat on the edge of the cot and looked out at the rotund officer staring back at her; she turned and closed her eyes.

Help me, God, she muttered, desperate and humbled enough to except whatever help he'd be willing to offer.

It had been hours when a large, uniformed man ambled into the station. He glanced in the direction of the cell and smiled when he saw Jennifer. "What do we have here?" He walked over to her cell, looking her over, licking his lips. After taking a long, bawdy look, he walked to the desk of the stout officer named Dominguez. "What's with the princess in the cell?"

"Says her car was stolen. We found her wandering the highway with no ID."

"And what do you think?" His tone was mocking as he spoke loud enough to make sure Jennifer could hear him. She quickly looked around the station for the officer that had grabbed her. He'd been polite when the other officer acted like a creep.

"If you're looking for Rubio, he's gone." Dominguez got up and walked toward her. "He's got himself a nice wife, two little girls, a regular family man. He clocks out every night at 6:00 p.m. We're the only ones here now. Just you, me, and Ruiz."

Jennifer felt ill when she looked at the maniacal smiles on the faces of the two men. She would rather die than let them touch her.

"So tell me the truth, senorita." Dominguez moved closer and hung on the bars of her cell, his heavy accent making his words sound even more menacing. "What were you doing out there all alone?"

"I told you. My car was stolen." She faced the wall refusing to look at him.

"I don't think so. You know what I think? I think maybe you were dumped off by an angry boyfriend . . . or maybe an unhappy customer."

She tried to ignore him, his broken English, and his disgusting comments.

"Come on. What'd you do? Pick up some tourist looking for a good time, and then try to roll him? Or maybe he just didn't want to pay for services rendered?" His laugh was filthy and repulsive.

Ruiz was looking at her hard while Dominguez continued his harassment. His eyes were unsettling, making Jennifer look away. He got up from where he was sitting and approached her with a steely look, pushing Dominguez out of the way. "What'd you say your name was?"

She turned at the change in tone, startled that Ruiz was now scrutinizing her from only a few feet away. "Melissa." She spoke into her chest, afraid of making eye contact with him.

"And what were you doing out in the middle of the highway?"

"Like I told them, someone stole my car."

"Describe it to me."

"It was a silver Toyota Corolla with California plates."

"Toyota with California plate," he repeated. "I think I might have seen such a car."

"Really?" Jennifer turned to him, feeling hopeful.

"I need to call someone and see if I got the right car. But if I do, we'll have this cleared up in no time." His tone changed from menacing to calculating. Jennifer wasn't sure which was worse.

His words should have been reassuring to her, but something about his tone, his look, told her he wasn't to be trusted. Dominguez turned back toward the cell, wanting to continue his harassment.

"Leave her alone," Ruiz snapped at him as he moved to his desk.

Dominguez glared at him, but something told him not to argue. He sauntered away and took a seat behind his own desk, watching her the whole time. It was obvious Dominguez took his orders from Ruiz, and at the moment, Jennifer was grateful for his intervention.

Ruiz leaned back in his chair and stared at Jennifer the whole time he was on the phone. She strained but she could not hear what he was saying. It wouldn't matter. He was speaking in Spanish, his words quick and muffled, but his eyes never moved off of her.

THE PHONE RANG IN CALDERON'S STUDY.
"She's in jail."
"One of ours?" Calderon questioned Frank.
"We should have her by 9:00 p.m."

JENNIFER HAD BEEN SITTING IN THE CELL for what felt like an eternity. She'd watched the sun go down through the barred windows across from her, and she began to feel the effects of being out in the sun all afternoon. Her shoulders were beet red and stinging, and her face felt hot and tight. Although her body was in pain, she was grateful she hadn't had any further run-ins with the two sleazy officers. They had talked in hushed tones so that she couldn't hear and had leered at her from across the room, but that was it.

She now had a new dilemma occupying her thoughts. She needed to use the bathroom. She'd held it as long as she could, hoping that Juan would show up, but she couldn't hold it any longer.

"I need to use the bathroom," she said abruptly as she got to her feet.

Dominguez looked at her from across the room. "That's what the can is for." He pointed to an old rusted can under her cot. Now she knew where the rancid smell had been coming from.

"We'll, I'm not a man. I need a bathroom." Her voice was insistent as she crossed her arms, feeling the heat of her skin.

Dominguez smiled and got to his feet. He walked to the cell, turned the key in the lock, and swung open the door. When she tried to step out, he stopped her by putting his chest in her face. He grabbed her arm, causing her to wince as he slapped a cuff across her left wrist, pinching it tight. He yanked her out of the cell by the other cuff, causing her to stumble. Her limp was pronounced as she crossed the station. She hadn't dared to look at her foot, knowing that her three hour trek in the dirt and the heat had reopened her wound. It was taking all her self-control to keep her composure, not wanting the two revolting officers to see that she was in pain. She wouldn't give them the satisfaction.

As she reached the desk where Ruiz was sitting, he looked up at Dominguez with warning in his eyes. "Hacer no estupido."

He laughed. "What, me? I'm a perfect gentleman. I wouldn't think of doing anything to our guest." His words were overstated and unconvincing.

They walked around the corner, where he pushed open a door and pulled her into the cramped quarters of a bathroom in shambles. The floor was filthy, its boards splintered and stained. There was no lid on the back of the toilet, and the water in the bowl was a disgusting shade of yellow. He handcuffed her to a bar next to the toilet and stood outside.

After the humiliation of having to relieve herself with Dominguez only a few feet away and the pain of seeing her blistered face in the clouded mirror hanging over the cracked sink, she was returned to her cell to wait for Juan.

She felt the hard plastic of the calling card in her back pocket and debated if she should ask to make another call. *But what good could Harrison do? He's probably back in Santa Monica by now, telling the FBI everything he knows about me. Sure they would come and get me, but where would I be then? I'd be a sitting duck for someone on Carlos Calderon's payroll. At least now, waiting for Juan, I have a chance of getting out of here and maybe getting away.*

She decided she had no choice but to bide her time.

She had only to wait another hour before Juan Sanchez burst through the door. His eyes quickly darted from right to left. When he saw Jennifer sitting on the cot, he rushed to her cell. She jumped up and nearly skipped to the bars. Before she could say anything, he gave her a reassuring smile and squeezed her hand.

"Are you okay?" He looked at her blistering shoulders and reddened face.

"I'm okay. Just get me out of here."

"Don't worry, I'll straighten this out. You'll be out of there in no time."

He turned before she could say anything else and approached Ruiz's desk.

"You say you know this woman?" Ruiz questioned Juan while rubbing his chin. Dominguez continued to watch them intently. "What is her full name?"

"Yes, I know her. Her name is Melissa Dower. She's an American and I can vouch for her and the description of her car." Juan was talking with authority and firmness. He put his hands on Ruiz's desk and leaned forward. "You have nothing to hold her on. She's been victimized enough and needs to be given a chance to talk with the American authorities."

"She ran. She must be guilty of something!"

"She ran because she was afraid."

"Why should she be afraid unless she did something wrong?"

Juan's pleas turned to threats. His voice was loud and intimidating, yelling obscenities and speaking of police harassment and abuse. Dominguez approached the desk as if to restrain Juan, but Ruiz waived him off. Jennifer stood listening, afraid that if Juan didn't control himself, he too would find himself behind bars.

Finally Ruiz pushed himself up from where he'd been sitting, as Juan continued to talk to him with an abusive, disrespectful tone. He handed Juan a piece of paper and said, "Sign here." He slowly walked to Jennifer's cell, unlocked the door, and motioned to her that she was free to go.

"I am sorry for inconveniencing you, senorita, but we can never be too careful with foreigners without their proper papers. I suggest you get to the American Consulate and get some emergency papers as soon as possible."

"But what about my car? You said you thought you'd spotted it somewhere?"

"I was mistaken."

You're lying, she thought to herself but didn't dare say it out loud. She moved to Juan's side, controlling her instinct to run out the door. He tossed the papers on Ruiz's desk and grasped her hand. She clutched onto the lifeline he offered and walked as quickly as she could to his car. She jumped in the passenger's side, looking behind her, afraid that Ruiz and Dominguez would come running out and pull her back inside.

"Can you hurry, please?" she urged Juan as he got into the car. He reached across to calm her, taking her hand in his. "I'm not going to give them a chance to arrest me for reckless driving. Just relax. You're safe now."

He pulled away from the dirt lot and slowly headed down the highway. Jennifer was still gripping his hand, her head pressed against the seat, the pulsing in her forehead causing her eyes to blur.

He held her hand, stroking her wrist with his thumb. The repetitive motion was soothing, just what her racing heart needed. Neither one of them spoke. Jennifer knew Juan had to have all kinds of questions, but she didn't feel as if she could speak at the moment, and he was respecting her silence.

They'd been driving for awhile when Jennifer finally opened her eyes. "I don't know what to say. I must look awfully desperate to you, calling you when we'd only spoken for an hour or so. I just didn't know what else to do. I had your card in my pocket, and I thought since you were a citizen, they would trust you." She was rambling, her words tumbling out of her mouth.

"It's okay, Melissa." He squeezed her hand. She looked at their hands, realizing he was still holding onto her. She casually slipped her hand from his and raked her fingers through her hair, causing her to grimace.

"You have a pretty bad sunburn. We need to get something on that before it blisters." She looked at her shoulder, moving the strap of her tank top aside, seeing the obvious color difference.

"They didn't hurt you, did they?" he asked looking straight ahead. "I might be proud of my heritage but that doesn't mean I'm blind to everything around me. I've heard about what goes on in these jails, especially to women." He glanced at her for a brief second before turning his eyes back on the road.

"No. I'm fine." She dropped her eyes to her lap. She'd been humiliated, but she was thankful that was all.

He gave a sigh of relief.

They drove again in silence, Jennifer's mind trying to formulate what she was going to do next.

"Where are we going?"

"Guadalajara."

"Is that where you live?"

"No. But that's where the nearest American Consulate is."

Jennifer froze, her body becoming still and rigid.

"Are you all right?" Juan asked curiously. "You do want to go to the authorities, don't you?"

"Well, yes, of course. It's just that . . . I mean . . ." She stuttered and stammered, not knowing what to say.

"You are in trouble, aren't you?" When she didn't answer immediately, he slowed, pulled over to the side of the road, and put the car in park. He waited for her to say something, but his patience was running short. "Okay, spill it. I just risked getting thrown in jail for you; I think I deserve the truth."

Jennifer looked away from his intense stare, the gleam of the door handle catching her eye. He hit the automatic lock button, getting her to turn her attention back on him. "Don't even think about running because I'll hunt you down and turn you in myself." His tone was angry, almost resentful.

"Okay. You're right. I am in trouble. Melissa's not my real name. I made it up."

"Why?" he asked, not looking the least bit shocked.

"Because I was picked up for shoplifting last week in Tijuana." Her voice was convincing or at least she hoped it was. "It wasn't my fault." Her words were hurried as she made up a flimsy story and spoke it at the same time. "The shopkeeper lied, said I took something that I didn't. I tried to explain to the officer what happened, I even let him look in my purse, but he wouldn't listen. He started making crude remarks and told me how much trouble I was in, and I got scared. So I ran. He chased after me, but not for long. I didn't realize until later that he'd taken my license out of my purse."

"So what's your real name?"

"Amy . . . Amy Brown."

He drummed his fingers on the steering wheel, not saying a word, not even looking at her. Jennifer could tell he was thinking . . . about what, she wasn't sure.

CHAPTER TWENTY-FIVE

Juan kept a firm grip on Jennifer's elbow as they headed to their hotel room. She wasn't sure if he was trying to be helpful since her steps were unsure or if he were afraid she was going to make a run for it. She sensed he no longer trusted her and felt the pangs of guilt. He'd done nothing but help her, and she continued to repay him with lies.

She had convinced him to wait until morning before going to the consulate. It would buy her some time, but what she would do with it she wasn't sure.

Juan unlocked the door and allowed Jennifer to step in before him. He brushed his hand against the wall, searching for the light. The room was washed in an amber glow, illuminating the upscale accommodations.

Jennifer gazed around at the fine furniture and luxurious bedding. It reminded her of the hotel she and Harrison had stayed at in New Mexico. The emotion she felt thinking of Harrison took her by surprise. She was angry at him for betraying her; at least she thought she was. But inside where her emotions battled against each other, her heart waged war against her mind.

Her attention was quickly turned back to Juan when she heard him drop the deadbolt in place and chain the door. He looked at her with curious eyes, and she became even more aware of their current circumstances. She had already told him once she wasn't looking for a relationship, but she couldn't help but wonder if he felt he was deserving of a show of gratitude because of his willingness to help her.

"Let me see your foot," he said as he crossed the room with insistence in his tone.

Jennifer sat on the edge of the bed while Juan pulled up a chair and brought her foot up to his lap. He unwrapped the filthy bandage that had been blackened by her expedition and shook his head in frustration. The wound he had so neatly stitched and cleaned just two days ago was red, swollen, and once again seeping with infection. He stood.

"Come on; we need to get that washed out. Your foot is filthy." He slipped his arm around her and helped her stand. When his shoulder pressed against hers, the heat of her sunburn ignited. She bit her lip to hold back her gasp and relied on his strength as her own weakened.

Even in her pain, Jennifer couldn't help but notice the extravagant amenities the bathroom had to offer. A marble vanity, a glassed-in shower, and a huge Jacuzzi tub nestled in the corner. Lush, white towels hung from gold towel racks, and crystal decanters of bubble bath and soaking salts decorated the corner of the tub.

Juan sat on the edge of the bath, running water over his hand until the temperature was just right. He turned to look at her, taking in her overall appearance.

She stood bracing herself against the large marble countertop. The fatigue from her walk and the effects of the sun were making her feel weak and nauseous.

"You know," he said in a low, sultry tone, "instead of just washing off your foot, why don't you take a nice, relaxing bath?"

"No. I'm fine." She tried to stand up straighter. Though a bath sounded wonderful, she didn't want to put herself in a more vulnerable position than she already was.

He grinned at her and raised one eyebrow. "Come on. This room cost me a fortune. We might as well enjoy its finer qualities." Jennifer found his emphasis on "we" unsettling.

The noise of Juan turning on the jets made her jump. He laughed at her surprise and moved to stand dangerously close to her. He brushed his finger against the redness of her cheek and down her sunburned shoulder, causing her to shudder.

"Need a hand?" he whispered as he tugged slightly at her sleeve.

"No. I can do it." Her answer was quick.

"Are you sure, because I don't mind." He leaned in, but she quickly stepped away.

He was amused by her shyness and gave her a conciliatory smile before he left her to herself and closed the door. She sighed in relief that he hadn't continued his advances.

Jennifer quietly turned the lock on the doorknob before undressing. She inched herself into the swirling water, first adjusting to the pain in her foot, then the heat and the motion of the water. The jets pulsed against her flesh, massaging away the aching and soreness in her muscles. The warm water on her shoulders stung, but she was finally able to bite back the pain and rest her head against the folded towel behind her neck.

She laid there, wanting nothing more than to relax and enjoy the soothing pulse of the water jets. But with her world racing out of control, she had no time for relaxation. She weighed her options and possibilities knowing she didn't have many choices. Juan seemed more than willing to offer his help, but with the attention he was already showing her, she knew he would expect something more than a simple thank you in return.

She sunk lower in the water trying to convince herself that spending time with Juan wouldn't be so bad, especially if he would be willing to side-step the authorities and take her at her word. He was extremely attractive and so far had been gentle and charming towards her. She could show him a little affection, be a little more accommodating if it meant buying her some more time. *I can handle it.* She told herself it was survival; she had no choice.

Who are you kidding? she chided herself inwardly. She had always told herself she would do anything to survive, except for prostitution, but that was precisely what she was contemplating. Although she wasn't exactly standing on a street corner offering her body to a lonely stranger, the outcome would be the same. She would be offering herself for something in return—sex for safety, companionship for shelter. She closed her eyes in disgust, hating herself for even considering such a thing, but then again, what was she saving herself for?

Before she could think much more about it, there was a light tap on the door. "Are you okay, your highness?" Juan's tone was playful. "I would feel terrible if the queen was to drown in a bath that I had drawn."

"Stop calling me that." Jennifer snapped at Juan's good-natured teasing, not wanting him to be so gallant, so kind, when all she planned to do was use him.

"As you wish, Ms. Dower, but I am here if you are in need of any assistance." He continued to speak with a regal tone.

Jennifer shut her eyes, confused and bewildered at her circumstances. She replayed the few conversations she'd had with Juan, trying to convince herself that she could be attracted to him if it wasn't for her feelings for Harrison. Then, something struck her. He called her Ms. Dower. *How does he know my last name?*

Jennifer sat upright in the tub, splashing water over the edge, trying desperately to remember her exact conversations with Juan. She replayed them over and over, coming up with the same conclusion each time. She'd told him her name was Melissa. She had never used the name Dower. *Did I tell him over the phone when I called for help?* She thought hard about her phone conversation from the police station, squinting her eyes shut as if that would improve her memory. *No, I never used the name Dower.* She had strained to hear the phone conversation between him and the officer. Even if she didn't know Spanish, she would have recognized her alias being used, and she was sure it hadn't been.

She remembered the way he barged into the station, demanding her freedom, vouching for her by name. *How did he know if I didn't tell him, and if I didn't, then who did?*

A chill enveloped Jennifer's body as she stepped from the tub, but it wasn't the climate of the room causing her to shudder. Somehow, Juan knew she was going by the last name of Dower. Someone had told him. Jennifer fumbled with her clothes, dressing quickly as she thought of the possibilities.

Maybe Juan had reported treating her at the clinic. Maybe there was some kind of paperwork doctors had to file when they treated foreigners. No, that couldn't be it or he would have asked for her full name at the clinic.

She thought again about their conversations, straining to remember every detail. Had she given him her assumed name? Because if she hadn't, and the authorities hadn't, that left only one other possibility and the reality of it made her double over in horror.

The thought of her father knowing where she was, who she was pretending to be, and the predicament she was in was more than she could handle. Her rapid breathing and already weakened state were causing her to hyperventilate. She began to gasp, seeing pinpricks of light flash in her eyes. The room was spinning out of control. She lost her balance, stumbling against the wall with a thud. She heard Juan pounding on the bathroom door, his voice harsh as he asked if she was all right. She was unable to catch her breath long enough to answer. The last thing she remembered was hearing the splintering of wood and seeing Juan lunging towards her as she sat on the cold tile floor, her head between her knees.

Her skin was cold and clammy. Juan helped her from the floor and led her to the bed where she laid down without protest. She could sense Juan hovering over her. He pressed a damp cloth to her forehead which she proceeded to push away.

"What happened?" She tried sitting up, but Juan restrained her with gentle but firmly paced hands to her reddened arms.

"You must have passed out. I think your sunburn has turned into a mild case of heat stroke." He was sitting on the edge of the bed, pressed up against her hip. Jennifer laid there, remembering her last thoughts and the real reason she'd collapsed. She studied Juan as he handed her a glass of water and helped her tip her head enough to sip at it. Her eyes were fixed on him, looking for the slightest hint or clue that he knew more about her than he was letting on. He pressed a stethoscope to her chest, pulling slightly at the collar of her soiled tank top.

"I don't think that's necessary," she said as she brushed his hand aside and pulled her shirt back in place.

He chuckled at her embarrassment. "I am a doctor, you know. I do this kind of stuff all the time." He removed the scope from his ears and set it on the nightstand.

"By that do you mean taking advantage of people who pass out or bringing strange women to high-priced hotel rooms?"

He looked at her with only slight amusement as he leaned closer, placing his hands on either side of her head, pinning her to the pillow.

"You know, for someone who's in a lot of trouble, you don't seem that appreciative of my help."

"Maybe I'm beginning to worry what that help is going to cost me." She looked for anything in his eyes, in his expression, that would show her he knew exactly what she meant, but instead her comment was met with laughter.

He pushed away from her and pulled something from his medical bag. "Hey, I've been a complete gentleman. I've offered you nothing but bedside care." He squeezed a clear gel from a little white tube and began dabbing it on one of her blistering shoulders. Jennifer winced and flinched as he rubbed in the chilly gel.

"So why are you being so helpful?" she asked him pointedly.

"The Hippocratic oath. I take it very seriously."

"That explains why you're putting that putrid smelling stuff on my shoulder and stitched up my foot the other day, but it doesn't explain why you would drive for hours to get a complete stranger out of jail."

He ignored her, continuing with the ointment on her other shoulder. She watched him watching her. She looked in his eyes and in an instant decided to change her tactics. If he truly was working for her father, there was no way he would be allowed to take advantage of her or make good on his advances; her father wouldn't permit it. So . . . she decided to call his bluff.

She leaned in closer to him, allowing her fingers to play with the buttons on his shirt. "I really do appreciate all your help, Juan. I know I haven't shown it, but that's because I was angry and hurt." She saw the confusion register on his face as she moved closer. "Maybe we could start over. Like you said, no sense letting this beautiful hotel room go to waste." She slipped her hand inside his shirt and pressed a kiss to his neck.

Juan pulled her hand away and got up from the bed.

"What's wrong?" Jennifer questioned. "I thought this is what you wanted?"

"I do . . . I did." He tossed things back into his medical bag as he tripped over his words. "But not like this. You're sick and exhausted. You passed out just a few minutes ago, and you're running a fever."

"So what!" Her words got insistent as fear began to rise inside her. She knew the more he refused, the more he was proving what she already suspected. "I want to show my appreciation. Is that so bad?"

He didn't answer. He just avoided eye contact with her and rummaged around in his medical bag, looking nervous and tense.

She got up and paced to the other side of the room. "You're just like Harrison. He would get me all heated up, and then bam, he'd go cold on me. You men are all alike. You talk a big talk, but that's all you're good for. What a disappointment you turned out to be."

Juan did not like his virility being insulted. He had Jennifer in his clutches in two short strides and shook her as he spoke. "Look, I could nail you right now if I wanted to, but I'm not into rebound sex. I'm not going to be anyone's substitute."

She snapped her arms out from under his hold, her sunburn stinging and pulsing, her mind reeling. She walked back to the edge of the bed and slumped on it. She had to think. She had to figure out a way to get away from Juan. He was holding back from her, and it had nothing to do with a proper bedside manner.

Juan tried to act casual as he walked around the room, parting the curtains slightly, when he thought Jennifer wasn't watching. When she caught him glancing at his watch, she knew she was running out of time. He was expecting someone tonight.

She sat on the edge of the bed and looked at Juan. "I'm sorry for what I said. I can't blame you for turning me down. I must look like such a loser to you."

"Forget about it," Juan said casually as he paced a little more. "Why don't you just lay down and relax. You're going to have to be rested and in your right mind when you try to explain to the authorities how it is you have no I.D., no money, and no one who can vouch for you."

"You're right." Jennifer curled up on the bed. "It exhausts me just to think about it." She closed her eyes and rested her head against the pillow.

She listened as Juan continued to pace and roam around the room. She chanced opening one eye and saw him once again peering through the curtains. She closed her eye, feeling like she was going to jump out of her skin. The way Juan was watching the window meant he was expecting someone tonight. She'd be lucky if she even saw tomorrow.

She rolled over on the bed with a heavy sigh, wanting Juan to believe she was asleep, hoping he would let his defenses down or get distracted, something that would give her the chance to get out.

It only took another 20 minutes for Jennifer to get the break she was looking for. Juan stepped into the bathroom, the splintered doorframe no longer allowing the door to latch. She could hear his voice, low and muffled, and she realized he was talking on the phone. This was her chance. She needed to get out now.

She scooped up her shoes at the foot of the bed and quietly moved backwards towards the door, keeping her eye on the beam of light coming from the bathroom. She carefully slid the chain from the door and unlatched it as her other hand quietly turned the dead bolt. The streak of light grew larger, and she knew she only had seconds to get away. She slipped through the door and was one flight down when she heard Juan yell to her from the balcony.

She never looked back. She just ran as fast and as hard as she could. She ran between buildings and around street vendors. It was pitch black and hard for her to see where she was going, but it didn't matter. It didn't matter where she was going, only that she was getting away.

Finally, after zig-zagging through several city streets and getting further and further away from the nice store fronts and large hotels of the resort area of Mexico, Jennifer found herself in a darkened alley, crouched in the doorway of a boarded up store. She sat there, catching her breath, her eyes darting from side-to-side to see if anyone was watching her. When she was convinced that Juan had not been able to follow her, she slid to the cold concrete beneath her and wrapped her arms around her knees. With her head down and her shoulders shaking with emotion, she questioned God. *How much more God? How much more are you going to dump on me? Where is the hope and the peace and the love that Harrison talked about?*

Do you believe I am who I say I am?

Jennifer jumped to her feet, ready to run. She looked around to see who was there, but found that she was still alone. *Great . . . now I'm losing my mind*, she scolded herself as she wiped tears from her cheeks.

She hunched back down on the cold pavement and felt overwhelming despair. She closed her eyes in exhaustion. *I can't go on*, she thought to herself. *I have no where to go and no one to help me.*

Let me help you.

There it was again—the voice. She opened her eyes and looked around, but a feeling in her soul told her that the voice wasn't coming from without but from within. She looked towards the sky and began talking to the God she had tried for so long to ignore.

JENNIFER WAS AWAKENED by the noise of two garbage cans crashing together. Through the light from the early morning sky, she could see a man in soiled clothes rummaging around in the cans behind what looked to be a small, rundown restaurant.

She got to her feet, stretching and wincing. Her entire body was sore and stiff, and she could only imagine how she looked after spending the night huddled in an alley. The blisters on her shoulders were open, and her hair was mangled and sticking to the puss seeping from them. When she tried to walk, she gritted her teeth from the pain. It felt as if she was walking on cut glass; her foot cried out from all the punishment she'd put it through. She hobbled down the alley with one goal in mind, to find a phone. She decided she would call Harrison. She really had no choice. With her father's men after her, the thought of being brought in by the FBI sounded better than what might happen when her father found her.

She did her best to blend in, but it was hard since she had strayed away from the normal tourist routes. Her obviously fair, but blistered skin and disheveled clothes made her stick out like a sore thumb, even among the other street people. It was obvious she was an American and didn't belong.

She stayed close to buildings, keeping her head down, trying not to make eye contact with any of the locals and ignoring the whistles and comments coming from the men on the streets. She cautiously crossed a narrow road and made her way down another alley. She could see a gas station sign up ahead and headed for it, hoping they would have a phone she could use. She was almost to the end of the alley when three men stepped out from behind a broken-down fence and blocked her way.

They spoke to her in Spanish while their eyes traced over her body, and their smiles twisted with lust. She didn't know what they were saying, but it was clear to her what they wanted.

She began to back away from them, when one of the men lunged at her and pulled her towards a fenced in yard. She struggled against his hold as the other two men sneered and laughed, blocking her way with their bodies.

Not like this God. Please, not like this.

Just when it seemed as if the men were going to be able to overpower her and pull her from the alley, an idea came over her.

In a deep, gravely voice, she began to bark. The men stopped their taunting and looked at her, stunned. She barked some more, lunging at the men, snapping at them with her teeth. They didn't know what to make of her behavior.

They looked at her like she was crazy and then looked at each other like they weren't sure what they should do next.

One of the men grabbed at her mouth, clamping hard on her cheeks, yelling at her in Spanish to shut up, but that didn't stop her. She shook free of his hold and continued barking, howling, and lashing about like a mad person. One of the men stepped away from the others, saying something before disappearing down the alley. Obviously he didn't want to deal with a loco woman.

Now she was left with two of the men, one of them getting angrier at her behavior. He moved behind her, wrapped his arm around her neck and yanked her up against his chest. He rattled off something in Spanish, Jennifer unable to understand him as he tightened his grip. He began pawing at her clothes, pulling at the button on her jeans, getting more and more excited as he held her tight. The other man was watching, eyes bulging, mouth open wide with anticipation.

Jennifer's mind reeled. What could she do? There was no way she would be able to fight off two men with her being so weak and them looking so possessed. She struggled against the man and with a newfound burst of energy was finally able to twist free. She began barking again and dropped to her knees on the grass. She pulled at clumps of grass and shoved them in her mouth. The men looked at her with horror and began to back away. She heard the word "loco" again and again as they spoke to each other right before they disappeared around the side of the fence.

Jennifer quickly got to her feet and ran for the alley. She was spitting out dirt and grass as the gas station came into view. She slipped behind the station and looked around. It was old and dingy, but still being used. Some of the windows were covered in an oily soot while others were boarded up with plywood. She inched around the side of the building and nearly burst into tears when she saw the frame of an old telephone booth, glass broken out, leaning against the peeling wood of the station. *Please work, please work,* she mumbled to herself as she hurried to the booth. Her hands were shaking as she picked up the phone and put it to her ear. The dial tone was the sweetest thing she'd ever heard.

CHAPTER TWENTY-SIX

H arrison was listening to Bill as he gave the instructions of the day when one of the other agents who was on the phone, rushed to the T.V. "You're going to want to hear this," he said as he changed channels and turned up the volume.

A reporter was speaking, when the picture of a man appeared over his right shoulder. The report was in Spanish, so Harrison stood perplexed, not understanding the importance of the report. Bill's head sagged between his shoulders as the reporter finished and passed off the anchor to the pretty brunette sitting next to him.

"What? What was that all about?" Harrison asked puzzled.

Bill looked at Harrison with hesitation. "The man they were talking about, the picture, it was of a Dr. Juan Sanchez. He was just found murdered in his hotel room."

"The same guy who said he'd helped Jennifer?" Harrison grimaced in unbelief.

"Yes." Bill massaged his forehead before dragging his hand down his face in uneasiness. "An American woman was seen running from the hotel room." He turned to Harrison to see if he was getting the full picture.

When Harrison saw Bill's look of concern, he barked. "You don't think Jennifer had anything to do with this do you?"

"She fits the description." Bill volunteered.

"That's ridiculous. What would Jennifer be doing with the doctor that treated her a few days ago, and why wouldn't he have called us and let us know he was with her?"

Bill's eyes looked distant, worrisome. "Maybe someone else got to him first?"

"You mean Calderon?"

"It's possible. Like I said before, Calderon's tentacles are far reaching here in Mexico. Maybe he used the doctor to flush out Angelica."

"But Jennifer . . . killing him?" The thought was more than Harrison could assimilate.

"She's already done it once." Bill's words were an accusation. Harrison was ready to fire back when Bill held up his hand to stop him. "Harrison, I know you care for her deeply, but I don't think you know the extent of her character. She is a fighter, a survivor, a manipulator. She's going to do whatever it takes to keep fighting, to keep running, to survive, even if it means killing. I think you have to come to the realization that Angelica Calderon is dangerous and isn't going to let anything stand between her and her freedom."

Harrison sat in a chair, his head between his hands, the portrait of Jennifer that Bill had just painted twisting at his stomach. Bill's attitude had shifted from helping Jennifer to explaining that she was now considered armed and dangerous.

Harrison's phone vibrated in his pocket. His heart raced as he dug it out and held it to his ear. "Hello?"

"It's me." Jennifer's voice was low and trembling.

"Jennifer, where are you?"

Everyone in the room jumped to attention.

"I don't know," she whispered and began crying.

"Don't cry, Jennifer. It's going to be all right. We're going to find you."

"It's too late, Harrison, there's no time." She cried quietly but tried to regain her composure.

"What do you mean? Are you hurt? Are you okay?"

"My father knows where I am, Harrison. A man . . . Juan Sanchez, he's after me. He helped me the other day, but now I think he works for my father, or my father is using him. I don't know. I got away from him last night, but I know he won't give up. I have to get out . . . "

"Jennifer, listen to me. Juan Sanchez is dead."

"What?" She felt as if she'd been punched.

"He was found last night, murdered. You were seen running from the hotel. Jennifer, what happened?" Harrison's voice was soft, and he lowered his head, bracing himself for her confession.

Jennifer held the phone tighter to her ear. "I didn't do it, Harrison, I swear I didn't," she pleaded, begging for Harrison to believe her. "I don't know what happened. I ran when I realized I was being set up. You've got to believe me. I didn't do it. It had to have been my father. It wasn't me." She kept repeating herself as she sobbed.

"It's okay, Jennifer, I believe you," He sighed with relief, knowing Jennifer wasn't the dangerous person that Bill was trying to make her out to be.

Jennifer needed to refocus so she could tell Harrison what she wanted him to know before it was too late. "Look, Harrison, I just wanted to tell you," she ran her hand across her face, wiping her runny nose and wet cheeks, "if I don't make it, I'm going to be okay. I don't want you to worry about me."

"What do you mean, if you don't make it? I'm here, Jennifer. I'm here in Mexico. Tell me where you are; we'll come and get you."

"It's too dangerous, Harrison. I just wanted you to know, I'm going to be okay."

"What do you mean you're going to be okay?" Harrison was confused. "Are you somewhere safe? Is someone helping you?"

"Yes." Jennifer cleared her voice. "You were right, Harrison. I needed to believe in someone other than myself. God saved me last night, Harrison. I talked to him. He was there with me in the alley. He saved me. I know now, even if I don't make it, I'm going to be okay. He helped me get away last night and again this morning."

Harrison couldn't believe what he was hearing. Jennifer had finally surrendered her life to God. And though he should be ecstatic, he was frightened by the sound of exhaustion and futileness he heard in her voice. "Jennifer, you can't give up now. Focus . . . look around, describe to me where you are. You can't be too far from the hotel where Sanchez was found."

Jennifer took in her surroundings. Maybe it wasn't too late. Maybe Harrison could still help her.

"Come on, Jennifer." Harrison's voice was gentle. "Explain to me where you are, what do you see?"

"I'm at a gas station. It's an old, brown building with the paint chipping off of it."

"What's the name of the station?"

"I don't know. It just has a big sign that says "Gas." I can't see a name anywhere."

"What else, Jennifer? Are there any other buildings around?" Harrison was scribbling down Jennifer's description of the building for Bill while he tried to coax more information from her.

"There's a building across the street that says," Jennifer strained with her Spanish diction. "Levar y secar."

Harrison look up, repeating her words to the men around him. One of the men quickly answered. "A laundromat."

"What else, Jennifer?"

"There's a bar." She squinted to read the sign that would normally be lit up at night, but now was only fluorescent tubing. "Lil Pepe's Cantina."

Again Harrison repeated her words to the agents that hovered nearby.

"Oh, no!"

Harrison heard Jennifer gasp over the phone.

She watched as she saw the familiar face step from the black Lincoln that had just pulled up to the curb across the street.

"It's too late, Harrison," she whimpered softly into the phone that was pressed tightly to her cheek. "They found me. Frank found me." She tried to shrink from view as she watched the man of her childhood nightmares walk around the side of the car and go into the bar.

"What's happening? Where is he, Jennifer, what's going on?" Harrison got up and started pacing; whispering Frank's name to his friend. Bill acknowledged with a nod that he knew who he was talking about while Harrison was feeling panicked at what it was he could not see. At the same time, one of the agents yelled that he knew where she was. He knew the station and the bar. She was only 10 minutes away.

"Hold on, Jennifer. We're coming. We know where you are. You've got to stay put."

"I can't; he'll see me. I've got to go."

"No, Jennifer. You need to stay there. We're coming for you." He said this as everyone scrambled around the room, gathering equipment, getting ready for what could be an all-out war.

"I love you, Harrison." Her voice was heavy with emotion. "Just know that I love you, and I'm sorry that . . ." her words choked her. "I'm sorry that I didn't listen to you sooner. You were right. I know now that God loves me and has a place for me. I just wish it could have been with you."

"But Jennifer, we're coming, we're . . ." Harrison realized he was no longer talking to Jennifer. She was gone.

He jumped into action with the rest of the men but was met with Bill's hand pressed against his chest. "You're staying here, Harrison. It's too dangerous. Frank Mancino is Caldron's right-hand man. If he's here, he's not alone. You've got to stay here."

Harrison lost all control. He swung at a table lamp, sending it crashing to the floor. He then turned his aggression on Bill and slammed him up against the wall. Before he could do or say anything else, two agents had rushed him and pinned him to the ground. Harrison lashed about as he yelled, "I have to go. Jennifer will run from you. She won't know who to trust. I've got to go. I've got to be there."

The men wrestled to keep Harrison under control, but Bill waived them off. Harrison jumped to his feet, and with intensity and a great amount of self-control, he stared at Bill. "Please, Bill. I've got to be there. Don't do this to me."

Bill said some choice words and flung his hands in the air. "Okay, but only on one condition."

JENNIFER SLOWLY WALKED BACKWARDS from the dilapidated phone booth, hugging the wall, trying to be invisible. She never took her eyes off the door of the bar and watched as Frank sauntered out and stepped back into the Lincoln. She slumped behind the trash dumpster pushed up against the back fence of the gas station and watched as Frank's car disappeared from sight. She took a deep breath, feeling a rush of relief. She crouched behind the dumpster, keeping the phone booth in sight. Harrison told her to stay put, that he was coming. She watched and prayed. Maybe it wasn't too late.

Jennifer had no sooner imagined what it would be like to see Harrison and feel his safe and protective arms around her, when she saw the front end of the Lincoln pull up to the gas pumps just yards away from her. She looked around her, seeing where she could go, where she could run. She squeezed through a missing plank in the broken-down fence that separated the gas station from the open field behind it. Instinctively, she knew she should run, run for all she was worth, but emotionally, she was drawn to the phone booth, straining to keep it in view. It was her only link to Harrison and a part of her knew that it was her only chance to see him again.

Frank walked up to the building, talking to the attendant that was asleep in the office. He strolled around the side of the building and saw the receiver of the pay phone swinging at the end of its cord. His head snapped up and before Jennifer could make a move, he'd spotted her between the cracks in the fence.

She heard Frank hollering as she started racing across the field. The screeching of tires and the yelling of voices told her that several men were after her. Part of her wanted to collapse in the overgrown brush and hope that they wouldn't see her, but her determination wouldn't allow her to stop. She kept fighting against the prickly weeds that whipped at her face and grabbed at her clothes, all the while praying that God would rescue her just one more time.

She looked back briefly as she crossed a narrow dirt road. She didn't see the steep decline on the other side of the road and stumbled to the ground. She thudded against a large boulder, hearing something crack against the impact. She couldn't catch her breath or get to her feet. She grabbed at her side and tried to crawl for cover. She could hear the men gaining on her and knew it was only a matter of seconds before they had her in their sights. That's when she saw the large drainage pipe that ran under the dirt road.

She quickly dragged her body to the pipe and peered in. The stench nearly threw her back on her heels and light was swallowed up by the darkness inside it, but she had no choice. It was the only place she could hide.

She began crawling through the sludge that gathered at the bottom of the pipe. Every time her stomach constricted and fought against the smell of the filth she was sliding through, her side screamed in pain, making it hard for her to breathe. She heard the faintness of footsteps and voices above her and knew she couldn't take the chance of making any noise. She carefully turned to sit in the mire of the darkened pipe and gasped as a pain shot through her side. She covered her mouth and sat completely still. She saw feet rush past the entrance of the pipe and prayed that they would keep going.

Moments passed and with it came feelings of claustrophobia and panic. The sweltering heat and the constricting position she was sitting in was beginning to play with her mind. She was sure something was crawling on her. She could feel something on her feet, and again against her cheek. She placed her head against her knees, and had to will herself not to move, not to scream, not to give herself away. Her self-preservation lasted only a matter of minutes.

"Hello, Angelica." The voice was undeniably Frank Mancino's—a voice she would never forget. She opened her eyes and turned her head to see Frank hunched down, his hand up against his face, trying to block the stench. He was staring at her through the small circular pipe opening. When his eyes met hers he lowered his hand and smiled. "It's time to go home, Angelica. Your father is waiting for you."

She looked in the other direction to see if there was one last chance of escape. She heard a click, as Frank cocked his gun and knew instinctively that it was trained on her. "I wouldn't do that if I were you. I'm supposed to bring you back in one piece, but your father would understand if there was an unfortunate accident. He would believe me if I told him you killed yourself before I could catch up to you."

She turned back to him, knowing it was over, knowing there was nothing left for her to do. She emerged from the pipe slowly, covered in a mixture of sweat, muck, and blood, squinting her eyes against the raging sun.

Frank turned his head and cursed when he got a whiff of the rancidness that seemed to envelop her. His disgust didn't last. Soon his face twisted into a menacing smile. Other men gathered around them, guns drawn, panting and out of breath. Frank raised his hand and Jennifer prepared herself for the impact. But instead, he ran his fingers down the length of her cheek. "Well, well, well, Angelica. It's been a long time." He stepped back to take in her whole body with a self-satisfying stare. "Even covered in garbage, I can see that you're as beautiful as your mother was. I'm going to enjoy every minute of making up for lost time." He moved closer to her, bending to brush his bristly jaw against hers. When he turned to kiss her, she twisted her face to the side. He laughed at her attempt to deny him.

"That's okay, Angelica, we have plenty of time for that." He pawed at her arm as if petting a beloved pet. "You're mine now. We have all the time in the world."

His caress turned to a painful grip on her arm, but Jennifer didn't feel it, she was numb. She would never allow Frank to hurt her, not where it mattered, not in her heart or her soul. Those two places could only be touched by God—God and Harrison Lynch.

Frank dragged Jennifer along with him as his men followed. They were almost back to the fence when the sound of weapons cocking came through the dense weeds.

"Freeze, Mancino. There's nowhere for you to go."

The three men that surrounded Frank pulled their weapons, giving Bill and his men no recourse but to take them out. As they collapsed to the ground in a hail of gunfire, Frank swung Jennifer around in front of him, using her as a shield. He locked his arm around her neck and held his gun to her temple.

"You're going to have to go through her to get to me!" Frank didn't know who he was yelling at. Bill and his men were still hidden behind the cover of weeds.

"Give it up, Frank! There's no way we're going to let you walk away from here." Bill's voice was booming from right in front of him.

"Then I guess you give me no choice."

In a confusion of motion and sound, Harrison rushed from cover, yelling at Frank and waving his arms. Reflexively, Frank pointed the gun at Harrison, dropping him in one shot. Jennifer screamed as she saw Harrison collapse to the ground as other shots rang out. She felt herself being pulled to the ground by Frank. When his grip on her loosened, she scrambled to get to her feet and stumbled forward to Harrison's still form.

Immediately a man she didn't know gently grabbed at her shoulders and moved her out of the way. He carefully rolled Harrison over and began speaking to him. Jennifer crawled back to his side and gasped when she saw his eyes fluttering.

"Harrison." Bill tried to get his attention. "Harrison, don't move. I need you to lay still." Bill unzipped the windbreaker Harrison was wearing. Jennifer didn't understand what was going on. She saw Harrison shot. She saw him go down.

Bill removed the windbreaker emblazoned with the initials FBI that Harrison was wearing to reveal a bulletproof vest. Bill could see the dent the bullet had made and carefully removed the vest. He bent close to Harrison's mouth and listened as he tried to take a breath. He pressed at his side, making Harrison wince in pain. "Sorry, Harrison, just lay still. You're going to be all right."

Bill saw the confusion in Jennifer's eyes.

"He's going to be okay. He might have some cracked ribs, but he's going to be fine. Either way, we need to get him to a hospital."

She grabbed for Harrison's hand and squeezed it tight. She held her side with her other hand and bent close to his face. "I'm here, Harrison. Everything's going to be okay."

His eyes opened and focused on Jennifer. He tried to say something, but it came out as a gasp. Instead, he squeezed her hand, tears running down the sides of his face. Jennifer brushed at his tears, trying to disguise her own pain.

Bill was yelling orders and the entire scene became a mixture of procedure and confusion. "Angelica, I'm going to need you to come over here." Bill helped Jennifer to her feet and led her away from Harrison's side. It was then that her body buckled with exhaustion.

JENNIFER LAID IN BED, her eyes roaming around the room. She'd been in a fog for what seemed like days. Every time she woke up, she was assured that Harrison was doing fine and that she was safe from her father. It was enough to allow her to fall back to sleep.

She heard hushed voices and opened her eyes to see Harrison and the man who introduced himself as Bill Dennison standing at the foot of her bed, talking in whispered tones.

"Hey." Harrison smiled and slowly moved to her side when he saw she was awake. He winced slightly as he bent over and pressed a kiss to her forehead. "How are you feeling?"

"Okay now." She reached for his hand and clutched it, needing the physical contact to know she wasn't imagining him. She thought about the last time she saw him in the field, unable to talk to her, and it brought tears to her eyes.

"Hey." He squeezed her hand. "Why the tears?"

"I thought you were dead."

"But I'm not. I'm going to be fine." He sat on the bed along side of her, himself needing the physical contact after feeling as if he had lost her forever.

"Look," Bill cleared his throat and made his way to the door. "I've got some phone calls to make, and you two have some catching up to do. I'll be back in a little while." He made eye contact with Harrison. "Don't overdo it." His stern composure broke into a smile as he left the room.

Harrison turned his attention back to Jennifer. He brushed his fingers across her haphazardly cropped hair and smiled.

She brought her hand up to the nape of her neck and nervously played with her choppy hairstyle. "It will grow . . . and the color will wash out eventually."

He leaned in closer, his lips dangerously close to hers. "I wouldn't care if it was green with pink stripes. All I care about is that you're here with me, and that I'm never going to let you out of my sight again." He closed the distance between them and showed her exactly how glad he was to have her back.

After their moment of intimacy, Harrison pulled up a chair alongside Jennifer's bed and slowly lowered himself into it.

"Should you be up?" she asked, looking at the way Harrison shifted to get comfortable.

"I'm fine, just a little sore."

Jennifer waited for him to find a comfortable position before hitting him with the questions that had swirled in her mind each time she'd woken up.

"How did you know I was in Mexico?"

"Bill traced your call to the gas station where you bought the calling card. The lady at the counter gave us a description of you and your car. Bill had a hunch you were headed for Mexico. The border patrol was alerted, but you'd already made it through."

Jennifer's mind drifted back to the night of Kelly and Robert's wedding. She tried to explain what had happened.

"When I realized Kelly had lied to me about Denali, I knew something wasn't right." She turned panicked-filled eyes toward Harrison. "I didn't mean to kill him, Harrison. We struggled and the gun just went off. I didn't know what else to do, so I ran."

"I know, but how did you come up with Melissa Dower and all of this so fast?"

"I always had a back up plan, in case I'd ever been found out. I had a duffle bag with a new identity and some money at the bus depot and a car hidden in a storage facility downtown. I cut my hair and changed its color, then headed for Mexico. Everything would have been fine if I hadn't hurt my foot." Jennifer nodded her head towards her right foot.

"Is that how you would have wanted it?" Harrison asked somberly. "To disappear in Mexico?"

She looked at the emotion in his expression and realized that if her plan had succeeded she never would have seen Harrison again and maybe never would have realized her need for God.

"I didn't mean it like that. I just meant—"

"It doesn't matter. You're safe now," he reassured her as he stroked her arm.

She wanted to believe him. She had to. She didn't have the energy to run any longer. "What are we going to do now? My father won't stop looking for me now that he knows I'm alive."

Harrison carefully reached for something just out of Jennifer's sight. He handed her a Mexican newspaper with the headline *Disparar Fuera Matar Ocho. Caledron Familia Implicar.*

A gruesome picture of slain bodies accompanied the article.

Jennifer read what she could understand. Harrison explained that the article described how a professional hit put out by the Calderon family went bad, eight dead and no survivors.

Jennifer strained at the photo. She could make out the face of Frank Mancino, lying grossly disfigured in the open field. There were other bodies slumped on the ground, two of them being Harrison and herself. She gasped, bringing her hand up to her mouth, feeling as if she was going to be sick. "I don't understand!" Jennifer looked confused, the picture too much for her to absorb.

"They were staged. Well, some of it was." Harrison looked at the picture and shuddered at the harsh reality of what could have happened. "Your father's men will take the blame for botching your capture. The article states that you were shot in the crossfire between U.S. federal agents and known gunman with mob ties. The United States government has already issued a statement regarding the loss of two agents and two American citizens in Mexico. While they didn't disclose what the agents or the citizens were doing in Mexico at the time, they have confirmed what Mexican officials had already reported."

Jennifer let the paper fall to the sheets on top of her. "Why?" She looked at Harrison, "Why did Kelly do it?"

Harrison dropped his eyes. "For the money."

Jennifer looked at him, trying to understand why an heiress would sell her out.

"It was because of Robert. He was in debt to a bookie for over half-a-million dollars, with the total escalating every day he didn't pay it. She didn't want to go to her father with it because he already had his apprehensions about Robert. So she figured out who your father was and sold you out for one million dollars."

Jennifer laid with her eyes transfixed on the blurred photo in the newspaper and the information that Harrison had just told her. "So, what now?"

"We start over. But this time, we're going to do it together."

CHAPTER TWENTY-SEVEN

"**M**r. and Mrs. Templeton, nice to see you again," the pastor greeted the now familiar couple as they exited the small chapel.

"Your sermon was quite thought-provoking, pastor. I enjoyed it a great deal, but please, it's Sarah and Kyle. Mr. and Mrs. Templeton sounds so formal."

The pastor smiled. "Okay, Kyle and Sarah it is."

The cool breeze of Prince Edward Island played with Sarah's bangs as Kyle and the pastor discussed the morning message.

"It's always great to see you in the congregation, Kyle." The pastor shook his hand firmly. "Will you be with us next week?"

"Yes, we don't have any travel plans for a while."

"And how was your trip? France, right?" The pastor turned his attention to Sarah.

"It was wonderful." Sarah blushed slightly as she thought of what made the trip so special. "Paris was beautiful, but nothing compares with coming home." They had been gone for more than three months and were now looking forward to spending some time at home.

The pastor nodded in agreement and smiled. They said their good-byes and soon were heading home to their small cottage on Rustico Bay, Sarah enjoying the scenery as Kyle drove.

It had been three years since the death of Harrison Lynch and Angelica/Jennifer/Samantha Wilder in the shoot-out in Mexico. It had been nine months since the trial that convicted Carlos Calderon, sending him to prison and his empire to ruins.

For Harrison, it had been a tumultuous time. His love for Jennifer was never in question, but to follow her into the witness protection program meant separating himself from his family, never getting a chance to say good-bye.

The "death" of Harrison had been the eye-opener that Robert needed to get his life turned around. After finding out that Kelly had indeed set up Jennifer, he filed for an annulment, spent two months in a stupor, and then turned his life over to Christ. Along with his father, he began managing the holdings that Harrison left behind and was finally becoming the man of God and the brilliant entrepreneur Harrison always believed he could be.

Harrison's mother and father were devastated by the news of their son's shocking death. Robert filled them in with some of the details that the police didn't know regarding Harrison and Jennifer's relationship. He explained to his parents how very much in love Harrison had been. It didn't eliminate their grief, but it did make Mrs. Lynch thankful to know that her son had experienced true love before his death. It took her some time to accept the loss of her son. Slowly, she was beginning to move forward once again.

After the FBI took down Calderon with the ledger copies Jennifer had sent to Weissler, Schuler, and Lynch, they went to work on fabricating the life that Harrison and Jennifer would make together.

They now lived a quiet existence on Prince Edward Island, in a waterfront community that knew them as Kyle and Sarah Templeton. Kyle spent his time as a financial analyst and freelance advisor, and Sarah dabbled in the world of photography. Though there were a few couples in the church they enjoyed spending time with, they had the reputation as being free spirits, world travelers, and a couple very much in the newlywed stage of their marriage. They were in-separable and lived in each other's eyes.

Kyle relaxed in the hammock that was draped between two trees in the backyard as Sarah worked on the small garden she had planted in the spring and now needed to revive after their latest trip.

"How about Paris?" Harrison suggested as Jennifer laughed out loud.

"Paris? I'm not going to name our little girl Paris."

"But it would be so perfect." Harrison laughed. "It was where she was con-ceived after all." His mischievous grin tugged at the corner of Jennifer's lips. She pulled off her gardening gloves and tossed them at him playfully before nestling up next to him in the swinging hammock.

He gently laid his hand across her tummy and began speaking to the most precious thing in his life other than his relationship with God and with Jennifer. He caught the serious look on her face and tipped her chin up to look into her eyes.

"It's going to be okay, Jennifer. God didn't bring us this far just to let us down. "

"I know. It's just that we really didn't plan for this." Jennifer had been shocked to find out what she thought was a touch of the flu while in France was in fact morning sickness. "Do you think it's fair to bring a child into the world under these circumstances?"

"Are you kidding me? It's a miracle!" His eyes were wide with excitement as he wrapped his arms firmly around her, his heart racing with anticipation.

They drifted from side to side in the hammock for several minutes while they each contemplated silent thoughts.

"So, come on." Harrison gave her a nudge. "What do you think about Paris as a name? I think it's perfect."

Jennifer glanced back to look into eyes of love. "Okay, but remind me of one thing."

"What's that?" he asked as they swayed in the breeze.

"The next time we decide to go on vacation, remind me why Turkey would not be such a good idea."

About the Author

TAMARA TILLEY resides with her husband Walter and their children John, Christopher, and Jennifer at Hume Lake Christian Camps in the Sequoia National Forest. They have served on full-time staff and ministered at Hume for 13 years.

Tamara manages one of the retail stores at Hume Lake, which serves thousands of kids visiting the conference center on a daily basis.

Tamara is an avid reader and enjoys other hobbies such as, scrapbooking, designing greeting cards and invitations, and enjoying God's creation from her front porch.

Contact the author c/o:
Evergreen Press
P.O. Box 191540
Mobile, AL 36619